Se

Could

Two sensational stories about smouldering
desire and exploding passion as two women
are seduced by what they want...

The first in the *Seduce...Surrender...Satisfy*
trilogy, *Seduce* is guaranteed to get things off
to a sexy, seductive start!

CARA SUMMERS

The Proposition
"A lush, suspenseful story"
—*Romantic Times*

LESLIE KELLY

Wickedly Hot
"Spicy and sensuous"
—*Romantic Times*

SEDUCE...SURRENDER...SATISFY

Seduce

How far will you go?

Cara Summers

Leslie Kelly

*M&B™ and M&B™ with the Rose Device
are trademarks of the publisher.
Harlequin Mills & Boon Limited, Eton House,
18-24 Paradise Road,
Richmond, Surrey TW9 1SR*

Seduce © by Harlequin Books S.A. 2006

The publisher acknowledges the copyright holders of the
individual works as follows:
The Proposition © Carolyn Hanlon 2005
Wickedly Hot © Leslie Kelly 2004

ISBN 0 263 85082 X

055-0806

*Printed and bound in Spain
by Litografía Rosés S.A., Barcelona*

The Proposition

CARA SUMMERS

Dear Reader,

Cop Natalie Gibbs prides herself on being able to handle men on the job and off...until Chance Mitchell comes into her life and she finds she wants her hands on the sexy insurance investigator a bit too much. When Chance proposes one night of no-strings, no-complications, no-etiquette sex, the very practical Natalie sees his proposition as the perfect way to get him out of her system for good.

The problem is that one night with Chance Mitchell isn't nearly enough, and after three months Natalie decides that she's willing to run any risk to lure him back into her bed – even if she has to disguise herself to do it...

This is just the beginning of Natalie and Chance's adventure. I hope you'll come along for the ride and watch them ultimately take the biggest risk any two people can take when they risk their hearts.

Developing *The Proposition*, *The Dare* and *The Favour* has allowed me to write about three fascinating triplet sisters who have very different dreams, talents and goals. But they have one thing in common – they're willing to risk everything to get what they want. I hope you will look for Rory's and Sierra's stories, *The Dare* and *The Favour*, and that you will enjoy reading them as much as I have enjoyed writing them.

I would love to hear what you think about these stories. You can e-mail me through my website, www.carasummers.com.

Happy reading!

Cara Summers

Prologue

HARRY GIBBS was a man who'd spent his life taking risks and loving every minute of it. For an international jewel thief, risks were a part of the game, and Harry had always played the game very well.

Of course, he'd been born smart and lucky. As for his other talents—such as his Houdini-like knack for opening locks and his gift for disguise—well, those he'd honed to perfection over the years.

And look where his chosen profession had gotten him. Standing on the balcony of his Tuscan villa, Harry watched as the summer sun bathed the vineyards below in a golden light. Although he had a small cottage outside of Dublin and an apartment in Paris, this was his favorite residence in between jobs.

Some would call his the perfect life.

Harry bit back a sigh. No life was perfect, and he had reason to know this better than most men. Life, he'd discovered, boiled down to a series of choices that you either embraced or rejected. Ten years ago, he'd made a big decision—to leave his wife and ten-year-old triplet daughters behind so that he could resume his career as a master thief.

His wife Amanda had wanted Natalie, Rory and Sierra to have a "normal" life. He'd wanted that for the girls, too. So for ten years, he'd tried, but in the end he just couldn't accept that "normal" life for himself.

As the light pouring over the valley slowly darkened and the shadows lengthened, Harry finally let out the sigh he'd been holding back. There wasn't a day that passed when he didn't miss his family. And on this particular warm summer night, the twentieth anniversary of the day the triplets were born, he missed them more than ever.

He moved into the salon, then crossed to the bar and poured champagne into a flute. Six more years—he and Amanda had agreed on that. He wouldn't contact the girls or try to see them until their twenty-sixth birthday.

Tonight, the six years seemed like forever, and lately he'd begun to feel that perhaps time was running out for him.

He crossed to his desk and opened the photo album to three pictures he'd taken of his oldest daughter, Natalie. Then he raised his glass in a toast.

"To my courageous Natalie," he murmured. "Happy birthday."

In many ways, she was the most like him. Sipping the icy liquid, he continued to study the images arranged on the page. They were his favorites. The first was one he'd taken when she'd had her tonsils out. She'd been twelve, and though she hadn't known, he'd joined Amanda to sit by her side the night she'd spent in the hospital. The second was of Natalie getting her diploma at her high school graduation. That was just one of many days that he'd missed being with his girls.

His agreement with Amanda hadn't stopped him from secretly attending important events in their lives and doing his best to watch them grow up. He just hadn't ever been able to let them know he was there.

When they were small, his girls had idolized him. The last thing Amanda had wanted for them was that they would romanticize the career path he'd chosen. He didn't want that either.

Harry bent to get a closer look at the picture he'd snapped of Natalie during her first day at the police academy. He grinned. No way was his oldest daughter going to follow in his path. If anything, she seemed determined to uphold the laws that he had lived his life breaking.

And that was his Natalie to a *T*. From the time she'd been able to walk and talk, she'd taken on the responsibility of both defending and ensuring just treatment of her sisters. A series of images streamed through his mind. In each of them, Natalie would stand in front of her sisters like a warrior. By the time she was ten, Harry could see that his oldest daughter had inherited not merely his red hair, but also his knack for opening locks and his talent for disguise. She would have made a great jewel thief.

Raising his glass, Harry drank to that. Of his three girls, Natalie had always been the biggest risk-taker, and he couldn't help but wonder if being a cop would help her to come to terms with that side of her nature.

If he could just talk to her...

And what the hell good would that do? Harry set down his glass. What could he say? The problem was he wanted his girls to be able to have their cake and eat it, too—but he and Amanda hadn't found a way to do that.

His gaze shifted to the framed photo of his wife, one he'd snapped at the girls' graduation. Reaching out, he ran a finger down the side of her cheek. He'd never stopped loving her.

And he'd never stopped loving his daughters. Thinking of Natalie, Harry reached for a sheet of paper and a pen and sat down at the desk. His risk-taking daughter, his seekers of justice, wouldn't hesitate to take action. There had to be something he could say to her. Even if he couldn't send the letter now, he'd find a way to get it to her eventually.

Harry took another sip of champagne in a toast to his oldest daughter. And then he began to write.

Dearest Natalie…

1

CHANCE MITCHELL had never before been obsessed by a woman in his life. He glanced down the table to where Detective Natalie Gibbs was sipping a glass of white wine. He continued to study her as she tucked a stray curl behind her ear. The two women seated next to her could be described as equally attractive, but ever since he'd joined his friends for a celebration at the Blue Pepper, his gaze had returned to Natalie.

At nine o'clock the popular Georgetown bistro was crowded. Customers were lined up three deep at the bar, and a salsa band was playing on the patio. In some corner of his mind, Chance was aware of that, just as he was vaguely aware of the ongoing conversation at his table, but his focus remained on the fascinating detective.

Her hair fell past her shoulders, and in the dim light of the bar, the red-gold curls looked as if they might burst into flames at any moment. He wanted to touch those curls. He wanted to touch her, slowly and thoroughly.

Chance took a long swallow of his beer, but it did little to cool the heat that burned inside of him. Oh, he was obsessing all right, and he wanted to know why.

What he felt for Natalie had begun the first moment he'd seen her. They'd both been working undercover for different agencies, and she'd been disguised when she'd walked into his art gallery. From the instant their eyes had met, there'd been a connection. He'd felt a curious shock of recognition that had registered like a punch in his gut.

So far, he hadn't acted on the attraction. During the three days that he and Natalie had joined forces and worked as partners, the cool, aloof redhead had kept him at arm's length. And he'd let her. That's what he couldn't quite figure out. He was a man who knew how to get what he wanted, but Natalie Gibbs had him hesitating in a way he couldn't recall doing since he'd been a teenager.

Perhaps it was time he put a stop to that. She didn't look quite so cool tonight. Maybe it was the clothes. When they'd worked as partners, she'd always worn a jacket and slacks, the standard uniform of a woman who worked in a man's world. But tonight, the blouse she wore left her arms and throat bare, and the lacy, sheer fabric revealed curves as well as skin.

His eyes shifted to the V-neck that ended just where he imagined the valley between her breasts began. He let his gaze lower to the tiny, pearl buttons that marched in a narrow line to her waist. He could imagine unbuttoning them one at a time, very slowly, drawing out the pleasure for them both.

As the images filled his mind, the tightening in his gut turned raw and primitively sexual. Why in hell was he hesitating? Desire was something he was familiar with. He could handle it. Or he could walk away. Couldn't he?

He took another swallow of his beer.

"You all right?"

Chance tore his gaze away from Natalie to face the two men seated beside him. Tracker McBride had asked the question. But it was Lucas Wainwright who was studying him thoughtfully. Seven years ago, Tracker and Lucas had worked with him in a Special Forces unit, and in the past two weeks, they'd had the opportunity to work together again to crack a smuggling ring operating in D.C. Tonight, they were supposed to be celebrating the successful closure of the case, and this was the second time he'd lost track of the conversation, thanks to Detective Natalie Gibbs.

"I think he has his eye on the fair detective," Lucas said.

Tracker's look turned speculative. "Really?"

Knowing that the best defense was a good offense, Chance said to Tracker, "Have you and Sophie set a date yet?"

Tracker's gaze went to the tall blonde sitting to Natalie's right.

Lucas grinned. "I hear from Mac that Sophie is talking about a fall wedding."

Chance mentally shook his head at the satisfied expression on Tracker's face and shifted his gaze to the third woman who sat at the other end of the table, Dr. MacKenzie Lloyd Wainwright. Mac and Lucas had been married for a year, and they were expecting a child. He'd never envisioned either of his friends marrying and settling down.

"Now that Lucas and I are pretty much spoken for, it's your turn," Tracker said.

Chance held both hands out, palms up. "Not a chance in hell." Then he laughed as his friends winced at the pun. He just wasn't the marrying kind.

It wasn't that he didn't like women. He did. And you could italicize the plural. Not that he had ever involved himself with more than one woman at a time. Going down that particular path had always seemed to him to be way too complicated if not downright suicidal. He'd always made sure that his relationships were simple, uncomplicated and a lot of fun while they lasted. *Permanent* wasn't a word that existed in his vocabulary. Hell, nothing was permanent—not in this life.

"I don't know," Tracker said. "Sophie says that there's a real spark between you and the detective."

The sudden ringing of a phone had all three men reaching for their cells. Whoever was getting the call, Chance figured he was saved by the bell. Lucas opened his and a second later said, "I'm going to have to take this in a quieter spot." Rising, he signaled Tracker to come with him. The two friends worked together now. Lucas ran his family's company, Wainwright Enterprises, and Tracker headed up security for him.

Chance sipped his beer and found his gaze returning to Natalie. When she glanced up and met his eyes, there was a moment, a long moment, when everything else faded. A heated discussion at a nearby table, laughter from the bar, even the low sound of a saxophone became just a buzz in his ears. The faces of the other two women at the table blurred, and all he could see was Natalie.

Twin sensations assaulted him—a hard punch to his gut and a strange flutter just beneath his heart. No, this wasn't the reaction he had to just any woman. Why did this particular woman have this kind of effect on him? A part of him wanted to find out; another part of him wanted to run.

The realization had a spurt of panic moving through him. No woman had ever made him want to run before.

"Hey." Tracker's amused tone only penetrated when he felt the nudge to his shoulder. Turning, Chance discovered that Lucas had moved to help Mac from her chair. "Our party's breaking up," Tracker said. "Mac's tired so they're driving home now. Sophie and I are going to walk back to her place. Do you need Lucas to give you a lift back to your hotel?"

"No," he said as he rose from his chair. It had been years since he'd allowed himself to run away from anything. That part of his life was over. He was flying to London in the morning, but there was one thing he was going to do before he left. Chance moved with Tracker down to the other end of the table.

"Sorry to be such a party pooper," Mac said, stifling a huge yawn.

"I'm the one who yawned first," Sophie said. "The last few days have been hectic." Then she smiled at Natalie. "But you should stay. Chance is an excellent dancer, and the music is good."

"No, I—" Natalie began as she rose from her chair.

"Sophie's right on one point," Chance said. "The music is very good."

"Please. Don't let me break up your evening," Mac said, taking Natalie's hand and squeezing it. "Stay and have at least one dance. If I weren't asleep on my feet,

I'd drag Lucas out. There's nothing more romantic than dancing under the stars."

"What's one dance?" Sophie said softly as she kissed Natalie's cheek.

Chance waited until the two couples had taken their leave. "We don't have to dance if you're afraid of that Latin beat."

Natalie's eyes narrowed as she met his. "I can dance to that if you can."

It was just the reaction Chance had hoped for. The one thing he'd learned from working with the beautiful detective was that she was never afraid to take a risk. That was his key, he realized as he took her hand and led her toward the patio. If he framed his proposition in the right way, they'd be taking a different kind of risk together before the night was over.

NATALIE KNEW she was making a mistake the moment that Chance took her hand. It wasn't that he hadn't touched her before. He was a very physical man. In the brief time they'd worked together, he'd taken her arm, or placed a hand at her back. But he'd never before held her hand. His was hard, his fingers callused, and just the pressure of his palm against hers had little ribbons of heat uncurling up her arm.

The intensity of the sensations had her wondering what it would feel like when he really touched her. And she'd been thinking of that since they'd first met in that art gallery. He'd been a possible suspect in an art theft ring, and it had been her job to keep an eye on him.

Natalie sent him a sideways glance as he made a

path for them through the crowd. Keeping an eye on Chance Mitchell was nice work if you could get it.

He was a man any woman would look twice at. He had a long, rangy body that wore jeans and Armani suits with the same careless ease. Hair that looked brown one minute and blond the next. Eyes that were trapped somewhere between a smoky gray and blue. And a face that wasn't quite handsome until he smiled in a certain way.

But for the three days they'd worked side by side, it was his hands that she'd become obsessed with—hands that held a priceless sculpture or a gun with equal skill. More than once, she'd struggled with fantasies of how those long, clever fingers might pleasure a woman.

And she knew enough about men to know that he was fantasizing just as much as she. The fact that she and Chance had been assigned to protect Sophie Wainwright from a ruthless killer had helped both of them keep their focus. But now…Sophie was safe. The case was over. There was nothing to divert her attention from this man. And she wanted him with an intensity that she'd never felt for anyone else.

Why?

Natalie found part of her answer the moment Chance drew her into his arms. Heat streamed through her and every nerve in her body began to throb. No one had ever made her feel this way, and she knew that this was only a promise of what he could make her feel if she would just let him.

Why was she so hesitant to do that?

"We fit perfectly," he murmured.

Hadn't she known they would? She was tall, but he was taller. His chin brushed her hair, and as he guided her across the small dance floor, his thigh pressed briefly against hers. The shock to her system had her stumbling even more closely against him.

"Relax." His voice was just a breath in her ear as he ran those clever fingers up and then down her spine.

"Just listen to the music and let yourself go."

Let yourself go. Natalie bit back a sigh as she struggled against doing just that. She'd always prided herself on her control where men were concerned. Two years of working on a D.C. police special task force had given her plenty of experience handling males, both on the job and in the bedroom as well. In the two serious relationships she'd had, her lovers had both been intimidated by the fact that she was a cop, and she'd learned from experience not to invest too much of herself in a relationship.

Instinct told her that Chance was different. He'd have the ability to break her control, and the idea of that tempted her almost as much as it made her wary.

When Chance drew back a little, Natalie barely kept herself from protesting.

"Much better," he said. "Relaxation is the key."

Of course, it was easy to relax when her bones were melting. But Natalie kept that to herself. Instead, she made herself focus. "You really do know how to dance. Where did you learn?"

"Here and there. I've found it a very useful tool."

She raised her brows. "Tool?"

Chance smiled at her. "Absolutely. Dancing is the easiest method I know for getting a woman into my arms, and second only to my cooking for getting a woman into my bed."

Bed. She should have had a quick comeback for that. Or at least she could have snorted. But the image, as well as the way he'd leaned close to her ear to say it, had a fresh wave of desire streaming through her.

The rhythm of the dance changed abruptly, and Chance slid his hands to her hips, pulling her close for one brief contact. Heat flashed through her as she felt the long hard length of him. The lower part of her body burned and melted. "Oh, yes," one part of her mind said—even as another part said, "Get away while you can!"

But the negative voice in her mind was losing strength, and Natalie suddenly realized that she wasn't going to play it safe. Hadn't some part of her made that decision when she'd chosen her clothes tonight?

The admission sent a hot erotic thrill moving through her. A sliver of panic followed. It wasn't like her to be thinking this way. Just as it wasn't like her to dress with the intention of tempting a man. As the oldest child—by a few minutes anyway—she'd always been the responsible one, and she'd always had to control that wild, reckless streak inside of her that she'd inherited from her father.

"I want you, Natalie." The words were nothing more than a breath in her ear, but her knees turned to water. She was suddenly aware that he'd steered her off the dance floor and into a darkened corner of the patio. Potted trees surrounded them; a brick wall pressed against her back. And he stood before her, the heat of his body so close…

"I want to take you to bed, I want to touch you—all over."

She couldn't prevent the quick thrill the words brought her any more than she could prevent her heart from beginning to hammer.

"I—"

"No." He pressed a finger against her lips. "Let me finish. I have a proposition for you. I'm flying to London tomorrow morning. If I'm lucky, the assignment will take three months. If not, I'll be gone even longer. So there's just tonight." He drew his finger down that line of her throat to the vee of her blouse and then down the tiny pearl buttons one by one. She was sure that her heart skipped a beat at each one.

"Spend just one night with me," he said.

SHE HAD TO SAY YES, Chance told himself. He'd chosen his words very carefully. He always did where women were concerned. One night with no strings was just the kind of proposition that the cool, logical Natalie Gibbs he'd come to know would find irresistible. He figured she was cautious when it came to men because she didn't want complications.

But as he stared into those cool, green eyes, he couldn't get a hint of what she was thinking. She had to have felt at least part of what he'd experienced when they'd been dancing—the incredible promise of what they could share. And she had to be experiencing at least some of the desperation that he was feeling right now.

When he saw her lips part to speak, he raised his fingers to rest them there. "Don't say no. I—" Chance broke off the moment that he realized what had nearly slipped out of his mouth. He'd almost said, "I need you." And that wasn't true. Being a little obsessed was one thing, but need?

Taking a quick breath, he spoke around the bubble of panic that had risen into his throat. "Just think about it. When was the last time you had sex for the sheer fun of it—no strings, no complications? No worrying about the morning-after etiquette? C'mon. What do you say?"

For a moment his question hung in the air between them. One night with Natalie Gibbs—that was what he wanted. And he wanted it very badly. That was all. Need had nothing to do with it. Chance Mitchell hadn't needed anyone for a very long time.

Natalie took his fingers and removed them from her mouth. "That's your proposition? No-strings, no-complications, no-etiquette sex?"

"Exactly." Chance made himself stop with one word. Because he was very much afraid that he was going to babble. Worse still, he just might beg.

Her grin was quick and wicked. He'd never seen that look on her face before, and his heart did a little stutter.

"Proposition accepted," she said.

Chance's heart stopped altogether.

NATALIE LED the way down a narrow flagstone path to the back of a Federal-style house just three blocks away from the Blue Pepper. Lantern lights hung on either side of the door to her apartment.

She'd never before brought a man here—to her own space. But when Chance had suggested her place be-

cause it had to be closer than his hotel on Sixteenth
Street, Natalie hadn't argued. If she was going to give
herself over to one night of reckless, no-strings, no-
etiquette sex, she might as well do it in familiar surroundings.

Chance had said nothing since they'd left the Blue
Pepper. He hadn't touched her either, but she'd been
very much aware of him walking at her side. When she
drew the key out of her purse and slid it into the door,
he laid a hand on hers.

She turned to look at him then. The full moon
poured brightly into the garden behind him, but
Chance's face was caught in shifting shadows. His
eyes were dark, and she couldn't read what he was
thinking.

"Second thoughts?" he asked.

The kindness of the question had some of the nerves
in her stomach settling. But she'd made her decision,
and she wasn't going to run away from it. Shaking her
head, she said, "You?"

"No."

She led the way into the narrow foyer. After shut-
ting the door with his foot, Chance moved quickly,
using his arms and body to cage her against the wall.

"It's not a night for any kind of thought," he murmured as he lowered his mouth to within a breath of
hers. "Tonight we're just going to feel."

Any lingering doubts streamed away in that first
touch of his lips to hers. His mouth was firm, but giving, his hands almost gentle as he ran them up her arms
and slipped them into her hair. And his taste—there
was a dark sweetness there that she hadn't expected.

Natalie had one long moment to take a heady sample of it before he moved in even closer. His body, rock-hard, pressed against her, and she felt her own body soften and yield in response. He nipped her bottom lip then slid his tongue over hers.

Heat, one glorious, scorching wave of it, rushed up and over her. If she'd ever been more aware of a man before, she couldn't recall it. Everything about him was hard—his chest, his hands, the angle of his hip and the long length of his thigh. Even his mouth had grown harder, more demanding, as if he was determined to find some flavor that she was hiding from him.

It wasn't sweetness she tasted anymore, but a hungry desperation. Was it his or hers?

And all the while those clever, glorious hands raced over her—tracing the curve of her throat, cupping her breasts, and gripping her bottom to pull her even closer. Fire licked along her nerve endings as one sensation after another pulsed through her. Her body had throbbed before, but not like this. Her heart had hammered before, but not as if it intended to burst right out of her chest.

"More."

Had she said the word aloud? The question had barely formed in her mind, when he answered it by slipping fingers into the vee of her blouse and ripping it open. Then in a lightning move, he jerked what remained of her blouse down her arms, trapping her hands at her sides.

Vulnerability. It was a feeling she'd fought against all of her life. But Natalie welcomed it now, along with the deeply erotic thrill that shot through her. She'd prided herself on always being in charge—on the job, in bed. Now, as those hard hands moved over her again, she couldn't remember why she'd even wanted to be in control. When he began to use his mouth on her, she gave herself over to a fresh storm of sensations—the hot, rough texture of his tongue at her throat, the scrape of his teeth at her shoulder. One instant she burned, the next, she shivered.

Someone laughed. She didn't recognize the low, sultry sound, and then his mouth closed over her breast. Fire, furious flames of it, sped along her nerve endings. There was another rip of cloth as she tore her arms free from her blouse. Then she threaded her fingers through his hair and tried to drag his mouth back to hers.

"More," she repeated.

Her whispered plea became a drumbeat in his mind as hunger and need tangled inside of him. He'd been right that it wasn't a night for thinking. He couldn't seem to grab on to one coherent thought. Nor could he resist returning for one more sample of her mouth.

Would he ever get enough of the sweet, drugging flavor of her surrender, that throaty gasp of pleasure that ended in his name? And her scent—something wild and exotic that made him think of taking her quickly on a deserted, moonlit beach while waves thundered furiously over the sand.

Another second and he would simply drown in her. Drawing back, Chance fought to breathe, to clear his mind.

"Hurry. Please."

Her words started his blood pounding in his head.

Helpless to resist, he covered her lips again with his and plundered. This time it wasn't sweetness he tasted, but a hunger as sharp and desperate as his own. The hands running over him were as eager and determined to possess as his. The change in her from surrender to fevered urgency swamped his senses, and need sliced through him.

His fingers fumbled as he tore her belt free and sent her slacks pooling to the floor. He ran his hand down her, pushing aside the remaining barrier of silk. Hanging on to a thin thread of control, he lifted his head—because he had to see her, needed to see her, as he slipped two fingers into her heat. She locked around him, and he watched her eyes darken and cloud as she absorbed the pleasure he was giving her. He knew the moment her climax began, and when she reached the peak, it was his name she breathed. The sound sliced through him and sharpened an ache deep inside him, sharper than any he'd ever known.

Even as the last ripples of her climax moved through her, Natalie knew she had to have more of him. Of this man. Of Chance. She pulled his shirt free and tugged at his belt. Together, they struggled to free him of slacks, T-shirt, shoes until the only barrier between them was the thin black fabric of his briefs. Unable to take the time to pull them down, she closed her hand over him.

"The bedroom." His voice was ragged.

"Here," she replied.

They dragged each other to the floor. Once they were there, she lost no time. Rolling herself on top of him, she began to explore him with her mouth, using her tongue and teeth on his shoulder, his throat, his chest. She couldn't get enough. Her heart had never beaten this hard. Her body had never ached this sharply.

Rising to her knees, she straddled his thighs, dragged down his briefs. Hands clamped at her waist. He lifted her clear of the floor, and then she was sinking onto him. The moment he filled her, they began to move. Through a haze, she saw his smoky eyes, locked on hers as he filled her, withdrew, then filled her again. Pleasure, waves of it, engulfed her as they both increased the pace. As her vision grayed, she leaned down to cover his mouth with hers.

"Now," she murmured against his lips. "Come with me, now."

In one lightning move, he rolled her beneath him. Then he drove her, drove them both, until together they reached that peak and shattered.

2

Three months later...

WITH ONE HAND, Chance Mitchell reached into the cooler at his side and pulled out a beer. He was being watched. It was nothing that he could see in his brief scan of the shoreline—not yet. Still, the moment the boat he was on had rounded that last curve of the coast, all of Chance's senses had gone on alert.

"The hair on the back of my neck tells me that I'm posing for pictures," Tracker said from his position behind the wheel.

"Yeah," Chance replied. That cinched it. If there was one person whose instincts he trusted more than his own, it was Tracker's. "I'm getting the same feeling."

Chance twisted off the cap on his beer and took a long swallow, all the while keeping a tight grip on his fishing pole. To any observer he looked like he was enjoying the fishing that the waters off the south Florida coast provided. That's exactly what he wanted the security people he knew were watching him to believe.

And if they checked into it—as he was sure they were doing right now—they would find that the boat was registered to Lucas Wainwright III, CEO of Wainwright Enterprises, and that the man himself had indeed flown in from D.C. to spend the weekend in Boca Raton and had had his boat brought in from his place on the Keys.

Chance pulled his hat down hard. Luckily, he and his old friend Lucas were the same height and build, so all he'd had to do was use temporary black dye on his hair. But there was no telling how powerful those cameras were, and he didn't want anyone on shore getting a good look at his facial features.

Something hit the line hard. The pole bent nearly double, then twanged upward. Chance nearly laughed out loud. Sometimes, he really loved undercover work. Here he was, on a job staking out the isolated Florida estate of Carlo Brancotti—a millionaire who'd made his fortune stealing from others—and he was going to have the pleasure of battling and landing a big catch. He couldn't have planned it better for the audience that he was sure was recording his every move.

The only thing that might please him more was to land Carlo himself. Two years ago, a huge yellow diamond, the size of a baby's fist, had disappeared from the Ferrante private collection in Rome, and Chance had been on Brancotti's trail ever since. The theft had occurred while the jewel was in transport between the Ferrante palace and the museum where it was to be displayed. The real diamond had been taken and an amazingly accurate fake had been substituted.

From the moment he'd been called in to investigate the heist, Chance had been sure that Brancotti was the mastermind behind it. He'd been tracking the man for a long time, and Brancotti's trademark was to leave an almost undetectable fake in place of the real jewel. By the time the theft was discovered, Brancotti would have found a buyer, and there would be no evidence to connect the man with the crime.

In this case, the substitution had been discovered within days because Count Ferrante had insisted on an appraisal of the diamond for insurance purposes just before the exhibition was opened to the public.

Chance had sold the insurance company and the count on offering a reward for the diamond, one large enough to tempt Brancotti to give it back. And Brancotti had taken the bait. It had been a good idea. If it had worked, the count would have gotten his diamond back, and Chance would have settled an old score and put Brancotti behind bars.

But the plan had gone terribly wrong, and Chance had lost his partner, Venetia Gaston.

The fish pulled hard on his line, and Chance dragged his thoughts back to the present. Mindful of the telescopic lens he was sure was aimed at him, he began to play the fish, releasing the tension on the line and then gradually pulling it taut again.

For two long years, he'd waited for news of a large yellow diamond to surface, and a week ago it had. Through one of his contacts, he'd received a tip that Carlo Brancotti was inviting a very select group of men and women to a weekend at his retreat in south Florida and that the Ferrante diamond would be auctioned off to the highest bidder.

The heightened security along the shoreline of Carlo's estate cinched it. Carlo Brancotti was meticulously careful. That was why he'd never been caught.

Tilting his head slightly, Chance kept one eye on his pole as he scanned the shoreline. The south Florida sun beat down, sending sparks skimming across the backwash the boat was creating, but he didn't miss the flash in the thick cypress trees that lined the shore, light reflecting off a lens. Someone was definitely watching them. He felt the quick kick of adrenaline that he always experienced when he knew the hunt was about to begin.

"Showtime," he said to Tracker. "I'm going to need your help with this fish. It's big."

"Damn. You have all the luck."

A second later, his old buddy was at his side. He'd been pleased when Tracker had agreed to help him with the case—they made a good team. Together, they watched the fish leap out of the water in a huge, graceful arc. The pole bent nearly double again as the fish dove below the surface.

"You spot anything?" Tracker asked as he grabbed Chance's chair to steady it.

"One of them is at two o'clock as you face the shore."

"Got it," Tracker said. "There's another one about a thousand yards to the left."

The fish cleared the water again.

"A lot of security," Chance remarked as he reeled in the line.

"Must be something needs guarding," Tracker said.

"That's the way I figure it, too. Keep a watch, will you? Landing this fish is going to require all of my attention. And if they're watching me, maybe you can pick out a few more of them."

"Right," Tracker said.

For the next few minutes, they said nothing as Chance let out the line and then drew it in, over and over. By the time Tracker dipped the net over the side of the boat and they hauled the fish in, the boat had moved past the Brancotti estate.

Chance waited until they'd turned and were headed back. Tracker kept the throttle open, and Chance stood at the wheel with him while the video camera on the stern side of the boat recorded every inch of the shoreline. This time there was no telltale flash of light. Evidently, their cover had held. The photos that would make their way to Brancotti would show a very happy fisherman, heading home after a satisfying catch.

"Can you get in along the shore without being detected?" Chance asked.

Tracker grinned. "Is the Pope Catholic?"

"Carlo doesn't leave anything to chance."

"Getting you *off* the estate will be the easy part. You've got the tough job. You've got to get *on* the estate by getting invited to the party. And you have to steal the diamond."

Chance smiled at his old friend. "I've got an invite already, thanks to a contact of mine. As for stealing the diamond—that will be the fun part."

Turning, Tracker studied his friend for a minute. "This is more than a job to you, isn't it?"

"Carlo and I go back a long way." Longer than Chance would ever admit to anyone. He and Carlo had lived in the same orphanage for a year—one long year when he'd been a scrawny twelve-year-old and Carlo had been seventeen and his only friend and mentor. Of course, their names had been different then. Chance had hero-worshipped the older boy. But the friendship had died the night that Carlo had robbed the orphanage and made sure that Chance got the blame for the theft. That had been twenty years ago.

Tracker shot his friend a look. "If it's personal between you and Brancotti, that could get in your way."

"I won't let it."

"Is there any chance he'll recognize you?"

"No. I was twelve the last time we saw each other."

Tracker frowned, then said, "Why don't I go in with you? I could pose as your bodyguard or your personal assistant."

Chance grinned and shook his head. "Thanks, but I already have a partner in mind, and you won't fit into the wardrobe."

"There's a wardrobe?"

"An expensive one. I'll be posing as Steven Bradford. You probably haven't heard of him because he's very low-key, but he's a software genius who made his billions in the high-tech boom. And as Steven, I'll be bringing along my latest companion, a model type who, with my backing, is hoping to jettison her career into supermodel status."

Tracker grinned. "The nerd and his arm candy."

"Exactly." Chance paused, then said what he'd been thinking about ever since he'd accepted the assignment. "I'm going to ask Natalie Gibbs to work with me."

Tracker thought for a minute. "She's a looker all right."

"She's the right body type and with blond hair she'll be a dead ringer for Catherine Weston, who now calls herself 'Calli.'" But it wasn't just her looks that had kept Detective Natalie Gibbs in his mind and in his dreams for three straight months.

"I did some research on her." He'd run a thorough check on Natalie, partly to figure out why she'd gotten to him. "Her father, Harry Gibbs, was an international jewel thief. One of those legends who's the prime suspect in every big heist, but who never got caught. He died in an accident about six years ago."

"The father's a jewel thief and the daughter becomes a cop. Interesting."

Fascinating was the word Chance would have chosen. The hell of it was, the more he'd learned about Natalie Gibbs, the more intrigued by her he'd become. "She's not the only daughter. She's the oldest of a set of triplets." According to one source he'd talked to, Natalie took her position as the oldest quite seriously, especially since their mother had passed away six years ago.

"She evidently inherited some of her father's talents," Chance continued. "She worked her way through college cracking safes for various law enforcement agencies."

Tracker eased the boat around a curve of land that cut them off from the Brancotti estate, then turned to study his friend. "Sophie's pretty sure that there's something going on between the two of you. Or that there could be something. She swears that sparks fly whenever you're in the same room together."

Chance shrugged. "It won't interfere with the job."

"It could interfere with your thinking. Take it from someone who's been there."

"The bottom line is I need her for the job. She's got

a cool head." Except for when she was exploding in his arms. "Plus, she has a gift for disguise and a knack for undercover work."

Tracker hadn't taken his eyes off Chance. "You're sure about this?"

Chance met Tracker's eyes steadily. "She's exactly what I want." That was nothing less than the truth. Even before that one night in her apartment, he'd wanted her more than any other woman he'd ever met. The mistake he'd made was to think that having her once would get her out of his system. His miscalculation about that wasn't the only error he'd made that night. He'd never been so rough with a woman before. Hell, he'd ripped her clothes off and taken her on the floor of her foyer. And he hadn't been much gentler later in her bed.

To top everything off, he'd left before she'd awakened and flown off to London without so much as a note or a phone call to say goodbye. Chance liked women, and he prided himself on treating them well. But he hadn't treated Natalie very well.

Truth be told, his response to Natalie Gibbs had scared him. It hadn't been just the lack of control he'd had over his physical response to her. No. There'd been a moment when he'd stood in the doorway of her bedroom watching her sleep when he simply hadn't wanted to leave. Ever.

That was unprecedented. Chance Mitchell never stayed in one place, never intended to settle down. He changed his name as often as he changed locations. But something about Natalie Gibbs pulled at him. That was why he hadn't called or sent flowers. Now, three months later, he wanted her to help him catch Brancotti. And he still wanted her, period.

"You haven't run any of this by Natalie yet?" Tracker asked.

"No."

Tracker grinned. "I'd say you have your work cut out for you—on more than one front. She struck me as the straight-as-an-arrow type and I don't have to tell you that you've always taken the riskier approach."

"Yeah." Tracker was the one who'd nicknamed him "Chance" when they'd worked together in a Special Forces unit.

"Have you got a plan?"

"Not yet." Three days ago, he'd called her department, but at the last minute, he'd asked to talk to her partner, Matt Ramsey, instead.

"She didn't strike me as the type who could be easily conned," Tracker said, his grin widening.

"No." Chance bit back a sigh. If he was going to convince Natalie Gibbs to join him, he was going to have to pull off some fancy moves all right. And so far, he hadn't come up with a plan that had a chance in hell of succeeding.

"Tell you what," Tracker said. "Sophie's throwing a party at her antique shop on Friday to showcase some local artists. Natalie will be there. Why don't you come?"

Chance thought for a minute. If he ran into Natalie at a party, she couldn't refuse to see him. She'd have no choice but to talk to him at least.

"I'll take you up on that," Chance said. That gave him about forty-eight hours to come up with a strategy. Deadlines always sparked his creativity.

"Good. I was sure I was going to be bored. Now, I'll have the chance to observe a master con man at work."

"HERE ARE THE latest acceptances to your party."

Carlo Brancotti didn't glance up from his computer screen as his personal assistant, Lisa McGill, placed a manila folder on his desk. He was a careful man. Some judged him to be too careful, but he hadn't remained at the top of his profession by letting down his guard. Anything out of the ordinary was reported to him instantly, and his surveillance team had phoned him the minute the boat had been spotted so close to shore. They'd already traced the license plate. It belonged to Lucas Wainwright. Frowning, he tapped his fingers on his desk. Wainwright…the name was familiar, but the details escaped him.

Suddenly, the information appeared on the screen. Carlo scanned it quickly. Lucas Wainwright, CEO of Wainwright Enterprises, owner of a resort hotel in the Keys and another in South Beach, frequently used his boat to fish.

Satisfied, Carlo turned his attention to Lisa. "Report."

"All of the usuals, Sir Arthur and Lady Latham, the Moto brothers, the Demirs and Hassam Aldiri."

"And the first-timers?"

Lisa frowned a bit. First-timers made her nervous because there was a chance, always a chance, that one of them would be a plant, someone that a big insurance company or a law enforcement agency had gotten to. Carlo was looking forward to that very possibility. Foiling those who thought they could catch him was half the fun of the business he was in. More than anything, he enjoyed the game. He always had. The money was just a very pleasant side benefit.

"Risa Manwaring, Armand Genovese and Steven Bradford have all accepted, and they will arrive on Sunday."

The disapproval in her voice had him biting back a smile as he opened the file she'd placed on his desk. He wouldn't show any disapproval for her concern, for it was her job to worry and to keep him safe. "You've put them under surveillance?"

"Of course."

Carlo nodded in approval as he examined the photos in the file. Lisa had already run background checks on all three—Risa Manwaring, the retired film star, who now lived in seclusion; Armand Genovese, the Italian businessman, with rumored ties to organized crime; and Steven Bradford, the software genius, who reportedly had money to burn. Each would have his or her own reasons for wanting to acquire the Ferrante diamond. Which one, he wondered, would have that special craving for it that would run up the price?

Taking out the photos, he lined them up in a neat row, then pulled a magnifying glass from his desk. Not one of them offered a clear, accurate image. "These were the best you could get hold of?"

"Yes. I'm still working on it."

He nodded in approval, but he didn't expect her to find any better pictures of his future guests. He'd chosen these three specifically because all three shunned the media.

Which one would the man who called himself Chance Mitchell be impersonating? That was the question.

There wasn't a doubt in his mind that the insurance agent who'd come so close to tripping him up on his last job would take the bait. The man was good. Too good. After their last encounter, Carlo had made it his business to learn everything he could about the freelance insurance investigator who went by the name of Chance.

Carlo doubted that was the man's real name or that he even used it very often. There was even a possibility that Chance was a woman. In the past seven years, Chance Mitchell had become a legend of sorts in certain circles, the one person feared by anyone in Carlo's business.

But Carlo wasn't afraid. No, indeed, he thought as he smiled. He was looking forward to going up against Chance Mitchell again. Lately, he'd found that life offered too few challenges. With one long finger, he tapped each of the photos in turn. Which one would Chance choose to appear as? Risa, Armand, Steven or the woman on Steven's arm? He lowered the magnifying glass to decipher the name. Calli.

"Run a check on this Calli also."

"Yes, sir," Lisa replied.

Carlo set down the magnifying glass. He would know each one of his invited guests intimately before they arrived at his estate. Which one would turn out to be the one he would have to kill?

$$3$$

NATALIE SPOTTED her sisters the moment she stepped into the Blue Pepper. Rory, as usual, was in the thick of things, having an animated conversation with the reservation hostess. Natalie had no doubt that in spite of the crowd, Rory would get them a table. With her pixie face and short, dark hair, Rory had always reminded Natalie of Puck, the mischievous fairy in Shakespeare's *A Midsummer Night's Dream*. She had a knack for muddling things up the same way he had.

As Natalie edged her way through the crowd, she searched for a glimpse of her youngest sister, Sierra. Sure enough, Sierra was seated next to the reservation desk, looking on and jotting something down on one of the blue note cards she never seemed to be without. Natalie bit back a sigh.

With her straight blond hair and innocent air, Sierra had always made Natalie think of Alice in Wonderland. Though the academic Sierra was more intellectual than Alice and more shy, she was every bit as curious. However, Sierra never ever just tumbled into things the way Alice had. Instead, from the time she was little, she'd mapped out everything she did on blue note cards.

Well, Natalie believed in plans, too, but she drew the line at listing steps on note cards of any color. And she worried a bit that Sierra, who'd been sick a lot as a child, was a little too organized and too cautious in her approach to life. But whenever she broached the subject to Sierra, her sister would point out that her planning had gotten her two Ph.D. degrees and a tenure-track position at Georgetown University.

Ever since their father had left them, Natalie had always believed that it was her job to look out for her sisters, and she couldn't help worrying about how they were going to take the news that she was bringing them tonight.

Outside on the patio, a saxophonist blew a trill of notes, and Natalie stopped short as the image of Chance Mitchell slipped, unwanted, into her mind. That was all it took for her body to respond. Annoyance streamed through her. It had been three months since she'd been here with him—three long months since she'd thrown caution to the winds and spent the night with him. And she still couldn't get him out of her mind.

One night. That's what he'd offered and what she'd agreed to. He'd promised no-strings, no-etiquette sex, and he'd certainly delivered. Just the memory of what he'd done to her, what they'd done to each other, was enough to have her skin heating and something deep inside of her melting.

It certainly wasn't Chance's fault that she'd never before experienced anything like it. Nor could she in all fairness blame him for the fact that she wanted to experience it again.

Her glance shifted to the patio where they'd danced and where he'd made her the proposition. Oh, there was a part of her that wanted to blame Chance, a part of her that wanted to pay him back for the fact that since she'd spent that one freeing night with him, she'd felt restless, unsatisfied with her job and with her life.

And dammit, she'd been perfectly satisfied before. Her work on a select task force that handled high profile crimes in D.C. was exciting, but lately she was… just plain bored.

"Detective Natalie! Greetings, greetings, greetings."

Natalie smiled at Rad as he rushed up, grabbed her hands and rained kisses on the air several inches above her knuckles. The young restaurant owner was a full head shorter than she was, and he changed his hair color as frequently as he changed his ties. Tonight he was wearing his pale blond hair in spikes that were tipped with orange. She noted that the shade matched one of the swirls in his psychedelic tie.

Holding her hands a few inches out from her sides, Rad's smile faded as he gave her outfit a thorough look. The linen suit she wore was khaki colored, the T-shirt beneath was black, and she could sense a fashion critique coming her way.

"How's George?" she asked in an effort to deflect Rad's attention. George, Rad's partner, was a bronze-skinned, gentle giant of a man who managed the bar while Rad ran the restaurant.

Rad waved a hand. "George is gorgeous. Perfect, as usual. You, on the other hand…" He broke off to press a hand over his heart. "It cuts me to the quick to see you in such drab colors. Aquamarine would do wonders for you. Or mint-green." He tapped a finger to his lips as he considered. "No, pink. You should really think *pink*."

Natalie suppressed a shudder. A cop wearing pink? Not to mention what the color would look like in contrast to her red hair. She thought not. In a second attempt to distract Rad, she said, "Nice hairdo."

He flashed her a grin. "Thanks. There's a lot of product up there."

"Excellent match with the tie."

Rad fluttered his hand an inch above the spikes. "I had to work on the color for over an hour. I could do something quite wonderful with yours."

"I'd rather you found me a table."

Rad glanced over to where Rory was beaming at the reservation hostess. "I think your sister has taken care of that. I'll run interference for you."

Straightening her shoulders, Natalie followed Rad through the crowd. Tonight she and her sisters were going to celebrate their mutual birthdays, and she was bringing them a surprise present.

The envelope she carried in her purse had arrived this morning. It had contained a note from her father's attorney and three separate sealed envelopes for Harry Gibbs's daughters. Inside were messages from their father—messages that he'd written six years ago and had wanted them to read on their twenty-sixth birthday.

All day long the letters had been weighing on her mind and her heart. She still wasn't sure how she felt about them. Harry Gibbs had walked out on his family when she and her sisters were ten years old. When they were twenty, he'd died in a fluke climbing accident. Her father had always been taking risks. Within six months of receiving the news of Harry Gibbs's death, their mother had died, too.

Natalie had always known that her parents had loved one another—and there wasn't a doubt in her mind that her mother had died of a broken heart. But ten years before their deaths, Harry and Amanda Gibbs had split up because of "irreconcilable differences."

In this case the difference they couldn't reconcile was the fact that Harry Gibbs was a master jewel thief who found it impossible to settle down, and their mother Amanda wanted to raise her daughters in a stable, conservative environment.

Six years ago their father had suddenly decided to send them some kind of message they would receive on their twenty-sixth birthday? Personally, Natalie felt half pissed and half saddened by that, and she suspected that her sisters would feel the same.

Just then, Rory spotted her and called out, "Nat! This way."

Not content with waiting for Natalie to reach them, Rory grabbed Sierra by the hand and began to muscle her way through the crowd. The picture that they made moving toward her was one she'd seen so often—Rory rushing forward and Sierra having to be dragged along. Natalie had sometimes wondered why Rory hadn't made it first out of the womb.

"Happy birthday," Natalie said when they reached her.

"Happy birthday," Rory echoed.

"Ditto," Sierra said as they exchanged hugs.

"It's not every day we all turn twenty-six," Rory said in an undertone. "When I explained it to the hostess, she agreed that we should have a table on the patio. C'mon."

The patio was the last place Natalie wanted to be, but she didn't have the heart to spoil Rory's delight with herself. Still, as they moved down the short flight of stairs, she had to put some effort into keeping her eyes from straying to the spot behind the potted trees where Chance had drawn her to make his proposition.

"You all right?" Sierra asked as they followed Rory across the dance floor.

Natalie managed a smile. "Absolutely. How's the research going, Dr. Gibbs?"

"It's going. Of course, all the data isn't in yet."

"Don't pay any attention to her. Her research is going brilliantly," Rory said. "It always does. The big news is that my job at *Celebs* magazine is going well. A first for me. There's a senior reporter there who's taken me under her wing and I'm really enjoying the work."

"This calls for champagne," Sierra said.

"Agreed," Rory said as she sat down and picked up a menu. "And I'm starved."

Natalie waited until they were all seated before she said, "Maybe we ought to hold off on the celebration."

"What is it?" Sierra asked.

As Natalie explained the package she'd received that morning, she took the sealed envelopes out of her purse and placed them on the table. For a moment, all three of them simply stared at the white rectangles.

"To open them or not to open them, that is the question," Sierra finally said.

"Exactly." Natalie could always depend on that fine analytical mind of Sierra's to cut to the bottom line.

"They're from our father," Rory pointed out.

"So what?" Natalie said, letting a little of her anger show. "We agreed to stop calling him 'father' when we were ten because he left us."

Silence stretched between them again.

"It's been sixteen years since we last saw him and six years since he died." Sierra placed one finger on the corner of her envelope. "Why now?"

"Exactly," Natalie said again. "He's never once gotten in touch with us—not when we were sick, not for a birthday or a graduation. Not for anything. Why did he instruct the attorney to get those letters to us now?"

A waiter appeared, pen poised at the ready. "Drink orders, ladies?"

"A martini," Natalie said without taking her eyes off the envelopes. "Very dry with an olive."

"I'll have what she's having," Sierra said.

Rory sighed. "Ditto. Champagne just isn't going to do it. And bring us one of those appetizer samplers with three of everything. I'm definitely going to need food before I deal with this."

After the waiter hurried off, the silence descended again for a moment.

"Neither of you has to deal with this right now," Natalie finally said. "But I think I do have to open mine. I've got too much of Harry in me just to throw it away."

"We all have too much of Harry in us," Rory said.

Sierra drew in a quick hitched breath and let it out. "I'm afraid to open mine."

Natalie reached for her sister's hand. "Are you all right? Do you need your inhaler?"

Sierra shook her head. "I'm not having an asthma attack. I'm just a coward."

"No, you're not." Natalie and Rory spoke in unison.

"Tell you what," Natalie said. "We'll make a plan and you can jot it down on one of those note cards."

Rory nodded in agreement. "Even I could use some kind of plan for this."

Sierra pulled a blue card out of the canvas bag she always carried with her.

"We'll go in the order of our births. I'll go first," Natalie said.

Rory patted Sierra's arm. "Number one—Natalie, our fearless leader. And put me down for the number two slot."

"And I'm number three," Sierra said as she added her name to the list.

"And I'm the only one who's going to open her letter tonight." Though Natalie could sense that Rory might want to open hers tonight, she willed her to go along. "The two of you can wait. For a few weeks, a year, five years—take all the time you need. Harry certainly took his time getting these to us."

"Good plan," Rory said.

As Natalie slipped a finger under the flap, she could see some of the tension fade in the way Sierra was gripping her pencil. Finessing the envelope open, she took out the letter. Then clearing her throat, she read it out loud.

Dearest Natalie, my warrior and seeker of justice, Happy birthday. You're probably wondering why I'm sending you this letter on this particular birthday, and the answer is a bit complicated. Your mother and I were exactly twenty-six when you came into our lives. Ten years later, I gave you up. Your mother and I agreed when we separated that I would cut off any contact with you until you were twenty-six. We thought that was for the best. I now know that leaving you and leaving your mother was the biggest mistake I ever made. If something happens to me and I can't be with you on your twenty-sixth birthday, I want you to know this: Don't make the same mistake that I did. When you see what you want, trust in your talents. Risk anything it takes to get it. And most importantly, hold on to it.

Love,

Harry

"Well," Rory said.

Natalie placed the letter down on the table and ran her finger over the signature. She couldn't put a name to any of the feelings swirling through her. "You've got to hand it to him—he's a man who walked his talk. He went for what he wanted, and we all paid the price."

"Look." Sierra pointed at the envelope. "There's something else inside."

Natalie pulled out three photos. One was taken at her high school graduation, another on her first day at the police academy. The third one was from when she was twelve, and she'd had to stay in the hospital over-night to have her tonsils out.

"He was there," Rory said. "I'd figured he'd forgotten all about us."

Sierra studied the photos when Natalie passed them to her. "I'd always suspected that he and Mom made some sort of deal that he had to stay away. She was so afraid that we would take after him."

"And now he seems to be advising you to do just that," Natalie said. "'Trust in your talents…risk anything it takes….'"

"That's exactly what you want to do, isn't it?" Sierra asked as the waiter set their drinks and a platter of appetizers in front of them. "That's what's been bothering you for the past three months, right?"

Natalie stared at her. Sierra was the most observant of her sisters, but Natalie hadn't thought she'd been that transparent. "I don't want to become a jewel thief, if that's what you're asking."

"But…" Sierra urged.

Natalie sighed and turned to Rory. "It was a mistake to let her get that Ph.D. in psychology."

"You're just evading the issue," Rory said around a mouthful of shrimp. "You haven't been yourself lately. Even I've noticed that. But I don't think it's because you're thinking of ditching law enforcement for a career in grand larceny. I'm betting it's a man."

"I've sworn off," Natalie said with a frown.

"Here, here." Rory lifted her glass. "I'll drink to that. Ever since Paul the jerk dumped me, I've decided that the only men I'll allow in my life are the ones I create in my fantasies."

Sierra laughed and joined in the toast. "Which particular man have you sworn off, Nat?"

Natalie slanted Sierra a look. "You should have been a cop." Then with a sigh, she set down her glass. Who better to talk to than her two sisters? "The man is the one I worked with on that smuggling case three months ago. I haven't been able to get him out of my mind."

"So what's the problem?" Rory asked. "I've never known you to have any trouble getting a man if you wanted him?"

Natalie turned to face her two sisters. "That's just it. I don't want to want him. Besides, the feeling doesn't seem to be mutual. I haven't heard from him in three months. Not that I expected to. We had an agreement—for one night. That was all."

"That is a problem," Sierra said.

Natalie sighed. "That's not the only one. Ever since I worked with him on that case, I've begun to be restless at my job. I've been grumpy with my partner, Matt, my office seems to be closing in on me and I want more than anything to escape."

Shocked at what she'd just admitted, Natalie stared at her two sisters and found them staring right back at her. "I am just like Harry."

"Of course, you're like him," Rory said, helping herself to a crab puff. "We try to deny it, but we're all like him. I count on luck to get me out of scrapes. Sierra uses that marvelous brain she inherited from him. And you take the risks that he thrived on, though you try very hard to keep a lid on that tendency. But, face it, we can't escape our genes."

"Sierra," Natalie said, "you want to help me out on this one? Tell her she's wrong."

Sierra shook her head. "I can't. Rory's right. We are, all of us, his daughters—for better or worse. But if you want my advice…"

"I need something," Natalie said, waving away the shrimp that Rory offered her. "And I don't mean food."

"I think that you ought to follow his advice. You've seen what you want. Why not trust in your talents and take a risk?" Sierra said.

Natalie turned her gaze to Rory.

"You're not going to get any argument from me. You like this guy who hasn't called you in three months. I say go get him. And if you want to give up your job as a cop, do that, too. For years, you've been the responsible one, holding down a steady job, helping Sierra apply to another graduate school, helping me write yet another résumé. But Sierra and I are officially all grown-up now. You can stop worrying about us and escape."

"I'm not giving up my job." The thought had a little curl of panic tightening in her stomach. "I heard this afternoon that he's going to be at the party Sophie Wainwright is throwing at her shop on Friday."

"Excellent," Rory said. "Sierra was invited, and she's bringing me as her guest. We'll be there to cheer you on."

Natalie drew in a deep breath, then let it out. "I'm just not sure…."

"Do you want him?" Rory asked.

"Yes." She couldn't deny that. It had been three months, and she hadn't gotten him out of her head.

Rory selected another mushroom. "Then I say follow Harry's advice and take a risk. What have you got to lose?"

Natalie said nothing as the curl of panic tightened in her stomach. As a cop, she was used to facing her fears. As a woman, she was less sure of herself. Except for that night she'd spent with Chance. She lifted her hands and dropped them. "We had an agreement—for one night."

"Agreements can be renegotiated." Rory sipped her martini.

"Whose idea was it to make it one night?" Sierra asked.

"His," Natalie replied.

"Figures," Rory said.

"In many primitive cultures, the woman is the hunter when it comes to mate selection," Sierra said.

"Whoa." Natalie lifted her hands, palm outward. "I'm not on the hunt for a mate. I'm more in the mood for a fling. And I was in total agreement about the one night."

"And all you want is one more night?" Sierra asked.

"Yeah," Natalie said. One more night. Maybe then, she could get him out of her system and get her life back to normal.

Sierra cleared her throat. "Then I have a suggestion. For my current research project, I've been researching the sexual fantasies of different cultures."

"That's our girl," Rory said, lifting her glass.

After they toasted again, Sierra continued, "One of

the most universal fantasies is sex with a stranger—someone you don't know and never will know." Pausing, she cleared her throat again. "So why don't you just pretend that you're someone else for the night?"

When her two sisters turned to stare at her, Sierra hurried on. "It makes sense. You love undercover work and you're good at it. So just come to Sophie's party as someone else."

"That's a great idea," Rory said, waving a shrimp.

"I don't think—"

"That's your problem, Nat," Rory said. "You overthink everything. Sierra's got a great idea."

"You're so good at disguise," Sierra continued. "You could just let yourself *be* this other person. That way you can put Natalie Gibbs's fears and hang-ups away for the evening and be free to make a play for this man as a totally different person."

"You're serious, aren't you?" Natalie asked.

"Absolutely." Sierra leaned forward. "It's the age-old concept of Mardi Gras. For one night you put on a mask and do things that you would never do as your real self. Very freeing."

Rory shot Natalie a look. "Freeing? Does this sound like the baby sister we used to know and love?"

Natalie shook her head, seriously considering her youngest sister's idea. She glanced down at her drink. The glass was still half-full, so she couldn't blame the martini. Her gaze shifted to the letter and her father's words.

When you see what you want, trust in your talents. Risk anything it takes...

Natalie ran her finger over her father's signature

again. She wanted Chance, and if she took Sierra's suggestion, she could go after him with a clean slate. She wouldn't be Natalie, the woman he hadn't called for three months.

"Think about it," Sierra said.

If she did decide to follow Sierra's advice, she knew two things for sure. Chance Mitchell wouldn't recognize her. And he wouldn't know what hit him.

CHANCE STOOD outside on the flagstone patio at the back of Sophie Wainwright's antique and collectibles shop and scanned the crowd through the window. From what he could see, the event was a success. Three musicians were tucked away in a corner playing Mozart, and a white-jacketed waiter offering flutes of champagne was threading his way through the crush of guests.

In between the potted trees and terra-cotta urns bursting with pansies and geraniums, Chance spotted a prominent senator, a congresswoman and several well-heeled collectors who'd been frequent clients at the gallery down the street where he'd worked undercover.

The person he hadn't spotted yet was Natalie Gibbs. He'd told himself that he came through the back alleyway because of the line of guests waiting to get in the front door of the shop, but the truth was he was stalling. He still wasn't sure how he was going to handle Natalie when he ran into her.

Damn if his hands weren't damp. With a frown, he rubbed them on his pants. A woman hadn't made him nervous since junior high school. He'd spent two days thinking of ways to convince her to go with him on the Florida caper. The best scenario he'd come up with was to play it by ear. Not that he was worried about that part. He wasn't a planner by nature, and he'd gotten himself out of plenty of scrapes by improvising. He wasn't worried about the job—she'd come with him to Florida, all right. It was on the personal level that he wasn't quite sure how to handle Natalie Gibbs.

Later, he couldn't have said what it was that drew his gaze to the small balcony on the second story of Sophie's shop. But the moment he saw the woman, he felt his mind go blank and then fill with her. Her hair was blond, parted in the middle, and it fell in a straight, smooth curve almost to her shoulders. The tiny black dress revealed curves in all the right places and left more bare than it covered. The summer sky was finally beginning to darken overhead, but even in the less than perfect light her skin had the pale perfection of an old-fashioned cameo. Chance let out a breath he hadn't known he was holding.

She was the kind of woman who would get a second glance from any man, but Chance couldn't seem to get past the first one. The quick tightening in his gut was unexpectedly raw and hot, but what surprised him most was the flicker of familiarity, recognition almost, that pushed at the edges of his mind. He could have sworn he'd never laid eyes on her before. If he had, he certainly would have remembered.

And then her eyes met his, and for the second time in as many moments, Chance felt his mind empty. The primitive streak of desire that moved through him had him scanning the iron railing, looking for a staircase,

a ladder—or tree branch that extended far enough to…
He hadn't realized that he'd moved closer to the balcony until he bumped smack into a waiter. The man's
tray tilted, two champagne flutes began a downward
slide. Chance barely managed to catch them.

"Sorry," he murmured as he settled them on the
tray.

"No problem, sir."

"I'll take one of those, if you don't mind." He took
a long swallow of the icy wine before he raised his
gaze to the balcony again.

She was gone.

Disappointment warred with astonishment. Had he
really been thinking of doing the Romeo thing and
scaling a balcony? What in hell was the matter with
him? Shakespeare's star-crossed hero had been all of
about sixteen. Chance was twice that age. Hormone-
driven foolishness was a thing of his adolescent past.
Or it should be.

Still there was some similarity between Romeo and
himself, he thought as his lips curved in amusement.
In a way, he *was* crashing a party. He hadn't gotten an
engraved invitation from Sophie, merely a verbal,
secondhand one from his friend Tracker. But that's
where the parallel would end. He hadn't come here to
meet some woman he was going to lust after at first
sight and then fall madly and tragically in love with.

He was here to make an offer to Natalie Gibbs that
she would not be able to refuse. Taking another sip
from his glass, Chance made his way to the French
doors that opened into the shop. But it took more effort than he liked not to glance back up at the balcony.

4

WITH A HAND firmly pressed against the nerves jittering in her stomach, Natalie closed the door to the balcony behind her and took two steps into the office above Sophie's shop.

So much for the hope that the attraction she felt for Chance Mitchell had faded with time and distance. His absence from her life might not have made her heart grow fonder, but it had sure increased the lust factor.

One look, one meeting of eyes at a distance of some twenty feet had her nipples tightening and muscles she hadn't even known she had clenching deep inside of her. If he could do that to her with a look, what would happen if he touched her, kissed her, made love to her again? At the image that filled her mind, an arrow of pleasure, hot and sweet, streaked right to her center. Natalie lowered her hand from her stomach to the spot where she throbbed and reminded herself to breathe.

There was no need to panic. She could handle this—because she was Rachel Cade. Drawing in a deep breath, she moved toward the antique mirror in the far corner of the room. All she had to do was get into character the way she did for a job. She met the eyes of the woman who stared back at her from the silvered glass and let the tension ease from her shoulders. She could barely recognize Natalie Gibbs at all. Rachel Cade had straight blond hair. Natalie's hair was red and had a tendency to curl. Rachel's eyes were blue. Natalie's were green. Rachel was wearing a dress—what there was of it—that Natalie never would have bought.

In front, the thin black silk covered her from breast to midthigh, and the back was bare from neck to waist except for a narrow strap that went over the shoulder. Oh my, no. She smiled at her reflection. Natalie Gibbs would never have worn this dress because she held men at arm's length and dressing like this would have been counterproductive.

Rachel Cade didn't have any hang-ups about men. Thank heavens! With a smile, she watched Rachel push her hair back behind her ears. It wasn't a wig. Midsummer in D.C. was far too hot for that. So she'd had it dyed and flat-ironed. Her hairdresser had had to double up on his anxiety medication, but she'd been firm about the color change. Besides, if she was going to take Sierra's advice and *be* someone else, even for a short period of time, she was going to go all the way. For the next few days, she *was* Rachel Cade. She'd arranged to take the time off that her partner, Matt Ramsey, had been pushing her to enjoy. No sense in doing something unless you were willing to *risk anything it takes.*

She shook her head and watched her hair settle back into place. This was her chance to see if blondes really did have more fun and if gentlemen preferred them.

After fishing lip gloss out of her bag, she slicked

it on. This was what she'd always most enjoyed about being a cop—the opportunity it gave her to become someone else for a while. It was a weakness, she knew, but it was also very liberating. And becoming Rachel Cade was especially so. When she did undercover work, the persona she created was often dictated by the job, but she'd had complete freedom with Rachel. The tall blonde staring back at her from the mirror was a distant cousin of the Gibbs sisters. She'd come from her home in South Florida to visit for two weeks.

Natalie had never been to South Florida in her life, so she'd read up on it. Not that she expected Chance to give her a pop quiz, but in a good undercover operation, one always had to be prepared, just in case.

Just thinking about him had an image of Chance slipping into her mind. The tuxedo he was wearing certainly enhanced that long rangy body….

No. She wasn't going to go there, or she'd be stuck in this room all night imagining what it would be like to get her hands on him again. Natalie might be satisfied with a fantasy life, but Rachel preferred the real thing. She gave herself one last glance in the mirror as she reviewed her plan. Rachel Cade—blond ambition and material girl all rolled into one—wanted to have a hot, wild and mutually satisfying night—or two or three—with Chance Mitchell. He would have fun. She would have fun. And they could go their separate ways.

Luckily, that would never bother a girl like Rachel. She would just move on to the next man. Oh, she was going to like being Rachel Cade. After beaming one last smile at the girl in the mirror, Natalie walked to the door.

"YOU DON'T LOOK like you're having a very good time."

As usual, Chance hadn't seen or heard his friend Tracker approach. "I haven't yet spotted my quarry."

"She'll be here. Her sisters arrived about twenty minutes ago with a cousin who's visiting from South Florida. Sophie took them on a quick tour. She's outdone herself with this place, don't you think?"

Chance glanced at his friend, intrigued by his tone that contained a mix of pride, approval, and… Searching for a word, all he could come up with was loyalty. "You haven't even tied the knot yet, and you're beginning to sound like an old married man."

"Yeah." A man of few words, Tracker thought for a minute. "Yeah." He didn't sound a bit displeased. "By the way, I developed those pictures we took on our fishing trip. Looks like there are only the two sentry stations we spotted, but I'm betting he has other guards patrolling the beach. It won't be a piece of cake, but I can get you off the place by water. Any word on when you leave?"

"Day after tomorrow."

Tracker shot him a look. "You're cutting it close. What if Natalie doesn't agree to go?"

"I'll just have to make her an offer she can't refuse." Chance's gaze drifted to the flight of stairs that ran up the far wall of the store. He knew there was one display room on the second floor and another, smaller space where Sophie kept an office. His mystery woman had to be up there.

"Natalie's sisters are right over there if you want to ask them when she's expected to arrive."

Dragging his eyes from the stairs, Chance shifted his attention to where Tracker was pointing.

"The blonde is the academic," Tracker said. "Her name's Sierra and Mac says that there was quite a buzz when both the anthropology department and the psychology department at Georgetown hired her. And the short dark-haired one is Rory. She's a freelance writer. If you want, I can introduce you— Uh-oh, Sophie's giving me a signal. You're on your own."

The moment Tracker began to make his way through the crowd, Chance opted to edge his way along the wall to where the two Gibbs sisters were standing and surveying the party. But reaching them was easier said than done. Two major hurdles stood in his path—a group of women and a tall potted tree. He began to edge his way around the women.

"This is such a crush," a tall brunette said. "I'm going to have to come back when I can really see this place."

"Me, too," another woman said.

"Look, over there. Isn't that Mame Appelgate who writes a column for the *Washington Post?* All it will take is a mention from her, and it'll be a crush here tomorrow, too."

Chance found himself temporarily wedged between the wall and a potted palm. Through the leaves, he could see Sierra's cheeks were flushed, and she shook her head as Rory offered her something from the well-stocked plate she was holding.

"I can't eat," Sierra said.

"Relax. Natalie will be fine," Rory managed around a mouthful of pastry.

Sierra glanced at her watch. "I think you should go upstairs and check on her."

Though he hadn't meant to eavesdrop, Chance moved closer.

"Uh-uh. I value my life too much," Rory said. "Besides, she said she only needed a few minutes to get in character. You know Nat. She doesn't like to appear as a new 'persona' until the disguise is perfect and she's had a chance to assume her new persona. Harry was like that, too. Remember the game he played with us when he would show up at the door and we wouldn't be able to figure out who he was?"

"Nat always knew," Sierra said.

"Just like I always knew when he was bluffing at poker." Rory paused with a shrimp halfway to her mouth to sigh. "You know, I still miss him."

"Me, too," Sierra said. "Have you thought about when you're going to open your letter?"

"No. I figure I'll know when the time is right. But I'm going to wait until Natalie has had her adventure. I'll need both of you there when I do."

"Yes," Sierra agreed. "I will, too."

Rory studied the food on her plate and then offered it to Sierra again. "Come on. You'll feel better if you eat something."

"I'm too nervous," Sierra said. "I just feel so responsible for this. I suggested the plan."

Rory reached out a hand to pat her sister's arm. "I'm sure Dr. Frankenstein felt the same way right after he threw the electrical switch for the first time."

"Not funny."

Rory rolled her eyes. "Nat is going to be fine. And your plan is brilliant. Pretending to be someone else is the perfect ticket for her. For a little while, she can leave all of her responsibilities behind and be someone entirely different. As soon as my job at *Celebs* is more secure, I may try a masquerade thing myself." She tossed a morsel of food into her mouth. You've really got to try these crab puffs."

Masquerade. Chance tried to make sense of the thoughts swirling through his mind as he replayed the snatch of conversation he'd just heard. Natalie Gibbs was adopting a new persona? She was going to be someone else for a while? Chance scanned the crowd, this time more carefully than he had before. He'd seen Natalie Gibbs in an undercover disguise twice. She was good, but he should be able to spot her.

He made one full circuit of the store and came up empty. Frustrated, he moved out onto the patio. Immediately, a ripple of awareness moved through him. Natalie. But when he turned, it wasn't Natalie he saw. It was his blond mystery woman from the balcony. Even then, he might have continued his search for Natalie. But the blonde chose that particular moment to shove her hair behind her ear, something that he'd seen Natalie Gibbs do countless times. He dropped his gaze to her feet. Sure enough, one of them was tapping. That was another habit Natalie had.

Then he simply stared. Could it be? Was this the disguise that Sierra and Rory had been referring to? Could his blond mystery woman be Natalie Gibbs?

Chance accepted a drink from a passing waiter and

sipped without tasting what he'd chosen. He had to think, and the first step would be to unglue his eyes from his mystery woman's legs. He was not going to find the answer to his question there. He shifted his gaze slowly upward.

Gestures aside, this woman was a sharp right turn from the Natalie Gibbs he knew. But his gut instinct, which rarely failed him, was telling him that the detective he was searching for and the blonde he was looking at were one and the same person. The light was no better than it had been before, but he was closer, and there was no balcony blocking his view.

Over the years, he'd honed his observation skills, but they'd seldom brought him more pleasure. Her eyes were heavy-lidded, her mouth slick and cherry-red. During the time he'd spent with Natalie, she'd either been disguised as a man, or had been wearing muted makeup colors. He wasn't close enough to make out the color of her eyes. Natalie's, he recalled, were a deep shade of bottomless green, but he was willing to bet that the blonde's were a different color. When a professional put on a new persona, he or she went all the way and changed everything that could possibly be changed.

Like the hair. Natalie's was red and long and curly. He'd thought of an exploding sunset the first time he'd seen it. The blonde's hair, shorter and straight, with the finish of newly spun silk, held its own attraction. The slick fall of it tempted a man to touch, and once he did, there would be all that smooth skin to explore. Then there were those legs—his gaze slipped back to them. They were nothing short of miraculous.

It occurred to him that he'd never seen what Natalie Gibbs looked like in a dress because she'd always hidden her feminine figure beneath trousers and a jacket. His mystery woman didn't seem to believe in hiding anything. The contrasts fascinated him. Natalie Gibbs was all work. His mystery woman shouted "play." Detective Gibbs's sex appeal, out of sight beneath pantsuits, was muted like the steady hum of a current along a wire. The blonde's sex appeal snapped and crackled around her like static electricity.

A man was bound to be burned if he got too close. And he was being drawn as inevitably as a moth. He'd already moved halfway across the patio toward her, and he still hadn't decided how he was going to handle her. Oh, this was Natalie Gibbs all right. Hadn't he known it on some level from the first moment he'd spotted her and felt that tiny click of recognition? This Natalie was the one he'd discovered when they'd made love in her apartment that night three months ago.

Just what kind of a game was she playing?

A warning voice told him to wait until he'd weighed his options and come up with a strategy. But the inner voice he'd always trusted was reminding him that he did his best work when he played it by ear.

5

NATALIE KNEW the moment that Chance spotted her, and she struggled to keep the tension out of her shoulders. It was bad enough that her stomach was jittering again.

She could feel his eyes on her and sensed the instant they moved from her face down her body to her legs. Though it took some effort, she stopped tapping her foot. He was sharp, and he knew all about disguises. This would be the supreme test of just how good her persona was. She signaled a passing waiter and took a glass of champagne. As yet no one had known who she really was.

As a preliminary test, she'd asked Sierra and Rory to introduce her to Tracker McBride and Sophie Wainwright. They'd been pleased to meet the Gibbs sisters' cousin, but she'd detected no gleam of recognition in their eyes.

When the short, bald man to her left said something, she shoved her hair behind her ear and smiled down at him. Before she could catch his name, she found herself surrounded by the two other men he was with. Instantly, she was ankle-deep—no, make that waist-deep—in a discussion of a new water pollution bill that was going to the house floor the next week. Because it was part of her job to know who was who in the nation's government, she recognized all three of the men. One was a congressman who'd been elected as an environmentalist; the two others were senators who had coauthored the bill under discussion.

"Darling, I've been looking all over for you," said a voice at her side. Then Chance took her arm in a firm grip, and shot a five-hundred-megawatt smile toward the three men who'd boxed her in. "Sorry, gentlemen, but I have to borrow back my wife. I have a proposition to make her. We're still newlyweds."

Natalie made no protest as Chance led her back into the store. Instead, she used the time to remind herself that she was Rachel. And Rachel Cade would never object to a man who looked like Chance leading her away. Nor would Rachel Cade care a fig if Chance Mitchell saw through her disguise. And any minute she would know if he had or not.

When he stopped in front of one of the display cases, he turned to her. "Aren't you even going to thank me?"

"For what?" she asked in the low voice she'd chosen for Rachel.

"I saved your life. Another five minutes and they would have bored you to death."

She felt her lips twitch, and some of her tension eased. She saw no hint of recognition in his expression. He hadn't seen through her *yet*. "What if I told you that I find environmental problems sexy?"

"I'd immediately find a job with the E.P.A."

She couldn't prevent the laugh, and she didn't stop

him when he placed a finger under her chin and tipped her face up so that their eyes met for the first time.

"Blue," he said. "I wondered."

For five whole seconds, Natalie held her breath. Chance's dark, smoky gray eyes held no knowing look. All she could see was curiosity…and the tiniest flare of heat. The heat she understood because his hand on her arm had created a flame that was spreading over her entire body. "Why did you wonder about my eyes?"

"Because I couldn't tell from across the room. Who are you?"

The blunt question had the rest of her nerves easing. He wasn't suspicious yet. It was up to her to make sure he stayed that way. "Rachel Cade."

He smiled and held out his hand. "Chance Mitchell."

She raised her brows. "Did I ask?"

Chance withdrew his extended hand and pulled an imaginary arrow out of his chest. "And after I saved your life."

Natalie laughed—not just because of what Chance had said but because she knew that she was in the clear. Her disguise was working, and she could feel the freedom move through her. If she were Natalie and Chance was flirting with her, she would make some excuse to leave and check on her sisters. But as Rachel she could eat it up. In fact, the only way to keep him believing in her persona was to do just that.

Chance reached over to tuck her hair behind her ear. "You know, I hate to use such a corny line, but when I first came in, I saw you standing on the balcony that overlooks the patio, and I thought for a moment that I'd seen you someplace before. Except if I had, I'm sure I would have remembered it."

The man had more than his share of charm. Natalie would have been wary of it. Rachel could simply enjoy it, just as she was enjoying the fact that his hand was still lingering on the sensitive skin behind her ear. "Nicely put. I'm told that I bear some resemblance to my cousins, the Gibbs triplets. Perhaps, that's what you see."

He studied her for a minute, and Natalie held her breath.

"Well, that's one mystery solved. On to another. Just who is Rachel Cade?"

Natalie smiled, trying not to let any trace show of the relief she was feeling. Now that the first hurdle had been cleared, it was time for step two of her plan. Seduce Chance Mitchell before he knew what hit him. She ran one finger down the lapel of his jacket.

"Who is Rachel Cade?" she repeated. Perhaps it was time to explore that question thoroughly. One thing she was discovering—Rachel wasn't nearly as patient as Natalie. And for some reason, Rachel seemed to be even more vulnerable to the attraction she was feeling for Chance. The moment he'd touched her, every nerve in her body had seemed to come alive. And the way he was looking at her now had her melting inside. She had a short bio all set to deliver, but suddenly she didn't want to waste the time. "That's a long, boring story. I can think of something we could do that would be much more fun than exchanging life stories."

CHANCE COULD almost hear some of the synapses in his brain disconnect. There wasn't much chance of making a snappy comeback when that happened. He heard his heart skip one full beat and then begin to pound until the noises of the party—the chatter, the clink of glasses, the music—all of it faded to a hum. And all the while, he simply couldn't take his eyes off of her. As if the combination of cherry-red lips and startlingly blue eyes weren't lethal enough, she now had a slew of very improper images flooding his mind. Thoroughly fascinated by this side of Natalie, he could barely wait to see what she would do next.

She filled in the silence by taking the fingers that were still at her ear and raising then to her mouth. He felt the warmth of her breath, then the cool brush of her lips just before the heat scorched through him. Even after she released his hand, he felt as if the skin had been singed by a candle.

"Where are you staying?" she asked.

"The Meridian," he said.

She ran one finger from his tie down the front of his shirt, stopping at the waistband of his pants. Then she traced the buckle of his belt. "You know, the moment I saw you, I thought to myself—when was the last time I made love with someone just for the fun of it? And I couldn't remember."

She was seducing him in the middle of a crowded party. And he wasn't doing a thing to stop her. He wasn't even taking over the task. He didn't want to. In some dark corner of his brain, Chance recalled that he'd come to this party with a job to do and that he was on a deadline. But none of that seemed to matter anymore.

Her fingers had slipped below his belt and were resting lightly on his erection. "Am I moving too fast for you? I have a tendency to do that."

"I think I can keep up."

She smiled at him. "Good. I'm only in town for a few days, and I'd hate to waste my time here."

"Time management just happens to be my specialty." Chance took the hand that was toying again with his belt and linked her fingers with his. "Let's go."

By the time he'd led her through the gate and down the alley to where he'd parked his car, he'd organized his thoughts a little. At least he thought he had. But when they reached the sleek red convertible, Natalie turned so her body brushed against his, and his brain seemed to switch off.

"You know, we're about to go off and have a bout of hot, wild sex," she said. "At least I hope we are. But we haven't even kissed yet. Maybe we ought to try it to see if we have the right chemistry."

Oh, they had the right chemistry all right. The luscious red lips were only inches away, and he was sure he could smell his synapses frying again. He had to get some kind of handle on his response to her.

He had not come to Sophie Wainwright's party to seduce Natalie Gibbs. He'd come to convince her to come to Florida with him. He needed her help, and what he was about to do might blow his chances of ever convincing her to help him catch Carlo Brancotti.

But from the moment she'd looked at him through those baby-blue contact lenses and told him that she wanted to do something a lot more fun than exchange life stories, he'd been unable to think about anything else. He might be about to make the biggest mistake of his life, but he wanted this Natalie just as desperately as he'd wanted the woman who'd haunted his dreams for the past three months.

But that didn't mean "Rachel" was going to have it all her way. Two could play the little game she'd started. He moved forward, just enough to push her back against the car and bring his body into full contact with hers. The quick hitch of her breath gave him a great deal of satisfaction. "If I kiss you now, really kiss you, I won't stop," he murmured, bringing his lips to within a breath of hers, "until I'm inside of you."

He saw the quick flash of heat in her eyes, felt it in the way her body melted against his. He rested his mouth against hers, just long enough to sample the yielding softness. Then he drew away. His words had conjured up in his mind a very clear image of what it would be like to take her right there on the hood of his car. He was ready. He'd been ready since he'd first spotted her on the balcony. And he could very easily find out if she was ready. All he had to do was slip his hand beneath the hem of her dress and up the satiny softness of her thigh. He had no doubt that she would be hot and wet and welcoming. The alley was deserted right now, and the party was in full swing. The sounds of string music and muted laughter carried clearly on the still night air.

When she looped her arms around his neck, and pulled his head just that little bit closer so that his lips were brushing hers again, he nearly gave in to the temptation to taste her. Later he would thank the blast of music from a car driving past the alley for saving them both. Placing his hands on her shoulders, he drew back. "We could get arrested."

"Arrested?" The cloudy mix of desire and confusion in her eyes nearly snapped his control.

"Yeah. Mug shots, fingerprints, one phone call. It could really take all the fun out of the evening."

"Yeah." She gave her head one quick shake to clear it, then pushed her hair behind her ear. Though he couldn't have said why, he found the nervous gesture endearing.

"I'll take a raincheck on that kiss," he said.

"Ditto."

He managed to get her into the car without touching her again. That was the easy part. The hard part was the drive to his hotel. They'd no sooner pulled out of the parking lot when she scrambled onto her knees and began to loosen his tie.

"Rachel, getting into an accident is another way to take the fun out of an evening."

Her laugh was quick and breathless in his ear. "I'm just trying to save us time. You did say you were into time management."

"Yeah." His tie was off, and her fingers were already slipping beneath the buttons of his shirt, leaving a trail of ice and heat on his skin. "Two rules. You keep your hands above my belt, and I'll promise to keep both of mine on the wheel."

Laughing, she closed her teeth around the lobe of his ear. "Deal. But don't they say rules are meant to be broken?"

NATALIE HADN'T convinced him to break the rules, but it had been a close call. She could tell by the quick way he handed the car keys over to a valet and drew her with him into the hotel. The Meridian was one of D.C.'s more posh accommodations for travellers. Many of the rooms boasted a view of the Washington Monument and the Mall, though she didn't think that she and Chance were going to spend time looking at either. She could feel heat radiating through her body from where his hand was pressed at the small of her back.

His touches, his kiss, had been tame so far, and she was beginning to crave him. When his body had brushed against hers in the parking lot, it had been hard, solid. In the three months since she'd last seen Chance, she'd spent some time imagining exactly what that body would feel like pressing into hers. Natalie, of course, had pushed those fantasies out of her mind. Rachel, on the other hand, couldn't wait to make those fantasies and more come true. Had Rachel always been living inside of her? That was something she would consider later. Right now, she was going to focus all her attention on Chance.

She said nothing until they were in the elevator and the doors were sliding shut. Then she turned to him. "Are you ever really going to kiss me?"

"Soon." He settled his hands at her waist, but instead of pulling her close, he turned her instead, so that she could see them both reflected in the mirrored walls of the elevator. Then meeting her eyes in the mirror, he moved one hand to her breast, the other to the hem of her dress. The sight of those long, lean fingers mov-

ing on her skin only doubled the sharp stab of pleasure moving through her. She was on fire where he
touched her, and she was sure that her knees had turned
to jelly.

"I've wanted to touch you like this ever since I first
saw you on that balcony."

His fingers slipped beneath the bodice of the dress
as his other hand began to push up the hem of her skirt.
He moved so slowly. She wanted him to hurry. She
wanted the sensations to go on forever. When her dress
was up to her hips, he ran his finger along the lacy edge
of her panties, from the top of her thigh to the narrow
vee that disappeared between her legs. "When we were
standing in the parking lot, I was tempted to do this."

Natalie watched his finger slip beneath the band of
her panties.

"And this."

He pinched her nipple at the same time that he
slipped a finger inside of her.

The orgasm that moved through her in one long,
crashing wave had her sagging against him. Later, she
couldn't recall exactly how they'd gotten out of the elevator and down the hall to the room. But by the time
Chance had opened the door, she'd gotten some of her
strength back. And she was thinking more clearly.

A sudden feeling of déjà vu struck her as he drew her
into the narrow foyer. It grew sharper when he used his
body to trap her against the wall. She recalled that he'd
used the same move when they'd entered the tiny foyer
of her apartment three months ago. He'd kissed her and
then taken her, or they'd taken each other, on the floor.

Natalie had surrendered without a second thought,

just as she'd surrendered in the elevator a few seconds ago.

"Now, I'll kiss you," Chance said as he pressed his body more fully against hers.

But she didn't have to be Natalie. Tonight, she could be Rachel. Despite that her body was heating, melting against his, she avoided his mouth at the last moment. Her voice was breathless when she said, "Not yet. Turnabout's fair play. Now it's my turn to touch you."

6

BEMUSED, CHANCE STEPPED back and then followed Natalie into the sitting room of the suite.

"Ahhh. Mirrors. Just what I need." There was a wicked gleam in her eyes when she turned to face him.

Chance studied her for a moment. The woman in the elevator had been the Natalie who'd haunted his dreams for three months. He would have bet his life on it. But the woman who'd driven him crazy in the car and the woman facing him now was "Rachel." And he wanted her just as much.

He moved toward her, cupped a hand at the back of her neck. "I want you now."

She placed a hand on his chest with just enough pressure to preserve the distance between them. "You can have me. But what's the rush?"

His eyebrows rose. "You were in a hurry in the car."

She smiled up at him. "What happened in the elevator sort of took the edge off for me."

He increased the pressure on the back of her neck, and she moved closer so that her body was in contact with his.

"It only built the pressure for me."

"Yes, I can feel that. But I do have a solution."

He felt his heart quicken against her palm, saw her eyes darken when she felt its rapid beat, too. She slipped a finger beneath the top button of his shirt and freed it. "You're going to enjoy what I'm going to do to you. I promise."

Chance felt his mind begin to cloud as she continued to unbutton his shirt. Each time her fingers brushed against his skin, ribbons of heat fanned out across his skin. She pushed the shirt off of his shoulders and it slid to the floor.

"I wanted to do this right in front of everyone at Sophie Wainwright's party."

And she very nearly had, Chance recalled. Her hands were spread out along his waist now, and with her thumbs touching, she drew them upward over his ribs until they were resting just at the bottom of his rib cage.

"Watch what I'm doing in the mirror."

He could do that. His arms were beginning to feel heavy, but he could still move his eyes.

She rubbed her palms over his nipples and he sucked in a breath.

"You like that," she murmured as she did it again.

He felt his nipples harden. Her skin was so fair against the darker color of his. And the sensation—

"Let's try this." Leaning forward, she moistened one nipple and then the other with her tongue. "I love your taste," she murmured then repeated the process.

His breath was backed up in his lungs or he would have told her to stop this torture now…or never.

She wrapped her arms around him, slipped her hands beneath the waistband of his trousers and dug her nails into his hips as she began to suckle, first on one nipple and then the other.

When he felt the scrape of her teeth, Chance groaned. What was she doing to him? He'd desired her before. And the strength of that desire had made him reckless and rough. But what she was doing to him now made him weak. No other woman had made him feel this way. Fear mixed with a need so deep that he felt paralyzed.

"You still have too many clothes on," she murmured.

In the wall of mirrors, he watched her move around him. Her tongue stroked lightly on the skin at the back of his neck, then trailed a damp path down his spine. His skin felt icy and hot at the same time. He couldn't think, could barely breathe as he watched her strip him of his belt and send his trousers to the floor. Next she removed his briefs. Then she moved around so that she was facing him again.

More than anything he wanted to grab her, pull her to the floor and bury himself in her. But his arms still felt heavy, and he wasn't sure that he could raise them.

"Watch," she said. "I'm going to touch you now."

He was helpless to do anything else as she closed both of her hands around him. Her fingers were hot, and she was doing something magical, twisting gently with one hand at the base of his penis as she pulled with the other.

"I'm going to make you come," she said.

He wanted to crush her to him. He wanted to feel her beneath him on the floor. But he couldn't take his eyes off what she was doing to him in the mirror. The steady movement of her hands and the incredible waves of pleasure she was bringing him.

She moved closer to him then until her lips were brushing his. "You can kiss me now. Why don't you kiss me while you're coming?"

Whether it was her words or the fact that she kissed him, Chance felt strength and power return to his arms. He gripped the front of her dress and ripped it down the center. Then she was beneath him on the floor.

They rolled as one, mouth to mouth, body to body. Triumphant, Natalie gave herself over to Chance and to the needs that consumed her. This was what she'd wanted from him—this consuming hunger. She could feel the power of it as his hands raced over her, molding, pressing, bruising. She rolled on top of him and devoured. His skin tasted darker and more dangerous now. But she only got a sample before she was crushed beneath him again.

And then he was poised above her.

"Look at me while I take you."

She stared into his eyes and saw herself. *I need you.* The words pulsed through her as he drove himself into her. And she gave herself over to the madness.

CHANCE WINCED as he stepped beneath the cold spray of the shower. He was hoping it would clear his mind of the woman he'd just spent the night with. He needed to think.

Just who the hell was she?

As he lathered his shoulders and arms with soap, Chance considered that very fascinating question. The blonde with the sky-blue eyes was definitely Natalie

Gibbs but in her new persona, she was different. "Rachel" was more playful, more inventive—he frowned, searching for the right word—more free.

It wasn't that one woman was any sexier than the other. They were simply two thoroughly delightful sides of Natalie Gibbs, a woman he'd wanted with a desperation that had taken him to the limits of his control—and beyond.

Still, the differences between Natalie and "Rachel" fascinated him. Detective Gibbs had the cool head and the detachment of a cop. He'd admired that from the first time they'd met. And even in the way she made love, she was focused. "Rachel" seemed more impulsive. She had a talent for absorbing herself entirely in the moment. Damned if she hadn't tempted him into doing the same. In fact, he'd been so absorbed in her that instead of coming up with a plan to convince her to join him on his Florida job, he'd just given himself over to exploring the pleasure they could bring to each other.

The whole night had been a battle, and Chance still wasn't sure who'd won. He could vividly recall the way her hands had torn at his clothes and his had torn at hers, the way he'd finally dragged her to the floor and she'd wrestled him across it.

He wondered if he would ever forget the way her body had bucked and shuddered beneath his, or the way she'd cried out his name as they'd both drowned in pleasure. Each time when they'd finished with each other, they should have been content. But they hadn't been. Their appetites had been insatiable.

Never had the need to possess a woman been so intense. It should have scared him. He should have wanted to get out of there—and fast. On some level, he was sure that he did. But overriding that fear was the determination to have Natalie Gibbs with him when he went to Brancotti's estate.

Turning around, he let the cold water slap him in the face. The night was over. He had to get it out of his head and decide how to approach her about the Florida job.

Would she admit to him this morning that she was Natalie Gibbs, or would she continue to pretend that she was Rachel Cade? That was the question.

It might be fun to have them both along on the Florida job. But having fun wasn't the issue. Catching his old childhood nemesis was. He couldn't allow himself to jeopardize that.

After stepping out of the shower, Chance grabbed a towel and rubbed himself dry. The night was over. If Natalie didn't put an end to the masquerade, he would. The situation might be a little difficult at first—especially if she didn't want to be unmasked. But Natalie, the cop, was someone he knew how to deal with because they were a great deal alike.

Still, he thought with a smile, he was going to miss Rachel.

NATALIE SURFACED SLOWLY, her senses awakening one at a time. Rain—the steady sound of it lulled her. Keeping her eyes closed, she let herself drift, savoring the protection of the warm cocoon she was still wrapped in. This was one of her favorite parts of the day, the brief span of time in the morning before her alarm rang when she could feel the sunlight splashing across her bed, see the lightness of it beyond her eyelids and still not have to face it.

Burrowing more deeply into her pillow, she drew in a deep breath. Something was different. For a moment she couldn't put a name to it. How could she feel sunshine and hear the soft, steady fall of rain at the same time? Even as the question formed in her mind, she realized it wasn't the scent of her vanilla candle she smelled. It was…Chance.

Opening her eyes, she sat up as everything came flooding back into her mind. A quick glance around the room told her that she hadn't dreamed the night she'd just spent with Chance Mitchell. She was in a suite at the Meridian, and the rain that had lulled her was the sound of the shower.

When it had stopped, she pushed hair out of her face and felt a little flutter of panic. At any moment Chance could step into the room.

And then what?

The second flutter of panic was strong enough to have her throwing back the covers and grabbing one of the hotel robes. As she was tying the belt, she caught sight of herself in the mirror and dropped her hands. She wasn't Natalie Gibbs. Lifting a hand, she toyed with the ends of her hair. She was Rachel Cade. Natalie might have concerned herself with morning-after etiquette, but Rachel Cade didn't.

A smile curved her lips. After living in Rachel's skin for one long glorious night, Natalie knew that her alter ego didn't concern herself with much of anything but the pursuit of pleasure.

Raising her arms over her head, she stretched. Each little twinge of muscle brought back images and sensations from the night she'd just spent with Chance Mitchell.

He *had* kissed her—finally. And the man had an incredible mouth. She ran her fingers over her lips and sighed. Nothing had ever come close to what she'd felt or what she'd done during the two nights she'd spent with Chance Mitchell. Natalie might have worried about that. But Rachel was already wondering about stretching the experience into another day at least— and perhaps a night.

Natalie laughed. She was going to have to thank Sierra for her suggestion. Sex was a lot more fun when you didn't have to bring your personal baggage along.

A buzzer sounded at the door of the room and she heard a muffled voice say, "Room service."

When she opened the door, the waiter rolled a cart in and positioned it near a window that offered a view of the Mall.

"Rolls and glassware are on the lower shelf. Will there be anything else, ma'am?"

Natalie waved a dismissive hand, but she couldn't take her eyes off the spread that the waiter had delivered. Four white plates with silver covers were arranged on a cheery yellow cloth and in the center stood a pitcher of orange juice, a thermal container of coffee and a champagne bottle in a silver bucket.

A funny little feeling moved through her as she ran a finger over a single yellow rose that lay on one napkin. This kind of care wasn't something she'd come to expect from a man.

She peeked under one silver lid and saw crisp bacon and plump sausages.

"I didn't know what you'd like, so I ordered a bit of everything."

Natalie turned to see Chance walk into the room. He was wearing trousers, but not his shirt. His feet were bare, his hair still damp from the shower. Her throat went dry. Incredibly, she wanted him all over again.

"I'd like *you*," she said.

THE VOICE, the look she was giving him told Chance it was still Rachel he was dealing with, and if she continued to look at him in that way, the breakfast he'd ordered was going to get very cold.

Business, Chance reminded himself. *Keep it light.* "I thought it might be nice if we shared a meal—since we never got around to eating last night. That way we can talk and get to know one another."

She laughed. "So we have a night of wild, sweaty sex and then we have a date?"

It occurred to him that he'd never had a date with Natalie in either of her personas. "Something like that. I'd like to get to know you."

It was nothing less than the truth. In spite of his resolution to end the game she was playing, he was still intrigued by this side of Natalie. What could it hurt to delay the unmasking until after breakfast?

Natalie lifted one of the silver covers at random, then settled herself into a chair. "An omelet. I guess I could use the protein for energy."

It was his turn to laugh as he took the seat across

from her. Oh, it was definitely Rachel he was dealing with. He was going to miss her. "I was beginning to think you had an unending supply."

She sliced into the eggs. "Well, we could certainly test your theory."

Chance concentrated on the practical matter of lifting silver covers until he found what he was looking for. Then he scooped yogurt into a bowl and added fresh fruit and a little wheat germ.

"I'm sorry," she said.

He glanced up startled. "What for?"

"That." She pointed to his bowl of yogurt. "You must have ordered that for me. Here." She pushed her plate toward him. "Have some of the omelet. It's delicious."

"Thanks, but this is what I eat every day."

"You're kidding."

The horrified expression on her face made him smile. "I like to be careful about what I put into my body."

"And here I'd pegged you for a risk-taker." She met his eyes. "But I guess you're doing something right. You've got a great body."

She was making it hard to stick to the date plan. "What do you usually eat for breakfast?"

She shrugged as she lifted another forkful of eggs. "I'm a cop, so you get one guess."

"Donuts?"

She pointed a fork at him. "You got it. I prefer them day old so I can dunk them in the dreadful coffee they serve at the station."

Chance's eyes narrowed. "So…you're a cop like your cousin Natalie?"

As she set her cup down, some of the coffee spilled onto the saucer. "Yes. Fort Lauderdale."

For a few moments, she busied herself with eating, and Chance wondered if admitting to being a cop had been a slipup. Perhaps, now was the time to tell her that he knew who she was. He could reach over, take her hand and say, "Natalie, I know."

But once he did that, would "Rachel" disappear? "Do you like being a cop?"

"Sure." This time when her eyes met his he saw a trace of amusement. "Is this the part where we exchange bios?"

Chance shrugged as he set down his spoon. "Standard first date talk. You interest me, Rachel Cade. Ever do any undercover work on the job?"

She hesitated only an instant. "Some. You should see me in my hooker clothes."

A vivid image filled Chance's mind, but he shoved it away. "I've heard your cousin Natalie is good with locks. Any chance that you're good with them, too?"

Her eyes narrowed slightly. "Anything Nat can do, I can do better. You know, this is beginning to sound like a job interview."

Chance couldn't help thinking that Rachel's mind was every bit as sharp as her "cousin's." "How long are you going to be visiting your cousins?"

"I'm not sure." She lifted her cup and drained it. Then she sent him a provocative smile. "Why do you ask?"

Because at some point in their conversation, Chance had scratched his original game plan and come up with a new one. He wasn't at all ready to lose Rachel Cade yet. He wanted her in Florida with him. His head might tell him that he was taking a dangerous risk by not ending Natalie's masquerade right now, but something much closer to the bone was telling him that he was going to need both women to catch Brancotti. "I've got a little proposition to make you and it will involve about a week of your time."

She reached over and ran a finger down the back of his hand. "Sounds perfect. Especially, if it's anything like the proposition I made you last night.…"

Chance shook his head. "It's more of a job offer, and it's dangerous." He saw something flicker in her eyes, just once. Surprise or something else? "You'll have to wear a disguise."

She said nothing, but her expression had stilled and the woman studying him now was Detective Natalie Gibbs through and through.

"I was thinking of asking your cousin Natalie. I need someone who's good at disguise and it wouldn't hurt at all if you could break into a safe. If you're interested, I think we could work very well together."

She said nothing at all, but he could almost hear the wheels turning in her head. Chance felt a little sinking sensation in his stomach. Would she tell him that she was really Natalie? With the seconds ticking away, he watched her closely. If there was any struggle going on inside of her, he saw no evidence of it. Oh, this was the cool, sharp detective all right. But he couldn't help remembering the impulsive and incredibly responsive woman he'd spent the night with. How many other facets were there to Natalie Gibbs?

Finally, she said, "I might be interested. Tell me what it involves."

Leaning forward, Chance did just that. He explained everything just as he had to Tracker—the missing Ferrante diamond, its resurfacing and the upcoming auction for a select group of invited guests. Then he told her about the cover. They would go in as a billionaire software nerd and his current piece of arm candy. The only things he left out were Venetia Gaston's death and his personal relationship to Brancotti.

"Brancotti's estate is in South Florida. Have you heard of him?"

Natalie shook her head. "We wouldn't if he keeps himself as clean as you say he does."

Smooth, Chance thought. But of course, she wouldn't lie unless she had to. No one who had lived undercover and had to tell lies for long periods of time ever told more than necessary.

"What do you say?" Chance asked.

YES. NATALIE HAD to bite down hard on the inside of her cheek to keep from saying the word out loud. As much as the "Rachel" part of her wanted to agree, she knew that she had to think. More than that, she needed to make a few phone calls and find out more about this Brancotti. She couldn't just up and run off to Florida and pretend to be some high-tech billionaire's arm candy. Could she?

Of course not. She never acted on impulse. Oh, she took risks, certainly. But she always weighed her options, ascertained the consequences and made plans accordingly.

But she was so tempted to throw caution to the wind and say yes. Chance was offering her just the kind of assignment she'd always dreamed of. She could use her talents, and she would be working with one of the best men in his field.

She lifted the pot and refilled her cup. There were other things to consider. There had to be. For one thing, he thought she was Rachel Cade. She should tell him right now about the trick she'd pulled on him. But if she did, would he become annoyed and withdraw his offer?

Plus, she wasn't at all sure that she wanted to give up being Rachel Cade.

The voice came then, pushing past the fears and doubts skulking around in her mind like a shadowy thief. *"Trust in your talents."*

Chance chose that moment to take her hand in his and raise it to his lips. "What do you say, Rachel?"

It was Natalie who was dithering, and she knew in an instant what Rachel would say.

"What time do we leave?"

SHE HAD TO BE CRAZY, Natalie thought as she lifted the ten-pound weights that Chance had given her. He selected heavier ones for himself, then turned to face her.

"Do what I do," he said as he raised his arms until they were level with his shoulders, held for a count of five and then lowered them.

She did. Although she'd told him that she was in good shape, he'd insisted on putting her to the test. The moment that she'd agreed to go with him to Florida, he'd told her that they were going to take a five-mile run through Rock Creek Park. He'd even bought her some shoes and workout clothes in one of the hotel's gift shops.

When she'd asked why he was testing her, he'd merely said that he needed to make sure she could keep up with him if they had to make a run for it. The run had lasted well beyond five miles. After forty minutes she was still matching him stride for stride, and he'd been the one to call it quits.

Now they were using the hotel gym. It was located on the lobby level, and offered weight machines, treadmills, free weights and a large pool that started indoors and ended outside. Four glass walls made the room about as private as a fishbowl.

Lifting the weights to her shoulders, she began to follow Chance's lead through a combination of lunges and squats. When he finally set down his weights and took hers, he said, "You're good."

Her brows shot up. "I'm a cop, remember."

"Not all cops stay in shape." Then turning, he led the way to a mat. "Let's see what you can do in hand-to-hand combat."

For a moment she stared at him. "You're serious?"

He smiled at her. "Unless you think you can't take me."

Unable to resist the challenge, she stepped onto the mat and began to circle slowly. He knew what buttons to push. She'd have to remember that and push a few of her own. He was bigger than she was and stronger. On the job when she'd had to use physical force, she'd always been able to play the looks-like-a-fragile-woman card. That wouldn't work here. So her best option was distraction.

Keeping her eyes on his, she said, "What's next? Target practice?"

He laughed, and she very nearly allowed herself to be distracted by the sound as she moved in and hooked her foot behind his. Once she had him off balance, she aimed her elbow at his stomach. An instant before it connected, she found her arms pinned to her side and before she could blink, she was lying beneath him, facedown on the mat.

While she struggled for a breath, she was vaguely aware of applause. But she was much more aware of Chance's body pressing hers into the mat, of his voice in her ear. "You'll have to work on your eyes. They give you away."

She would work on that, she vowed as she got to her feet.

This time she let him make the move, and she blocked it.

"Good," he said. "Now try this one."

He moved fast as a snake, but she moved faster. He didn't talk after that, and neither did she. She wasn't even sure how much time had passed as he made one move after another and she attempted to block them. She lost count of how often she ended up pinned to the floor. But each time, he helped her to her feet and taught her the countermove that would have stopped him.

He was very good, better than any martial arts instructor she'd ever trained under. But she would have bitten her tongue out rather than tell him. Nor was she about to tell him that she'd never before responded to martial arts instruction like it was foreplay. Her mind might be calculating countermoves, but her body had become very sensitized to his touch. In the course of their workout, his forearms had brushed against her breasts. His hands had gripped her calves, her thighs, her hips. Twice when they'd rolled on the floor his leg had been between her thighs. When he finally called it quits and grinned at her, in spite of her annoyance, she wanted to jump him.

If there hadn't been an audience with their noses pressed against the glass walls surrounding them, she might have. Instead, she smiled at him, shook his hand. As they walked together toward the shower rooms, she bided her time. When he was least expecting it, she gave him a quick shove into the pool.

Then with the applause of the spectators in her ears, she waited until he surfaced and grinned down at him. "Thanks for the tip about the eyes."

"Anytime," he said as he gripped the side of the pool. "I don't suppose you want to give me a hand out of the pool."

She grinned down at him. "Do I have the word Sucker written on my forehead?" Then she turned and walked away.

CARLO BRANCOTTI sat in his office, looking over the file that Lisa had just handed him. Sun streamed through the open French doors and a breeze from the ocean played with the wind chimes on the patio. When he finished reading Lisa's report, he glanced up. "So— which one of these would a clever insurance investigator choose to impersonate?"

"I don't know. I wasn't able to eliminate any of them."

Carlo studied her for a moment. Lisa was a very cautious woman. He paid her to be just that. "Take an educated guess. If you wanted to trap Carlo Brancotti, which one of these people would you attempt to impersonate?"

She thought for a moment. "I'd choose Steven Bradford. But you don't pay me for guessing."

"Why Bradford?"

"I suppose because he's so squeaky clean. He's never entered this kind of a market before. Plus, he avoids the press. The only picture I was able to come up with was from his college days. If Interpol wanted to slip someone in, we'd be hard-pressed to see through the disguise."

It wasn't Interpol he was worried about. Carlo studied the picture of a thin young man with long, brownish-blond hair. Bradford would be twelve years older now, a man instead of a boy. The body would have filled out, the hairstyle changed.

"Good choice," he murmured. Then he glanced at the photos of Steven Bradford's current girlfriend.

She hadn't been a model long. The one layout that Lisa had come up with featured a tall blonde modeling a bathing suit while playing volleyball. She was wearing sunglasses in each picture. He picked one up and studied it more closely. Steven Bradford was a lucky man. "What about the woman? This…" he paused to find the name, "Calli? The government doesn't always send a male agent."

Lisa frowned. "But you won't invite her to the actual auction. She won't have access to the diamond."

True. Still, he wasn't going to dismiss the possibility that the model known only as Calli wasn't as harmless as she appeared. He was going to enjoy getting to know her better when she arrived. He picked up the next picture. "What about Armand Genovese?"

"He would be my second choice. He's wearing a hat and sunglasses in every picture, so we can't be sure what he looks like either. Also this is his first venture into the black market."

Now Carlo smiled. "Only because he has other sources for stolen art and jewels. Ones that don't always require top dollar."

"True. Which makes it a little surprising for him to contact you. Perhaps because of his methods of acquisition he's made a deal with the government."

"Good point." This was precisely why he paid Lisa McGill a very good salary. She had a razor-sharp mind as well as a knack for computers and research.

For the first time since she'd come into the room, Lisa relaxed slightly. "Thank you, sir."

Carlo turned his attention to the third photo. When it had been taken, Risa Manwaring had been the toast of Hollywood. That had been at least twenty-five years ago. "And why might a very clever insurance agent choose to impersonate Risa Manwaring?"

"Because once she married that British lord, she shunned the press, so no telling what she looks like now. And as you said yourself, the government doesn't always send a male agent."

"True. Good work, Lisa," Carlo said as he slipped the file into a drawer and locked it.

"Thank you, sir."

"When Bradford arrives, we'll put him in the Venetian room. That way we can keep very close tabs on him. Signore Genovese will stay in the Tuscan room, and Ms. Manwaring in the Neopolitan room. Make sure that all three rooms are wired and that the security cameras in the walls are well hidden."

"I'll see to it myself, sir."

When Lisa left the room, Carlo rose from his desk and turned to the painting that hung behind him. After moving it aside, he opened his safe and took out two velvet pouches. One was red and the other was black. After setting them on his desk, he removed a diamond from each pouch, then carried them out through the French doors to his patio. It was early, not yet eight o'clock, but the sun was pouring directly into the courtyard. It shot light into both stones and the facets in each captured that light and seemed to glow from within.

Both were a rare shade of canary-yellow, and only one of them was real—the Ferrante diamond. The other was a very carefully crafted fake. Only a skilled gemologist would be able to tell the difference.

Carlo smiled as he looked down at them. He would use them both to set a trap for "Chance Mitchell." There was nothing that he enjoyed more than a game of cat and mouse with a worthy opponent.

Too bad that he would have to end the game for good this time.

7

BY THE TIME Natalie arrived at the Blue Pepper, second thoughts were attacking with a vengeance. Not that the "Rachel Cade" part of her was having any. No, it was good old Natalie who'd called her sisters for an emergency meeting. She'd told Chance she had to talk to her "cousins" and inform them of her change in plans.

The restaurant was crowded. And the number of patrons, more than the quick glance she gave her watch, told her that she was running more than half an hour late. And she was never late. At least Natalie wasn't ever late. Plus, she was exhausted. Both conditions, she blamed completely on Chance Mitchell.

During a long, grueling day of cramming, shopping and packing, she'd discovered a whole new side to the man—one that made her think of Simon LaGree. Not in a million years would she have suspected that the laid-back man she'd known as Chance Mitchell would turn into such a taskmaster.

The run in Rock Creek Park and the workout had just been the beginning. When she'd passed those little tests, he'd dragged her back to his room at the Meridian to study. He hadn't been satisfied until she'd known everything there was to know about Carlo Brancotti.

He'd even quizzed her. Of course, she'd passed. She prided herself on her sharp memory.

Brancotti wasn't the only name he'd ever used. There were at least half a dozen other aliases, and the man hadn't limited his dealings to art and jewels. Over the years, he'd trafficked in just about every black market commodity he could lay his hands on, including drugs and arms. Brancotti's trademark as a jewel thief was leaving a high quality fake jewel in place of the real one, and usually by the time the theft was discovered the trail was cold.

By the end of the cramming session, the cop part of her had known that she hadn't made a mistake in agreeing to Chance's proposition.

It was the feminine part of her that was having second thoughts. Pushing past the crowd clustered around the hostess station, she scanned the restaurant and spotted her sisters seated at a small table on the upper level. They were looking in her direction, but when she waved, they didn't seem to see her.

Of course, they were looking for Rachel Cade. And she wasn't Rachel anymore. Thanks to Chance Mitchell, she'd been transformed into "Calli," a wannabe supermodel who'd been cohabiting with software billionaire Steven Bradford for the past six months.

"Welcome to the Blue Pepper."

Natalie glanced down to see that Rad had suddenly appeared in her path. "Hi." Though she smiled at him, he didn't grab her hands or kiss the air near her cheeks. The disguise must be working with him, too. But then he wasn't looking at her face. His eyes were riveted on the skinny tank top she was wearing.

"Oh my, oh my, oh my." He pressed a hand to his heart as he stepped back to run his eyes down her. "Oh my, oh my, oh my."

Several people turned to stare, and Natalie glanced down, praying that everything about the skimpy outfit she was wearing was still in place. Both the pink shorts and top were cut high, leaving plenty of leg and stomach bare. She tugged the edge of the shorts down a bit, hoping there wasn't anything showing that might get her ticketed for indecent exposure.

"What's wrong?" she asked.

"Nothing. You are perfection! The hair, the shoes. And that color is soooooo you!" Rad clapped his hands together. "I have a friend who should be wearing this color. I've told her over and over to think pink."

As Rad began to circle her, she caught a glimpse of herself in one of the mirrored columns that flanked the bar.

She had to hand it to Chance. It was the perfect outfit for her new alter ego. The hair, the earrings that fell to just above her shoulders, even the ankle-breaking sandals suited "Calli" to a *T,* and the whole package together sent out a promise of hot, steamy sex.

Rad had completed his circle, and he was facing her now. "*Love* the hair! Where did you get that cut?"

Beginning to enjoy herself, Natalie tucked a curl behind her ear as she leaned down to whisper. "Arturo at the Meridian."

"He is an artist!"

"Thanks. I'm looking for the Gibbs sisters."

"Wonderful! Then you'll get to meet my friend, Detective Natalie. She's not here yet," he said as he began to cut a path through the crowd for her. "You must tell her about Arturo."

Natalie recalled that Chance had slipped Arturo an enormously large tip to layer her hair and pile on the products until it looked like she'd just got out of bed with a man. But she hadn't gotten a chance to see if she could achieve the look naturally by doing just that. Chance, the taskmaster, hadn't made a move on her since she'd agreed to work with him on the Brancotti job.

There hadn't been much time, of course. Still, the change in him had started her thinking. Had he gotten his fill of Rachel Cade in one night just as he seemed to have gotten his fill of Natalie?

Would the same fate await Calli?

As they reached the stairs, she shot a quick look over her shoulder and caught her reflection again in the mirror. Calli might have something to say about that. Rachel definitely would. Perhaps the two women would have to tag-team him. A quick laugh bubbled up at the direction her thoughts had taken. On her own, she would never have come up with that idea. She was beginning to enjoy the different persons she was discovering within herself.

Rad stopped at the top of the short flight of stairs and pointed in the direction of her sisters. Pushing all thoughts of Chance out of her mind, Natalie made her way to the table.

"Do you mind if I join you?" she asked.

"Sorry," Sierra said, glancing up at her.

"We're waiting for our sister," Rory explained.

"She won't mind," Natalie said as she settled herself in the empty chair.

"Now, wait just a minute," Rory began. "You can't just…"

"Wait." Sierra cut off her sister by squeezing her hand. In the space of five beats, Natalie saw the recognition seep into her youngest sister's eyes.

Three seconds later, Rory said, "Who in the hell are you supposed to be?"

"The name is Calli, and I'm a wannabe supermodel."

"Okay," Rory said, intrigued now. "I can buy that. The question is *why?*"

Natalie sighed and signaled a waiter. "It's a long story, and I need a drink."

"What'll it be, ladies?"

"A martini, dry with an olive," Natalie said.

"Make that three," Rory said not taking her eyes off of Natalie. "And we'll have the appetizer sampler." The moment the waiter hurried off, she said, "Whatever the story is, I vote you wear that outfit every time we come here. We've never gotten service this fast before."

"What I want to know is what happened to our dear cousin Rachel?" Sierra asked. "Didn't the disguise work?"

"Oh, it worked. Maybe too well." Then Natalie leaned forward and told them everything, pausing only when the waiter served their drinks. Once she'd finished, Rory drained the last of her martini and said, "You were getting bored with your job. This man has offered you the kind of assignment you've always secretly dreamed of having. On top of all that, you're attracted to him. What's the problem?"

Natalie shifted her gaze from Rory to Sierra.

Sierra shook her head. "Don't look at me. I think Rory summed the situation up nicely. Unless you don't think you can pull it off."

Natalie shook her head. "The job isn't the problem. I can do it. It's Chance. He's the problem."

"So?" Sierra asked. "Is he going to be any less of a problem if you change your mind and tell him Rachel doesn't want to turn herself into Calli and fly to Florida tomorrow?"

Natalie thought for a minute. "No, but…"

"You'll only regret it if you let this opportunity slip by," Sierra said.

"And you won't just be saying goodbye to the job. You'll be kissing off the guy, too," Rory pointed out. "Are you ready to do that yet?"

Natalie sipped her martini, then set her glass down. That was the real problem. She wasn't ready to cut Chance adrift. Not yet.

"I thought spending another night with him would get him out of my system," she said.

"That's one of the problems with our society," Sierra said. "We want quick fixes, and sometimes that's just not possible."

Narrowing her eyes, Natalie glanced from to Sierra to Rory. "I wanted the two of you to talk some sense into me."

Rory shot her a bland look. "I thought that's exactly what we were doing."

"We think you ought to go," Sierra said.

Natalie ran her finger around the rim of the martini she'd hardly touched. "I should probably tell him that I'm Natalie."

"Why? It's Rachel he invited along," Sierra pointed out.

Rory grinned at her. "Do you really want to go back to being Natalie yet?"

"No." She wasn't ready to give up being Rachel Cade yet. "But I've never tried to be two people at once before."

Rory rolled her eyes. "You can't have forgotten that Halloween when you were Wonder Woman and you kept slipping away from us so you could reappear and terrorize us as Jason from *Friday the Thirteenth*. You did it three times before we figured out it was just you."

Natalie laughed. "I had forgotten that. Still, this is a little different."

"Do you still want Chance Mitchell?" Sierra asked.

"Yes, but…"

"That's Natalie talking," Sierra pointed out. "How does Rachel feel about it?"

Natalie grimaced. "She's the one who said 'yes.'"

"What about Calli?" Rory asked.

"*She's* got her bags packed."

"There you go," Rory said. "Two to one—they've outvoted you."

Sierra reached over to take her hand. "Calli and Rachel are parts of you. Maybe it's time you trusted them."

Grinning, Rory lifted her glass in a toast. "To quote Harry, 'trust in your talents.'"

Sierra smiled and raised her glass. "'Risk anything it takes.'"

CHANCE STRODE into the bedroom and checked the suitcases for the third time since Natalie had left. The designer name luggage looked well used. Brancotti would notice that. He was a man who noticed everything. Not even a small detail would escape him. And new luggage would give rise to questions.

That had been the reason that he'd urged Natalie to pack some of Rachel's clothes as well as the new things they'd purchased for "Calli." He'd insisted on stopping by Natalie's place where "Rachel" was staying so she could collect her belongings. Flipping open the top of one of the smaller pieces, Chance fingered a lace camisole in a shade of icy pink. He'd often wondered what Detective Natalie Gibbs had worn beneath those tailored suits. In his mind, he'd pictured the stereotypical black lace, but for some odd reason, he found the pale pastel shade even more alluring. Of course, he'd known that Natalie had her vulnerable side. What he hadn't known was that it would appeal to him just as much as her strength did.

When he caught himself reaching for Rachel's cosmetic bag, he stopped himself. He'd already checked it and assured himself that it contained a mix of new and old makeup—just as any woman's would. The only question he wanted in Brancotti's mind was how much Steven Bradford would pay for the Ferrante—the diamond that had already caused the death of a fellow agent.

For a moment, he let himself think of Venetia Gaston, the woman who'd been his partner during his last encounter with the man who now called himself Carlo Brancotti. For two years, he'd blamed himself for Venetia's death. He'd set up the meet, and it should have gone smoothly. Carlo was to bring the diamond he'd just stolen and Venetia was to turn over the money. Then Interpol would move in. But Venetia had never reached the spot where the exchange was to take place. Carlo had intercepted her somehow. When they'd found her body, the money had been gone, and she'd had a fake diamond in her purse.

Chance firmly pushed the image of Venetia out of his mind. Dwelling on a past mistake was not going to help him now. He drew his thoughts back to the present and lifted a skinny little tank top that he'd had "Calli" model for him earlier in the day. This time he wasn't taking any chances. He was going to face his old nemesis himself, and he was taking someone in with him that Brancotti would have no way of knowing. Chance's lips curved slightly. How could Brancotti know that the sexy woman known as Calli was also a tough cop who was equally adept at handling a gun and opening safes?

Chance dropped the tank top and closed the suitcase. The suite had suddenly seemed empty when she'd walked out. Her request to meet with her "cousins" had surprised him, but it had made sense. Of course, she would want to let her sisters know that she was leaving town. But what if she had second thoughts? How could he handle them if he wasn't there?

Turning, he strode back into the living room of the suite. He'd just have to handle them when she got back. He wasn't going to Florida without Natalie Gibbs. The file he'd shown her that afternoon was still spread out on the coffee table. He doubted she was aware of it, but when she worked she was all police detective. The intensity of her concentration and the strength of her endurance—both were qualities he'd come to admire throughout the long and grueling day he'd put her through.

She hadn't once flinched or complained. And not so much as by a twitch of a muscle had she let it be known that anything in his old enemy's file had shocked her. She'd looked up from it once to say, "You lost your partner?"

"Yes," he'd said. She deserved to know the truth. "Brancotti killed her."

"I'm sorry." Then she'd gone back to reading the rest of the file. When she'd finished and met his eyes, there'd been the look of a warrior on her face.

Recalling it now, he felt more reassured than he'd been since she'd left. The woman who'd read that file wouldn't back out on him. She wanted to bring Brancotti to justice almost as much as he did. Isn't that why he'd wanted her with him in the first place?

Or at least partly the reason, he thought as his gaze moved to the foyer, one of the many places in the suite where they'd succumbed to their desires the night before. How many times during the day had he wanted to make love to her again? Hell, he'd nearly pulled her into the woods at Rock Creek Park and taken her there. The truth was he wanted Natalie/Rachel/Calli—all of the women who made up Natalie Gibbs—with an intensity that had him being…cautious. No woman had even made him cautious before.

When the doorbell rang, Chance strode forward to

answer it. But it wasn't Natalie he found on the other side. It was Tracker and Lucas, carrying a brown bag.

"Are we interrupting anything?" Lucas asked.

"No." Chance hoped that he was hiding his disappointment as he stepped back from the door.

"We thought you might be busy with that blonde you left Sophie's party with." Tracker removed a six-pack of imported beer from the bag.

"'Beware of Greeks bearing gifts,'" Chance quoted as he took the one Tracker offered to him. "What's up?"

"Tracker is worried about you," Lucas said.

Chance raised his brows. "I'm touched."

"I've been doing a little digging on Brancotti, alias Phillipe Sagan, alias 'Damien.' The two of you go back a long way."

Chance didn't even let a flicker of surprise show. He'd known that Tracker was about the best there was when it came to running background checks, but he hadn't expected him to unearth the "Damien" alias. Still, there was no way he could have traced Damien back to that orphanage. "I've been tracking him for a long time."

"And you lost your partner in Rome two years ago," Tracker said.

"Yes, I did."

"Besides being dangerous, this man has the reputation of being very smart." Tracker raised a hand when Chance opened his mouth to give his opinion. "Let me finish. Lucas and I will concede that you're a very smart man, too. The thing is you nearly had Brancotti for stealing this diamond two years ago. He's not a man who'll forget that. Put yourself in his place. There's a good chance that he took the time to find out exactly who was on his trail then, and that he's kept tabs on you. He could be expecting you."

Chance took a swallow of his beer. "I'm sure he is."

"It could be a trap," Lucas said.

Chance met his old friend's eyes. "It could be. But I wouldn't be where I am today if I ran every time I suspected a trap."

Lucas glanced at Tracker. "I told you we wouldn't talk him out of it."

"Relax," Chance said. "There's no way he can suspect my cover. We've built it very carefully. Both Steven Bradford and his current love interest have agreed to go into seclusion until this is over. Their private plane will arrive here tomorrow morning. They will be whisked off in a hired limousine and delivered here to this suite where they will stay until the job is done. Steven is shy of the press. I won't have any trouble passing for him."

"I want to go in as your bodyguard," Tracker said. "Someone who hides from the press as much as Bradford does would be eccentric enough to insist on a personal bodyguard."

Chance shook his head. "The invitation was very specific. One guest. If Bradford tries to bring anyone besides his girlfriend at this point, it could mean he'll be refused admittance to the estate, and I won't risk that. Besides, Natalie Gibbs is perfectly qualified to be my bodyguard."

Tracker and Lucas exchanged looks again.

"You convinced Natalie Gibbs to be your partner then?" Tracker asked.

Chance hesitated for only a second, then cursed himself for it. "Yes." He knew that both of his friends were studying him more closely now. In another minute they'd demand to know the whole story.

"Natalie never did show up for Sophie's party, and you left with a blonde," Tracker pointed out.

"It's a long story," Chance said.

Tracker passed a beer to Lucas and took one for himself. "If we're your backup and rescue team, we deserve to be filled in."

Since he couldn't argue with that, Chance took another drink of his beer and then laid it out for them. By the time he was finished, both men were frowning and regarding him intently.

"So she doesn't know that you know she's really Natalie Gibbs?" Tracker asked.

"Right," Chance said.

"Why the masquerade in the first place?" Lucas asked.

"I couldn't ask without letting her know I saw through the disguise," Chance said.

"Right," Tracker said. "That much makes sense. What doesn't make sense is why you didn't inform her that you knew who she really was."

Chance's brows shot up. "Hey, I didn't see through her disguise at first. Neither did the two of you." He'd like to think that he would have seen through it even if he hadn't overheard her sisters talking. "Even though I quickly realized it was Natalie, that doesn't change the fact that a very sexy and attractive blonde made a play for me. By the time my brain was functioning again, things had gotten…complicated. I wanted Natalie on this job with me for a number of reasons. My chances were slim to none if I got her pissed at me for not fessing up that I'd known it was her almost from the get-go."

Lucas's grin spread slowly. "In other words, you made your bed, and now you have to lie in it."

"Yeah." Chance sighed. "Something like that."

Tracker took a sip of his beer and then asked, "Is she aware of the dangers?"

"She's read the file. She knows about my last partner. And she knows what kind of man Brancotti is."

"Okay, so both of you are aware that you're dealing with a very nasty guy. Have you considered the possibility that there's someone on the inside of the insurance business who's on Brancotti's payroll?" Tracker asked.

Chance met his friend's eyes steadily. "I've had two years to think about how he got away with the diamond the last time. He had to have been getting inside information to steal the diamond in the first place. That's why I insisted that no one could know the route that Venetia was taking that day except me."

Tracker frowned. "And Venetia. You think she was the traitor?"

"I've given it some consideration. Carlo's quite a ladies' man. Perhaps he used her, then killed her because she'd served her purpose and he didn't want to share. This time I'm working on my own. No one at the insurance office knows I'm going in as Bradford. I haven't even told them that the Ferrante diamond has resurfaced."

"I told you he'd be on top of it," Lucas said, then glanced at Chance. "Tracker here's a real worrywart."

"Humor me," Tracker said as he passed a slip of paper to Chance. "That's my private cell phone number. You're the only person who can call me on it. As long as you're on that estate, I'll be close by."

Chance glanced at it, memorized it and handed it back.

"You better make sure that Natalie memorizes it, too," Lucas said, "just in case."

"Done," Chance said.

Tracker leaned back and for the first time since he'd entered the room, he smiled. "One other thing."

"Yeah?"

"What happens when Rachel finds out that you've known all along she's really Natalie?" Tracker asked.

"I'll handle it," Chance said. And he wished to hell that he felt as confident as he sounded.

8

"YOU'RE SURE you've got it?" Chance asked as the limousine pulled away from the Meridian. There wasn't even a hint of the sun in the eastern sky, and the streetlights they passed offered only intermittent illumination in the car.

Natalie gave him a sharp salute. "Aye-aye, sir. From the time we step on the plane we are no longer Chance Mitchell and Rachel Cade. We are Steven Bradford who's just made another million or two this morning and his new best friend, Calli." She tilted her head to one side. "You really think Brancotti might have Steven Bradford's plane bugged?"

"It's been sitting on the runway since yesterday evening. I'm banking on it."

Her eyes narrowed. "You're hoping he bugged it, aren't you?"

"I want to give Brancotti every opportunity to assure himself that we are who we say we are. Most of the others he invited for his little auction are returning clients. Steven Bradford is an unknown, and Brancotti is very cautious."

Natalie had to hand it to him for thinking of allowing Brancotti to wire the plane. Everything so far about the cover that Chance had built for them had won her admiration. As far as she could tell, nothing had been overlooked. The small purse she carried contained a driver's license, passport and several well-worn credit cards that identified her as Catherine Weston. The driver's license was from San Diego, California, and would expire in eight months. But if Brancotti ran a check on Catherine Weston, now "Calli," he would find that she'd been born and raised in a small town, nestled in the foothills of the Blue Ridge Mountains.

Under Chance's careful supervision, she'd spent three hours boning up on Catherine Weston's background instead of sleeping. And once the real Calli had arrived at the hotel, Natalie had spent another three hours studying and talking with her.

Natalie stifled a yawn. She hadn't slept more than two hours, but how could she complain when Chance was being just as thorough as she always was when she adopted a new persona. A perfectionist. That was the one word she would use to sum up Chance's approach to this job, and she had no choice but to admire him for it.

She glanced at him and saw that he was using a pocket flashlight to read the open file on his lap. The Steven Bradford disguise was excellent, and as Natalie studied him, she marveled again at how far it went beyond the wrinkled tan suit he was wearing.

The tiny lines that furrowed his brow as he frowned at something he was reading were new. So was the way he ran his fingers absently through his hair. Body language, she knew, was as important as the costume in creating an authentic disguise. She watched his fingers toy with the edges of the manila folder on his lap, folding the edge back and forth. She would have been willing to bet that Chance Mitchell had never fidgeted in his life. He was the most self-contained man she'd ever met. The only time she was certain of what was on his mind was when they were making love.

What would the man sitting across from her be like in bed? Would the perfectionist streak in Chance force him to carry the impersonation of Steven Bradford that far?

One thing Natalie did know from the time she'd spent with the real Catherine Weston—the woman's relationship with Steven Bradford went beyond her ambition to become a supermodel. The dreamy look in her eyes when she'd spoken about Steven was a dead giveaway. Natalie would have bet good money that Catherine Weston had fallen hard for the software billionaire.

Did Chance's Steven Bradford have similar feelings for his Calli, she wondered? If so, she had no doubt that Chance would have carefully noted it in that mental notebook she suspected he carried with him. What would the perfectionist in him force him to do with the knowledge?

One thing Natalie knew for certain—her Calli was not going to wait much longer to find out. One of the many things she'd learned about her namesake was that she had boundless energy and enthusiasm—and Natalie was sure it extended to the physical side of her relationship with Steven Bradford. Gut instinct told her that Catherine Weston had even fewer hang-ups than Rachel Cade. And she couldn't wait to try out that facet of Calli's personality.

A sliver of pure excitement shot up her spine. For the first time, she admitted to herself how much she really wanted to work at Chance's side during this operation. She was definitely her father's daughter, and for the first time in her life, she wasn't going to feel guilty about embracing that part of herself. Instead, she was going to enjoy it, and she was also going to enjoy exploring a relationship with Chance.

There'd be a price to pay. There always was. But as she watched Chance turn his flashlight off and insert it in the breast pocket of his shirt, she knew that however she was going to pay for saying yes to Chance Mitchell's proposition, she was sure it was going to be worth it.

And she had plans for him. He'd evidently been satisfied after one night with Natalie. And last night he'd been able to resist making love to Rachel. But his one-night stand days were over. Calli was going to see to that.

CHANCE WAS very much aware of Natalie's eyes on him. Just as he was fully aware of the excitement radiating from her in little spurts. She might look like Calli, but right now her body language was totally Natalie's. Her arms were folded across her chest and her foot was tapping. He knew exactly what she was feeling because he felt it, too. He was equally impatient for the adventure to begin. There was nothing like going up against a worthy and challenging opponent.

What worried him a little was that challenging Brancotti wasn't all that was on his mind. He was also thinking of being with Natalie. And those thoughts were distracting him from the file he was reading. It was taking him twice as long as usual to memorize Tracker's latest surveillance map of the Brancotti estate. Swamps bordered the estate on two sides, and they were kept well stocked with alligators. That left two avenues for escape in an emergency. Through the entrance gate on the western side or by boat on the ocean side.

A red dot just inside the southern edge of the swamp marked where Tracker had hidden an inflatable boat. Hopefully, all would go well, and they could use it to meet Tracker once they had the Ferrante diamond.

Pocketing the flashlight, Chance closed the file and for the first time since they'd entered the limo, he met Natalie's eyes. "Ready?"

"What did you have in mind?"

The grin she flashed him and the quick arch of her back told Chance he was dealing with Calli now. As Rachel, Natalie was slower moving and much more aware of her effect on the opposite sex. She knew to a *T* what she had in her arsenal, and she matched the weapon to the man.

Calli was more spontaneous, and her heart ruled her head. She didn't even think about attracting men, but everything she did, including the back stretch, was incredibly sexy.

"You're very good at impersonation," he said. So good that he was wondering how being Calli would affect her response the next time he touched her.

"So are you." She pushed her hair behind her ear.

"Right now I'm wondering what it will be like to make love to Steven Bradford."

"Rachel, I—"

She leaned closer, and he caught her scent.

"Aren't you wondering what it will be like to make love to Calli? We could find out." She reached for his tie, but before she could pull it off, he grabbed her hands.

"We're almost to the airport. If you've got any questions about the plan once we get to the estate, now would be a good time to ask them."

Natalie raised her brows. "Plan? I wouldn't call what we have a plan exactly."

"Sure it is," Chance said easily. "Find the safe, pick a time to crack it, replace the real diamond with the fake one that Brancotti left behind the last time, and then leave."

"It's a little short on the details," Natalie pointed out.

Chance was beginning to enjoy himself. Whether she realized it or not, Detective Natalie Gibbs was beginning to shine through, and he found he'd missed her. "You'll just have to trust me. We'll improvise the details as we go. If you're nervous, you can just follow my lead." He regarded her steadily for a moment. "Unless you think you can't keep up."

Her chin lifted, and Chance had to bite back a grin.

"I'm way ahead of you," she said. "My plan is to charm Carlo into giving me a tour of the house and see if I can spot the safe."

Chance frowned. "It'll be better if we take the tour together."

As the limousine pulled to a stop, she shot him a Calli smile. "Relax. I'm pretty sure my plan will work faster."

"You can't be too obvious."

Her brows shot up. "I can be very subtle when I want to."

Natalie didn't worry him. It was Calli who made him nervous.

Before she got out of the car, she patted him on the knee. "You'll just have to follow *my* lead."

NATALIE GIBBS slept like a rock, Chance thought as he sat across from her, watching her. She'd curled up on the seat across from his the moment the aircraft had reached cruising altitude. When they'd hit some turbulence over Virginia, she hadn't stirred, not even when he'd pressed his hands briefly against her to keep her on the couch.

He'd been tempted to do more than touch her, but he'd resisted—just as he'd resisted making love to her last night. It had been late when she'd finished her session with Catherine Weston, and he'd pretended to be asleep when she'd slipped into bed beside him. Oh, he'd been tempted then to turn and see which of the two women had joined him—Rachel or Calli. But he'd resisted. And he would be wise to continue resisting until the job was done.

Of course, that was much easier said than done. She was stretched full length on the seat across from his, and she was wearing "Calli" clothes—a stretchy, midriff-baring tank top and shorts. Looking at her was not helping to strengthen his resolve. Taking a quick sip of the ice water he'd poured for himself, he decided to take a break from his self-imposed torture and browse through his file on Brancotti once more.

NATALIE CAME AWAKE in stages the way she always did, and out of habit she remained perfectly still until all the layers of fog in her brain had disappeared. The hum of the jet's engine told her where she was, and she could feel Chance's presence as well as smell him. Was he looking at her? She'd selected her outfit with the main purpose of making him do just that. And she'd posed herself on the couch to tempt him while she slept.

That was step one of her plan. Now it was time for step two.

Keeping her eyes closed, she stretched and felt the tank top inch its way upward. Then in one smooth movement, she sat up and opened her eyes.

Humph. He wasn't looking at her. Instead, he was sitting, shoulders hunched, poring over his file. And he had horn-rimmed reading glasses perched on the bridge of his nose. For some reason, just looking at him wearing them had a little tendril of lust uncurling itself in her stomach.

Oh, it was more than time for step three.

"Steven?" she said in her high, effervescent Calli voice.

"Hmmmm?" Chance didn't even glance up from the papers he was reading.

It was damned hard to seduce a man when he wouldn't even look at her. Good thing she had a fool-proof plan.

Taking the file out of his hands, she slid onto his lap. "Hi."

"Calli—"

"Shhhh." She cut him off by pressing a finger against his lips. "I've been wanting to do this ever since I came back to the hotel last night."

He closed his fingers around her wrist and drew her hand away. "We'll be landing in a very short—"

This time she cut him off by pressing her lips against his. The heat ignited immediately, leaping from her to him and back again. Drawing away, she said, "I can be very quick." As if to prove it, she slid to her knees and pulled his belt free, unbuttoned his trousers and slid the zipper down.

When his hand covered hers again, she drew back a little and tugged her tank over her head. "I want you, Steven." She touched him then, taking him into her hand. "You want me, too. You always want me, don't you, Steven?"

HE DID. Later, Chance told himself that if he'd had a moment to think before she'd taken him into her hands… If she hadn't called him "Steven," or looked at him in that particular way… Or maybe if he hadn't been looking at her for the past hour and fantasizing about taking her on the floor of the airplane… Maybe then he would have been able to resist her and stick to his resolution.

He couldn't think at all when she rose to her feet and wiggled out of her shorts.

She was wearing nothing underneath. His hands came to life then, pulling her so that she could straddle him. And then she was taking him into her. Only then did she lift his glasses off and set them on the table.

"We wouldn't want to fog these up, would we?" she asked before she found his mouth again and began to move.

9

THE LATE-AFTERNOON SUN beat down mercilessly as the limousine turned onto a sleekly paved drive. The limo had been waiting for them when the plane touched down on Brancotti's private landing field. The driver, a tall blond muscle builder in his mid-twenties, had assured them that the twenty-minute ride would be as cool and as comfortable as he could make it. In her persona as Calli, Natalie didn't have to hide the fact that she was totally impressed with the chilled champagne and the fruit and cheese tray that awaited them in the plush interior of the limousine. Mozart poured out of a speaker, and she sat cross-legged on the carpeted floor, turning the knobs on a small TV.

Unless and until they could be absolutely certain that they weren't being bugged, they were to stay completely in character. That was the plan, and Natalie decided that being Calli was liberating. The woman didn't seem to have any hang-ups.

And seducing Steven Bradford had been almost as exciting as seducing Chance Mitchell. There'd been an added kick to realize that initially he'd tried to resist her. It occurred to her that she'd never before tried to seduce a reluctant man. But once Steven had gotten over his initial resistance, he'd been a more than willing participant. And if she hadn't known better, she would have sworn that the man she'd made love with on the airplane was different than the one she'd made love to two nights ago. As a lover Steven was gentler, or perhaps sweeter was a better word.

Did Chance feel the same way about Calli—that she was a different lover from Rachel? Which woman did he prefer? The thought fascinated her. Gazing over her shoulder, she studied him for a minute. It was definitely Steven she was looking at. What would it be like if she could make him lose control and become Chance when he wanted to be Steven Bradford?

Running her hand along the lush carpeting, she considered what it might be like to discover the answer to her question right now. Right here.

Turning, she sent Chance a slow smile. "Want to fool around?"

Without taking his eyes off of the papers he was poring over, he threaded his fingers absently through her hair. "Later. I have a call with Harold scheduled for five o'clock, and I need to get through these."

The call would be with Tracker McBride. That much Natalie knew. The conversation would sound like business, but there would be a coded subtext. Right now the subtext of his message to her was to keep her mind on the job.

But wasn't part of her job establishing the fact that she was totally besotted with Steven Bradford? Knowing that the driver was listening and probably watching through his rearview mirror, Natalie twisted around and placed her hand on Chance's thigh. "You know what they say about all work and no play."

In a quick move that she didn't anticipate, Chance closed his hands over her shoulders and drew her close for a long, hard kiss. Then even as heat flared to life, he moved his mouth to her ear and whispered, "You're playing with fire."

She laughed. "I hope so."

She felt his lips curve as he brushed soft kisses at the corners of her mouth. There it was again, that unexpected gentleness. Was it part of Chance or merely a layer to the persona of Steven Bradford? She was leaning forward when he slipped his hands out of her hair and set her away from him.

"Too late. We're here," he murmured.

Glancing through the window, she saw that they'd stopped at a mammoth gate set in a tall stone fence. The moment it opened, the limo slid through and continued up a winding narrow drive. Flowers bloomed on either side. To the right, there were three tennis courts where two hardy souls battled the heat and each other. Through the tall cypresses to her left she caught a glimpse of a landscaped patio area surrounding a huge pool. A few guests sat sipping drinks in the shade of red-and-white striped umbrellas.

Then as the car swept around a curve and the main house came into view, Natalie let her mouth drop open. The building was huge, three stories high with wings on either side. The entire structure was built out of slabs of gray marble streaked with shades of rose and pink. It reminded her of an Italian villa as she supposed it was meant to. At its right stood a low-slung build-

ing—an old carriage house, she guessed. Now it probably served as a garage and servants' quarters.

"Wow," she said as the car pulled to a stop. Though
she didn't repeat it, she might have said the same about
the man who descended the marble steps to greet them.
In person, Carlo Brancotti was even better-looking
than he'd been in the photos Chance had shown her.

Tall and broad-shouldered, he wore black trousers
and a white shirt with the sleeves rolled up. But it was
his face that drew and held her attention as Chance
guided her out of the limo. The slash of cheekbones
and the hair hanging loose to his shoulders made her
think of ancient warriors. The hint of the savage in contrast with the elegant clothes and surroundings made
for a devastating effect. She had a moment to absorb
the impression as he shook hands with Steven Bradford. When he took her hand and looked into her eyes,
a quick prickle of unease moved through her.

For a second, just until he released her hand, she
had the uncanny sensation that he could see right
through her. It passed the moment he smiled at her.

"I'm so glad I made an exception and allowed Steven to bring you along."

"So am I." The smile she sent him was genuine.
"You have a lovely place."

"It's even lovelier now," he said. Lifting a hand, he
signaled for a man who wore a uniform identical to the
one the driver had worn. "Show Mr. Bradford and
Miss Calli to the Venetian room." Then he turned to
Steven. "Make yourselves at home in any way you
wish. I'm giving a small party tonight so that my
guests can get to know one another."

Steven frowned. "I'm a busy man. I didn't come to party."

Brancotti smiled and shook his head. "So American. You'll have to learn to relax and enjoy my hospitality."

Then he turned and led the way into the house.

A PRICKLE OF UNEASE had worked its way up Chance's spine the moment that Carlo had said the words *Venetian room.* It moved through him once more as he read the same words on the engraved brass plate that adorned the door to the suite they were shown into. Venetia and *Venetian.* Was the name of the suite a coincidence or Carlo's way of letting him know that he was aware of who he was?

A part of his mind said no. There was no one at the agency who knew that he was coming here as Steven Bradford. Still, his mind raced as he watched Natalie move around the suite and peer through the French doors that led to a small balcony. She was playing her part beautifully, just the right mixture of sex kitten and wide-eyed innocent. And he was finding the combination fascinating. So damn fascinating that in spite of his resolution, he hadn't been able to resist her when she'd begun to seduce him on the plane.

"Look, we have a view of the pool and the ocean." Then she was skirting around the valet who'd escorted them to the room, and opening the door to an adjoining bath.

"Wow!" she said. "The shower takes up the whole wall, and there's a hot tub."

"Will there be anything else, sir?" the valet asked.

"No." Chance followed the valet to the door. Before he closed it, he glanced once more at the brass plate.

Brancotti might suspect any one of the guests he'd invited to the estate. He might even put Steven Bradford at the top of his list. But he couldn't know for sure.

Still, he should tell Natalie that they might be under suspicion. When he turned back into the room, she was moving through the suite, running her hands over the polished surfaces of old antiques, oohing and aahing. If Brancotti was listening, he'd hear a girl raised in the foothills of the Blue Ridge Mountains nearly going into ecstasy over his home. He might be rattled, but Detective Natalie Gibbs was doing her job, checking for any hidden cameras or small microphones.

Emotions streamed through him—admiration and something he couldn't quite put a name to. She was getting to him, and for both their sakes, he couldn't let that distract him from the job he'd come here to do.

"This is so lovely," she cooed as she climbed onto the bed and ran her fingers over the carved headboard. Then she stretched out on the mattress and sent him a quick grin. "Any idea about what we could do to while the time away until that dinner party?"

"You could take a swim in the pool," he suggested.

"Too hot." She made a face as she rolled over and then dropped her chin on her hands.

"I need to work," he said.

She made another face. "Too boring."

Moving to the bed, he took her hand and drew her up and off the mattress. "Why don't you try out the hot tub?"

She locked her arms around his neck. "Why don't we try it out together?"

"I really need to get some work done." But he leaned closer, caught the lobe of her ear between his teeth and whispered, "What did you find?"

Keeping her arms looped around his neck, she drew back and mouthed the words. "No cameras, two mikes here in the bedroom. One mike in the bathroom." Then she said aloud, "Oh, Steven, you worked on the plane."

"I need to talk to you," he whispered right against her ear. "Tonight, during the party, find an excuse to entice me away for a while. We'll walk along the beach."

"Oh, Steven." Her voice was a throaty purr as she drew back again. "You're always working. Can't we play? Just a little?"

Pursing her lips in a little pout, she pulled his tie loose. Then before he could even think to stop her, she was working on his belt.

"Calli."

"I want you."

Quite suddenly, he wanted her. Calli, Rachel, Natalie. They were all parts of the same woman, and he wanted them all. But they had a job. They should both rest.

The thought slipped away as her hand enclosed him.

"You know I can't go for very long without sex. It's a curse." She kissed him then, making sure that every soft curve of her body was pressed fully against his.

Chance flipped on the stereo beside the bed to mask the noises he knew they would make and then eased her back onto the mattress. "Then we're both damned."

NATALIE HAD to hand it to Carlo Brancotti. The man knew how to throw a party. Dinner had been a sump-tuous seven-course affair served in a room that re-minded her of a medieval dining hall. Her dinner partner had been a portly British gentleman, Sir Arthur Latham, who'd seemed sincerely interested in Calli's aspirations in the modeling field. The woman on her left had looked vaguely familiar, but it wasn't until Sir Arthur had introduced her that Natalie realized she was Risa Manwaring, a retired actress who had married a British lord.

By the time they'd finished with dessert, Risa had the name of her agent as well as a list of her most re-cent modeling jobs.

At the far end of the table, "Steven" had been seated to Carlo's immediate right, and as far as she could tell, the conversation between the two men hadn't flagged once.

Were she and Chance being tested—or was she just being paranoid? Natalie had always found that when she was doing undercover work, a little paranoia was a good thing. But hers had been increasing steadily from the moment she'd looked into Carlo Brancotti's eyes that afternoon.

She was pretty sure that Chance was feeling the same way. She'd felt the tension in him escalate the moment they'd entered their suite. There'd been that urgent request that she lure him away from the party. And she'd sensed an even greater urgency when they'd made love. What did he need to tell her?

Whatever it was, he was willing to wait until they

could be absolutely sure that no one was eavesdropping. So it was important, but not urgent.

The gathering at dinner had been small—under a dozen in all. Besides Sir Arthur and Lady Latham and the retired film star, there'd been two Japanese gentlemen, the Motos—father and son. Natalie recognized them as the two men she'd seen playing tennis earlier in the day. She'd also been introduced to the Demirs, a distinguished-looking businessman and his wife from Turkey, and another man with very hard eyes— Armand Genovese. Carlo's personal assistant Lisa had rounded out the number. Though she wasn't sure why, Natalie had expected more guests.

Once Carlo had led the way from the dining room to the conservatory for after-dinner drinks, the men had retired to the patio to sample some of his cigars. Natalie had toyed with the idea of joining them and insisting on sampling one herself, but had decided at the last moment that it wasn't something that Calli would have done.

Instead, she joined the four other women as Lisa led them on a guided tour of the flowers growing in the conservatory. It wasn't difficult to keep her expression awestruck as she admired more varieties of orchids than she'd ever seen. The fact was, she wasn't finding it difficult at all to be Catherine Weston.

Maybe it was the fact that the woman was about as uncomplicated as they came. She'd come from nothing and her ticket to the big time in modeling was Steven Bradford. Natalie Gibbs might not have gone about it the same way, but she could certainly admire Calli's single-minded determination to make a different kind of life for herself.

After all, wasn't that what she'd tried to do with her own life? For twenty-six years she'd lived with the fear that she was her father's daughter—that she might be tempted to follow in his footsteps. She'd joined the D.C. police because she'd wanted to make sure that she satisfied her desire for adventure on the right side of the law.

And now as Calli she had the opportunity to have her cake and eat it, too. A diamond heist—it didn't get much better than that.

She was even beginning to like the wardrobe that Chance had picked out for Calli. Natalie fingered the spaghetti straps that held up the silky white sheath she was wearing. Whether or not they made the man, clothes definitely made the woman. Each time she dressed in one of the outfits, she felt that she came to a deeper understanding of the part she was playing. Or perhaps, she was coming to a deeper understanding of herself.

When she'd slipped into the silky white dress that Chance had selected for her tonight, she'd instantly felt both beautiful and desirable. Natalie Gibbs rarely allowed herself to feel either of those ways.

But then the old Natalie would never have worn a dress that stopped at midthigh. Nor would she have thought of seducing a man twice in one day. No, three times. She had plans for that walk on the beach.

"It's a lovely room, isn't it?"

Natalie turned to smile at Sir Arthur's wife, Lady Latham. "I've never seen anything quite like it."

The glass walls and ceiling of the conservatory allowed a view of a starlit sky, and the air was scented with exotic flowers and candle wax. A small band tucked in a corner and surrounded by potted palms was playing a movie theme she couldn't quite place.

"But you're missing your young man?"

Natalie smiled. "A bit."

"Carlo is European and old-fashioned. He still honors an old tradition that men and women separate for a time after dinner. That is not the case in America, am I correct?"

"Yes, that is not the case in America."

Lady Latham smiled at her. "Well, maybe you were right to fight for your independence. But don't tell Sir Arthur I said that."

Natalie pantomimed locking her lips and then throwing away the key. She was beginning to like Lady Latham very much.

"You ought to go out there and lure your Steven away. A man with someone like you doesn't need imported cigars or the poker game that Carlo will entice them into next."

Natalie studied the woman for a minute. Though she was well into her sixties, she could see that Lady Latham must have been quite a beauty in her day. The smile she saw in the pale gray eyes looked sincere. "I promised Steven to be on my best behavior tonight. He wants to conclude his business with Carlo as quickly as possible."

Lady Latham's brows shot up. "There won't be any business done until tomorrow or the next day. Hassam Aldiri's plane was delayed, and he won't arrive until tomorrow afternoon at the earliest. Carlo will wait for him. Hassam has a lot of money. Even if he decides

that he doesn't want the diamond, I doubt that Carlo
will want to offend him."

"Well…in that case." Flashing Lady Latham a con-
spiratorial smile, she moved toward the doors she'd
seen the men exit through earlier. The night air was
warm in spite of the breeze from the ocean, but one
quick glance told her that the patio was empty. Hurrying toward the balustrade that separated it from the
sprawl of gardens below, she caught sight of the men
seated at tables in a small candlelit gazebo.

"I understand Steven has a weakness for poker."

Natalie pressed a hand to her heart as she turned to
face Carlo. She hadn't heard him approach. "Yes, he
can never resist a game. How did you know?"

"I make it a point to get to know the people I do
business with."

Though she couldn't see his eyes as clearly as she
had earlier, Natalie felt the intensity of his gaze. "I was
hoping to lure him away for a walk on the beach."

Carlo held out his arm. "Perhaps you'll allow me
to stand in for him?"

"No, I don't think so," Natalie said with a shy smile.
"I had more than walking in mind."

"Ah." Lifting a hand, he drew a finger down her
cheek. "I would be delighted to be his substitute for that
also."

"Oh no. I could *never*…" She and Chance had discussed the possibility that Carlo would make a move
on her, but she hadn't expected it to be so soon.

For a moment he said nothing. Natalie waited. She
was pretty sure that Carlo Brancotti was not a man who
accepted rejection easily. This might blow her chance

of ever getting that private tour. Finally, she saw the quick flash of his smile. "I admire loyalty. It's a precious commodity."

Natalie eased away a step so that he was forced to withdraw his hand. The last thing she wanted to do was alienate Carlo Brancotti, but she had no choice except to react to the situation the way she believed that Catherine Weston would react. "I don't want to interrupt Steven's game, so I think I'll retire to my room," she said.

"I apologize if I offended you. I want you to feel perfectly comfortable and enjoy your stay here." He smiled again and held out his hand. "Could we, as you Americans say, wipe the slate clean and begin again?"

"Sure." She put her hand in his and felt the warm press of his palm before he released hers.

When she turned to go back into the conservatory, he placed a hand on her arm. "Please. I will feel that I have failed as a host if you retire so early. How about if I offer you a tour of the gardens or the house—or both?"

Natalie hesitated, then smiled. "I'd love to see both. Steven has a couple of great homes—a ranch and a house he just built outside of L.A.—but I've never seen anything like this place. How old is it?"

"It's relatively new." He didn't touch her but merely held his hand out to indicate the direction. "I bought the house from a Saudi Prince two years ago, but the gardens are new. Flowers are my passion."

"I admire anyone who can grow things," she said enthusiastically as he guided her down a circular stair. "Not that I have a green thumb. I don't. But I love flowers."

"It's a passion that we share then," Carlo said as he urged her toward a door beneath the stairs. "Shall we start with the house and save the best until last?"

10

CHANCE HELD three royal ladies in his hand, but the woman who held his attention wasn't in the cards he'd been dealt. She was standing on the patio talking to Carlo Brancotti. And she could handle herself. Wasn't that the reason he'd been so determined to get Natalie Gibbs for this job?

"Are you in, Mr. Bradford?"

Silently cursing himself, Chance glanced back down at his cards.

Natalie was focused on the job. He was the one who was allowing himself to be distracted. The truth was that whenever he made love to her he became so drawn into the moment that he almost forgot that he was here to do a job. When he glanced back up at the patio, it was empty.

Chance ruthlessly suppressed the mix of panic and anger that tangled in his stomach. Natalie had made her plan clear. She was going to persuade Carlo to give her a tour. Obviously, the plan was working.

But Venetia had been following a plan, too.

"Are you in or out?" Armand Genovese's voice was thin with impatience.

"Give me a minute." Chance tore his gaze away

from the patio and found four pairs of eyes staring at
him. What he read in them ran the gamut from annoyance and mild curiosity to speculation and amusement. It was the speculation that bothered him the
most because it came from Sir Arthur Latham, the
man he suspected would report his every move to
Carlo.

Get a grip, he warned himself. He could hardly
throw down his cards and go running after Natalie.
One of Steven Bradford's weaknesses was poker. He
had a group of friends, ones who went back to the
founding of his company, that he regularly played
with. Chance had to believe that Brancotti's dossier on
Bradford would have included that little known piece
of information. So he could only conclude that the
poker game had been arranged to keep "Steven" occupied and separated from "Calli" for the evening.

"Mr. Bradford?" The question came from the Turk-
ish man who was also clearly annoyed.

"I think that Mr. Bradford may be thinking of other
ways that he could be spending the evening," Sir Arthur said. "And I can't say that I blame him."

Chance pushed a pile of chips into the center. "I'm
in."

For the rest of the hand, he kept his attention focused on the game. Natalie was doing her job. If he
wanted to keep her safe, all he had to do was concentrate on doing his.

"YOU DID SAVE the best for last," Natalie said as Carlo
led the way down a winding path bordered on either
side by jewel-colored flowers.

"You delight me. Most women are more impressed with the main salon or the gallery," Carlo said.

"They were lovely, too. But the paintings in the gallery made it seem more like a…museum." She sent him an apologetic smile. "I'm not much on museums."

As they continued down the path, Natalie reviewed the tour Carlo had just given her in her mind. He'd taken her through all of the rooms on the first floor—except for one that had a coded access pad. His workspace, he'd said as he'd guided her past it. Then for the length of a long hallway, he hadn't spoken. Natalie suspected that he was waiting for her to ask to see it. She hadn't. Instead, she'd stopped to "ooh" and "aah" over a marble-topped table with a mosaic inlay.

Gut instinct told her she was still being tested. Did he suspect that she wasn't the real Calli or was he always this careful?

The main salon took up the entire first floor in the wing opposite the conservatory. Marble floors gleamed, mirrored walls caught the reflections of carved pillars and crystal chandeliers. French doors opened onto patios with a view of the ocean. Natalie had spotted at least two surveillance cameras.

"The masquerade ball will be held in here tomorrow night," Carlo had said. "Who will you come as?"

Natalie had realized that she didn't know so she'd shot him a flustered look. "I can't tell you that. Steven says the whole point of a masquerade is that no one knows who you are. For one night you get to be someone else entirely with no consequences."

"How will I find you?" Carlo had asked. "All I would ask for is a dance."

Hoping for the best, Natalie had allowed herself to remain a bit flustered. "I really can't tell you. Steven hasn't even told *me* what costumes he brought."

Carlo had laughed. "You're charming. Steven is a very lucky man. But I will still try to figure out who you are."

Which wouldn't be much of a challenge, Natalie had thought. She'd spotted two cameras in the hallways, and Carlo would see them leaving the Venetian room in whatever they were wearing.

"I do love playing games. I believe your Steven does too," Carlo had said as he'd taken her arm and drawn her back to the main hall. "Come, I want to show you something."

The something had been a small room down the hallway. Oval in shape, it boasted two ornately carved pillars at the midpoint of the room.

"This gallery is my favorite place. We'll have the auction here. What do you think?"

"Wow," she'd said as she'd let her gaze sweep the room. Furniture was positioned to form conversation areas on richly hued oriental rugs, and settees were placed at intervals along one wall. Across from them hung the paintings.

Natalie had counted ten, and she'd been hard pressed to keep her mouth from falling open. She'd recognized several of the painters, but she hadn't been sure that Calli would.

"It's like you have your own museum," she said. And while Calli had stared in awestruck wonder, Natalie had catalogued the pieces in her mind. There were two van Goghs, a Manet and what she was pretty sure was a Renoir. But there were other works whose artists she wasn't as familiar with. Just how many of them had Carlo Brancotti acquired legitimately?

As if in answer, Carlo had stopped midway down the length of the room, leaned against one of the pillars and told an amusing story of how he'd won one of the van Goghs in a poker game.

Watching him, Natalie had felt a kind of prickling at the back of her neck, one that she hadn't felt in a very long time. She hadn't dared look around to figure out what had caused it because she'd had to appear utterly fascinated by Carlo's story. The pillar he'd leaned against was ornately carved and right behind his head was what looked to be a bronze sundial. The prickling sensation had increased.

The moment Carlo had finished his story, she'd smiled. "If you're that good at poker, you should be out with Steven and your other guests."

"Then I would have missed this opportunity to share my most prized possessions with you," Carlo had replied as he'd led her back outside.

His most prized possessions. Now, as they toured the gardens, the phrase lingered in her mind. And what was in that room that had made the back of her neck prickle like that?

"The gardens are boring you," Carlo said.

With a start, Natalie jerked her thoughts firmly back to the present. "No, they're magical. Sorry." She made the first excuse she could think of. "I guess I'm just missing Steven."

"You're in love with him, aren't you?" Carlo asked.

"No—I—" To her complete astonishment, Natalie felt herself blush. "We're just…I…he doesn't want…"

Carlo put one finger under her chin, tipping her face up so that he could see it.

Natalie felt a skip of panic as she stared up into those dark eyes. What would he see? For an instant there, she hadn't been sure whether she was speaking as Natalie or as Calli.

She held her breath through a stretch of silence before Carlo dropped his hand and said, "Steven is a very lucky man."

Carlo then gestured her forward, and for a while they walked in silence. The garden path was covered with a soft green mulch and bordered by lights. At regular intervals miniature streetlamps were nestled between palms.

"How clever of you to install the lights," she said finally. "I feel as if I'm walking through a fairyland."

"I had them installed because the temperatures are often so hot here in South Florida, and I wanted my guests to be able to enjoy the gardens once the heat of the day had passed."

The streetlamps also offered the perfect places to install video surveillance equipment. Natalie was certain she'd spotted a tiny camera beneath the ornate shade of the light they'd just passed. She bet there were microphones, too. Carlo Brancotti was a very suspicious and very careful man.

Turning, she shot him a very steady look. "And yet you offer entertainment that keeps your guests otherwise occupied."

He smiled at her. "Sometimes I prefer to enjoy the

gardens under less crowded conditions. Come, there's a new orchid I want to show you over there."

Though she kept her pace slow and her attention focused on the varieties of blooms that Carlo was pointing out to her, Natalie was thinking about the man walking next to her. Not once since he'd told her that he admired loyalty had he tried to touch her in any kind of personal way. Yes, he'd made it clear he wanted to dance with her, but even when he'd tipped her chin up to study her face, his touch had been impersonal. He was being a charming host and very much the gentleman—a persona that was a far right turn from the man she'd read about in the file Chance had compiled.

But there were reasons other than romance why he might want to separate her from Steven. There'd been that moment in the gallery and another when he'd bypassed his "workspace" that she'd felt something. Did he suspect that she and Steven weren't who they pretended to be? She couldn't rid her mind of the certainty that this whole tour was some kind of test.

Natalie the cop would use this opportunity to pump him for information, so she didn't. Instead, she yawned, then glanced guiltily at Carlo. "I'm sorry. It's not the company. Steven woke me very early for the flight here."

"Come. I'll take you inside."

"And Steven?"

"Sometimes the poker games go on into the morning hours."

She allowed disappointment to show in her eyes before she glanced away. "Oh."

"If you wish, I'll send him to you," Carlo offered as he led her back along the path.

She shook her head. "No. He loves the game. It's his one vice."

When they reached the door that he'd escorted her through earlier, he opened it. "If you go in this way, you can avoid the others in the conservatory."

She met his eyes again. "Thank you. Your home is lovely."

Natalie walked down the hallway without a backward glance. And she made very sure not to glance at the door with the coded access pad that led to Carlo's "workspace."

CHANCE FOUND himself glancing at his watch for the fourth time in two hours. Natalie had not reappeared on the patio, and neither had Carlo Brancotti. He'd managed to keep his mind on the game, and he'd even managed to win a few hands. But he hadn't been able to shake off the urge he had to go to Natalie. The rational side of him told him that she was perfectly capable of handling a man like Brancotti.

But each moment that ticked by made him feel less and less reasonable. Chance shoved a pile of chips into the center of the table and waited for the other bets to be placed. When Sir Arthur turned over his full house, Chance laid down his cards and pushed himself away from the table. "I'm finished, gentlemen."

There were a few grumbles. Chance paid them no heed as he let himself out of the screened gazebo and strode back toward the house. He might be making a mistake. He'd been weighing the odds of that for the past two hours. Logic told him that Steven Bradford would stay at the game. But gut instinct told him that he had to go to Natalie, and he hadn't gotten where he was by ignoring his instincts.

Let Carlo Brancotti make what he wanted of the fact that Steven Bradford was so besotted and so hot for Calli that not even a high-stakes poker game could keep him distracted for very long.

The conservatory was empty when he moved through it. At another time, he might have paused to enjoy the orchids, but now he only quickened his stride. There were surveillance cameras everywhere. Not surprising since there were expensive pieces of pottery and sculpture on display even in the hallways. But then, Chance didn't think that anyone Carlo invited to his estate would dare to steal from him.

No. The state-of-the-art surveillance equipment was for keeping tabs on his guests' movements. Chance took the stairs two at a time. If Carlo was watching, he would see a man who was desperate to get to his woman. And Chance was. He needed to see her, to satisfy himself that she was all right.

He needed *her.* Chance felt himself rocked by the realization. Before he had time to absorb or reflect on that, he reached the door to the Venetian room. It was locked. As it should be, he told himself as he swore silently and searched in his pocket for the key.

NATALIE PACED back and forth inside the suite. Since she'd come back to the room, she'd gone over everything that had happened that evening—from the time Carlo had appeared on the balcony to when he'd let her into the house, making sure she walked by his office again.

He'd definitely wanted to know about her relationship with Steven Bradford. And she had to hope that it had rung true. She'd blushed, for heaven's sake. And she was almost positive that it was Natalie's cheeks that had heated, not Calli's. When panic threatened to bubble up again, she ruthlessly pushed it down. She was not going to worry about that now.

Natalie paused in front of a mirror and faced her reflection. She was playing a game. That was all. Calli was in love with Steven Bradford. But Natalie was not falling in love with Chance Mitchell. What she felt for Chance was lust. And professional respect. The emotions tumbling around inside of her had no relation to what Catherine Weston felt for Steven Bradford. She couldn't afford to let the different roles she was playing merge. Giving herself a nod, she began to pace again.

Gut instinct told her that Carlo Brancotti had not only been testing her, he'd also been playing some kind of a game with her. Her mind kept circling back to the fact that the tour had been his idea. He'd wanted her to see the layout of the house, his "workspace," the salon and his gallery. Why?

She stopped pacing and began to tap her foot. It was in the gallery that her neck had begun to prickle. She often got that feeling when something meshed for her on a case. She and Chance had assumed that the Ferrante diamond would be locked in a safe in his office. Could it be in the gallery?

A quick glance at her watch told her it was midnight, the witching hour. There was no telling when the poker game would break up, and she needed to talk to Chance. Foot still tapping, she considered her options. As Natalie, she'd have to think of a plan. At the very least, Rachel would have to run through the possible repercussions. Thankfully, all Calli had to do was to go down to that poker game and tell Steven that she needed a walk on the beach before she could sleep.

She was at the door when she heard the knob turn, and she opened it just as Chance was fishing out his key. What she saw stopped her short for a moment. His hair was mussed, his expression impatient and just a bit dangerous. Her mouth began to water. But it was what she saw in his eyes—the mix of frustration and desire that had her heart taking a tumble. For just a second, she couldn't move, couldn't even think.

CARLO STUDIED the TV screens in the security room adjacent to his office. One of the security men had buzzed him the moment that Steven Bradford had left the poker game. And now Bradford was standing in the doorway to his room.

"What do you think?" he asked Lisa.

"He's a man who prefers his woman to a poker game," Lisa said.

"But it's well known that poker is his weakness. He plays twice a month with old friends. He doesn't rush home to be with his Calli."

"Perhaps that's because he's playing with friends. Or perhaps he was overcome by jealousy when you spent over an hour giving his Calli a tour of the house and gardens."

Carlo glanced at her sharply. Something in her tone told him that she didn't approve, but it wasn't like her to criticize him. "Are you jealous, too?"

She met his eyes, but said nothing.

"You don't think the tour was wise."

"No. You haven't yet decided who the plant is, and yet you showed her the gallery where the safe is."

Carlo smiled then and lifted a hand to trace it along her cheek. "Where one of my safes is."

"You're playing with fire."

"It's just a bit of misdirection, my dear Lisa. And I know what I'm doing. If they think the Ferrante diamond is in the gallery safe, it will make the game more interesting. And you can stop being jealous. My other guests will receive the same tour."

"I still don't like it," Lisa said.

He leaned down and brushed his mouth over hers. When her lips warmed and softened beneath his, he drew back and raised her hand to his lips. "Come. I think we can leave the lovebirds to themselves. And perhaps I can make it up to you for spending so much time with Calli."

FOR JUST A SECOND after Natalie opened the door, Chance couldn't move. Feelings swamped him. She was here. She was safe.

And he didn't have any idea which woman he was looking at. That realization fueled both his frustration and his desire. Stepping forward, he urged her back into the room, closed the door and locked it. Then he grabbed her arms, drew her up on her toes and closed his mouth over hers. Heat. He could feel it shoot from her to him and back again. He wanted, no, he needed...

Drawing back for a moment, he stared at her in the moonlight streaming into the room. *Who are you?* he wanted to ask. He wanted to shout it. But he couldn't.

What he said was, "I want you." Then before she could answer, he pushed her back against the wall and kissed her again. By damn, he was going to find out which part she was playing. He had to.

The flavor would give her away. Rachel was slightly tart. He tasted that. Calli was sweet—like wild honey—and he found that, too. He nipped her bottom lip and discovered the dark exotic flavor that had haunted him for three months. Natalie. Even as all three tastes flooded through him, he was desperate for more. Changing the angle of his head, he took the kiss deeper.

When he dragged himself back this time, they were both panting. In another moment, he would have pulled her to the floor and taken her right there. Scooping her up in his arms, he carried her into the bathroom and kicked the door shut behind him.

He didn't set her down until he'd twisted the knobs of the shower. There was a small mike on the ledge of the hot tub. He wanted to make sure that the spray would block any sound. He said nothing as he began to strip out of his clothes.

Natalie waited, watching as he removed his shirt and allowed his trousers to pool at his feet. In the moonlight pouring through the balcony doors, he looked like a god. She moved closer. Then, placing her hands on his shoulders, she drew his head down and spoke into his ear. "There are cameras throughout the garden, probably microphones, too. And I've been everywhere on the first floor. I know where Carlo's office is."

He gripped her hips and set her far enough away that he could see her eyes. They were a bit puzzled, but focused on his. Did she believe that he'd brought her in here to hear a report? She was thinking of the job and all he was thinking of, all he *could* think of, was her.

"Do you care if that dress gets wet?"

He couldn't hear his own words over the noise of the shower, but she must have read his lips because she turned and pointed to the zipper.

It extended all of three inches down from the small of her back, and as the silk parted, his fingers brushed against soft, damp skin. She shrugged her shoulders, wiggled her hips, and the dress slid to her feet.

She was wearing nothing beneath it. Chance's mouth went dry as a bone. He'd wondered, of course. So had every other man at dinner. But he hadn't known and hadn't truly believed that the woman he'd known originally as Natalie Gibbs would have gone to a dinner party, wearing nothing at all under her dress. Even Rachel Cade had worn underwear, hadn't she? To think she'd spent one hour alone with Carlo Brancotti wearing nothing but that thin swatch of silk.

Turning, Natalie looped her arms around his neck and pulled his ear to her mouth. What was she going to tell him now? That she knew where Brancotti's safe was?

He gripped her shoulders hard. "You can give me the damned report later. First, I want to know who the hell you are."

She didn't answer him immediately, but he could see the way her eyes darkened, the way the pulse at her throat fluttered. Then she smiled and suddenly her mouth was at his ear again. "I can be anyone you want."

Not quite gently, he clamped one arm around her waist and kept the other gripping her arm as he pulled her into the shower with him.

"I can be Rachel." She nipped his earlobe. Somehow she'd managed to get hold of the soap, and her hands slid over his skin leaving trails of ice and fire in their wake.

"I love touching your body." Her voice had become a breathy whisper. "Do you like it when I touch you here?" Her hand slithered from his shoulders down his chest.

"How about here?" Her fingers drew a line to his waist and then lower. "Or here? Do you like this?"

He closed his eyes as her slick, hot fist enclosed him.

"Or I can be Calli." She dropped a quick line of kisses along his jaw and began to pump him gently.

"Or I can be both." Her laugh was a breath in his ear before her tongue darted inside. And then she was whispering, "I could be two women at once. Is that your fantasy, Steven?"

He felt his head literally spin, his strength drain away.

"I could give you your fantasy," she breathed. "Right now, I'm Rachel."

Chance felt the subtle change in her posture. Her hand grew firmer on him and began to move more quickly.

"All during dinner, I thought of doing this. And this." She ran a slick hand over his shoulder and down his back to spread her fingers over his buttocks. "If you'd been sitting next to me, I would have found a way to touch you—even with Lady Latham watching us from across the table. Can you imagine it?"

Her whispered words had the image filling his mind.

"We might have been caught while I was slipping down your zipper, inch by inch. And then I would have done this." Her hand stilled, then milked him in one long pull.

With a moan, Chance slammed one hand against the shower wall to steady himself.

"You like that. Would you like me to make you come this way?"

This was madness. As he lifted his head and tried to clear it, she was all he could see—those wide eyes, the color now as dark and mysterious as the sea at night. That soft, soft mouth. In the misty steam that swirled around them, she made him think of a mermaid, and for the first time in his life, he understood how mythical sirens had lured sailors to their deaths. Those men simply hadn't cared about anything else.

Then she smiled, and releasing him, she stepped closer until the length of his hardness was pressed against her softness. Her mouth was at his ear again.

"Now, I'll be Calli. I'm not nearly as experienced as Rachel, but I read. When I was on the patio watching you play poker, I thought about this wickedly sexy book I read. It was all about what went on in this Victorian brothel. On Friday night, the men would gather in the parlor for a game of cards, and the lady of their choice would crawl under the table, and slip between the gentleman's knees...can you picture that?"

As the image formed in his mind, she slithered down his body and took him into her mouth. He couldn't think, couldn't breathe. He was drowning in her. Everything he was became centered on the sensations she brought him—the movement of that soft, hot mouth, the sharp press of her fingernails as she kneaded them into his backside.

He'd never felt a pleasure so intense. He wanted it to go on forever. But he wanted to be inside of her when he came. The struggle between those two desires was brief and vicious. But he finally found the strength to free himself. He knelt with her on the floor of the shower.

Water sluiced over them. Her wet hair clung to her forehead in jagged wisps, making her look different once again. The thought had barely entered his head, when she drew his ear to her mouth again.

"I'm a stranger you've just met. You don't even know my name." Her quick, wicked laugh only punched up the heat that was boiling inside of him.

"We have no history, no future, no expectations. You just know that you want me. You do want me, don't you, Chance?"

Later he would wonder if it was her use of that name that pushed him to the edge. He didn't know exactly who she was. When he looked into her eyes, all he saw was himself, trapped. All he was certain of was that he needed her with a desperation that threatened to slice him in two.

She smiled, but it wasn't Rachel's smile this time. Nor was it Calli's. "I want you. Now."

Chance was sure that he heard something inside of him snap as he dragged her to him.

HIS MOUTH crushed hers. The kiss wasn't loverlike. It was hard, demanding, and Natalie reveled in the onslaught of sensations sprinting through her. This was what she'd wanted, the mindless passion that only he could bring her. She could almost feel the barriers crumbling inside of her. He made her so aware of herself, so free.

No other man had ever made her feel this way. It was forbidden. It was delightful.

Even as his mouth devoured her, his fast, clever hands were everywhere, molding, pressing, possessing. Pleasure, hot spiky arrows of it, pierced her at every contact point.

When he drew back, she was trembling. Then he dragged her close again. "You're mine." His voice was a harsh whisper in her ear. "Mine."

Mine. The word echoed in her head as his mouth returned to hers. She'd wanted this madness, craved it from the moment she'd opened the door and seen him standing there. Now, he gave her no time to think, to breathe—no time to orient herself or anticipate. He ran his hand up her thigh and slipped two fingers into her, and her hips bucked to meet his touch. When he began to move his hand, her body moved with him, her muscles bunching, straining until her release, hot and hard, rocked her system. Only then did he drag her beneath him and drive himself into her on the floor of the shower.

"Look at me."

Shuddering, breathless, she opened her eyes to him. Water poured down, but even through the mists, she could see his gaze—dark and fixed on hers. Her vision and her body were filled with him. Her whole world had narrowed to him. There was nothing that she would have refused him.

"Say my name," he said.

For a split second, she hesitated, trying to clear her mind enough to remember who she was supposed to be. But he'd stripped all of those women from her.

Swearing, he withdrew and thrust into her again. "Say my name."

"Chance," she said. And she knew that it was Natalie who'd said the word, Natalie who was giving herself to him.

He nodded even as he began to move.

Wrapping her legs and arms around him, she gave herself over to the ride.

11

WHEN NATALIE opened her eyes in the morning, she found herself staring at Chance's sleeping face. Even as her mind readjusted to reality, recalling the job, the danger, the events of the night before, she kept studying him.

In sleep, he looked different. There was a hint of vulnerability, a hint of the boy that was seldom there when he was awake. Both pulled at her, and she felt her heart take a slow tumble.

Not good, she thought, as she pressed a fist against her chest. She was pretty sure the heart gymnastics thing had nothing to do with hot, sweaty sex or fantasies about what went on in Victorian brothels.

Where had that one come from anyway? She'd never read a Victorian porn novel in her life. And she'd better remember that the Victorian scenario hadn't been the only fantasy going down here. This whole thing she was playing out with Chance was a fantasy. He didn't even know she was here. He thought he was with Rachel and Calli. He certainly had no idea that the woman who'd given herself to him in the shower and all last night had been Natalie.

Suddenly, she frowned. No, she hadn't given herself to Chance. The word *give* was too closely associated with the heart acrobatics. And Natalie Gibbs was much too smart to give her heart to anyone. Maybe Calli was that type. As for Rachel, well, Natalie hoped that any cousin of hers would be wiser than that. But at least Natalie knew the kind of heartbreak that came when you allowed yourself to take that long fast fall into love. She'd seen what could happen up close and personal. Love had left her parents pining for something they could never have. And love for her dead husband had killed her mother.

No. She was not going to even think about the *L* word. *L-O-V-E* was not in her vocabulary. But as she lay there staring at him, she felt the little flutter near her heart begin again. Panic bubbled up. She had to get away from him to think.

After easing herself off the bed, she tiptoed backward to the closet, grabbed shorts, sandals and a shirt, then slipped as quietly as she could from the room.

SHE WAS GONE. Chance stood in the bathroom and struggled to keep panic at bay. When he'd woken up in an empty bed, he'd assumed she was in the bathroom. Their clothes were still lying where they'd dropped them, and her damn scent was still there. But there was no sign of Natalie. After moving out onto the balcony, he let his gaze sweep the grounds below. Relief streamed through him when he spotted her hurrying off in the direction of the beach.

Relief was pushed out by anger as he moved back into the bedroom for his clothes. What in the hell was she doing going off by herself? He dragged on trousers and pulled a shirt off of a hanger. They had roles to play, a job to do.

The next emotion to sweep over him was guilt. He should be lecturing himself on that score. Obviously, she was upset by what had happened between them during the night. Facing himself in the mirror, he tucked in the shirt and slipped into shoes. He could see the reflection of the bathroom door and the shower beyond. What had happened in there and later when he'd carried her into the bedroom had nothing to do with the masquerade they were involved in—or the job. He'd let his hormones take over.

No, that wasn't the whole truth. Placing his hands on the dresser, Chance leaned forward and met the eyes of the man staring back at him. Self-deception was not something that he'd ever let himself indulge in. It hadn't been merely hormones that had made him leave the poker game early. It had been feelings—feelings that he couldn't name, let alone sort out.

And he'd been swamped by feelings again in the shower. Calli, Rachel, Natalie—all three of them had gotten to him. But in the end it had been Natalie he'd made love to. Natalie he'd dragged to the floor. Natalie he'd demanded say his name. He was certain of that.

What he wasn't certain of was who Natalie had been making love to. Was it all role-playing for her? That was the question that he wanted to ask her, and it was not the question that should be foremost in his mind.

It was the job that should have his undivided attention.

Chance straightened and headed toward the bathroom. When he'd convinced Natalie to come with him to Brancotti's estate, she'd thought she'd be working with a professional. He'd have to make sure that she was. Until they had the Ferrante diamond and were safely off the estate, he had to find a way to stop touching her.

But even as the thought went through his head, he knew that keeping his hands off Natalie would be next to impossible.

SHE WASN'T ACTING like a professional. Natalie admitted that to herself as she reached the water. The sunlight glinted off the surface so intensely that she lifted a hand to shade her eyes. The quiet water and light breeze signaled that the day would be hot. The one thing that she'd always prided herself on was that she never let anything interfere with a job.

But last night, they'd…for the life of her, she wasn't sure what name to put to what they'd done to each other in that shower. All she was sure of was that when she'd seen Chance standing there in the doorway, she'd forgotten all about the job. All she could think of was having him.

Shoving down a fresh bubble of panic, she turned and started up the beach. What she needed was a bit of time to analyze what had happened. More importantly, who had allowed it to happen. From the time she was a child, she'd always loved pretending to be someone else. Her sisters had always enjoyed playing dress-up too, but for her it had always been about more than putting on outfits. She loved the whole process of getting into another person's psyche. For as long as he'd lived with them, her father had always encouraged her to develop her skill for what he called "slipping into other people."

With a dry laugh, she angled her path closer to the shoreline. Well, she'd "slipped" into some doozies last night. And the worst of it was, she'd enjoyed it. Never in her life had she felt so uninhibited, so wanton, so desirable. It had been wonderfully exciting until—

The cry of a gull had her shading her eyes and looking out over the water again. The white bird contrasted sharply with the wide expanse of blue sky. It called out again as it soared higher.

Freedom, Natalie thought. "Slipping into other people" offered her the freedom to escape from herself. Oh, she was her father's daughter all right. But last night she hadn't been able to completely carry off the charade. In the end, it had been Natalie who'd made love with Chance—in the shower and again in the bed. And…she'd lost a part of herself.

Stumbling, she pressed a hand against the tension in her stomach. Hadn't she known from the first time she'd looked into his eyes that he could touch her as no other man could?

It wasn't just the sex. It never had been just about the sex. That was why she hadn't been able to get him out of her mind for three months. That was why she'd decided to don a disguise for her next encounter with him. She'd done it to protect herself and it hadn't worked.

Natalie increased her pace and moved toward a part of the beach where tall grasses edged closer to the shore. She just needed to think. To plan. Choosing a spot near a lone palm tree, she sat down, drew her knees up and wrapped her arms around them.

What in the world was she going to do about Chance Mitchell? With a sigh, she rested her head on her knees. She supposed the answer to that question was simple and quite out of her hands. In a few days, the job would be over, Chance would go off to work on another case, and she would revert to being Detective Natalie Gibbs. Everything would return to normal, except that the job she'd loved for the past three years no longer held any appeal for her.

With one hand she scooped up white sand and let it flow through her fingers as she considered another question. Who was Natalie Gibbs? A part of her was her father's daughter, someone who loved dressing up and accepting the call to adventure. But she'd never before tried to analyze just what that said about who she was as a person. Why did she need to escape into other people? Or were they really "other people?" Just how much of Natalie Gibbs was in the people she slipped into? She scooped up more sand. There was a lot of her in the Rachel she'd created, and probably more of her than she'd thought in Calli. And if parts of her really were those other women, then did she know who she was at all?

Natalie wished that her father was with her so that she could talk to him about it. It wasn't often that she allowed herself to wish for him. At eleven, a year after he'd walked away from them, she'd locked those feelings away. For the sake of her sisters and her mother, she'd had to be strong and in control. But every so often, the need and the emptiness slipped past her guard and filled her as they did now. Even if her father couldn't tell her what to do, surely he could sympathize. Had he ever wondered who he was?

SWEARING UNDER his breath, Chance jogged along the beach. In the time it had taken him to get down the stairs and out of the villa, Natalie had disappeared from his view again. The moment he found her, they were going to have a talk, and he was going to get her word that she wouldn't go off by herself again.

Then he saw her, sitting with her head on her knees, her shoulders slumped and he increased his pace immediately. Something was wrong. Natalie never sat like that, and for that matter, neither did Rachel or Calli. He thought of the woman he'd squared off with on that mat in the Meridian's gym. She hadn't given an inch. He thought of the woman he'd been with last night, the woman who'd matched each of his demands with one of her own.

Something was definitely wrong. Quickening his pace, he knew the minute that she sensed his presence. Her shoulders stiffened and she lifted her head. But her gaze remained fixed on the water as if she needed a moment to gather herself.

When he reached her, neither of them spoke. He wanted to reach out a hand and stroke her hair, but once he touched her, he wasn't sure he could stop touching her.

"You shouldn't go off like this on your own," he finally said.

Then she did look at him, and there was nothing of the sadness that he'd sensed in her posture.

"I needed to think." With a smile, she patted the sand at her side. "And we need to talk."

She was Rachel. Chance was as certain of that as he was that she'd been Natalie when she'd been sad. Suddenly, he wanted the role-playing to stop. He wanted to talk to Natalie, find out what was bothering her.

But telling her now that he'd known all along that she was really Natalie Gibbs could put their whole job in jeopardy. Oh, she'd help him steal the Ferrante diamond. But there wasn't a doubt in his mind that Natalie would hate him for deceiving her. And Carlo Brancotti was good at reading people. Even the subtlest change in the relationship between Calli and Steven Bradford might make him suspicious.

"We'll have to be quick." She glanced past him down the beach. "I doubt that we'll be allowed to be here alone for very long. And I want to tell you where I think the safe is."

Chance cursed himself under his breath. As usual, she had her mind focused on the job. He didn't. Chance tabled the war going on inside of him. Now wasn't the time for his personal problems, but there was one thing he could do.

He took her hands. "I was too rough with you last night. You drove me crazy. I'm sorry."

Her eyes widened in surprise. "You don't have to apologize." Then she smiled, and he caught a glimpse of that light in her eyes that was so characteristic of Natalie. Chance once again found himself stifling the urge to grip her by the shoulders and tell her that he knew who she was.

Leaning forward, she brushed her lips against his. "I wasn't very gentle with you either."

Her scent filled him and sent images tumbling into his mind.

"I could be gentle." The words were a whisper against his skin, and then she used her tongue to trace his lips. "I could be very gentle if that's what you'd like."

Chance had slipped his hands into her hair and was about to take control of the kiss when he realized that it was happening again. All she had to do was touch him this way, and every other thought shot out of his mind.

He set her firmly away from him. "I think that until we get the diamond, we'd better keep totally focused on the job."

"I can multitask."

"I…" Chance paused for a second as he recalled just how good she was at multitasking. Then he cleared his throat. "I'm not as good, I'm afraid. It's not you. You're…" He paused again, battling both anger with himself and frustration. "Hell, yes it *is* you. You…distract me, and I want it to stop. I've waited a long time to get Brancotti. Can you understand that?"

"YES." Natalie studied him through narrowed eyes. She thought she understood a great deal more than what he was saying. He'd spent one night with Natalie and disappeared for three months. Then he'd spent one night with Rachel and turned all business.

Now, he'd spent a day and a night with Calli, and he was all set to run for the hills again.

Chance raked a hand through his hair. "We can pretend we've had a fight. You've run away to the beach and I've followed. That will give us an excuse to keep our distance, and tonight I'll sleep on the couch in our room."

Not going to happen, she thought. This time, she was going to have something to say about it. She had a hunch all three of the women inside of her would.

"Do you turn tail and run every time you have great sex?" she asked.

"No." There was shock in his eyes, followed by a frown. "What are you talking about?"

Keeping her eyes steady on his, she leaned back against the palm tree. "Well, you spent one night with me when I was Rachel and backed off. Now, you've spent a day and a night with Calli and you're ready to back off again. My cousin Natalie never said you were a coward."

His gaze narrowed. "I'm not. I'm concerned about the job. Don't tell me that you aren't having some of the same misgivings. Otherwise, why would you have run away down here to think?"

In spite of the jitters in her stomach, she raised her brows and sent him a cool look. "Sure, I came out here to think and, yes, I find you distracting, too. But not enough to change our game plan. We've set up Steven and Calli as lovers who are passionately involved and just a bit unpredictable. Tonight at the masquerade ball, I figure we're going to need an excuse to slip away together so that we can pin down the location of the safe. Sex is something that Brancotti understands, and we've laid the foundation for it." She reached over to pat his hand. "Stop worrying about the sex and let's concentrate on getting the diamond. I think I know where the safe is."

"He showed you his office?"

"Twice. When he finished showing me the gardens, he let me into the house through the wing where he keeps his 'workspace.' He didn't take me inside, but he made sure I saw the coded keypad."

"That's where the diamond is?"

She shook her head. "That's where he wants me to think it is."

Chance frowned. "Then you think he suspects you?"

She rolled her eyes at him. "Well, yeah. We're in a room where we can't even talk to one another unless we go in the bathroom and turn on the shower." She shrugged. "But I think he suspects everyone."

"Okay. So why don't you believe that the diamond is behind the door with a keypad lock?"

"Because of a couple of things. One, he's a man who believes that he's smarter than anyone else and constantly likes to prove that. And two, he told me himself that he likes playing games."

"So?"

"Well, I've been thinking. What if showing me the room with the coded keypad was just a bit of game-playing—or misdirection, if you'd rather call it that? Then because he's so smart and his ego is enormous, he couldn't resist showing me the room where he *really* keeps the things that are most precious to him."

"Where?" Chance asked.

"There's a small art gallery down the hall from the main salon where he keeps his collection of paintings.

He told me he's going to hold the auction there, and I think the diamond is in a safe in that room."

Chance thought for a minute. "It would be just like him to pull something like that. He's always been a risk-taker, and I agree that he's a game-player. In fact, he could have a diamond in both places—a fake in one safe and the Ferrante diamond in the other." He met her eyes. "Unless we get lucky on the first try, we'll have to break into both safes."

Natalie's eyes gleamed. "Yeah. That's the way I figure it, too."

"How many paintings are in the gallery?"

"Ten."

"Ten paintings…I don't suppose you have any idea which one the safe is behind?"

Natalie smiled. "Did I say I thought it was behind a painting? I think he's a bit trickier than that. I'm betting it's concealed behind a panel in one of the pillars. He stood right in front of one of them, and I got this… feeling." She rubbed the back of her neck.

"How sure are you about this?"

A small frown appeared on her forehead. "It's a hunch. But I'm sure enough that I'm going to lure you into that room tonight and seduce you. You'll have to take care of the camera. Then I want to poke around those pillars."

"How long will you need?" Chance asked.

"As much time as you can get me."

He raised her hand and pressed his lips against her fingers. "You're very good at this game of deception we're playing."

She gave him a quick glance and caught the intent

look in his eyes. For one moment, she wondered if he knew that she wasn't Rachel Cade.

"We'd better get back to the house," she said.

Chance didn't move. He merely studied her for a moment. He might be losing his focus, but she wasn't losing hers. He was very glad that he'd brought her to Florida with him.

"Carlo is going to wonder if we don't get back," she said.

"Let him," Chance said as he remembered the way she'd looked when he'd first seen her here on the beach. "Let's go wading first."

"Wading?"

The surprise on her face pleased him. "You take your shoes off and walk in the water."

"I'm familiar with the concept. I just don't get the purpose."

The dryness in her tone had him shooting her a sideways glance. "Fun. Once we go back to the house, we're Calli and Steven. Right now, we can be whoever we want. Didn't you ever skip school and play hooky as a kid?"

"No."

Chance grinned at her. It was his Natalie who'd answered. He was certain of it. "No. Of course not."

Her chin lifted. "And you played hooky a lot?"

"You might say that my early life was pretty much one long game of hooky." He walked to the shoreline, toed his shoes off and then leaned down to take off his socks.

"How so?" she asked, kicking off her sandals and joining him.

"It's a long story," Chance said.

"I can wade and listen at the same time," Natalie pointed out.

They began to walk. The sun beat down on their shoulders and arms, and the lukewarm water lapped at their ankles. "My mother moved around a lot, mostly within London and the south of England. But a few times, she followed a band to Scotland or Wales. She was what you would call in America a groupie—and she was especially fond of young groups that were just starting out. Sometimes, they'd give her work, repairing and laundering costumes or passing out flyers. I got to help with that."

Natalie frowned as she slipped her hand into his. "She took you with her?"

"She was only sixteen when I was born, and she didn't have any family. Most of the time she supported the two of us by waitressing. She thought that was the best kind of job because she could bring home food. Plus, it was something that she could do just as well in one town as another."

Chance shot her a look and saw that the frown had deepened on her face. "It wasn't as bad as it sounds. She was pretty and she laughed a lot. And she loved me. It wasn't until I got to the orphanage that I started to go to school regularly."

"Orphanage?"

Chance shrugged. He rarely let himself think about that part of his life, and he never talked about it. He wasn't sure why he was now except that what they were doing reminded him in a way of that early part of his life before the orphanage. "One night she never came home. Police came to the door the next morning. She'd been struck by a bus on her way home from a concert."

Natalie simply turned and wrapped her arms around him. "I'm sorry. How old were you?"

"Twelve." Chance found that it was hard to get the word out because once again feelings were swamping him. He felt his body stiffen, not in defense but in surprise. There was none of the fire that he usually felt when she held him. In its place was a steady warmth and a sweetness that seemed to squeeze his heart. Her head was pressed against his chest, her arms wrapped around him, and he could have stood like this, just like this for a very long time.

Slipping a finger beneath her chin, he lifted it because he had to see her eyes. He could see sympathy and affection and a question.

"Chance?"

He wanted more than anything to kiss her. To lower his head, press his mouth to hers and lose himself in her. But if he did, he knew he would lose something that he would never get back. At the last second he set her away from him.

She turned away, but not before he saw the hurt in her eyes. He had his mouth open, his hand outstretched when he realized that the name in his mind, on his lips, was *Natalie*.

He barely had time to swallow it when he heard the crack and felt the burning sting in his shoulder. The next shot hit the wet sand not three feet from them.

"Run." Grabbing her hand, Chance fixed his gaze on the line of palms half a football field away and dragged her with him.

12

NATALIE STRUGGLED to swallow her fear as they raced for the cover of the trees. Sand sprayed up less than a yard to their right, and Chance's grip on her arm tightened. "Sprint."

Fighting to keep her breathing even, she felt the pull in her calves each time her foot sank into the sand and struggled for traction. Fifty yards became forty…thirty…twenty. There was another spray of sand, this one to her left. Finally, they reached the first line of trees.

Chance kept up the pace until palm leaves closed in on them and the sand at their feet became completely covered over with vegetation. Beach had become swamp in an instant. They would have to go more slowly now or run the risk of falling or twisting an ankle.

"Follow me," Chance said. It was only when he took the lead that Natalie saw the blood on his shirt.

"You've been hit."

Chance pulled the shirt off his shoulder and glanced down at the wound. "It's just a scratch. C'mon."

Natalie pressed a hand against the knot of fear that had formed in her stomach. The mark was angry-looking and it was oozing blood. But he was right, she told herself. It was just a scratch. And she wasn't going to let herself think about the fact that it might have been worse.

They walked swiftly in silence for a while. Natalie tried to keep her mind blank and focus on putting one foot in front of another. Moving as fast as he could, Chance cut a path through the vegetation by tamping down palm fronds and grasses. Now only thin spears of sunlight pierced the darkening gloom, and damp heat pressed in on them. Natalie felt a trickle of sweat run down her neck.

Something moved under her foot. Stifling a scream, Natalie reached out to grab a fistful of Chance's shirt.

"What?" He stopped and turned so fast that she bumped into him.

"Nothing," she said.

When he merely studied her for a minute, she lifted her chin and repeated, "Nothing. Go."

She was just not going to let herself think of what might be under her bare feet, not while a gunman might be after them. Snakes had always scared her, but they weren't nearly as dangerous as whoever was using them for rifle practice.

"This way," Chance said and made a sharp right turn.

She hoped he knew where he was going, because the oval expanse of black water to her left had her thinking of another kind of danger that lurked in the Florida swamps. Alligators. Hadn't she read that wherever there was water, you could bank on finding one— or more?

No. She tore her gaze away from the water, fastened

her eyes on Chance's back and made herself think about who had shot at them. Brancotti? Had he somehow seen through their disguises? But how?

If it wasn't Brancotti, who else could it be? Keeping her gaze fastened on Chance's back, she pictured each one of the people she'd met at the dinner party the previous night.

Her favorite suspect would have to be Armand Genovese. A man with mob connections wouldn't even have to pull the trigger himself. He'd have easy access to a professional hit man.

And a hit man wouldn't give up until the job was done. He might even now be following them into the swamp.

Natalie risked one quick glance over her shoulder and saw only shadows. She stumbled, caught herself and refocused her attention on Chance's back.

Sir Arthur probably hunted, but even when she formed an image of him with a rifle in his hands, she found it hard to believe that he was a killer.

She didn't know as much about the other guests, but they were all very wealthy. Any one of them could have hired someone.

But why would any of them want to kill Steven— unless…

Chance stopped abruptly, and she walked smack into him again. Peering over his shoulder, she saw the trunk of a fallen palm tree blocking their path. He gripped her hand and guided her around it.

Once on the other side, they crouched down and Chance leaned close, his voice making no more sound than a breath. "If we're being followed…" He reached into his pocket and drew out a small gun. Together, they waited, listening. Gradually, she could hear other sounds above their breathing. No sounds of footsteps. Leaves rustled overhead, insects buzzed, and farther off, a gull shrieked. A minute stretched into two and then three. Natalie shivered as she watched a spider the size of her fist crawl down the side of the tree trunk.

Clamping her teeth together, she made herself wait another minute before she said, "I want to get out of here."

"Yes," Chance said. "'Calli' can get sick. I'll tell Brancotti that I want to fly you back to New York."

She stared at him. "Forget it. I was talking about getting out of this swamp. I'm not leaving you here alone."

His expression was grim, his eyes cold. "It's too dangerous. I don't want you here."

"Tough." She could make her eyes cold, too. "I don't cut and run until a job is finished. Besides, you need my help."

He said nothing for a minute. Because she was right. Natalie pressed her advantage. "We've decided that unless we get lucky and find the real diamond on the first try, we have to hit both safes. You won't be able to do that alone. Once the job is done, I'll be ready to leave. And instead of arguing with me, you'd best put your energy into figuring out who took that shot at us."

CHANCE SHOVED DOWN on the emotions that had been swirling through him since they'd narrowly missed that barrage of bullets on their sprint for the trees. He couldn't afford to let them cloud his mind, not now when he had to focus on protecting Natalie. Gathering his thoughts, he said, "I don't have to figure anything out. It was Brancotti."

She shook her head. "Not necessarily. It could be anyone he's invited to his house party."

Chance bit back his impatience as she ran through her little rogue's gallery of suspects, but he still wasn't convinced. "What's their motivation?"

"Any one of them could be worried that Steven Bradford might outbid them."

Chance shook his head. "My money's still on Brancotti."

"He's a businessman. He wants Steven Bradford here as competition. You'll drive the price up."

She had a sharp mind. Chance had to admit that, but she wasn't aware of all of the facts. "I've gone up against him before."

"I read the file. You lost your partner."

Chance nodded. "He could have put us in the Venetian room to let me know that he suspects who I really am. And now he's decided that the game is over."

Natalie thought for a minute. "I don't think so. Wouldn't he rather play the game out to the finish—let you get the diamond in your hand and then spring a trap?"

Chance remained silent. She could almost see his mind at work.

"Besides, if he kills Steven Bradford, he calls attention to this place. He can't want the police wandering through, questioning his guests or even worse, wondering why all these people are gathered here. It's too risky."

"But he didn't kill me," Chance pointed out. "He could still intend to play the game to the finish. Either way, it's too risky for you to stay."

Natalie studied him in silence for a moment. Then she said, "I'm not going unless you come with me."

"I'm not leaving without the Ferrante diamond."

"Then I stay, too."

Chance grabbed her wrist as she started to rise. "Haven't you heard a word I've said? It's too dangerous for you to stay. It's possible that Brancotti set this whole auction up to trap me because I came too close to catching him the last time."

She gave him a long, cool look, and when she spoke, her voice was just as chilly. "I've heard everything you said. But I don't desert my partners."

When he opened his mouth, she raised a hand to silence him. "You haven't convinced me yet that Carlo is on to us. Your history with him and the fact that you lost a partner may be clouding your judgment."

"You may be right, but—" He cut himself off as he looked into those cop's eyes. He owed her the rest of the truth. "There's more that I haven't told you. Carlo and I go back a long way—all the way back to that orphanage I told you about. His name was Damien back then, and he was my best friend, my mentor. I trusted him until he betrayed me."

"How?" Natalie asked.

"I was twelve and he was seventeen when I was placed there, and he took me under his wing right from the start. You've seen what he's like. I came to worship him. The nuns at the orphanage trusted him, too. He could go anywhere without being questioned.

He had a knack for opening locks and under his tutoring I found that I did, too. After lights-out at night, he'd come and get me, and we'd practice. Once a month they changed the combination on the safe in the headmistress's office. Damien would finesse the lock on her office door and then we'd practice on the safe. It took a while, but eventually, I was able to open it. Each month after that we'd have competitions to see who could open it the fastest."

Natalie couldn't help but recall that she and her father had had the same kind of competitions.

"One night, Damien excused himself while I was working on the safe. He said he had a surprise for me. I don't know how long he was gone. I was totally focused on listening to the tumblers fall. This particular night the safe was empty. I didn't even have time to wonder about that when Damien returned with the headmistress and the police. There'd been over a hundred thousand dollars in the safe—money from the annual fund-raiser. Looking back, I can see that Damien had laid his plans far in advance."

"They didn't suspect him?" Natalie asked.

Chance laughed dryly. "Why would anyone suspect St. Damien? He looked as horrified as the headmistress to find me there. He told them that he'd heard something when he was making his rounds and he'd called the police immediately. They found me in front of the open safe, and then they found letters under my mattress—from my accomplice. In them, I was told just what to do and I was even given the combination of the safe. The police assumed that I had tossed the money out the open window of the office to my 'partner' and that, thanks to Damien, I hadn't had time to make my escape. Looking back, I can see how stupid I was."

"You were twelve, a child. How could they have been so stupid to suspect you?"

Chance glanced down to find that Natalie had slipped her hand into his. He couldn't help wondering how his life might have turned out if someone at the orphanage had had even a little of that simple faith in him. "The nuns didn't think that being twelve was an excuse. And they didn't want to disbelieve Damien."

"What did they do with you?" she asked.

"I was taken away to jail. Of course, my accomplice was never found. Later, I learned that Damien left the orphanage shortly after that."

"And no one suspected even then?"

Chance shook his head, almost smiling at the vehemence in her tone. "He was close to eighteen, and he had a right to leave."

"What happened to you?" she asked.

Chance smiled. "Don't look so worried. The one thing I owed Damien for was that I'd become very good with locks. I spent one night in the town jail before I blew the place."

"You were twelve and alone on the streets?"

Because he couldn't resist her, he briefly touched his lips to hers. "The streets were a hell of a lot better than that jail. Now that you know what Carlo is really like, is there any chance that I can convince you to leave?"

"No."

There were some battles you could win, Chance thought, and some you retreated from so that you could fight another day. Tipping up her chin, he met her eyes steadily. "We're going to have to be very careful."

"Yes, we'll need some kind of a plan."

Chance could almost hear the wheels inside her head turning.

She glanced around. "I'll be able to think better once we get out of this place. If there's one creature that scares me more than alligators and snakes, it's spiders."

Laughing, Chance tucked his gun away, then pulled her to her feet and said, "Follow me."

"HAVE YOU GOT IT?" Natalie asked.

Chance glanced down at her as they stepped onto the circular drive that led to the house. There were smudges of dirt on her nose and cheeks, but she was totally focused on explaining the tack she thought they ought to take with Brancotti. It wasn't bad as plans went, Chance supposed.

"I'm going to be upset, angry, afraid," she said. "Someone shot at us, and I'm going to want answers."

Natalie Gibbs was a woman who seldom lost her focus, except when he was making love with her. Then that line of concentration disappeared from her brow, and that incredible mist would fill her eyes and darken them.

"Well?"

He filed away the image that had filled his mind and glanced down at her.

"And you're going to be—?" she prompted.

"I'm going to be upset and withdrawn. Let you take control. I don't much like that part."

She shot him a grin. "Steven Bradford's a bit of a weenie. That makes him very sexy to someone like me."

"I'll have to remember that," Chance said.

"I'd rather that you remember the plan—and stick to it."

He'd stick to it for a while, at least. Their best shot at leaving the estate with the diamond was to continue playing their roles. Natalie's instincts were good, and she was managing to keep her objectivity a hell of a lot better than he was. For the moment, he couldn't do better than to follow her lead.

"Ready?" she asked as they climbed the steps.

"Yeah. Are you ready?"

"Yes." She drew in a deep breath, let it out. And then Chance watched her turn into Calli.

Her step quickened and she slipped her hand into his. "The first thing I'm going to do is demand that you see a doctor."

"Whoa. That wasn't part of the plan you just outlined. I don't need a doctor," he said. "It's just a scratch."

"It's bleeding. A doctor should look at it."

She was being mother hen, Chance thought in some disgust. There was a lot of Natalie, the big sister, in Calli.

They stepped into the entrance hall just as Lisa entered from one of the hallways.

"I demand to see Carlo," Natalie cried. "Someone just tried to kill Steven."

"This way," Lisa said, gesturing them into the hallway she'd just stepped out of. "Carlo has already been informed of the incident. He's talking to the security people right now."

Chance let Natalie draw him down the hallway. Lisa stopped at a door with a coded keypad. Figuring that this was the same room that Carlo had shown Natalie on her tour, he took a quick survey as he stepped through the door. He spotted the guard right away, just outside the doors that opened onto a patio. Natalie strode forward and placed her hands, palms down, on Carlo's desk. "What is going on here?"

Carlo glanced at Chance, then back at Natalie. "I'm working on it. My men are searching for the shooter. I hope to hear shortly that they have apprehended him."

"And why should we trust you?" Natalie asked. "How can we be sure that it wasn't one of your men who shot Steven?"

For a moment there was silence in the room as Carlo looked from Natalie to Chance and back again. Chance could see the anger in Carlo's eyes and in the pulse beating in his temple. For a moment, he wondered if Natalie had gone too far.

Finally, Carlo moved around his desk and took one of Natalie's hands. "You're upset. Understandably so. Please." He glanced at Chance and gestured to the two chairs in front of his desk. "Sit down. Lisa? Pour our guests some brandy."

As Lisa did his bidding, Natalie and Chance sat while Carlo picked up his phone and punched in numbers. "I'm calling my own personal doctor. She lives right here on the estate. You'll want to have the wound looked at."

"It's only a scratch," Chance said. "Give me some antiseptic and a Band-Aid and I'll be fine."

"Thank you. He'll see a doctor," Natalie said.

Carlo gave orders over the phone, then hung up and waited for Lisa to distribute the brandy snifters.

He took a quick sip of his before he spoke, and Chance used that moment to study his old enemy more closely. Carlo's hand wasn't quite steady as he set his glass down on the desk. He was either rattled or giving a good imitation of it. Of course, Chance was well aware that Carlo was skilled at deception.

But what would be the point of acting rattled? Unless he truly was. Was it possible that Natalie was right and Carlo wasn't behind the shooting?

Chance had no reason to give him the benefit of the doubt.

"I want to apologize." Carlo said. "Nothing like this has ever happened on my estate before. In answer to your earlier question, I don't usually invite people here to shoot them. This villa—" he gestured with a hand "—is a place where I conduct a very lucrative business. And most of my clients are repeat customers. If word got around that something like this could happen here…well, you can imagine the repercussions. That is why you may rest assured that I had nothing to do with this deplorable incident. You can also be certain that I will do everything in my power to get to the bottom of it."

It was a nice speech, Chance thought. There was a line of tension in Carlo's shoulders and a bite of fury in his movements as he lifted the glass and took another sip of brandy. It was a superb performance.

"You say the shooter isn't one of your men. But how could he have gotten past your security?" Natalie asked.

Bull's-eye, Chance thought as a muscle twitched in Carlo's jaw. Was that why Carlo was so angry?

"That is an excellent question. I will have the answer soon," he promised.

On impulse, Chance said, "I want to send Calli home."

She rounded on him. "No. If we go, we go together. I don't care about that diamond. I only care about you."

There were real tears in her eyes. Chance would have staked his life on it. And they hadn't discussed this scenario. He'd sprung it on her out of the blue.

"No. Please," Carlo said.

Ignoring him, Chance looked only at Natalie. "I can't put you in danger."

She reached for his hand. "I won't leave you here."

The phone on Carlo's desk rang. "Excuse me." He reached for it. "Yes?... I'll be there shortly." After replacing the handset, he said to them, "My security team has apprehended the shooter. I'll get to the bottom of this, I promise you. In the meantime, I want you to let my personal doctor look at the wound." He turned to Natalie. "I promise you that you will both be safe here. I don't want you to leave. I'll auction the diamond tonight."

Good, Chance thought. The sooner he got Natalie off the estate, the better.

Natalie kept her grip tight on Chance's hand. "Will you see the doctor?"

"Yes. All right," Chance agreed.

"Ah," Carlo said as a small round woman with gray hair and wire-framed glasses was ushered in. "Dr.

Canfield, I'd like you to meet Steven Bradford and his friend Calli. Steven has a bullet wound that I'd like you to take a look at."

"It's a scratch," Chance protested.

The woman stopped short and sent Carlo a stubborn look. "I have to report a bullet wound." Chance got the impression the outspoken woman wasn't afraid of anyone or anything.

"By all means," Carlo said. "I plan on making a report myself just as soon as I speak with my security team and find out why this unacceptable incident occurred."

"Just so we're straight." With a brief nod for Carlo, she bore down on Chance and set her black bag on the edge of the desk. Then she said to Calli, "Is he going to be a baby about this?"

Natalie raised her brows. "He's a man, so of course, he's going to be a baby."

Chance suspected Dr. Canfield was biting back a smile as she turned and opened her bag.

"I'm leaving you in good hands," Carlo said as he signaled Lisa to follow him out of the room.

13

"TWO THINGS." Natalie pitched her voice low, gesturing with the lollipop the doctor had given him as a joke after she'd dressed his wound. She sat cross-legged on the edge of the bathroom sink while he shaved. Behind them, the shower was thundering like Niagara Falls, so they could talk safely.

"First, I think the diamond might be in the safe in Carlo's office after all."

Chance let his razor pause in midstroke and shifted his gaze to Natalie. "Why?"

She paused for a moment to gather her thoughts, and a tiny line appeared on her forehead. Chance wondered if she was at all aware that she'd slipped into being Natalie. "Three reasons. Number one and two are related—the guard and the fact there was no camera in the room."

Chance continued to draw the razor down his cheek. She was good. There wasn't a second that they'd been in Carlo's office that he'd seen her attention waver from either Carlo or him, but she'd still managed to scan the room for recording devices. "It's not surprising that he wouldn't have a camera in his office. That's his private space. He wouldn't want someone even on his own security team seeing everything that goes on in there. Or overhearing everything he says on the phone."

"Yeah." She tapped the lollipop against her lips. "That's the way I figure it, too. But the presence of a guard could mean there's something very valuable in the safe to protect."

"Or the guard could be stationed there to protect Carlo."

She shook her head. "He didn't go with Carlo. He stayed in the room. I'm betting Lisa is Carlo's bodyguard as well as assistant. And I think she sleeps with him."

Chance shot her a questioning glance. That was something he hadn't noticed. "They're lovers?"

"I'd bet good money on it. There's something in the way that Lisa looks at him."

"Your third reason?" Chance rinsed his razor under the faucet.

She frowned. "It's harder to explain, but it goes back to games. You mentioned he's fond of misdirection. So at first, I thought that he showed me the office with the coded access pad to make me think the diamond's there when it's really in the gallery. But maybe it's the other way around—and he took me to the gallery to make me think it's there while it's in his office with a coded pad on one door and a guard stationed at the other. Does that make any sense?"

Chance nodded. "Perfect sense. But we'll still have to hit both safes."

Natalie sighed. "Agreed. But I think we should do the office first."

Chance said, "We'll see."

"We should have a definite plan."

"I'm working on it. You said two things. What else did you want to talk about?"

She straightened a bit and rotated her shoulders. "I'm more convinced than ever that Carlo wasn't behind the shooting."

"Be careful." Chance drew the razor on one final stroke along his jawline. "You're letting the man get to you again."

"No. But I do have to give him points for calling in his private doctor."

"Damage control. He doesn't want it to become public knowledge that guests on his estate run the risk of being shot. And you only liked her because she swabbed my shoulder with something that could take the finish off cars."

Her lips curved. "Don't be such a baby."

Chance took a towel off his good shoulder and wiped his face with it. "Remember, all of Brancotti's charm is on the surface. Underneath, he's as cold and ruthless as they come. And he's the most likely candidate. He knew we were both down on the beach—the security cameras would have shown him that. All he had to do was pick up a phone and give the order."

Natalie pulled the lollipop out of her mouth. "But he was rattled when we walked in the room. And furious."

"Because his men botched the job."

"Or because something happened on his estate that took him by surprise, something that he wasn't in control of. That would piss him off."

She had a point. He'd given it some thought himself, but he wasn't convinced. Chance studied her as he rinsed his razor under the running water. As she tucked a strand of hair behind her ear in a gesture that was pure Natalie, something tightened around his heart. When the job was done, he was going to miss working with her, pitting himself against the sharp mind of hers. He was going to miss her. Period.

"Carlo didn't like it at all when he thought we might leave." Pausing, she pointed the lollipop at him. "I didn't appreciate that little improvisation either. It wasn't part of the plan."

He shrugged. "I have trouble sticking to plans. I wanted to see his reaction." He recalled hers—the tears that had sprung to her eyes. Would she miss working with him? Miss him?

"Rachel…"

"Hmmmm?"

As she met his eyes, he watched that total concentration shift to him. If he told her the truth now—that he'd known all along she was Natalie Gibbs—he might be able to convince her to go.

"What is it?" she asked.

As he played with a strand of her hair, he knew that he wasn't going to tell her—for the same reason that he hadn't pushed the issue in Carlo's office. In spite of the danger, in spite of everything, he wanted her with him for as long as he could have her.

"I want you," he said.

The tiny line appeared on her forehead again. "We should nail down details for tonight."

"Okay." He hung up his towel and turned to her. It

was then that he noticed the line of dried blood on the top of her foot. "You didn't tell me that you were hurt."

She glanced down. "I'm not. It's just a scratch."

Chance plugged the sink and turned the faucets on. "That defense strategy didn't work for me." He paid no heed to her grumbled comments as he drew her feet into the water.

"Ouch."

"I thought it was only men who were babies." Ignoring her little huff of breath, he lifted the injured foot out of the water, placed the sole in the palm of his hand and began to massage soap gently over the scratch. It *was* merely a scratch, he discovered, but there was more than one.

"I can do that," she said.

"Yes," he agreed amiably as he slipped a soapy finger in and out between her toes. "But why don't you tell me what you believe would be a good plan for tonight?"

"I think we ought to…"

"Yes?" He ran a hand up her calf to the back of her knee.

"Since there are two safes…we should…"

Watching her, he moved his fingers up the inside of her thigh. "We're not sure there are two safes."

"There are. I'm sure…you're distracting me."

"Really?" He traced his fingers back down her calf and rinsed her foot. "You're the most focused person I know."

"Two safes…two people…the most…efficient way to handle it would be…"

Her last words had come out in a rush, Chance

noted as he lifted her foot and pressed his mouth to the scratch. He heard the quick catch of her breath. And when he turned, he saw the mix of desire and confusion in her eyes. It struck him then that he'd never once taken the time to seduce her. Oh, he'd made love to her, but it had always been fast and hot. Wonderful in its own way, but… He watched her eyes darken as he ran his tongue along the scratch, then took one quick nip at the arch of her foot.

"Chance, I…"

"You were saying that the most efficient way to handle it would be to…?" Lowering her foot, he leaned in and brushed his mouth over hers.

"I can't think when you…do that."

"How about this?" He traced her lips with his tongue. "You taste like cherry lollipop." Then he shifted his attention to her other foot. This time he ran his hand up to the inside of her thigh and let it linger there. "You were saying…?"

"You're making it…hard to think."

He was going to make it impossible. But he didn't say that. Instead, he traced little patterns on the inside of her thigh and savored the quick catch of her breath.

"Why are we always in such a hurry?" he asked.

Her lips were parted, moist and stained cherry-red. He leaned in for another sample. Heat shimmered. The moment it threatened to flare, he drew back.

"No." The plea came out on a sigh.

The sight of her, aroused and at his mercy, excited him in a way that hadn't happened before. Watching only her eyes, he skimmed his fingers higher up the inside of her thigh until he could touch the lace of her panties. This time he intended to go slowly. "Tell me more about your plan."

Natalie sucked in a breath and wished that she could gather her thoughts just as quickly. There was some important point that she had to make. But she couldn't quite grasp hold of it.

"Or you could just let me touch you," Chance said.

She shuddered as his fingers traced the lace on the edge of her panties. She waited, shuddering again in anticipation of when they would slip beneath the thin silk and enter her. But they didn't. They merely traced the same path over and over.

Sensations moved through her. And they were so new—nothing like the flash and fire he'd always ignited in her before. This was...softer...sweeter, and her blood felt as if it had turned thick as honey.

"I love the feel of your skin." His hand moved down the inside of her thigh to her knee and then slowly back again. He repeated the process on her other thigh.

She could have sworn that she was floating. Ridiculous. She was still sitting on the counter. She could feel the hard press of it against her bottom and the heels of her hands. But what Chance was doing to her with just his hands made her feel as if he'd magically levitated her several inches above the counter.

That was ridiculous. And she should put a stop to it. She opened her mouth, intending to do just that when he drew her feet out of the sink and shifted her so that her back was propped against the mirror and he was standing between her legs.

He pulled her shorts off and dropped them on the floor in one smooth move.

"Open your eyes."

She hadn't even been aware that she'd closed them, but she did as he asked. She would have done anything he asked.

"I want to touch you here." He ran one finger down the silk of her panties until it rested against the center of her heat.

She shuddered as a wave of pleasure pierced her, weakening her. Helpless to do anything else, she watched him, waiting, wanting.

For a moment, he didn't move at all. And she couldn't. Everything inside of her was melting.

"Please..."

His finger moved then, but only to trace the same erotic patterns he'd made earlier on her thigh.

"No...please." Gathering all of her strength, she arched toward him, craving more.

He drew his hand away, gripped her thighs and pulled her to the edge of the counter. Then leaning down, he began to trace the same pattern on the silk of her panty with his tongue.

Pleasure built to a knife-edged pain inside of her as she strained toward him. But she couldn't get close enough, and he kept the pressure so gentle. Too gentle. The torture was so exquisite, she thought she might die of it.

"I can't... Please."

He drew her panties off then and followed their path down her legs with his mouth. Then he began the journey back up. If she'd thought she might die before, Natalie was quite sure she would now as sensation after sensation battered through her. There was the scrape of his teeth at her ankle, the slick pressure of his tongue on her calf, and the string of kisses that drew closer and closer, only to stop before they reached their goal.

And then his mouth was just where she wanted it to be, and the pressure was just what she'd been craving. She called out his name as the orgasm erupted. His arms were around her as the pleasure careened through her with a force that built and built and built to a high, airless peak. As she shot over it, all she knew was Chance.

And then he was inside of her, moving slowly in and out, in and out. She couldn't feel anymore. She was sure of it, but then the heat started to build again. And still he went slowly, too slowly. Drawing on all of her strength, she wrapped herself around him and began to move. She knew the moment the pleasure built to the flash point for him, and she went with him into the fire.

"WHAT DO YOU THINK of the costume?"

Natalie stared at herself in the mirror and tried to think of an appropriate Calli response. Of course, Chance had sprung the costume on her out of the blue.

And they still didn't have a decent plan. Once she'd managed to gather up her brain cells after they'd made love, she'd suggested that they split up and each break into one of the safes. He'd rejected it, but what he'd replaced it with was sketchy at best. The only thing she was sure of was that they were going to break into the gallery safe first. In her mind, the sketchy details meant that he intended to improvise.

"Great, aren't they?"

Natalie dragged her focus back to the costumes. The fact that they were in the bedroom and being listened to kept her from saying what she really thought about them. She shifted her gaze to Chance's reflection in the mirror. He was Stan Laurel. Tall and lean, he looked the part right up to the dopey expression on his face. Very cute.

She, on the other hand, was a fat, pudgy and very disgruntled Oliver Hardy. Spikey little black bangs peeked out from the bowler hat she was wearing, and she had a mustache and chipmunk cheeks. Chance had made her stuff cotton rolls in them.

Finally, she let her gaze drift down to the stomach that felt as big as Kansas. The added padding around her middle held her tools and a second costume just in case they had to improvise at some point in the evening.

Just in case they had to improvise? Yeah, right. But she felt better knowing that at least Chance had some sort of a backup plan. Still, the added girth around her middle was going to slow her down.

"You really look like Oliver Hardy," Chance said, grinning at her.

She did. And Calli should have some reaction to that. Someone was listening, but her mind had gone suddenly blank. How would Calli feel about wearing this costume?

For some reason she'd been finding it harder to keep in character since they'd made love in the bathroom. She was pretty sure that the clutch of nerves in her stomach had more to do with the way that Chance had made her feel than the job they had to do tonight.

"I was sure you'd like it," Chance said.

Stalling, she fisted her hands on her hips and focused on her image in the mirror. But she didn't want to be Calli right now. And she didn't want to be Rachel Cade either. What she really wanted was to drag Chance back in the bathroom and ask him what he'd meant by making her feel the way he had.

He'd made her feel loved. The word had fear and panic slithering up her spine, but it was better to get it out and face it than to let it gnaw away at her.

He'd made her feel something that wasn't real, that she couldn't have. Better to get that harsh truth out and face it, too. Maybe then, she could get her mind back on the job they had to do.

"You love watching my collection of Oliver and Hardy films…" The expression on Chance's face was puzzled. He'd probably looked forward to throwing her this curve ball, Natalie thought.

Tilting her head to one side, she met his eyes and said, "Loving the films doesn't mean I want to dress up like them. And I don't see why I have to be the fat guy."

Chance grinned Stan Laurel's silly grin and flipped his tie at her. "Because I'm taller."

She rolled her eyes and ad-libbed. "I never should have let you pick out the costumes."

"You told me to pick a couple."

"I was thinking of a couple couple. Romeo and Juliet, Antony and Cleopatra…" Switching her gaze to her own image in the mirror, she frowned. "I think I ought to get a reward for wearing this."

He reached for her hand and raised it to his lips. "By

the end of the evening, you'll have the Ferrante diamond. You can bank on it."

She met his eyes then. "I will." And that was all she was going to think about for the rest of the evening—getting her hands on that diamond.

"Ready?" Chance asked.

The ringing of his cell phone prevented her from replying.

"Yes, Harold," Chance said.

It was Tracker checking in again. He would have facts and figures to give Steven on the latest merger that Bradford Enterprises was engaged in. Sandwiched in would be anything important that Tracker wanted Chance to know.

While she waited, Natalie checked herself one more time in the mirror and practiced walking back and forth.

"There's been a little shooting incident," Chance said. "Nothing serious, but you can cancel the fishing trip and expect me back in New York tomorrow morning."

Nicely done, Natalie thought. Now, Tracker would know that they had to leave the island tonight. Once Chance pocketed his phone, he turned toward her and handed her one of the feathery masks that Carlo had provided. "Ready?"

She felt her heart flip and tried to ignore it. This was a man who would never be hers, but they were about to embark on the adventure of a lifetime. This was why she'd signed on. Later, she'd test her ability to deal with a wounded heart. Right now, she was going to trust in her ability to pull off this job.

"Ready," she said and waddled toward him.

14

OVER THE TOP. That was the phrase that popped into
Natalie's mind the minute she walked into the main
salon. Carlo had brought the room to life as surely as
if he'd been the prince who'd awakened Sleeping
Beauty. Crystal chandeliers glimmered overhead, and
the wall of French doors stood open to the night.
Across the room, tables draped in white linen cloths
held silver buckets of champagne and trays of food.
And there were flowers everywhere, their scents
blending with candle wax and expensive perfume. A
band played in the far corner of the dance floor, and
she noted that the room was already more than half-
filled with people.

Carlo Brancotti's masquerade ball was *the* party to
be invited to in South Florida. She'd almost forgotten
that, and as Natalie let her gaze sweep the room, she
wondered how many politicians and other assorted
celebrities hid behind the glittering, feathery masks
that Carlo had provided. It was a night to pretend, to
do things you might not if you were yourself.

That's what she was going to focus on. Taking a
deep breath, she waddled at Chance's side as they
stepped into the line that was filing past Carlo and

Lisa. Carlo's assistant wore a blond wig and a long, white dress, glittering with sequins. Barbie, Natalie guessed.

But Carlo didn't resemble the rather preppy-looking Ken. He wore a tuxedo with the same flair and effect as James Bond. With his long hair pulled back and fastened with a gold clip at the back of his neck, and one diamond glinting in his ear, he looked to be what he was—a rich, powerful man. There was nothing on the surface to even hint at the ruthless lowlife beneath.

"Ah, the film celebrities..." He paused and turned to Lisa. "Let me present Oliver Hardy and Stan Laurel." As Chance took Lisa's hand, Carlo continued, "And my companion, Barbie."

Natalie was sure that Carlo recognized her when he took her hand. And she also noted that he wore a tiny listening device in his ear—a clever way to get updates from his security people. The moment they were out of earshot, she nudged Chance and spoke in a tone only he could hear. "He's got a receiver in his ear."

"And a microphone in his tie. He hasn't survived this long without being very cautious. Want to try the food?"

"No, thanks." She patted her stomach. "Right now, it's pretty jammed up with nerves."

"Then, we'll dance."

"Dance?" she asked as he drew her onto the dance floor.

"Yes. I take your hand, like this, and I put my other hand at your waist, like this."

"I understand the concept—but we're two men."

"It's a masquerade," he said as he guided her

smoothly into the rhythm of the music. "Anything goes."

"This is ridiculous," she said.

"No," Chance murmured as he steered her down the length of the ballroom. "I've decided that we're going to hit the gallery while Carlo is still tied up in the reception line."

Nerves jumped in Natalie's stomach. "It's too soon. We just got here."

"Call it a preemptive strike. He won't expect anything this soon. And if the real diamond is in the gallery safe, we'll be gone before he's even suspicious."

The moment they reached the far door, he drew her through it and down across the hall.

"If you try to disable the camera, he'll send the troops after us," she said.

"Got it covered. Just follow my lead." With his hand on the knob, Chance paused long enough to meet her eyes. "Ready?"

Ready? How could she be when she had no idea what he was up to? But in spite of the nerves dancing in her stomach, Natalie felt the wave of excitement move through her. "Let's go for it."

"That's my girl," Chance said, leaning in to press his lips to hers as he opened the door and drew her into the small gallery. An instant later, he spun her around and pressed her against the closed door. Then his mouth was at her ear. "I'm going to tell you to strip for me. Make sure that you toss something to cover the camera."

Before she could reply or even think, his mouth was on hers again. For one giddy moment, she wondered if Stan was kissing Ollie or if Steven was kissing Calli. Then she no longer cared as the heat shot through her. His mouth was as ruthless and demanding as the hands he was running over her. As her knees turned to water and her arms moved around him, her body strained toward his. But there were too many clothes, too much padding in the way.

Suddenly, he backed away, swearing in frustration. "I can't feel you through all of those clothes. Get rid of them."

Natalie stared at him. His hair was mussed from her hands, and his eyes were hot with a mixture of desire and frustration. She felt an odd little thrill move through her. So he wanted her to strip? Okay, she'd strip.

Not moving, she said, "Sit down."

"I said I want your clothes off."

She took the feathered mask off first, then she moved toward him until her padded stomach was pressed against his. As she ran a finger down the front of his shirt to the waistband of his trousers, she said, "I'm going to take them all off. But it's going to take a while, so why not relax and enjoy it?" Then with her finger still prodding him, she urged him into the chair closest to the security camera.

The tie came first. She took her time pulling it off and then she looped it around his neck.

"What do you want me to take off next, Steven?" she asked as she backed a few steps away.

"The coat. Take the coat off."

She smiled as she freed the first button. "I can do that." Then she took her time, freeing one arm from the sleeve and then the other. Finally, as she lifted it and twirled it over her head, she considered. It was too soon to aim it at the camera. Besides, the security team might find the whole scenario more convincing if they could share a bit in the show. Natalie sent the coat flying wild. Then she fastened her gaze directly on Chance's eyes and smiled. "What would you like me to take off next, Sugar?"

He raised a hand and flicked a finger. "The trousers."

"Sure thing." Natalie unfastened the belt slowly. In spite of the nerves dancing in her stomach, she was finding it erotic to strip for Chance—and for whomever was watching through that camera.

So far, she hadn't exposed any skin, but she could feel the heat of Chance's gaze right through her clothes. In one long smooth movement, she pulled the belt free and set it on the floor next to her. A muscle twitched in his jaw. She made it twitch again as she sent the trousers pooling to the floor. "You like this, don't you?"

"Shoes."

The request surprised her. Maybe he was letting her know that he approved of her plan to prolong the striptease. She toed the shoes off, then crossed to him and placed one foot on his knee. Inch by inch, she rolled her socks down and pulled them off. She was close enough now that she could tell his breath wasn't steady. It grew more ragged as she repeated the process with the other sock. Then propping her hands on either side of the chair, she leaned in. Her mouth was a breath away from his when she said, "What next?"

He reached for her then, but she slipped away and laughed. "Let me choose this time. The shirt." She made it last—one button at a time, then the sleeves. She'd never before realized that stripping was as erotic and arousing for the stripper as it was for the audience. But just the brush of the fabric as she pulled it down her arms was sensitizing her skin. Raising the shirt high above her head, she twirled it just as she had the jacket. But this time, she aimed for the camera.

Bull's-eye.

"Take off that damn padding."

She did and she immediately bent over to take out her tools.

"Come here," Chance said. "I want to touch you now."

His voice was ragged, but when she glanced up, she saw that he wasn't in the chair anymore. Instead, he was opening the window. For their escape, she thought. Then she turned to the column and prayed that the safe was where she thought it was.

Though she hadn't heard him approach, he was there, lifting the bronze sundial off the wall. At the sight of the small safe, she let her heart take one little leap of triumph before she put on the earphones and began work.

"Here. This is where you like to be touched, isn't it?"

He wasn't touching her at all, but Natalie found she had to use all of her powers of concentration to keep from feeling that he was.

"And here. Right here where you're so wet and slick and hot."

Immediately, she was. She could feel the wetness pooling between her legs. Damn him. Promising herself that she was going to get even, she listened for the last tumbler to fall into place. The moment it did, she decided that two could play at the game that Chance had started.

In the huskiest voice she could muster, she said, "Bite me there. Yes. Oh yes. Yes." Then on a breathy moan, she opened the safe. The sight of the red velvet bag had her heart leaping.

Chance reached for it before she could, and a second later, the largest and most beautiful diamond she'd ever seen caught the light. To the naked eye, at least, it appeared to be real. But Chance was already examining it with a jeweler's loop. Without taking his eyes off of the diamond, he mouthed, "Keep the scenario going" and stepped up close to her.

She let out a long breathy moan. It wasn't hard, not with Chance's thigh pressing hard between her legs. "Yes. Oh, yes."

Only seconds ticked by, but to Natalie it seemed longer. Then Chance shook his head.

Swallowing her disappointment, she watched as he slipped the fake diamond back into the red velvet pouch and replaced it in the safe. As he rehung the bronze sun, she replaced her tools in the small pouch she wore. Then before she could even breathe, Chance had her pressed back against the column.

She didn't even have time to absorb the sensation before he rained a string of kisses along her cheek to her ear and whispered, "Before we leave, we have to play out this little scenario to the end. Otherwise, they'll wonder why suddenly everything got so quiet."

Then in a louder voice, he said, "I love to touch you here. And here." He ran his hands from her throat to her breasts and then slowly, lower and lower, until he slipped his finger beneath her panties and found her.

"And especially here." His mouth was so close that she could feel his breath on her lips. And he was barely touching her. His finger hardly entered her before withdrawing.

"I love to touch you here." His eyes were so focused, so hot. His fingers pushed into her—not far enough, not nearly—then withdrew.

She should push him away. In some far corner of her mind, she remembered that someone was listening to every word he said. And they still had to get the real diamond from the safe in Carlo's office. But with the pleasure streaming through her, she couldn't find the strength to raise her hands.

"Come for me, Calli. I want to see you come. Now."

Afterward, she would wonder if he could have made her come simply by commanding her to. There was something in his voice, something in the way he was looking at her...

But he didn't leave it to chance. As the heat of his words coursed through her, he slipped his fingers into her again—deeper this time. "Steven." That one gasp was all she managed before the orgasm that had been building since she'd started the strip tease slammed into her.

He held her there, propped against the column until the last wave of it receded, then he whispered against her ear. "Get dressed. We have to go now." She took some satisfaction in hearing that his voice wasn't quite steady.

She pulled on the clothes he handed her, a flood of emotions pouring through her. Shock, wonder—those were the only ones she could identify easily. And just below the surface, racing through her veins, was fear. No one had ever had this kind of effect on her, this kind of power over her. What was she going to do when their adventure was over?

"Ready?"

The whispered question had her dragging her thoughts back to the present. Chance was stooping at the open window, planting a listening device. If and when Carlo sent security to check the room, they'd have some advance warning.

At least that was the plan as he'd described it to her in the bathroom.

Chance crossed to the chair he'd been seated in and tucked a small tape recorder under it. For as long as the tape lasted, all anyone would hear would be a couple making love. The plan had been to play the tape from the moment she'd finished her striptease and blocked the camera. But Chance had decided to improvise.

There'd be time enough to worry about that after they'd finished what they came here to do. She moved to the window.

As he joined her, she became aware for the first time that he was wearing a cape and a mask.

On some level, she'd been aware that the clothes he'd handed her fit like a second skin, but it was only when he handed her a mask that she realized they were wearing new costumes. A quick glance down at her own confirmed her suspicion. Batman and Cat Woman.

Clever, she decided. The outfits would help them blend into the darkness of night and if they were caught, the new costumes should buy them a little time.

Chance said nothing as he threw one leg over the window ledge. His movements were smooth as he twisted and drew his other leg out. Then he was gone.

The only sound in the room came from the tape as she murmured Steven's name. Even above the scent of flowers from the garden, she caught the smell of sex. Anyone entering would have to be convinced that someone had made love in this room. Was that why Chance had made her come? Was it simply his way of being thorough? Or had it simply been to buy them extra time?

Later, she promised herself. Later, she'd not only have answers, she'd have revenge. Natalie threw one leg over the edge of the sill, twisted, wiggled and let gravity pull her until only her fingers were gripping the window ledge. Then she dropped.

The impact was still singing up her legs when Chance grabbed her hand and they began to edge their way along the wall of the house.

CARLO SCANNED the ballroom as he listened to the report from his chief of security through the small receiver in his ear. The shooter they'd been interrogating all day had finally named the man who'd hired him. Hassam Aldiri.

The news confirmed what Carlo had already suspected. Aldiri had a reputation for ruthlessness and Carlo had heard that the man would do anything to get what he wanted.

Lifting a hand, Carlo rubbed at the knot of tension that had settled at the back of his neck. Soon it would turn into the same raging headache he always got when he had to suppress his anger.

He was angry—furious—because Aldiri had hired someone to shoot a guest on his estate. And he was also angry at himself for not anticipating that a man with Aldiri's reputation might try something like this.

"Before you dispose of the shooter," Carlo said into his microphone, "I want to know how he got past my security system."

"Yes, sir."

Carlo let his gaze sweep the room again.

"And about the other matter, sir?"

A couple dressed as Oliver and Hardy had slipped into his gallery fifteen minutes ago and were currently making love. Carlo knew from an earlier report that the couple was Steven Bradford and Calli. Thanks to his security staff, he knew the identity of every person in the main salon.

He also knew about Calli's striptease. Evidently, Bradford and Calli weren't as upset by the shooting as he was. His gaze rested on Risa Manwaring and Armand Genovese. They'd arrived together as Napoleon and Josephine, and currently they were dancing.

As far as he knew, they'd met each other for the first time at dinner last night. Had they teamed up to buy the diamond? That would surely make tonight's auction more interesting…and profitable.

Carlo rubbed at the back of his neck again. Part of his tension was due to the fact that he still wasn't sure if one of his new guests was Chance Mitchell.

"Should I send someone into the gallery, sir?"

Carlo dragged his attention back to the voice in his ear. "You haven't lost the audio in the room?" he asked.

"No. They're getting that loud and clear."

Carlo bit back a smile. He could imagine that the volume was turned up high in the security room, and there must have been a loud groan of protest when they'd lost the video. For a moment, he debated whether or not to send guards into the gallery. Doing so might embarrass the couple, and they'd already been shot at today.

Glancing at his watch, he said, "I'll handle it in about fifteen minutes. But let me know if you lose the audio."

"Yes, sir."

Out of the corner of his eye, he saw Lisa approaching with Hassam Aldiri at her side. So the man had tried to kill the competition. On one level, Carlo could understand and admire that. He wouldn't forget that the attempt had been made on his estate, but for tonight, he'd concentrate on business.

Turning, he smiled as Aldiri reached him.

"Ms. McGill tells me that you will be auctioning the jewel tonight?" Hassam said.

Carlo glanced at his watch again. "In about two hours."

"I will top any offer that you receive," Aldiri said. "I want that diamond."

A man who didn't mince words, Carlo thought as he watched Aldiri move away. For the first time all evening, Carlo felt some of his tension ease. If the price went up high enough, perhaps he could forgive Aldiri for trying to shoot one of his guests. Turning to Lisa, he said, "It promises to be a profitable evening."

CHANCE MOVED as swiftly as he could along the wall of the villa. The clock was ticking. The tape he'd set in the gallery would last for ten minutes—if Carlo let it run to the end.

Flowering trees grew so close that now and again, he had to lift them away so that he and Natalie could squeeze by. Taking the path through the gardens would have been quicker, but he had no way of knowing how many security men were monitoring the cameras or how often the various sites rotated on the monitor screens. He wasn't taking the chance of letting one of those cameras pick up anything suspicious. The longer they kept their attention focused on the gallery, the better.

Just ahead, a palm tree butted up so close against the house that he ducked low and drew her around it. They had about one hundred yards left to go before they reached the courtyard near Carlo's office.

Natalie followed quietly behind him. She hadn't said a word since he'd touched her. He'd already asked himself what he'd been thinking. But he hadn't been thinking at all. Bringing her to orgasm certainly hadn't been part of the plan. They'd had a recording that they were going to play for the benefit of the men looking at the monitors. His job had been to place the listening device while she opened the safe. But the moment she'd started stripping, something had come over him.

She'd come over him. His mind should have been totally focused on the job. Instead, it had been focused on her. It was Natalie's tug on his hand that made him stop. When he turned, she whispered, "Here."

He glanced at the top of the wall and spotted the camera. It was aimed into the courtyard. If she hadn't spotted it, he wouldn't have stopped, and they'd have gone past Carlo's office and then wasted some of the precious moments they had by backtracking. Later, he promised himself. Later he would sort out what had happened to him in the gallery. Right now, he had a job to finish.

Pulling the tranquilizer gun out of the pouch he wore around his waist, he handed it to her. If they were lucky, the guard would be stationed on the patio. It would take less time to put him out of commission if they didn't have to lure him out of Carlo's office.

Leaning down, he cupped his hands. After she placed her foot in them, he gave her a moment.

"Ready," she whispered.

He straightened and boosted her up the wall.

NATALIE DUG her fingers into the crevices in the wall as she shifted first one foot and then the other onto Chance's shoulders. When she was sure she had her balance, she moved her hands to the top of the wall and slowly straightened until she could see over the edge. The patio was dim, illuminated only by the light spilling out from the office. But the French doors were open.

And then she spotted the glow of a cigarette. The guard was standing in the shade of a palm tree three feet to the left of the open door. She could hardly make him out, and she was only going to get one shot.

Heart hammering, she reached into her belt and pulled out the tranquilizer gun. Drawing in a deep breath, she aimed it in the direction of the palm tree. All she could see was the glow of the cigarette, and it wasn't moving. Impossible to tell if the guard was standing to the left or the right of that glowing circle of light. Was he sitting or standing?

She picked up a loose stone from the top of the wall and pushed it onto the patio. The guard moved toward the sand, stepping out from beneath the palm. Natalie aimed and fired.

"What the—"

She saw him raise a hand to his shoulder, then fall to the ground. Chance's hands gripped her ankles, lifting her until she could work the top half of her body over the wall. While Chance climbed up the wall to join her, she crawled over to the security camera and pointed it out at the gardens. If they were lucky, the guard watching the monitors wouldn't even realize that it had been shifted.

"Ready?" Chance asked.

Yes," she said as she began to lower her body over the edge of the wall. They dropped together.

Chance glanced at his watch. "The tape I left in the gallery just ran down," he said as they moved toward the French doors.

Natalie felt a rush of adrenaline. The clock was ticking now.

Moving quickly, she entered Carlo's office. The safe was just where she suspected—behind the painting at the back of his desk.

Her stomach sank. "I've never opened this kind of a safe before. Maybe, you should—"

"You can do it," Chance said.

She took one moment to gather her thoughts and then focused all her attention on the combination.

15

CARLO WAS MORE FURIOUS than he had ever been in his life. The headache raging behind his eyes only intensified when he walked into his gallery with Lisa and two security guards and saw the scattered clothes and the open window. After striding toward it, he glanced at the ground below.

"They're not here." He spoke into the microphone that connected him with his security chief. "Secure the grounds. No one is to leave this estate until they're found."

He turned to Lisa and the two security men who'd followed him into the room. "Check the Venetian room and see if they're there."

When Lisa didn't follow the guards, he said, "Go back to the salon. I need you there."

"What is going on?" she asked.

"I intend to find out. Go."

He followed her to the door and locked it behind her.

Then with a sliver of fear skipping up his spine, he went to the column and removed the bronze sundial. His fingers shook as he opened the safe. When he saw the red velvet pouch, his frown deepened. They hadn't broken into the safe. Otherwise, surely the diamond would be gone. Unless…had they had time to open the safe and discover that the diamond inside was a fake?

Clamping down tightly on his anger, Carlo focused as he surveyed the room again. They'd convinced his security staff that they'd come in here for sex. And the room smelled of it. So why had they exited through the window? Why not put their costumes back on and rejoin the party?

Or had they simply decided to take their lovemaking to a more private place?

Carlo studied the room. Clothes had been tossed everywhere. Trousers covered the security camera, one shirt hung over the back of a Louis XIV chair, another draped a Chinese vase a few feet from where he was standing. Next to it was the undergarment that had given Oliver Hardy his added girth.

Squatting down, Carlo turned the garment over. No padding. Whatever had been inside was something they'd taken with them. A new costume? Safecracking tools?

Had they come in here merely to throw him off and give themselves extra time to break into his office safe?

His gaze shifted to the window. Once they'd dropped into the garden, they'd only have to circle the house to reach the entrance to his private wing.

As Carlo strode toward the door, his mouth curved in an appreciative smile. Clever, he thought as he replayed in his mind every scene, every impression that he'd taken in since Steven Bradford and Calli had arrived on his estate. They were a couple who couldn't bear to be parted for very long, who couldn't keep their hands off one another. And they'd managed to create the illusion that there was more between them than sex.

No one, not his chief of security, and not even *he* had been overly suspicious when they'd sneaked into his gallery for a "quickie."

Oh, yes, they were much more clever than he'd anticipated. One of them must indeed be Chance Mitchell. It had been a long time since he'd had to pit himself against such a worthy opponent.

A new thought occurred to him. Could he be wrong about Aldiri? Had this "Chance" arranged for the shooting this morning just to throw him off? If so, he or she was very clever indeed. As he exited the room and relocked the door, Carlo spoke into the microphone that connected him to his chief of security. "Meet me at my office."

But Chance wasn't clever enough. The safe in his office wouldn't be as easy to open as the one in the gallery. It was a new model, and he'd had to practice on it for hours before he'd become sensitized to the fall of the tumblers.

IT'S TAKING TOO LONG. Natalie tried to ignore the nagging little voice in the back of her head as seconds ticked away. The muggy night air defeated the air-conditioning in the small room. She'd taken off her mask, and still she could feel sweat trickle down the back of her neck.

If her fingers slipped at this point… Very carefully, she lifted them from the lock and wiped them on her costume.

"Here," Chance whispered as he handed her a handkerchief.

"Thanks," she said. Where was Carlo right now, she wondered as she wiped her fingertips. He'd had plenty of time to go into his gallery, open his safe and see that the false diamond was still there. If the real diamond was here in his office suite, he'd check on it. He could be on his way.

The sound of static drifted in through the French doors, and her heart skipped a beat. Someone was trying to contact the guard she'd stunned. Time was running out.

She closed her fingers over the lock again. She had three parts of the combination. And she'd only had to try once for the last number. All she needed was for one more tumbler to slip into place. Just one more tiny click.

Chance said nothing, but she could feel him shift behind her so that his back was to hers. That way he could face both doors. Time was just about up.

She began to turn the lock very slowly. Seconds stretched into minutes, but she heard nothing. An icy sliver of fear slid up her spine, and she lifted her hand again. "I think I missed it. I must have missed it. I have the first three numbers. Maybe you'd better give it a try."

Chance placed a hand on her shoulder. "Start over if you have to. I fixed the lock so they'll have to force the door. There's still time."

But there wasn't. They both knew that. Natalie drew in a shaky breath and let it out. "I—"

Chance squeezed her shoulder. "You can do it, Nat."

Natalie went perfectly still. Later she would wonder whether it was Chance's belief in her that did it. Or perhaps it was his hand on her shoulder—that simple physical connection. Whatever it was, she could feel her self-doubt drain away as swiftly as if someone had pulled a plug. Suddenly, her mind was crystal-clear and her fingers felt each and every groove on the lock.

The same thing had happened the first time that she'd opened a safe. From the time she was little, her father had let her play with the one he'd kept in his office. She couldn't have been more than seven or eight the first time she'd cracked it.

Opening locks had been a game then, something she'd done in the precious time that her father had spent alone with her. With Rory he'd played cards. With Sierra he'd read books. But during the time he'd spent with her, they'd worked on locks. Even that first time, the last number had given her trouble. She recalled how he'd put a hand on her shoulder and said, "You can do it, Nat. Trust in your talents. You can do anything you want."

And she could. After drawing in a deep breath, she held it and focused all her attention on the connection between her mind and her fingers. The only sound in the room was the soft whir of the overhead fan. But even that faded when she felt the tiny click.

Someone pounded on the door.

With steady hands, she opened the door of the safe, grabbed the black velvet bag, and checked the contents. In it lay a diamond, the twin to the one they'd found in the gallery safe. There was no time for the jeweler's loop this time. Chance barely had time to re-place it with the fake diamond they'd brought with them before the wood frame of the door began to splinter.

Together they closed the safe and replaced the painting.

The noise at the door grew louder, and wood splintered again.

Chance grabbed her arm and pulled her toward the French doors. Shouts came from beyond the patio wall.

They were trapped. For one moment they stood frozen in the frame of the open French doors. Shouts beyond the patio were getting closer, louder. The door to the office was about to give. Chance stripped off his mask and threw it toward the patio wall. Then he shoved her behind a floor-to-ceiling drape at the side of the door. A second later, Natalie felt her breath go out on a whoosh as he flattened her against the wall. Heart hammering, she waited.

The door gave first and there was the sound of guards rushing forward. Then the darkness fled as someone flipped on the lights.

"Get out of the way."

Natalie recognized Carlo's voice even when he slipped into Italian and swore viciously. He must have seen the guard lying on the patio.

There was a rush of wind to her left as guards entered through the French doors. For one long second, the drape covering them puffed out. Natalie could have sworn that her heart skipped three beats until it settled around them again.

"Tell me you've got them," Carlo said.

His voice was close now—inches away. Chance had gone still as a statue, but she could feel every muscle in his body tense.

"No, sir. There's no sign of them. All we got is this."

Carlo swore again. And again, the curtain shifted with the breeze. This time, out of the corner of her eye, Natalie caught a quick glimpse of Carlo standing in the doorway, taking something from the guard. If he turned right now, he would see them.

It came to her in a flash that Chance would be the one Carlo would catch sight of first. Chance would be the one that Carlo would shoot. She felt her heart stop and then the drape settled around them in slow motion.

"They can't be far. Cover the beach and the woods. I want them caught. Bring them to me alive, if possible."

In some part of her mind, Natalie knew that the guards had left and Carlo had moved away. The room had become silent except for the sound of the overhead fan whirring. Then she heard a scraping sound. Her heart skipped a beat. Carlo must be removing the painting so that he could check the safe.

Seconds ticked away. Natalie had to remind herself to breathe slowly, silently. What would happen if he discovered that the diamond in the pouch was a fake?

"Lisa?" Carlo had to be talking to Lisa on his cell phone.

"Everything is under control. I have the diamond right here in my hand. No. I don't have them yet. But I've issued orders that no one is allowed to leave the estate."

Chance shifted slightly. For one long moment, Natalie wondered if he would step from behind the curtain to confront his old enemy. The urge to do just that must be tearing him apart. She found his hand and gripped it tightly in hers.

"Tell Aldiri and the others that the auction will take place in an hour."

Carlo's voice was firm now, without a trace of the temper and anger that had filled it when he'd come into the room.

"You worry too much. I'm bringing the diamond with me. Tell them one hour from now in the gallery."

Natalie counted off ten beats as she listened to the sounds of Carlo closing the safe, replacing the painting and leaving the room. It was ten beats more before Chance stepped away from her and drew her from behind the drape.

She threw her arms around him then and held tight. A flood of emotions swept through her. He was safe. They both were for the moment, and she didn't want to let him go. Natalie wasn't sure how long they both stood like that before Chance drew away. "We have to go."

"I thought you were going to step out and confront him," she said.

Chance met her eyes steadily. "I was."

"But you didn't. Why not?"

"Because I knew my partner would follow right behind. Besides, I came up with a plan." He took a piece of paper from Carlo's desk and wrote one word. "Gianni."

Natalie understood exactly what he was doing. She thought of the young boy betrayed by his friend and sent to jail for something he hadn't done. Then she let herself imagine Carlo finding and reading that note— after the auction.

Meeting Chance's eyes, she said, "He thinks he still has the real diamond."

Chance smiled at her. "Ego. He didn't think that we could pull it off, and he found a diamond in each safe. So he didn't bother to check." He placed the note in the middle of Carlo's desk.

"And he won't find it until after the auction."

"Oh, I think the fake will be discovered before that," Chance said. "I can't imagine any of those prospective buyers parting with a cent until they authenticate the diamond."

"They won't be too happy with Carlo when they realize it's a fake," Natalie said. "And I don't think I'd want any of those characters unhappy with me."

"Hopefully, the fear of retribution will keep Carlo here on his estate until I can get Interpol to send someone to arrest him," Chance said.

She threw her arms around Chance and gave him a quick kiss. "I wish I'd known you when you were Gianni."

FOR A MOMENT, Chance said nothing. He simply looked at her. Her words and the simple gesture of affection unlocked something deep inside of him and released a flood of emotions. A thousand images flashed into his mind—a kaleidoscope of everything that had happened in the short time since they had begun this crazy adventure together.

She was the most amazing woman he'd ever

known. And the most complicated. There were so
many facets to her. In the moonlight that poured into
the room, he saw that her eyes were bright with excitement and triumph. He'd seen those eyes so many ways.
Filled with a cool, steady courage. Lighted with laughter. And darkened by passion.

And he'd seen the intensity in those eyes when she
was thinking only of him, feeling only him. He wanted
to tell her. He needed to—

A crack split the still night air, and Chance dragged
his thoughts back to the present. "C'mon."

"Was that gunfire?" Natalie asked as they raced
into the courtyard.

"Tracker's version of misdirection. One of his men
is presently escaping in the inflatable boat we were
supposed to use."

"Supposed to use?" Natalie asked.

Chance leaned down, scooped up the guard's
weapon, and tossed it to her. "That's one of the reasons I don't have much use for plans. They usually
have to be changed."

To what? But Natalie didn't ask the question as she
stuffed the gun into her waistband. Chance had already moved to the wall and was cupping his hands.
By the time he'd boosted her to the top and joined her,
they could hear running footsteps beyond the trees
that grew along the wall and farther away came the
rapid cough of automatic fire.

Together, they dropped to the ground.

"Where to?" Natalie asked. But Chance was already drawing her in the opposite direction from which
they'd come. As they edged their way between the

trees and the wall of the villa, Natalie realized one amazing thing. She was almost getting used to Chance's habit of improvising plans on the spur of the moment. Almost, she reminded herself when she realized they'd made a complete circle of the villa. By the time they reached the iron gate that closed off the kitchen wing, she could hear the music from the ballroom once more.

Then Chance stopped and drew out the cell phone he always used to communicate with Tracker. Holding it to his ear, he said one word, "Now."

A few moments later, the iron gate to the kitchen wing swung open and a white van moved forward. Natalie barely had time to read the words, "At Your Service," on the paneling before a large woman in a tight-fitting white uniform climbed out and said in a husky voice, "Catering to your every need."

Natalie was reaching for the gun at her waist when Chance grabbed her wrist. "It's Tracker. C'mon."

He drew her with him as the "woman" opened the back doors to the van. Natalie had a hard time recognizing Tracker McBride. He was wearing a blond wig, and unless she'd known, she wouldn't have guessed that the snug-fitting uniform hid the tough, athletic body that she knew he possessed.

"The security is tight here. The guard searched the back of the van when I came in because I wasn't on his list from the catering company."

"Do I want to know how you convinced him to let you in?" Chance asked, amusement clear in his voice as he climbed into the back of the van and held out a hand to Natalie.

Tracker patted the blond wig he was wearing and wiggled his hips. "My charm, of course. We developed quite a rapport."

"It'll be tougher this time," Chance warned. "Carlo has instructed the guards that no one is allowed to leave."

"I love a challenge," Tracker said with a grin before he shut the doors.

"He seems confident," Natalie murmured.

"If anyone can get us out, he can," Chance assured her.

"He'll want to search the van." Tracker spoke from behind the wheel at the front of the van this time. "Think you can handle it?"

"No problem," Chance said. "I've got my partner with me."

Partner. The sound of the word warmed Natalie and eased the jumping nerves in her stomach. Neither she nor Chance spoke as the van moved forward and eventually pulled to a stop at the gate.

"Lots of excitement," Tracker said to the guard, using his husky almost falsetto voice.

"Mr. Brancotti is a stickler when it comes to security, and there was a problem earlier today. I can't let anyone leave."

Tracker laughed. "Do I look like I pose any threat to Mr. Brancotti? And you checked me out earlier."

There was a pause, and Natalie wondered just what Tracker was up to.

"Be a sport," Tracker continued. "I've delivered the extra food they needed, and I have a date tonight. You can check the back of the van."

There was another silence, but Natalie could hear the guard and Tracker walking along the side of the van. It was dark and she could barely see Chance, but they moved in unison, flattening themselves into the corners on either side of the doors.

A moment later the doors opened and the guard, flashlight in one hand and gun in the other, stepped up into the van. Natalie slipped her foot out, and when he stumbled, Chance clipped him hard on the back of his neck. The man fell like a stone.

"Nice going," Tracker said as Chance leaned down to tie the guard's hands behind his back. "You guys make a great team."

Natalie turned to Tracker. "How did you convince him to take a look?"

Tracker shot her a grin. "Money. Sometimes, it works a lot faster than my charm—" he smoothed his hands over his hips "—though I can't imagine why."

NATALIE DRIFTED awake as if she were surfacing from a long dive. The scent of coffee was the first thing that her conscious mind identified. Then everything came back to her in a rush. She and Chance had stolen the Ferrante diamond from Carlo Brancotti, and they'd left a fake one behind. Mission accomplished!

Once they'd taken care of the guard at the gate, their escape with Tracker in the van had gone without a hitch. Carlo's security team had been focused on the beach area. For a moment, she allowed her mind to linger on those few charged moments in the van when she and Chance had been so in tune about how to take out the guard. They might have been working together for years.

The events after that had been less clear. At some point after they'd boarded Steven Bradford's plane, the adrenaline rush she'd been riding on all day had faded, and she'd fallen asleep. She vaguely remembered that Chance had carried her into the bedroom. Then nothing.

Opening her eyes, she saw that she was still in the bedroom on the plane. And Chance was gone. But he'd been here. At some point, she'd felt him lying beside her, holding her. The pillow next to hers still bore the indentation from his head. As she ran her hand over it, she realized that the plane was stopped.

Just when had they landed? Throwing the covers off, she noted that she was still wearing her Cat Woman costume. She checked the bathroom first, but it too was empty. After taking a moment to brush her teeth and run her fingers through her hair, she moved quickly to the door.

But it was Tracker and not Chance that she saw sitting at a table, tapping at the keys of his laptop. He glanced up immediately. "Good morning. Want some coffee?"

"Where's Chance?" A funny little feeling had settled in the pit of her stomach the moment she'd seen that the airplane door stood open.

Tracker handed her a mug of steaming coffee. "I was under orders to let you sleep."

"Where's Chance?" Natalie repeated.

Tracker shot her a smile. "Promise not to kill the messenger?"

At any other time, she might have been charmed. Hell, she might even have been amused. But the funny little feeling was making her stomach roll and her throat tighten. "He's gone, isn't he?"

Tracker sighed. "Yeah. I told him he should wake you, but he had to get the diamond back to the London office. He tried to get out of it, but there's some red tape he has to take care of in person."

In some part of her mind, Natalie listened to Tracker's explanation. It was logical, perfectly understandable. Chance's part of the job wasn't over. So he'd had to fly off to London to tie up loose ends. A sickening sense of déjà vu filled her.

"Chance has to move quickly," Tracker said. "He hoped you'd understand."

Natalie thought she understood very well. The adventure was over, and a man like Chance—a man so like her father—would want to be on to the next one as soon as possible.

"Yes," she said. She did understand. She'd signed on for the job, and now it was over. She felt the prick of tears behind her eyes, and she blinked—but it was too late. The first drop slid down her cheek.

"Shit," Tracker said as he pushed the laptop away and rose. "Natalie, don't." He drew her against him and held her. "I told him to wake you and explain it himself. But he—"

Natalie held herself stiff. She had to stop crying. There was no sense to it. She never cried. She hadn't, not once, since her father had left.

"He's coming back, Natalie. He told me to tell you—"

Tracker broke off when suddenly she used all of her strength to push away.

"What is it?" he asked.

She scrubbed tears away with the heel of her hand. "You called me Natalie."

For a second a puzzled expression crossed his face. "Yes…oh, shit. Shit. Shit."

"If you know I'm not Rachel Cade, then—" As Tracker continued to swear, Natalie remembered the moment when she'd been trying to hear the last part of the combination to Carlo's safe. Chance had used her father's exact words. "You can do it, Nat."

He'd called her Nat. The sharp band of pain tightening around her heart had her rubbing her chest with her fist.

"He's known all along, hasn't he? That I'm Natalie, not Rachel Cade?"

"He…I…." It was pure panic that she saw on Tracker's face now. Later, much later, she was going to remember that with some amusement. She promised herself that. But right now, there were too many other emotions spiking through her. One of them was anger, the cold, icy kind. That was the one she latched on to.

He'd known who she was from the beginning. And he'd played along with her because he liked the game. It had all been a game.

"He wanted to stay and explain—"

Holding up a hand, she said, "Enough. You don't have to explain. I get it." Then she held out her hand palm up. "Since I had to leave the Brancotti estate without packing, I'll require cab fare to my apartment."

16

"OOH, DETECTIVE NATALIE! Your hair! What have you done?"

The moment Rad had caught sight of her, he'd clapped two palms to his cheeks and stared. Now the majority of the people waiting for a table at the Blue Pepper was staring at her too.

"You've cut it." Rad pressed the back of one hand against his forehead and the palm of the other over his heart. "You've *cut* your lovely hair!"

"Yes, I've cut my hair." Natalie fluffed the ends with one hand. The color was back to normal. And so was she. That's what she'd kept telling herself during the week she'd been back.

"It will grow in." Rad spoke in the hushed tone of voice one might use to express sympathy at a wake.

Because she was pretty sure he was comforting himself and not her, Natalie found herself biting back a grin. "Hair has a tendency to do that." Maybe her sisters had been right to insist that they get together for dinner. "Are my sisters here?"

"Sure thing." Rad's face brightened. "I gave them a table on the patio. They're already enjoying the appetizer sampler."

Natalie drew in a steadying breath as she followed Rad through the crowd and down the three steps. Being on the patio was a good thing. Better to face all your ghosts. Better to— Her heart nearly stopped as she stepped onto the dance floor. The salsa band was playing the same tune that she and Chance had danced to on the night that she'd taken him up on his first proposition.

Memories of that night and others streamed into her mind—the way he'd touched her, held her, filled her. The memories and the sensations hadn't dimmed any more than the ache in her heart had.

But they would, she told herself firmly. And maybe she wouldn't let her hair grow in. Maybe she could never be the same Natalie Gibbs she'd been before Chance Mitchell. So what?

Lifting her chin, she followed Rad off the dance floor.

"Here she is," Rad announced as they reached the table.

Any confidence Natalie might have built up faded the moment she looked at her sisters. She could tell by the expression on their faces that she wasn't quite back to the old Natalie Gibbs yet. In fact, what she saw in their eyes was what she'd been denying every time she let herself look in the mirror.

Rory had frozen in place with a stuffed mushroom halfway to her mouth. Rory never let anything interfere with her appetite.

Sierra had her hands clasped tightly together in front of her, the way she always did when she was really nervous or worried.

Hell. Natalie knew she looked like shit.

"Her lovely hair will grow back," Rad said.

When silence continued to stretch at the table, Rad cleared his throat and said, "Well. How about I bring the drink of the week—a frozen pineapple margarita?"

Rory cut him off by raising her free hand. "Three very dry martinis with olives. And keep them coming."

"Excellent choice," Rad said as he hurried away.

Sierra took Natalie's hand. "What happened to you?"

Natalie found she had to speak around a lump in her throat. "I'm fine."

Rory set her stuffed mushroom down. "You have black circles the size of Wyoming around your eyes."

"I've been working."

"And not sleeping," Sierra said. "Or eating. Tell us."

Natalie sighed. A triplet could never have secrets. Finally, she said, "Sometimes when you risk everything for something, you don't get it."

And then she told them the whole story.

"THIS ISN'T MY HOTEL," Chance said as Tracker eased the car to the curb in front of the Blue Pepper.

"We thought we'd have a drink first," Tracker said. "Lucas is buying."

Searching his mind for an excuse to bow out, Chance stepped onto the curb. Above the traffic noises on the street came the faint sounds of laughter and music from the patio. He recognized the song the band was playing. It was the same one that he'd danced to with Natalie three months ago. That's when everything had started between them. No, he corrected himself as nervousness twisted in his stomach. Everything had started between them the first moment he'd seen her. Had that been when he'd fallen in love with her?

Panic slithered in to join the nervousness. "You guys go ahead," he said. "I've got some business to take care of." Truth was he had a plan to make. And he was lousy at them. "I'll just take a cab—"

Tracker gripped one arm and Lucas the other. "Sophie's holding our table."

"And Mac will be very annoyed if we don't bring you," Lucas added. "Besides you owe us. I provided my boat and my chief of security for this little Florida caper of yours."

"Yeah," Tracker put in. "And don't forget the effort I put into saving your sorry ass. My arches are still sore from those high heels I had to wear. The very least you owe us is a drink and the rest of the story."

Chance sighed and let himself be led into the Blue Pepper. It was the last place he wanted to be. Memories of Natalie were already flooding his mind. The past week had been hectic, tying up the Ferrante diamond case in London and seeing to it that "Carlo Brancotti" was finally behind bars. Now, he needed a cool head to think.

"Ah, Mr. Wainwright. Welcome, welcome, welcome."

At first, Chance couldn't see who was speaking, but on the last "welcome," a short man with spikey red hair burst through the throng of people waiting for tables.

"Hi, Rad," Lucas said. "Is my wife here?"

"She's with Miss Sophie. This way," the man said as he waved a hand and led them up the stairs and into the bar.

At least they weren't going to have to sit on the patio, Chance thought. After greeting and being hugged by Sophie and Mac, he found himself wedged between the two women in the corner of a circular banquette.

Sophie poured a glass of beer from the pitcher in the center of the table and handed it to him. Then Tracker cleared his throat. "There's something you ought to know."

Something in the tone of his friend's voice had his stomach muscles clenching. "What?" He glanced around the table, noted the solemn expressions and fear streamed through him. "Has something happened to Natalie?"

"No." Mac spoke as Sophie laid a hand on Chance's arm. "She's fine. She's on the patio right now with her sisters."

Chance felt his throat go dry. "She's here." He wasn't ready to see her, and for the first time in his life he didn't trust himself to improvise. "I—"

Suddenly, he didn't care whether or not he had a plan. He had to see her. Hold her. Maybe the plan would come to him then.

"Let me out." He nudged Mac. "I need to see her."

"There's something you should know before you see her," Tracker said. "I—she knows you were aware all along that she was Natalie—that you were never fooled by the Rachel Cade disguise."

"You told her?" Chance asked.

"Hell, I didn't mean to. I slipped and called her Natalie."

Chance took a long swallow of the beer. "I take it she wasn't pleased."

"She wouldn't even let me drive her to her apartment," Tracker said.

"You don't have to lecture him," Sophie said before Chance could speak. "I already have. But you should have told her yourself."

"Before you took her to Florida with you," Mac added, then shook her head. "Pretending to believe that she was this Rachel Cade when all the time you knew she was Natalie…what were you thinking?"

Chance raised a hand, warding off their criticism. "I wasn't. But at the time, I—" At the time he'd been afraid she wouldn't come, and he'd wanted her with him. "I wasn't thinking clearly."

The two women exchanged glances, then Sophie spoke. "Tracker says you're nuts about her."

Chance pinned his friend with a look.

"Hey," Tracker said with a shrug. "I only calls 'em as I sees 'em."

"Don't look at me," Lucas said. "My advice is to plead the Fifth."

Chance glanced back at the two women. "Works for me."

Then to his surprise Mac and Sophie smiled at him.

"Since you are clearly nuts about her, we've decided to help you dig yourself out of the hole you're in," Sophie said.

Mac slid out of the banquette. "Go. Talk to her."

Chance felt his stomach plummet as he followed

Mac out of the banquette. Natalie was here. His intention had been to spend the night working out a strategy for what he knew he wanted to do. Maybe he'd call her in the morning. Or send her flowers and then drop in on her at work. Or…

Hell, it was the one time in his life that he dearly needed a plan, and he had no choice but to play it by ear.

"WELL, WHAT ARE YOU going to do about it?" Rory asked as she swirled her olive around in her drink and then popped it into her mouth.

"Do?" Natalie asked.

"Yes." Sierra reach over to pat her hand. "You always have a plan."

Natalie took a sip of her martini, then studied her two sisters over the rim of the glass. She'd just told them everything that had happened since she'd left Sophie's party with Chance, and they were looking a lot less worried than they'd been when she first sat down at the table.

"Right," Rory said around a mouthful of stuffed mushroom. "It sounds like you had a wonderful adventure down in Florida. But you're going to have to do something about Chance."

"No." Natalie shook her head. "I've had my adventure and I've had my fling. My plan is to go back to being Natalie Gibbs. Period."

"You're crazy about him," Sierra said in her quiet, certain voice.

"I'm…" The *not* stuck in her throat. Because Sierra was right. No one else in the world had ever made her feel the way Chance Mitchell had. She was very much afraid that she was in love with him. "I'm a mess," she finally admitted.

"Have one of these shrimp." Rory shoved the plate toward her.

Natalie shook her head, but she did take another sip of her drink. "He's walked out on me twice now."

"Yes, he has," Sierra said.

"The jerk," Rory said.

"I'll drink to that," Natalie murmured and did. For the first time since she'd walked off the plane a week ago, she didn't feel quite so numb. Perhaps it was the martini. Or maybe it was the little flame of anger that had flickered to life inside of her.

"He doesn't know who he's dealing with," Sierra said.

"No," Natalie agreed. He didn't.

"You've always been the one with courage. Harry was right when he called you his warrior. I've never once known you to walk away from anything," Sierra added.

Natalie's eyes narrowed. "You're trying that psychology stuff on me."

"She's trying the truth," Rory said.

"The way I see it, it all boils down to one question—do you want this man?" Sierra asked.

Natalie thought of all that had happened between them down in Florida. It hadn't just been about great sex. Finally, Natalie drew in a deep breath. "Yes, I want him."

"Then take a risk," Sierra said.

"And use your talents," Rory added.

Natalie glanced at her watch. Technically, she was

still on vacation. So there wouldn't be any trouble getting a few days off. Either Tracker or Lucas Wainwright should know where Chance could be contacted in London. And while she was finding out that information, she'd have time to plan.

"I've got to go," she said as she rose from her chair.

"Speak of the devil," Rory said.

Natalie felt the prickle of awareness at the same moment Rory spoke the words. Then turning, she felt that quick leap of her heart that only Chance could cause.

He was moving quickly through the crowd on the stairs. How long had he been in town? How had he known she was here?

The moment that his eyes met hers, she felt it right down to her toes. *I'm not ready for this.* That was the one solid thought that managed to tumble into her mind as she walked to meet him in the center of the dance floor. Couples moved around them. Natalie could see that he looked tired—as if he hadn't slept in a week. That made her feel just a little bit better.

For a moment, neither of them spoke.

Then Chance said, "Natalie," and reached for her.

She took a quick step backward and folded her arms in front of her chest. "Why? Why didn't you tell me that you knew I wasn't Rachel Cade?"

He frowned. "Don't you think I asked myself that a hundred times? I should have. I know that. But once we were down in Florida, I told myself that it would be safer if I didn't."

"Safer?" Her brows shot up and she began to tap her foot.

"Okay. I didn't tell you because I was afraid at first

that you wouldn't come with me and, later, that you wouldn't stay."

"So it was the job all along."

"No."

She saw the anger flash into his eyes, felt it in the way he grabbed her arms. But she planted two hands on his chest and held her ground.

"You were the one who masqueraded as Rachel Cade. Why did you put on the damn disguise in the first place?"

She lifted her chin. "Because you walked away from Natalie Gibbs."

"I didn't. I had a job."

She poked a finger into his chest. "You didn't leave a note. You didn't call for three months."

He held up his hands, palms out. "Okay. I plead insanity. But I'm not walking away this time."

In a move so quick that she couldn't prevent it, Chance pulled her onto her toes and kissed her.

As his taste, his heat, streamed through her, Natalie felt as if she were coming home. It would have been so easy to sink into that feeling, into him. But not yet. She hooked a foot around his ankle and gave him one good shove that sent him to the floor.

Couples scattered, and she heard a burst of applause. Out of the corner of her eye, she saw Tracker and Sophie on the side of the dance floor. Mac and Lucas stood behind them grinning.

"You go, girl!" Rory shouted.

"Trust in your talents," Sierra called, the laughter clear in her voice.

Natalie kept her eyes on Chance as he shot her a grin. It nearly melted her, but she wasn't through with him. Not yet. Planting her hands on her hips, she said, "You're a jerk."

"Okay. I plead guilty to that one."

There was another burst of applause from the crowd.

Chance held out his hand. "Help me up?"

Her brows shot up again. "Do I look like I have the word *Sucker* written on my forehead?"

CHANCE THREW BACK his head and laughed. This was his Natalie all right. He got up off the floor and faced her. "God, I've missed you. I liked Rachel. I've always had this thing for blondes."

"Really?" Her foot began to tap again.

Chance began to warm to his theme. "And Calli was really sexy. I had a real thing going for her."

"Yeah. I got that feeling."

She was softening. He was almost sure that he'd seen her lips twitch.

"But I missed you."

He waited a beat, and when she said nothing, he decided for the first time in his life to risk everything. "I have another proposition for you."

Her eyes narrowed and her foot tapped faster. "If you think—"

He raised a hand to stop her. "I thought we might go behind those potted trees over there—for old times' sake?"

"Forget it."

Oh, his Nat was back all right. He might have even begun to enjoy himself, if it weren't for the fear that had tied itself into a tight knot in his stomach. If he blew this— No, he wasn't going to blow it. He couldn't.

"Okay. I'll do it right here." He pulled the small box out of his pocket. Then he got to his knees and opened it.

"A ring? You brought me a ring?"

There was such astonishment on her face, in her voice, that a quick sliver of panic raced up his spine. Was he pushing her too fast? "Yeah. It doesn't have to be an engagement ring. It could just be a—"

Words slipped away as she dropped to her knees in front of him.

"Looks like an engagement ring to me," she said, meeting his eyes. "But if you're having second thoughts…"

"No." Chance met her eyes steadily and saw what he needed to see. "No second thoughts. How about you?"

She gave him a shaky smile. "Just about a thousand or so. I didn't plan on this." She drew in a breath and let it out.

He smiled at her. "Me either. But I'm good at improvising. So are you."

She looked down at the ring again. It was a big step, a huge one. And there wasn't a plan in the world that she could come up with to deal with it. But as Chance put his hands on her shoulders, she thought she could hear a voice telling her, "You can do it, Nat."

And then she heard Chance's voice. "I love you, Nat."

She met his eyes then and smiled. "I love you, too. So I guess we'll just have to make it up as we go along."

He kissed her then, and though she vaguely thought applause and shouts had broken out around them, the one thing that she was sure of was Chance.

Natalie's found her happy ending.
Now it's Rory's turn.
Don't miss the fireworks next month in
The Dare *by Cara Summers,*
part of the irresistible Surrender *anthology.*

Wickedly Hot

LESLIE KELLY

Dear Reader,

I just love Southern cities. Though I was born in Virginia, I wasn't really raised in the South. But I have always been intrigued by the rich culture, passion and romance of the region. One city in particular, Savannah, has always fascinated me. So when I decided to write a book about a sultry possible-thief, I couldn't think of any better city to put her in than Savannah.

Jade's not like a lot of my heroines. She's more self-confident, and a lot more mysterious. But I really liked exploring her quirky love of history, her legacy and ancestry, not to mention her wicked sense of revenge, which would allow her to tie a naked man to a statue…and leave him there.

Hmm…enter naked man. Ryan Stoddard. Northern, conservative, professional. But since he also has vengeance on his mind, he's more than up to the challenge of tackling Jade head-on. Handcuffs and all.

Hope you enjoy my atmospheric little visit to this lovely Southern city. I enjoyed it so much I think I'll return there in the future. In person. And in my books.

Best wishes,

Leslie Kelly

And to all the wonderful reviewers and webmistresses who help support this genre, particularly Barb Hoeter, Barb Hicks, Carla Hosom, Blythe Barnhill, Kathy Boswell, Catherine Witmer, Cynthia Penn and Diana Tidlund. We couldn't do this job without your enthusiasm and support.

Prologue

LYNNETTE GRAYSON HAD finally found the perfect woman for her grandson Ryan and she was utterly determined to bring them together. Whether he liked it or not.

"Brunette, his favorite," she murmured as she went over her checklist. "Intelligent, without question. Tall and slim, somewhat mysterious." And, most of all, *interesting*.

Ryan was altogether too comfortable, too spoiled, too at ease in his Manhattan apartment with his equally bored friends. He lived for his job with a high-stakes architecture firm, dated far too many women and cared for none of them.

He needed someone to challenge him. "Someone to spice him up a bit," Lynnette said, remembering the horridly cold creature Ryan had brought to dinner the last time his grandparents had come into the city.

Her grandson wasn't cold. That big, cold city might have made him forget he came from exciting, passionate, fascinating people who loved quickly and loved forever. Herself included, she had to admit with a smile. She'd led her husband, Edward, on a merry chase before marrying him, but she'd known he was the one from the first time he'd held her hand.

"Women nowadays," she said aloud with a dis-

gusted sigh. "No mystery. No subtlety. No unique-
ness."

Except for *her.* Jade Maguire, the young woman from
Savannah she'd met just last week.

Jade was exactly what Ryan needed. The perfect
woman at the perfect moment. Ryan was thirty years
old. It was high time for him to settle down, create a
family. Her other grandchildren were all happily settled, having followed family tradition by falling madly
in love with the right person as soon as they'd met
them. She wouldn't rest until the same thing happened
to Ryan—the oldest and, though she'd never admit it
aloud, her favorite.

Unfortunately, she had the feeling he would be a little stubborn about this.

She'd tried matchmaking before with, er, *unfortu-
nate* results. This wasn't the same. She wasn't inviting
him up for a weekend when she'd coincidentally invited a young woman she'd met at the bank. Nor was
it like the time she'd hosted a dinner party, with Ryan
and the granddaughter of a friend the only unattached
people there. This wasn't like the florist, or the school-
teacher, or that nice young girl who sold houses for a
living. None of whom Ryan had found the least bit interesting, much less fallen madly in love with in record
time.

No, this time she'd chosen wisely. Perfectly, as a
matter of fact. An art lover, a historian, a fascinating
young woman who'd built a business all on her own.
Even her business was exciting, unique and mysterious, like its owner.

Jade Maguire ran one of those wonderfully spooky
walking tour companies in the old Southern city of Savannah. Lynnette had never taken such a tour, but the

adventurous part of her told her she'd probably love being scared out of her wits while standing on a darkened street late at night. Jade had told them a few fascinating, ghostly tales when she'd come to see Lynnette about the painting that used to hang above the fireplace.

"Imagine," Lynnette murmured aloud, looking at the now-empty wall where the beautiful portrait of a young woman had hung. "We had stolen property."

Lynnette's great-great-grandfather had stolen the portrait from a plantation during the Civil War. Jade had produced positive proof—letters, a copy of a social column from an ancient newspaper, even a copy of the wrinkled, yellowed, hand-written bill of sale from the artist.

Jade had asked Lynnette and her husband to consider donating the painting to the Savannah Historical Society, either now or in the future. Lynnette had immediately agreed, not only because it was the right thing to do but also because she was already trying to figure out a way to get her grandson Ryan to go visit the painting in Savannah.

Not likely. He'd certainly never do it because she asked him to. He'd know something was up and would suspect a romantic fix-up.

So she had to be careful. Tricky. Never ever let Ryan know she was trying to bring him together with Jade Maguire.

"How?" she whispered, still staring at the empty place on the wall. And suddenly, as with most of her *really* good ideas, it simply popped into her head

She was smiling as she reached for the phone. Smiling as she dialed and listened to the ring. But when Ryan answered, she quickly mustered up a quivery, weak, old-lady voice and some tears. He wouldn't be taken in by much. Her grandson had always, however, had a soft spot for a woman who cried.

"Ryan?"

"Grandmother, what's wrong?"

"I need you," she said. "You see, I'm afraid I've been swindled." Crossing her fingers behind her back and sending up a promise to say an extra Act of Contrition the next time she went to mass, she proceeded directly to the biggest whopper of her life. "A dreadful con woman has stolen the painting my father left me."

1

JADE MAGUIRE CIRCLED the ballroom of the historic old Medford House Inn and Museum, socializing with the Savannah elite, but never taking her eyes from her prey. He stood out, impossible to miss amongst the ladies in glittering gowns and the men in their pressed tuxedos. Though he'd made the concession of allowing the customary gardenia bloom to be tucked into his lapel, he no more resembled the spoiled, wealthy pillars of Southern society than Jade resembled a Barbie doll.

Though his elegant suit fit his tall, hard form with tailored precision, it was a dark navy instead of the *de rigueur* black. That only drew more attention to his already striking looks. His shoulders and chest were too brawny to be considered tasteful. His dark hair too long over his brow for most men of high standing. His eyes—which from a distance appeared light, a nice contrast against his hair—moved constantly over the crowd. Searching, hunting, seeking, though she didn't know what.

His body shifted with an almost-disguised impatience that hinted at boredom. But every once in a while his gaze found her. And lingered. She always looked away, aware of the full force of his attention from across the crowded room. It was accompanied by masculine appreciation, which was good considering her plan.

But it also unnerved her. It dug at her, prying into her life, silently looking for answers to unvoiced questions. Hinting that he wasn't just a simple mark, an easy quarry for her scheme.

All in all, he was much too attractive for a miserable, loathsome creep.

"Ryan Stoddard," she whispered, tasting the hated name on her lips for the dozenth time today.

"Have you met him?"

She immediately turned her attention to Tally Jackson, local matriarch and Jade's godmother. Jade didn't have to ask who she meant. Every woman here tonight had been giving the tall, dark stranger second looks. And third ones. "No."

Tally flapped her fan, which matched her old-fashioned, hoop-skirted evening gown. She'd chosen to come in full costume, not mere formal wear, since she was representing the historical society at tonight's gala. "But you want to."

"Not particularly."

The older woman gave a sound of disbelief too elegant to be called a snort, but not far from it. "Well, he certainly appears to want to meet you." When Jade shrugged, Tally added, "Or just to *want* you."

"Maybe he's going to get his wish," Jade murmured. "But only when it comes to *meeting* me."

Tally smirked, obviously thinking the man could get around any woman's defenses. Including Jade's, which had been in place for quite some time now. "If you say so."

Tally was a distant cousin—like many others in Savannah—and seemed to think she knew Jade as well as she knew herself. Maybe that was true. The older woman had, after all, helped shape the woman Jade had become. A fixture in her life since childhood, Tally had long cultivated Jade's love for local history. Along with Jade's mama, and great-aunt Lula Mae, Tally had told her endless stories that had enthralled and captivated her as a little girl. The three women had instilled in Jade a sense of belonging, of home, of pride, until Jade had come to understand that Savannah's history was inextricably wound with her own.

This place defined her.

From her earliest childhood memories, Jade had felt the presence of generations of Dupré women who'd preceded her. She'd seen herself in every role—matriarch to mistress, slave to debutante. Like Savannah, the Dupré women were dark but graceful, sometimes ruthless but always elegant. Genteel but often boiling with emotion and passion.

When they loved, they loved hard, and usually only once. When they lost, they grieved but moved on. They seemed destined to never fill an emptiness inside that longed for a certain something out of reach—whether it was a way of life, or a loved one—but they found a way to live with it.

Jade had learned *that* lesson at a young age, too, when her father had died.

"Now, aren't you glad you came?" Tally asked. "If only to see that lovely man? I don't believe I've seen that look in your eye in a good year, young lady."

"You're imagining things." Then, because she didn't want to offend Tally, she added, "But yes, I'm glad I came."

Tally was the one who'd talked Jade into coming to this party tonight. Thank heaven she had, given Stoddard's presence. Normally Jade avoided such functions. But since she'd just helped arrange for the return of a long-lost sapphire necklace—which had been stolen from this plantation home during the Civil War—Jade had allowed Tally to persuade her.

"I wish you'd let me introduce you and reveal your help in getting the necklace donated."

Jade immediately shook her head. "Not part of the deal. I don't need recognition. You know that's not why I do this. Mama likes the spotlight, I don't."

Her work provided satisfaction enough. Researching and tracking down historical items and persuading their present-day owners to return them to their rightful places—well, it was merely a hobby, but it fascinated her. Just as she was fascinated by these stately homes with their seething pasts.

Besides, seeing that necklace so proudly displayed here in the small museum was all the payoff she needed.

Tally harrumphed, knowing she'd lose the argument again. Then she glanced at Ryan Stoddard. "Shall I slip him your phone number so you can pretend you're not making the first move?"

Jade tore her attention off the necklace—on loan here tonight before being moved to a larger local museum run by Tally's society—and frowned at her overly romantic godmother. "Absolutely not. I can arrange my own introduction, thank you."

"You need more than an introduction," Tally said in disgust. "Darlin', you need a shove into a naked man's arms."

Jade raised a brow. "I somehow don't think I'm going to land in a naked man's arms immediately after an introduction."

Something like that might happen to Jenny, the flighty member of their family. But not Jade. Not the mysterious one.

Tally smiled, catlike. "Well, now, that depends on who does the introducin'."

Tally had been looking for a love life for Jade for two years, ever since Jade had ended a relationship with a man she'd cared about but who'd never really understood her. He'd asked one too many times, *Who wants to make a living telling ghost stories?* Rick had never appreciated or respected the kind of life she'd chosen for herself.

Respect was important to Jade. Having come from a family who'd done without it a lot of the time, she was determined never to feel lower than anyone else. Any man in her life had to be one she respected in return. One who could match her in wits, challenge her in ideas, and keep her on her toes. He had to support her choices, no matter how crazy her life got. With her family, her life sometimes got *really* crazy.

And she had to love him beyond all reason.

So far, she hadn't met such a man. She certainly wouldn't here, tonight, with all the rich snobs looking down their noses at her—a member of *that* side of the famous local family.

"You never know what can happen at a first meeting," Tally said, apparently not noticing Jade's distraction.

"Actually I do," Jade said. "Remember the handsome guy who came on the garden walking tour a few years ago, saying he was looking for movie locations?"

"The producer?"

"He wasn't."

"He whisked you off to his fabulous place on the beach."

Jade crossed her arms. "Not his."

Tally sounded a little less enthusiastic as she asked hopefully, "He drove that beautiful sports car?"

"Rented."

"Well, darling, I hear *this* man," she nodded toward the dark-haired, blue-suited stranger, "is exactly who he claims to be. A nationally known, wealthy, professional architect. So if at first you didn't succeed…try again."

"No." Jade ignored the older woman's hopeful look. "And don't say a word to my mother about this. It's not what you think." She lifted her drink to her lips, murmuring, "It's a private matter. One I need to clear up with him."

"A matter of getting naked and between the sheets?"

Rolling her eyes, she ignored Tally's salacious chuckle. "No. Now go mingle. Be sociable. Rule the world through your glove-covered iron fist. I think I see someone wearing cream-colored shoes with a taupe dress. Go skewer her with that sharp tongue of yours."

Tally gave a delicate shiver. "Hideous. Money truly is wasted on the color-blind and those one generation out of the trailer park."

Jade chuckled, knowing Tally herself was only *two* generations out of the trailer park.

The older woman's eyes lit up, spying a wealthy older man who'd recently moved to town. Jade recognized the look. Tally was a fund-raiser supreme.

"Right on time," Tally whispered, greeting the man with a languid little wave of her hand. "That's Leonard something-or-other from Chicago. He's here with his wife who wears altogether too much jewelry. I have to make nice with them before somebody tells her only tarts and carpetbaggers' wives wear so much jewelry to an event like this."

"Nobody here would say it—except you. Now be nice or I'll warn your prey to hide his wallet."

That reminded Jade of her own victim. She began to look around for Ryan Stoddard, target of her search-and-destroy mission. Searching hadn't been tough—he'd certainly stood out. The destroying part might be more difficult. But he deserved it.

Anyone who broke the heart of her baby sister deserved destroying. He was just lucky Jade was only going to humiliate him, not castrate him like she'd prefer to do.

"There is one other person who could get away with saying such a thing," Tally said, after probably trying to decide whether or not Jade had been paying her a compliment. "Your mama. I wish she hadn't chosen this month to go on her cruise. I need her here."

"It *is* her honeymoon," Jade said, not bothering to keep a dry note from her voice.

"What's one more honeymoon to your mama?"

That sentence, in a nutshell, could probably explain Jade's entire life. They'd each had their own ways of dealing with Daddy's death more than a dozen years ago. Jade had grown mature before her time. Jenny had settled firmly into her role of spoiled baby. And Mama had just kept getting married, hoping she'd find someone else to love as much as she'd loved Daddy.

A shrink would probably say their past explained why Jade felt so protective of her sister, Jenny. It had been the two of them, facing the zaniness of their world with a much-married mother and a scandalous family, for a long time. Though only five years older, Jade had become so used to mothering her sister that she sometimes forgot they were just siblings.

It incensed Jade to remember the tears on her sister's cheeks. Jenny deserved some payback for what Ryan Stoddard had done to her. And Jade was going to see that she got it.

"Jade? Are you listening to me?"

She returned her attention to Tally. "Of course. But I have to say, this time I think Mama's finally met her match. A man with money who doesn't let her tell him what to do."

Tally nodded. "I have high hopes, too. But I do miss her. I needed her tonight. I don't suppose you..."

Jade narrowed her eyes and shook her head. "Don't even think about it. I'm not one of your society matrons. Most people in this room have no idea who I am, and I like it that way."

Tally frowned. The argument was an old one.

"Besides," Jade added, "if I want somebody to drop dead, I'll tell them to drop dead. Not, 'How delightful you look, sugah. Oh, I just love your hair. Why, it's almost exactly the shade and style of my grandma's French poodle.'"

Tally chuckled as Jade laid on a heavy Southern accent, which was nearly nonexistent in her everyday speech. "You're rather good at that."

"I don't want to be," Jade replied.

And she didn't. No matter how much her mother and her cohorts had tried to teach her, Jade had never learned to *enjoy* being sweet while cutting, honest while evasive. She much preferred direct insults to veiled ones, outright lies to such intricate games.

Though, tonight she was setting herself up for a very intricate one, wasn't she? The thought made her return her attention to the dark-haired stranger. She shivered a little. *Intricate games, indeed.*

"'Bye, darling, have fun," Tally said. Then she greeted the rich northerner with an air kiss and a gushing compliment on his clip-on tie, which Jade knew must be driving Tally mad.

Jade watched, then whispered, "Time to move."

As she sipped her drink—ginger ale with a twist of lime, which would appear to most to be alcoholic—she scanned the crowd again. Even if she hadn't been looking for the man when she'd shown up here tonight, she knew her eyes would have sought him out anyway. Just as any woman looked at something she desired but couldn't have.

Only, Jade meant to *have* him.

Earlier, his blue suit had stood out in the sea of black tuxes and brightly colored gowns, but she didn't spot him at first. Then finally she found him, leaning indolently against an arched doorway leading to another room.

Watching her.

He'd been watching *her.*

She flushed slightly. *Darn. Caught off guard.*

The man's eyes met hers from across the room. Blue. Or green. Surrounded by lush lashes and topped by dark brows that were slightly raised as he caught her stare.

Then he smiled.

Her legs wobbled. Good lord, no man had made her legs wobble since she was twelve and her Cajun second cousin had visited from New Orleans. Stoddard was altogether too big. Too ruggedly handsome. Too powerful-looking to play games with.

Yet that's exactly what Jade planned to do. Play games with him. And then leave him in the dirt.

But why is he here?

She didn't mean why was he here in Savannah. She knew why—for a big architects' convention, conveniently scheduled in her home city this year. The convention had saved her from traveling to New York to track him down.

But she'd expected him to stay at the hotel adjoining the convention center. Finding out from a friend at the hotel that he wasn't registered there had been a shock. Even more of a shock had been learning he was staying here at the Medford House.

Ryan Stoddard had no business being in this secluded, exclusive little piece of Savannah society. No business at all. He should be sitting in a loud hotel bar with the sounds of tinkling glasses and businessmen comparing last year's sales figures. Scoping out the women, flirting while they wondered how far they could go without technically cheating on their wives.

Not here, amid the husky laughter of bored millionaires and the scent of jasmine and magnolia that permeated the room from open French doors leading out to the lush grounds. Not in this place which many decades ago would have held tobacco planters and wounded veterans, as opposed to the bankers and stock brokers who comprised the elite set these days.

This was *her* turf. And damned if she wanted him on it. She'd planned to launch her attack on his ground, then slip away, back into the shadows of hers, where he'd never find her.

No way could she implement her original plan. A big chain hotel would have been simple—a pickup in a bar, a trip to his room, a heated encounter. Then walking out, laughter on her lips, leaving him naked and humiliated as he realized he'd been had. Realized he wasn't going to get off scot-free for breaking the heart of a member of her family.

"Jenny," she whispered, still missing her only sibling.

Her sister had gone off to try to be a star on the stage in New York City, against the family's wishes and to

Mama's utmost horror. She'd landed on the stage, all right—a raised platform in a diner where she served chicken noodle soup and pastrami on rye between showstopping numbers.

She'd seemed happy enough, though, at least until last week when she'd come home for Mama's wedding. Jenny had been crying about a man she'd met at the restaurant. She'd fallen *hard* as only a vulnerable, lonely twenty-one-year-old could. The stranger had swept her off her feet then dropped her flat.

Ryan Stoddard, aka the bastard.

It was time for him to pay. If Aunt Lula Mae found out, she'd likely want to punish him herself. And it still might come to that. If Jade couldn't publicly humiliate him, she just might have to get some of his hair and let Lula Mae do what she did best—curse him so he'd never be able to, uh, *perform* again.

But not until she'd given it a shot. Her way.

Which meant Ryan Stoddard was in for the most embarrassing night of his life.

RYAN HADN'T EXPECTED her to be so beautiful.

She stood out like an exotic jungle flower among a bunch of daisies. Her silky-looking dark hair was nearly black, skimming over her shoulders and down her back until it was lost against the color of her dress. A soft, red scarf draped loosely across her shoulders provided a dramatic contrast that drew the eye again and again.

Her skin was smooth and perfect, a warm tanned color like fine coffee full of rich, sweet cream. She was taller than most of the men who'd been eyeing her all evening, and held her slender jaw slightly up, indicating confidence and perhaps a bit of arrogance.

Though in a crowd, she seemed alone. Her detached attitude was enticing because of its mysterious quality, but off-putting because of her disinterest in her surroundings.

Her body was sin, her face was flawless, her eyes were wicked.

How appropriate for a thief.

"Mr. Stoddard, are you enjoying yourself?"

Mamie Brandywine, the owner of the bed-and-breakfast and museum, joined him. She briefly pulled his attention off his target, the woman he'd come to Savannah to find. Jade Maguire.

"Very nice, thank you."

"And you're finding your tours of the local plantation homes helpful in your research?"

"Absolutely," he said, trying to get his mind off the seductive, deceitful temptress and back on his job. Something he'd been putting on the back burner for the past few weeks while trying to get retribution for what had been done to his grandmother. Fortunately, his quest for justice had led him here, to the very city he needed to visit while writing an article on the architecture of the Old South.

"I'm truly enjoying the tours you've set up. Thanks so much for arranging for me to stay in some of the local inns," he added, trying to find some basic element of charm—or at least cordiality—within himself. It had been buried beneath a layer of anger for weeks.

That anger had increased the moment he'd seen Jade Maguire. She should have looked like a thief, a crone, a crook.

But she didn't. She looked like every man's fantasy. The kind of woman he'd always imagined but never found—mysterious, sultry, intelligent, almost unattainable. God, Ryan couldn't resist a challenge. And Jade Maguire screamed, "Look, but don't touch," a challenge no man could resist.

To his eternal shame, he wanted her in spite of knowing what she'd done. Wanted her with instant avarice and a healthy dose of anger. He wanted her under him, crying for mercy even as she cried out in passion and begged him to take her.

He'd never felt the heady mix of passion and anger before. Never understood its power, though he'd heard of it affecting other men.

Now he got it. It was nearly painful to be in the same room with a woman he'd desired on sight, but who'd swindled a valuable family heirloom from a helpless elderly woman.

Well, he could concede, his grandmother was not exactly *helpless*. She had a steel spine beneath her high-necked blouses—which made it even more imperative for him to get the painting back as soon as possible. The elderly woman was so embarrassed at having been tricked by the deceitful con artist that she'd refused to bring the police in on the case. She'd also forbidden him to tell Grandfather she'd let the painting be stolen. She'd concocted some story about it being on loan for an exhibit to keep the old man from asking any questions. She was relying on Ryan to bring it back before she could get caught.

"I can't tell you how pleased we are that *Architectural Digest* is going to devote an article to the construction of our fair city," Mamie said, interrupting his heated thoughts about the woman across the room.

The article. The reason Ryan was getting the red-carpet treatment here in Savannah. What perfect timing that he'd come here for an annual meeting, after being solicited to write a piece for the journal. He'd kill three birds with one stone.

The conference. The article. And the thief.

"Savannah has paved the way for other cities to save their historic treasures," he replied, completely in earnest. "Anyone who wants to preserve treasured buildings of the past would look to your city as a fine example."

The pudgy woman preened and not very subtly smoothed her hand over the low, tight neckline of her unattractive, fluffy green dress. Very tight. Very low cut. The wares were nearly spilling out, which was apparently what she wanted.

Ryan stiffened ever so slightly and took a small step back. His stance grew a bit more formal as he sent out a silent message that he hoped she'd get. He didn't want to have to flat-out turn her down and risk alienating the woman who owned the inn he'd be sleeping in tonight. Particularly because he imagined she had keys to all the rooms.

He had a sudden mental flash of a fleshy woman creeping into his bed in the dead of night. Talk about your basic nightmares. He'd had flings with older women—his university guidance counselor came to mind—but never *decades* older.

Then the picture in his oversexed brain changed, and it wasn't the proprietress face he imagined entering his room in the dark of night. He saw the thief—Jade—lovely and deceptive. Graceful and conniving. Intoxicating and completely ruthless.

The image of her dark black hair against his white sheets made him gulp a big mouthful of his drink.

"Are you all right, Mr. Stoddard?" Mamie asked as he coughed a bit into his fist.

"Fine," he murmured. "Just…went down the wrong way."

Everything about this situation had gone down the wrong way, from the minute his grandmother had told him she'd been robbed. First, tracking the wrong J. Maguire from Savannah, he'd wound up meeting the younger sister, Jenny, up in New York. He'd realized within hours that she wasn't the right woman. Thankfully, he'd only taken her out to lunch once. So she wouldn't have had any reason to mention him to her sister.

The second detective he'd hired—a *better* one—had found Jade, and his grandmother had confirmed the description. Ryan had taken the information and come to Savannah determined, in charge, using the cover of the convention and the article to get where he wanted to be—close to her.

Everything had gone fine. Right up until the moment he'd actually seen the woman he was after.

He could be in over his head with this one. It was somehow exciting, rather than disturbing, to imagine the sexy brunette sneaking into his room. Trying her tricks on him, creeping in to take something that belonged to him. Taking *him*.

He forced the traitorous thought away. Yes, she was damned attractive and he had to clench his fists to remind himself he had to *trick* her. Not *take* her.

Unfortunately.

"Well, if you need any help getting around," Mamie said, not noticing his distraction, "I'd be more than happy to help you in *any* way." She drew her hand to her throat again, flashing a big chunky rock on her ring finger and tapping her collarbone with the tip of her red-tinted fingernail.

Not on your best day, lady.

Since she hadn't gotten the nonverbal hint, he gave her a broader one. "I'm also enjoying getting to meet some of the beautiful *young* women of your city."

That seemed to get through. The woman was twenty years his senior, at least, with a husband dangling around here somewhere, probably downing drinks wondering how he was going to pay for her next party. Not to mention her next diamond.

"Well, there's no shortage of those." This time Mamie's smile was somewhat forced.

"What about her?" Ryan asked, nodding toward Jade, who stood talking with an older woman in a Southern-belle ball gown.

Mamie's mouth stiffened even more. "Jade Maguire. She can show you some things, all right. She owns one of those trashy tour guide companies that prey on out-of-towners who like to be scared out of their wits with silly ghost stories at night."

Nothing he hadn't known. The private detective he'd ordered to track down the *right* J. Maguire had sent a file on Jade's company, *Stroll Savannah*, which had become one of the most popular tourist traps since she'd opened it a few years ago.

He knew where she lived. Where she'd gone to school. What she liked to drink and when she liked to eat. Who she employed. Who she dated—nobody, really, which had been a surprise. When she traveled and where she went.

He'd been prepared for everything. Everything except how beautiful she was.

"You can find *better* tour guides," Mamie said.

The biting tone in the woman's voice was a surprise. Then again, he imagined a woman who looked like

Jade got a lot of jealous responses from overweight, aging society matriarchs. He was about to put the woman in her place, some unexpected instinct making him want to defend Jade, a woman he personally had hated for weeks. But before he could do so, Mamie continued.

"Her father was just an Irish bartender."

"So she's not a native of the city?"

Mamie shrugged, then grudgingly conceded, "She's actually part of a long lineage of Savannians. On her mother's side. Her father's name was Maguire, but her mother's maiden name was *Dupré.*" The woman leaned close, looking around to ensure she wasn't being overheard. "Some of those Duprés…well, they're not quite the *purest* family line, if you know what I mean."

He didn't. And for some reason, though he should want to gather more ammunition to use against Jade, he resented the woman's snide tone and didn't ask for details.

"The party's going well."

She frowned at the change of subject, looking disappointed that he hadn't taken the bait. Why hadn't he? *Stupid.* That'd been a stupid move. But he somehow couldn't find it within himself to regret it.

"I suppose." Then she put out her dark-tinted bottom lip in a small pout. "Are you going to be moving to the Winter Garden House tomorrow? You're sure we can't convince you to stay?"

Ryan shook his head. "Sorry. I must spend some time at all the inns I'll be writing about."

Not to mention the fact that Jade Maguire's tour company capped off their nighttime haunted history tour with a visit to the famous Winter Garden inn. Since he'd paid one of her employees to call in sick tomorrow night, he knew damn well who'd be leading the tour.

It was almost too easy luring the tigress into his den.

Hell, she was making it even *easier* because she'd been looking at him all night. Giving him these intense stares, studying him.

Ryan was used to the stares of women. Under normal circumstances, this woman's interest would have gotten exactly the kind of reaction he'd always had to a beautiful, seductive female. Instant heat. Hot pleasure. The kind of crazy passionate relationship he'd enjoyed more than a few times in his life. The kind that had kept him from settling down to anything more permanent—much to his grandmother's dismay.

Grandmother didn't believe he wasn't secretly interested in marriage, kids and all the suburban crap the women she introduced him to seemed to want. And he didn't want to force her to admit he didn't possess the love-at-first-sight gene that had downed so many of his family members.

So the least he could do for evading her marriage traps was reclaim a family treasure.

He hadn't realized, though, until he'd set eyes on Jade, that the job might be so very enjoyable. Getting her naked, helpless and at his mercy might prove to be fun. He just had to keep reminding himself this was a mission. Business, not pleasure.

Though, honestly, if some pleasure happened into the equation, he didn't think he'd protest too much.

2

"YOU'VE BEEN WATCHING ME," a smooth voice said, low and melodic and hinting at other words, more sultry words, that he'd rather not say in public.

Ryan Stoddard. God, he'd come right up to her. Jade hadn't expected him to make the first move.

"You've been watching *me*," she countered, sipping her drink and not turning around. She closed her eyes and did a rapid one-to-ten count to gain control. She couldn't believe he'd eased around the crowd and snuck up on her while she'd been watching Tally work her magic with the rich businessman.

On the positive front, she'd only been here an hour and already the object of her revenge scheme had approached her. She was getting almost too good at this clandestine thing. Though, she had to admit, the ability to be noticed in a crowd had come in handy on some of her treasure-hunting jaunts. Particularly with the *male* targets.

He moved closer. The fabric of his trousers brushed her bare legs, which were revealed well above the knee in a short jet-black beaded cocktail dress that didn't quite suit the dress code tonight. The contact stirred her, made something lurch within her.

"We've been watching each other," he admitted, his voice closer now. Close enough for her to feel his breath on her neck.

Goose bumps rose there. Goose bumps, for heaven's sake, as if she hadn't been practicing this man/woman/ sex thing since before she'd grown breasts. Every Dupré woman knew about seduction, just as every Dupré woman knew about the family history and the many ways to curse someone in the old language.

"If it makes you feel better to think so, go ahead."

He chuckled, obviously not fooled by her cool tone. How could he be when her whole body was practically arching toward him, shifting with imperceptible need? Was the warmth she felt caused by the hot summer night or by his nearness?

Or by her own anxiety about what she planned to do with this man very, *very* soon?

"You look wicked in that dress."

Nothing subtle about this man.

"Compared to the other ladies in their pastels and jewel tones, I mean."

She knew darn well he hadn't been talking about the color of her dress. He'd meant her. That *she* looked wicked.

Wicked as in *hot*. Not *bad*.

Which was good, since she didn't want him to know yet just how bad she could be. Particularly when she had payback on her mind.

"You mean I'm dressed inappropriately?" she asked, smoothing her hand across the front of her dress in a provocative stroke.

His response—a laugh—caught her by surprise. When she frowned, he quickly explained. "My land-lady tried the exact same move on me not ten minutes ago. Trust me, it works much better on you than it did on someone whose chins almost meet her cleavage."

Having no liking for Mamie Brandywine—who'd

been downright rude to Jade's mother on more than one occasion—Jade smiled, and forgave him for his laughter. "You should see her in a bathing suit."

He visibly shuddered.

"I'm sure she'd be happy to join you in the spa."

"I'd rather be boiled in oil."

"Warm oil. I'm sure she could arrange that, too. She's, uh, rather *fond* of her male guests."

He raised an offended hand to his chest and shook his head. "You mean, it's not just me? She wasn't bowled over by my manly charms and extraordinary looks?"

Jade couldn't help it. She let out a little snort, amused by his self-deprecating tone. "Don't flatter yourself. She'd be trying to get Attila the Hun naked in the hot tub if he were here. I think that's why she had it installed."

"I don't think the two of them would fit." Then he added, "And if she's used it a lot for her 'dates,' I think I'd better make a mental note—no hot tub for me."

Against her will, Jade reacted to his good humor. She liked his snappy comebacks and quick mind. Then she remembered what had gotten them on the subject of Mamie Brandywine to begin with. "By the way, I was *not* making a come-hither move."

"You weren't?" he asked, his voice growing husky. "You mean, you didn't deliberately move your open hand across your breasts, until your nipples got hard against your pretty black dress?"

She gasped. How on earth did he think he could get away with speaking to a complete stranger, in *public*, like that?

He didn't even pause. "You didn't intentionally run your thumb under the neckline, inviting a man to imagine the way your skin tastes?" Then he lifted her hand and laced his fingers through hers. "Not to mention your long fingernails just barely scraping across your skin, dipping between your breasts, inviting him to anticipate what it would be like to kiss you there, lick the hollow of your throat, then follow the path your own hand had taken?" He gave her a wicked look, silently daring her to lie. "*None* of it was intentional?"

Jade froze, her legs turning to lead and her lips parting to suck in breath. Lord have mercy, what had she gotten herself into here? This man used words the way an artist used paint. He'd woven a spell around her, as heavy and intoxicating as one of Lula Mae's brews. And he'd done it with only his voice.

She suddenly began to wonder if she'd made a very serious miscalculation.

Because instead of being the seducer, she was very much afraid she might end up the one seduced.

HE HAD HER. HE KNEW IT at that moment. The cool, confident goddess had turned into a stammering high school girl.

Women. Unbelievable what kind of verbal B.S. they fell for.

Though, he hadn't entirely been B.S.'ing. He'd had to force his voice to remain steady as he'd seduced her with words because, in truth, he'd meant everything he'd said. Though, in any other situation, he'd never have been so outrageous and suggestive with a woman he'd just met. The women he knew were the same cool, mature businesspeople he interacted with every day.

Not like her. Not like Jade. The kind who had him thinking of nothing but what her curves looked like under that black dress, how her mouth would taste, how her hair would feel spread out across his naked chest.

How she stole from your own family, asshole!

Yeah. That, too. This hot seductress used her Southern act to convince others she was intelligent, respectable, in control.

And honest.

She'd fooled his very astute grandmother into thinking she was a professional restorer of valuable art. That's how she'd conned Grandmother out of the beautiful Jules LeBeuf portrait. The elderly woman would never have handed over the painting, done by a lesser-known French Impressionist in the 1850s, without believing it was in good hands.

Such pretty hands. Such soft hands. Such talented hands…most especially when it came to things like picking locks. Or pockets.

"You seem to think you know how to charm a woman. I suppose you've had a lot of experience?"

Her voice was a little shaky. She was obviously still affected by the outrageous things he, a stranger, had just said to her. But there was also a hard note, as if she had her back up for some reason.

"No more than any other man," he said, lifting his shoulders in what he hoped looked like self-deprecation. Then he quirked a brow. "That's what I'm supposed to say, right? So I don't appear too confident?"

"I don't think that's possible. You wear your confidence like some men wear their clothes."

"Attractive and in good taste, I hope?"

"I was thinking more along the lines of flashy and overdone," she replied, though her insult lacked the punch she'd probably intended.

"Should I go away?" he asked, knowing the answer.

She shook her head. "So far you haven't done anything completely unredeemable."

No, she didn't want him to go away. She was still wrapped in the cozy, intimate place they'd stumbled into here in the midst of all these people. And she was still as affected as he was. He just hid it better.

Jade began rubbing her hand up and down one bare arm, as if warming herself. But the noticeable goose bumps on her skin weren't caused by cold—the room was sweltering.

No, their interaction was putting her entire body on high alert. But before he could call her on it, her attention was diverted by someone who paused to speak to her.

Ryan watched quietly, silently admitting that he, too, was on high alert. He tried to analyze it. This hot flush of awareness and excitement couldn't be brushed off as righteous indignation or the culmination of a couple of weeks' buildup. Being truly honest about it, he believed he'd have reacted just as strongly to Jade Maguire if this really had been a chance meeting at a party.

Ryan had known a lot of women over the years, and been involved with his fair share. Probably more than his fair share. He'd even come close to commitment, getting engaged to a Manhattan lawyer he'd met at a cocktail party a few years ago. But he hadn't been able to go through with it, and neither had she. They'd both figured out that while the two of them made a picture-perfect couple, they'd never shared the kind of deep, soul-stirring passion a marriage should have.

His grandmother would probably never believe it, and she'd laugh in his face if he told her. But one of the main reasons Ryan had never settled down—never even tried to feign interest in any of the women she, his mother and his sister had set him up with over the years—was because of the example his family had set. His grandparents were mad for each other. Ditto his parents. And Jane, his younger sister, was deeply in love with her husband.

Though he didn't believe he could fall madly in love at first sight—as other members of his family claimed to have—he did think he was capable of real love.

And he *wanted* it.

His family had set a high standard. Deep inside, he knew he couldn't settle for less. Unfortunately, so far Ryan had never felt that way about anyone. Never lost his mind, lost his heart or even lost control of his emotions over a single female he'd ever met.

Which made his instant reaction to this one that much more surprising. And intriguing. He'd never felt as sparking with energy, as...*alive* with a woman as he did in the brief time he'd known Jade Maguire.

Before he could take any longer to wonder about it, they were interrupted by Mamie Brandywine. "Well, here you are," she said to Ryan, giving him a broad smile. Then she turned her attention to Jade. "I'm surprised to see *you* here. This isn't your usual crowd, is it?" She shook her head and tsked. "And I must protest, you're monopolizing our special guest."

No love lost between those two, he'd already figured out by Mamie's earlier comments, so he wasn't exactly surprised by the woman's hard tone. Jade responded with a lazy smile and amused silence that practically dared Mamie Brandywine to push harder.

Mamie didn't push. And Ryan's interest in Jade went up another notch. *A woman with a lot of nerve, that one.*

Rather than losing the staring contest with Jade, Mrs.

Brandywine backed down and turned her attention back to Ryan. She took his arm, saying, "I want you to meet someone. The owner of the inn we were discussing is right over there."

The Winter Garden. The inn where he'd be staying, starting tomorrow. He did *not* want Jade to know he'd be there. It might be enough to make her suspicious when he put Plan B into action.

Plan A was to seduce her, get close enough to her and try to get her to reveal something that might lead him to the painting.

Plan B was...well...a little riskier and involved the inn.

And a pair of handcuffs.

"You won't mind if I steal him away, will you, Jade? Surely you can find some other way to amuse yourself," Mamie said. "There are lots of men here who might find your little ghost stories interesting."

"Of course there are, and I'm sure you've...*met*... them all," Jade said, her smile never fading. All three of them knew her hesitation had been intentional.

Mamie stiffened as Jade continued pleasantly, "By the way, you do look *lovely* in your dress. How funny, I think Auntie Lula Mae has a stuffed dead bird in exactly that color."

Ryan bit the inside of his cheek to hide a laugh as his landlady's heavily made-up face went a few shades paler. From behind Jade, he saw another woman—the one in the hoop skirts who'd been talking with Jade earlier—listening intently. At Jade's cutting insult, the woman grabbed her middle and laughed so hard she almost dropped her drink.

Okay, so at least one other woman here liked the sultry brunette.

Before the offended inn owner could muster up a suitable retort, she was joined by a middle-aged man wearing a slightly faded black tuxedo. His horn-rimmed glasses covered a weary-looking pair of eyes.

Those eyes lit up when the man spied Jade. "Jade, you look wonderful!"

For the first time since he'd joined her, Ryan saw the young woman loosen up and smile with genuine fondness. She stood on her tiptoes and kissed the man on the cheek. "Hello, Uncle Henry."

Ah, more relations. Another thing about the South, everybody was related to everybody.

"Your mama got off on her cruise all right? Gee, honey, I was so sorry to miss the wedding."

Mamie Brandywine's stiff mouth said she, for one, was *not* sorry to have missed the wedding.

"She's fine. Having the time of her life, I imagine."

"Better on the high seas than here causing trouble," Mamie interjected. "Though I hope the other wives on board keep their husbands close at hand."

Jade's jaw stiffened and her face flushed red. For the first time, it appeared the obnoxious Mamie Brandywine had scored a hit.

She opened her mouth to retort. But before she could do so, Ryan interceded. "If you'll excuse us, we were just about to dance."

Then, not taking no for an answer, he plucked Jade's drink out of her hands and put it on the tray of a passing waiter. Taking a strong hold of her arm, he led her away, heading toward the dance floor, feeling her fury and resistance with every step.

He should have known better than to think she'd let it go. After only a half-dozen steps, she planted her feet and refused to proceed.

So, instead of allowing the fireworks, he did the only thing he could think of.

He kissed her.

JADE HAD BEEN PREPARED for reasoning, an apology, a joke, anything a man might typically do to calm down an angry woman.

But not this. Not this amazing kiss. Not his mouth teasing the corner of hers, then moving over until their lips met completely. He wasn't holding her close, wasn't restraining her in any way. Yet she still felt completely touched. Held. Embraced. By nothing but his lips.

Somehow, she couldn't even bring herself to care that she was standing in a crowd of people allowing a complete stranger to kiss her. Maybe because it felt so incredibly good, an unexpected gift of pleasure like suddenly feeling the sun on her face during what had been a cloudy day.

He didn't try to deepen the kiss, merely playing with her mouth, letting her lips savor the pleasure of his as they shared breaths and as her anger eased away. Finally, after what seemed like forever, he pulled away and looked at her.

She couldn't say a word, could only stare up at him in confusion, her mouth falling open but no sound coming out. He touched her chin with his index finger, pushed her mouth closed and whispered, "Dance with me."

Then he slipped his arm around her waist and led her onto the crowded floor. Like Moses parting the Red Sea, his mere presence made people step to the sides, moving away to create room for them. He nodded his thanks, gave polite smiles and left the women groveling in his wake while the men lifted their chins in annoyance.

Good lord, no wonder Jenny had fallen for this man. He'd completely taken over this society party, as if he belonged. As if he'd been born here and could trace his ancestry back several generations—as Jade could—instead of coming from some cold northern city where people didn't know their neighbors' names, much less their great-grandparents'.

"I'm afraid I don't know the latest steps to elevator music," he whispered as their bodies moved together and began to sway. "But I don't think rigid as a board is the right position."

Jade couldn't prevent a tiny laugh from escaping between her clenched teeth. She had, indeed, been rigid and inflexible, still trying to deal with his words, with that kiss. Not to mention his...*presence.* That was the only word to describe it.

He was so unlike any of the men she'd known or dated. His looks were one thing—good looks were easy to find, and also easy to forget if they weren't backed up with personality. But this man had more than the looks and the personality. It was his aura, his power, his self-confidence, that she found nearly irresistible. He commanded respect. And, she suspected, he knew how to give it in return.

Almost against her will, she relaxed against him, the contact causing both instant pleasure and instant tension.

Bad idea.

His body was long, thick and hard.

All over?

She thrust the naughty thought away, lest it distract her once again from her mission. It didn't help, particularly when she realized that if things went as planned, she'd be finding out his secrets—size and all—in a very short while. She nearly shuddered at the thought, remembering how lost she'd been because of a simple kiss.

Maybe you can't do this after all.

Can't, however, was among Jade's least favorite words. It always had been. Nothing made her give something her all as much as being told she couldn't do it.

She *would* do it. Would leave Mr. Smooth quaking and humiliated by the time she got through with him.

Or she'd go down trying.

Go down. The image hit the wicked half of her brain with a vengeance and her legs started to shake again.

Stop it, Jade. Get your mind out of his pants!

All the muscles in her body tensed as she strove for control.

"You're stiff again," he said.

"Stiff. Yes," she murmured, still more than a little unsettled with the undeniably erotic direction her thoughts had taken. Pretty bad to have those kind of thoughts about a man she'd hated before laying eyes on him. It had obviously been *way* too long since she'd had sex.

"Relax. You're all tense because of silly Mrs. Brandywine."

"She deserves to be taken down a peg."

"Wasn't it enough for her to be told that her dress looked like a dead bird?" he asked, a twinkle in his eye.

Jade bit her lip, still unable to believe she'd given in and done exactly what she'd sworn to Tally she wouldn't do. The cutting insult had just fallen off her lips, as naturally as could be. She hadn't given it a moment's thought.

"I guess I do have a bit of my mother in me." Then, remembering what Mamie had said, went on to add, "Mrs. Brandywine hates my mother because Mama's first husband was Mamie's high school boyfriend."

"High school. Long time to hold a grudge."

Jade shrugged. "Long grudges aren't unusual down here. Go bring up the Civil War to some of the old-timers."

"No, I'm not that daring," he said with a laugh.

The small band segued into yet another slow, dreamy melody. As they moved together, his leg slid between hers in a move too perfectly aimed to be accidental. She gasped at the contact, not expecting him to be so deliberately bold again so soon.

He tried to claim otherwise. "I'm not the best dancer."

She sucked in a shaky breath. "You're doing okay." Then she repositioned herself and shot him a warning look, telling him she knew he'd done it intentionally. "But don't try it again."

He didn't even apologize. Not that she'd expected him to. Instead he remained just out of reach, a breath separating them, so only the fronts of their bodies touched from shoulder to hip. The near-contact was driving her out of her mind. Her earlier curiosity returned in full force.

Long. Thick. Hard. And more…*hot.*

He radiated heat and energy, from the intensity in his green eyes to the strength in his hands to the breadth of his impossibly wide shoulders. The man screamed masculine, sexual, powerful and untamed.

And she was really going to try to tame him? No, not tame him, *punish* him?

Yet another feeling of uncustomary uncertainty

flashed in her brain, which really irked her. She hadn't been uncertain about anything related to sex for a long time. Not since deciding to lose her virginity to her college-age neighbor when she'd been in high school.

"Where are you?" he asked softly.

She shook her head and forced a smile and a trill of light laughter. "Right here. Can't you feel me?"

He nodded, slowly, and pulled her tighter. A little too tight for propriety's sake. Warmth built inside her. She felt a trickle of moisture on her upper lip. And elsewhere.

"Has this happened to you before?" He nearly whispered in her ear, his voice husky.

"What?"

"Something this instant?"

He didn't have to elaborate. They both knew what he was talking about.

She answered with complete honesty. "No." Then, because she didn't want him getting too cocky, added, "Not *this* quickly, anyway. I think it usually takes at least a half hour and a glass of wine for me to determine compatibility."

"So, should I be scared or glad that you're drinking soda?"

"How did you know that?" she asked in surprise.

"I've been watching you very closely. All evening. Now, answer the question. Am I not worthy of wine yet?"

She chuckled, unable to resist his teasing expression, though she did worry about how observant he was. "I haven't quite decided yet," she said, needing to regroup and remind herself that the man was a pig and a creep and a despoiler of innocent young girls. Supposedly.

Jenny wouldn't lie.

No, her sister wouldn't outright lie. But she was something of a drama queen, which suited her desire to be an actress. Her tendency to exaggerate was well-known in the family, as well as to the Savannah police. Jade had gotten her sibling out of several scrapes, even stepping in to keep Mama in the dark when Jenny's outrageous behavior got her into serious trouble.

But she couldn't have lied about this. Jade had even seen a picture of them together. Though it had been poor quality, so his face was slightly blurred, she believed this was the man who'd been in the picture. He'd had his arm laid casually over Jenny's shoulders, she looking exquisitely happy—as any woman would when being held by a man who looked like pure sex wrapped in an Armani suit.

Jenny hadn't lied. Maybe he hadn't *meant* to hurt her. Probably he hadn't, given that even during their very brief acquaintance, she'd already realized that though he was a flirtatious, sexy playboy who turned on the charm with anyone female and breathing, he didn't seem the type to abuse his power over women.

Unfortunately, he'd turned that charm on a young woman unable to handle it, and broken her heart. He was a grown man, thirty at least. Old enough to know better than to mess with a twenty-one-year-old kid. So whether he'd done it intentionally or not, Ryan Stoddard had to pay.

He *would* pay. And he would definitely know better by the time Jade finished with him.

"Now, we haven't been properly introduced, have we?" he whispered, his breaths brushing her hair and tickling her ear. "Your name is Jade?"

She cleared her throat and replied, "Yes. Jade." She didn't offer her last name.

"I'm Ryan Stoddard."

Definitely no mistake then. A stab of regret dashed through her as an unspoken wish that he might *not* be the rotten man she'd thought he was—that she'd made some colossal mistake and some other amazing architect had shown up at the party tonight—disappeared. She looked into his eyes, so clear and honest-looking. Any woman could get lost in them. Including a very young, impressionable woman.

She was once again forcibly reminded of the reason for tonight's interaction. Revenge.

The crazy, sexy spell she'd been under dissipated. She finally managed to dig deep and reinforce her wavering determination by picturing Jenny in this man's arms. That mental picture hurt. Badly. Maybe not for the right reasons, but it worked anyway. She didn't pause to evaluate those reasons, sensing they could be based more on jealousy than family loyalty.

Family loyalty. It was all that really mattered when one grew up as she had. The name Dupré was associated with both power and loss, sadness and ancient scandal. The family had become adept at dealing with whispers and innuendo, envy and tragedy, until the Duprés had become almost a world unto themselves. That world was a safe haven where loyalty and love were valued above all. It was especially comforting to Jade that she was related to so many people here in Savannah.

One thing was sure, the Dupré women had withstood worse than playboys like Ryan Stoddard.

Back in control at last, Jade widened her lips into the smile perfected by generations of Southern women.

Warm but not effusive. Friendly but not precisely wel-coming. With a bit of Dupré woman thrown in—purely seductive.

"Well, welcome to Savannah, Ryan. I'll try my best to make your stay as…*memorable* as possible."

3

FOR THE NEXT HOUR, Jade concentrated on the plan. She put herself as a barrier between Ryan and any of the other women at the party who'd been giving him the eye. Tally, for some reason, seemed to want to help. She ran interference once or twice, including saying something to Mamie Brandywine that made the woman's face turn as red as her long, fake fingernails.

While standing in a shadowy corner, nibbling on canapés and sipping her drink, she leaned forward and touched him as often as she could. Laughed at the appropriate moments. Batted her eyelashes like a stupid twit and all in all did whatever one did to try to attract a man. It had been a long time since she'd wanted to.

She didn't want to consider whether or not she'd have been trying to attract Ryan Stoddard if she didn't have to bring him down. Because the answer would probably be *yes*.

"So how do you like our town?" She pursed her lips a bit, inviting him to stare and remember their kiss. "And its people?"

He tilted his head and arched his brow, staring at her mouth for a long moment—as he was meant to. Finally, he shook his head and tightened his jaw before coming up with a reply. "How do you know I'm not from here?"

"I know," she replied, certain she'd affected him. Men—they were all so utterly predictable. She gave him a warm laugh, inviting him to join in a gentle jibe at her hometown. "This is a small town for a modern city."

She didn't bother going into detail about how long her family had lived here, how many local families had ties to hers, and how her great-aunt was the local voodoo priestess who could name nearly every pure-blooded Savannah resident.

"It's interesting," he said. "Different from New York."

"Are you from there?" she asked, wanting to know more of his background, in case she needed to use it against him. She knew he'd met Jenny in New York City, but wasn't entirely sure that was where he lived.

"Yep. Born and raised. Now I live in Manhattan."

Manhattan. So he probably had money. He carried himself like a man completely comfortable with his finances.

She'd been to New York last month on one of her treasure-hunting trips, when she'd recovered an Impressionist painting from a very nice elderly couple who lived upstate. The painting had already been returned to the original plantation from which it had been stolen during the Civil War. The place now operated as a tourist destination outside the city and they were utterly thrilled to have the portrait back where it belonged.

For a second, she wondered if perhaps she'd spotted Ryan during her trip, and if that was why he'd seemed familiar to her when she'd first seen him tonight. Maybe her subconscious remembered him.

The picture, stupid.

Yeah, the picture of him with Jenny. No, it hadn't been a great one, and she'd only seen it briefly. But it'd obviously made an impression. As did the man.

"Let me know when you decide you want that glass of wine, okay?" he said, eyeing her empty soda cup.

She knew what he meant. It had already been more than half an hour. No wonder he was getting confident. There'd been no hesitation, no doubt in his voice. He thought he had her. Hell, maybe he did. At least for an hour or so.

Until she could get him naked.

"All right," she replied. "But for now, maybe we should just dance again."

"Suits me fine."

Suited her fine, too. Especially because, when they returned to the dance floor, he moved his cheek close to her hair and inhaled. She knew his head was filled with the special orange-blossom-and-almond condi-tioner Aunt Lula Mae made for her. His murmur of appreciation told her he liked it. He liked *all* of it.

Good. The man was making it incredibly easy. He'd sought her out—she hadn't even had to make a move on him. When he looked back on things later, he'd have to remember that much, at least.

"You truly seem to fit in here," he murmured as the music continued and they moved as carefully as possi-ble amid the crush of people.

"You don't."

He chuckled. "Why not?"

"Blue suit. Genuine smile. Interested look."

"That makes me stand out?"

"Like a June bug in a bowl of rice."

He laughed again, looking down at her, eyes spar-kling with interest. Dark green. Long lashed. Crinkled at the corners, probably from casting his wicked smile at any woman old enough to be affected by it.

He's a heart-breaking reprobate! She struggled to remember that as he continued to smile down at her.

"I like Southerners."

"We don't particularly care for you-all."

That made him laugh out loud.

She nibbled her lip, forcing her eyes to focus somewhere over his right shoulder so she wouldn't get caught up again in his good humor, wouldn't lose herself in his twinkling eyes and irresistible grin. Maybe dancing hadn't been such a good idea. Hard to remember silly things like family honor and vengeance when being held closely by a man as fine as this one.

"Honesty. I like that in a woman."

Well, darlin', you're not gonna like me very much, then.

"So tell me, how can I make myself fit in?"

"Got a few million dollars lying around?"

He shook his head.

"Genteel impoverished, but able to trace your lineage back to before the war?"

"Which war?"

She raised a brow and gave him a wounded look. "Whichever do you think?"

Their eyes met and she saw the laughter in his. He'd been teasing her, just as she'd been teasing him.

"I'm afraid I'm an Irish-English-German mutt," he replied with a mournful-sounding sigh. "Can't trace my roots further back than Ellis Island, for the most part."

"But I bet you have good taste in beer. Irish, English, German?"

He nodded, still looking amused.

"Unfortunately, that doesn't get you in with this crowd."

"How about with you?"

"Are you offering to buy me a beer?" she asked, leaping on the opening he'd provided. The time had come to get him alone. Now—before her defenses dropped even further and she forgot she wasn't allowed to like this man. "I doubt they serve it here."

"I have some in the fridge up in my room."

Ooh, cutting right to the chase. Trying to get her up to his room. How incredibly easy he was making this. And his smooth way of trying to get her alone reinforced her certainty that he was the creep her sister made him out to be, even though he'd been nothing but charming and friendly—if a bit flirtatious—all evening.

"I could meet you on the back patio for a cold one."

Okay, so he *wasn't* trying to get her to his room. She didn't know whether to feel relieved or disappointed.

She'd thought through several scenarios. The original one had involved his hotel room, a bedpost, her long red scarf and a wide-open door. Because he'd moved to the Medford House, she'd have to modify things a bit.

But the scarf was still included.

"How do you know I'm the beer-drinking type?" she asked as he waited for her answer.

His expression screamed confidence, as if he knew all there was to know about her after an hour of conversation.

"Let me tell you what I've figured out about you."

She smirked, daring him to be accurate.

"You've been nursing ginger ale all evening. Before I rescued you, you'd done nothing but look at the paintings, the furniture and that old necklace. You didn't return one glance at one of the rich guys who'd probably love to invite you to bathe in champagne back at their pampered palaces."

"Champagne bath? Sounds ticklish," she retorted, though the mental image created a surge of warmth low in her body.

He ignored her. "Your foot was tapping with suppressed energy and your fingers clenched and released about thirty times a minute."

"You were watching me that long, hmm?"

He didn't try to deny it. "You had my complete attention the moment I became aware of your existence."

There was a note of intensity, almost a growl in his voice, which surprised her. Again she wondered, briefly, if she'd ever met him before, perhaps on one of her trips to track down and retrieve artifacts stolen from local families during the war.

But she knew she hadn't. This was one man she would never have been able to forget.

"Your face, your mouth, your eyes, your body, they were all saying one thing," he continued, uncaring of the open ears surrounding them on the dance floor.

Take me?

"Bored."

That, too.

"Bored enough to want to do something different." His voice lowered, and there was an unmistakably suggestive tone in it. "Maybe something crazy. Which is why I decided to shock you out of your boredom during our initial conversation."

Oh, yeah, their initial conversation. The one that had included mention of her nipples and breasts, both of which were still aching as their bodies brushed against each other.

"I'm still not sure I've forgiven you."

"I don't think I asked for forgiveness."

Again that confidence. That suggestive—not salacious—tone. He was a self-assured man who'd noted their instant attraction and was acting on it without games, without the typical steps of flirtation. She liked that about him. Damn, she liked him more and more the longer she remained in his arms.

"Are you sure you're not a P.I. or something? You're pretty good at watching people," she said.

Her tone was teasing, though she was a teensy bit worried. If she didn't know for certain he was an architect, she might have thought the P.I. thing was nearer to the truth. The man was incredibly observant!

"You're very interesting to watch," he said, his voice low and only for her ears. "Fascinating." Then he lightened up. "Besides, it beats watching the white-haired guy with the ruffled shirt trying to look down the blouse of every cocktail server here."

She followed his glance. "Mr. Sherman. Disgusting, but harmless, especially since his wife tried to castrate him back in the seventies."

He stopped dancing, nearly stumbling on his own feet. His eyes were wide and she merely shrugged. The story was an old one.

"You're serious?"

"Why do you think none of the servers have slapped his face? Everyone feels sorry for the limp old thing."

He shook his head, drawing her close again to continue the dance. "What about the couple over by the buffet table? He looks thirty years too young to be her husband. I thought she was his mother until I saw them kiss on the dance floor."

Jade glanced over, unable to hide a frown of disgust when she saw the couple. "The latest divorced matron with her rebound boy toy."

"That kind of thing happens in the rich crowd even in the South?" He sounded truly surprised.

"Obviously you haven't seen or read The Book."

"The Book?"

"The tell-all novel that changed the image of Savannah in print and on film."

He nodded. "Ahh. *Midnight in the Garden of Good and Evil.*"

"Here, we just call it The Book."

"Okay. And actually, I have seen the movie. I assumed it was fiction."

"Some was. But not the eccentricities of the city's residents."

He shrugged, looking neither surprised nor disappointed. "It fits. Eccentricities, beautiful homes, fine things." He stared into her face, studying her eyes, her hair, her cheekbones. Jade resisted the urge to lick her lips, wondering if they were still as glossy red as they'd been when she'd touched up her lipstick earlier.

"I like looking at fine things," he murmured.

She sucked in a breath. The way he said the word *fine* made her shiver deep inside, as if he'd examined her, studied her, and declared her as lovely and desirable as a perfect piece of art.

God, what deceptive things come in pretty packages. Because she wasn't fine. She wasn't being honest. She wasn't *anything* he thought her to be.

For a brief moment, she wished they'd met under different circumstances. If Jenny had never mentioned Ryan Stoddard. If she'd never seen the man's picture—which had enraged Jade even more, considering how irresistible he'd be to a vulnerable twenty-one- year-old. If only...

If only there'd been a big mistake and he wasn't the man she'd sworn revenge on.

But he was. And it was time to get on with it.

"Okay, Ryan. I'll have that beer with you."

RYAN LEFT THE BALLROOM of the old mansion, telling Jade he'd meet her outside in fifteen minutes. She gave him a measured look, then nodded her agreement and stepped out of his arms. He'd had to stand there on the dance floor for a moment, to calm his pulse, to evaluate what he was doing, to make sure he wasn't about to make a mistake.

There was something so intriguing about the woman. Her strength, her charm. The way she stood her ground when surrounded by catty women whose dislike probably stemmed from jealousy more than anything else.

She seemed above it, somehow, not rising to it except for that one moment with Mamie. But even then, she'd regained her cool head pretty quickly.

He didn't know why, but he had a strong sense of misgiving about how the evening was progressing. He was supposed to be the hunter. So why was he suddenly feeling hunted?

"You're imagining things," he told himself. Things were going perfectly. It was only his overactive imagination—and overheated sex drive—that needed to be brought under control.

Unfortunately, someone else overheard. "Imagining things? No, you're not."

Ryan looked up and saw the woman in the hoop-skirted ball gown who'd been talking to Jade earlier. She should have looked ridiculous, but somehow, her innate grace made the silly dress work. At least in this setting.

"Tally Jackson," the woman said, extending her hand for a limp, ladylike handshake.

Ryan took it and introduced himself.

"Now, were you thinking you were imagining ghosts?"

Ryan raised a brow.

"You mentioned something about imagining it?"

"No, sorry, I was mumbling to myself."

She tsked. "Best be careful of that. Here in Savannah, you never know when one of your little quirks might end up in the pages of a *book*."

He grinned, having been forewarned by Jade about what book she probably meant.

"I just assumed you saw the ghost," the woman said.

"Ghost?"

"Well, Savannah *is* the most haunted city in the U.S. Oh, this house isn't spectacularly haunted, mind you. Not like the Lowe or the Winston house. But there have been a few occasions when guests swore they heard the sound of a man crying."

"A man?" He raised a disbelieving brow. Ryan didn't bother to hide the sarcasm from his voice, being well used to ghost stories about old buildings like these. "Are you sure you don't mean a poor spurned mistress or a child lost at a tragically young age?"

Tally didn't take offense. "No, no, definitely a man. Some say it was the millionaire who owned the house back at the turn of the century, crying over the woman he loved, who married another." Then she pointed to the curved staircase leading to the upper floors and bedrooms. "He hanged himself from that very banister on Christmas Eve, 1904."

Ryan looked up, wondering if he was supposed to shiver or shudder or feel someone walking over his grave.

None of the above. It was only a staircase. Stairs.

Banister. A normal, sweeping, curved staircase built so often in neoclassical mansions like these. The story was probably one of the dozens made up by con artists like Jade Maguire who made their living scaring the tourists, just like Mamie had said.

"Guess Christmas wasn't very merry that year," he replied with a rueful smile.

"You don't believe me?" Tally said.

"I'm certainly not calling you a liar," he said, trying to end the conversation gracefully."

Tally obviously heard the placating note in his voice and knew he was humoring her. "You don't believe in ghosts? Or is it that you don't believe a Southern woman could capture a man's heart so completely, he can never love another?" Her stare was so intense, so piercing, that he knew the question wasn't merely a casual one. Their eyes held for a long moment, hers asking questions. Before she could voice them, he beat her to the punch.

"Tell me about Jade Maguire," he countered, knowing that's who the woman meant.

"Touché," she said with a light laugh. "You've caught me. I saw you kiss her and nearly tripped over my hoops."

Considering the width of her hoops, that would have presented an interesting sight. "It was impulse. Trying to prevent her from going back to claw Mamie Brandywine."

Tally nodded, showing her disbelief. "Oh, I'm sure it was entirely selfless."

He couldn't deny it. "I won't say I didn't enjoy it…."

She laughed aloud. "Good. I'm sure she did, too."

"You're friendly with Jade?"

She nodded. "Her mother is my second cousin.

We've been best friends since childhood. I love Jade like a daughter."

Ryan heard a hint of warning in her voice.

"She seems...fascinating," he said. "Someone I'd like to get to know better."

Tally studied his face, as if gauging the truth of his words. Then she nodded. "Yes, I think you would. But remember, dear boy, you'd better treat her well. The Dupré women...well, let's say we know how to exact revenge if one of us is done wrong."

"Should I be afraid for my life?"

Or just my valuables?

Tally stepped closer and tapped his chest with the end of her fan, the strap of which she had looped around her wrist. "Not if you don't deserve it." Then she smoothed his jacket, tsking as she stared hard at the color. He guessed Jade had been right about the navy blue thing.

"My goddaughter can handle herself. But I shouldn't like to see her hurt, or give her any more reason to stay away from my parties. It's difficult enough to get her to come to events like these."

"Why?"

"Jade loathes these types of things. Her mother's cup of tea, not Jade's. And Patty Jean is a social butterfly. She also thrives on evenings like these as retribution for her side of the family being excluded from society in the old days."

This was getting interesting. "Excluded?"

Tally nodded, obviously as big a gossip as the owner of this inn. But this gossip might help him get inside the head of the woman he was chasing. Learn what made her tick and what buttons he could push, if it came right down to it.

He'd prefer to bring her down legally, but if he had to resort to blackmail, he'd do it.

"Patty Jean's from the Henri Dupré side of the family." She said it like that was supposed to mean something to him.

"Never heard of him."

Tally shrugged. "You wouldn't have, being a northerner. But that side of the family tree includes lots of scandalous branches."

Hmm. Maybe the family tree grew beautiful thieves. That would certainly explain Jade.

"So," Tally continued, "you'd best be careful with Jade. One of the most famous local Duprés is Lula Mae." The woman turned back toward the ballroom, smiling at someone inside.

"Are you trying to tell me something?" Ryan asked, suddenly feeling Tally wasn't a gossip at all. He sensed she'd been in control of this conversation from the very beginning and had given out only a teeny bit of actual information. Because, now that he thought about it, he realized she hadn't revealed much at all. And then, only what she'd wanted to, not what he'd asked for.

"Oh," Tally said, smiling at him over her shoulder. "Not really. Just wanted to warn you not to get on the wrong foot with Jade. Her great-aunt Lula Mae is a voodoo priestess."

She disappeared back into the crowd, leaving Ryan alone in the foyer. "Voodoo priestess, my ass," he mumbled, wondering why these Southerners loved their supernatural nonsense so much. And why Tally Jackson had felt it necessary to warn him about Jade.

Was her warning meant to keep him away from the mysterious brunette? Or to fascinate him even more? Because he had to admit, he was already pretty fascinated. He'd expected someone cold and calculating and instead had found a hot, sultry woman who turned him on right down to his bones.

Even more surprising, he actually liked her. Her wit, her confidence, her comebacks.

Her smile.

"Moron," he muttered aloud, knowing he'd let his defenses down way too quickly.

He needed to put them back up, and pronto. Because he wasn't backing away from Jade one inch. He had a score to settle, a debt he'd soon be calling in. He trusted her about as much as that little black dress covered her sweet figure, and that wasn't much.

As he went up to his room, he heard the trill of his cell phone in his suit pocket. Too late for a business call, and he'd told his friends he'd be unreachable for a week or two. So it had to be family. Probably not his parents, who were at their mountain place for the summer. And almost certainly not his sister, at home with twin four-month-olds.

That left grandmother.

"Hello?"

"Ryan. How are you? Where are you? What's happening?"

Yep. "I'm fine, Grandmother. Everything's fine."

"Have you found her?"

The anxious tone in the old woman's voice reinforced what his mind had been trying to forget during the hours he'd spent being charmed—and attracted—by Jade.

She'd hurt his family.

"I've found her."

The woman waited expectantly, then finally asked, "And?"

"And, I'm on her trail. Here in Savannah."

"Savannah! Oh, goodness, you found her right there in Savannah?"

"It wasn't hard. If you'd only remembered her first name originally, I wouldn't have been distracted by the wrong woman in New York."

His grandmother sniffed. She had been annoyed that he'd wasted time on the wrong Maguire woman, even though she'd been the one who'd given him only the minor lead of an initial for a first name. "The silly little waitress. Yes, yes. But now you've found her, the real McCoy."

"Maguire."

"Of course. What do you think of her?"

He heard a note of expectation in the old woman's voice and wondered if she didn't think him capable of handling someone as devious as Jade. "She's nothing to be afraid of, Grandmother, just a woman with secrets. I'll figure out where she stashed the LeBeuf. But you're sure you don't want to bring the police in on this, now that we know who she is?"

"Absolutely not!" Her voice sounded almost panicked. God love the old thing, so embarrassed at having been tricked.

"All right. I'll handle Jade Maguire."

Definitely handle her.

"She is beautiful, don't you think?" Grandmother said, her tone now more calm.

"Beautiful, yes. But only skin deep."

"And charming."

"Very charming. She'd have to be to swindle you out of your favorite painting."

"Well," Grandmother said, her voice wavering for the first time, "perhaps I was partially at fault…"

"Nonsense. You were robbed. Victims always wonder if they're to blame, but you're *not*. Jade Maguire is."

Though his grandmother sounded as if she wanted to protest, he didn't give her the opportunity. "It's late. Now go to bed, and let me worry about handling our thief."

"You're sure you can handle her? She is quite a handful, isn't she?"

Quite a handful indeed.

"I can handle her grandmother."

"And you won't tip her off! You won't let her know why you're after her. You'll be discreet. You'll just get close to her, spend time with her, stick to her like glue until you can…figure things out."

He smiled, hearing the worrying tone in the wavering voice. "Discreet as can be. I'll get as close to her as possible, then get the information without ever letting her know I'm on to her."

His grandmother's pleased laugh told him he'd provided the correct answer. "Good. And don't let her get away from you. She's slippery. You're going to need to stay close to that woman, day and night."

Day and night. If only his sweet old grandmother knew how very much he longed to stick with Jade day…and especially night. "I've got it under control. Now, good night."

His grandmother gave in with a reluctant sigh. "Good night. Keep your guard up. She's sinful. A man could get lost with a woman like that."

Yes, definitely lost, he thought as he disconnected the call and headed upstairs to his room. A woman like Jade could make any man lose his mind, give in to his senses. She silently cried out to a very basic, primal need he'd long since thought he'd suppressed—desire.

Flat-out, unrelenting want. The kind of hunger that made his mouth go dry and his hands shake.

Damn, what a vulnerable position to be in with a woman so skilled at deception. She was brilliantly skilled at it. As deceptive and seductive as a modern-day Delilah, and just as deadly. Just as dangerous. And his grandmother wanted him to stay *close* to such a creature.

If only she knew what she was asking of him. She wanted him to reach out to a hot flame, risk life and limb with someone who could burn him badly. Someone as adept at lying as she was at seducing, as good at stealing as she was at flirting.

This entire situation required acting without thinking, going on impulse and giving in to emotions he'd gotten used to controlling. That attitude had seen him through all his previous romantic entanglements, including his botched engagement. Not to mention his career, where he'd gained a reputation for a cool head, a steady hand, and a brilliant eye.

So why, suddenly, did he feel blazing hot, wildly off balance and blind when it came to the dangers he was about to face with Jade Maguire?

He didn't know. Almost didn't recognize the feelings in himself. Another thing to blame the woman for. She had him questioning himself in their short acquaintance and he damn sure didn't like it. He hadn't been unsure of himself in a long, long time.

And tonight certainly wasn't the time to start, no matter how the sexy brunette made him feel.

"Enough," he told his reflection in the mirror when he reached his room.

He quickly stripped off his jacket and tie for their meeting in the garden, then, remembering Jade's sticky fingers, he removed one more item from his back pocket.

His wallet.

4

WHILE RYAN WENT TO HIS room to get their beer—a drink for which Jade had no liking but would develop one quickly since it suited her purpose—she went outside to scope out her attack zone. She knew the grounds well. The Medford House was on the list of sites her company, Stroll Savannah, visited during their walking tours of the city. Jade had staff members who did most of the tours these days, but she'd visited the Medford place often enough to remember the layout.

The rear grounds were walled. The once-white wall, whose stones were now a soft milky gray, provided both a visual and a sound barrier from Taylor Square. It also seemed to provide a time barrier that removed this heavily treed back lawn from the modern world where traffic screeched along in present-day Savannah.

Here in the garden, the only concession to the twenty-first century was the spa the owners had added to appeal to their inn customers. She ignored the spa. Too obvious. Too close to the French doors leading into the ballroom. Too yucky, considering their conversation inside about Mamie Brandywine. He'd never feel comfortable enough to, um…get *comfortable* if he thought they could be so easily spotted.

Instead, she moved into the yard, stepping into the

soft grass, walking on her toes so her spike heels wouldn't slip down into the dirt. The ground was moist, the humidity which had hovered over the city throughout the day having misted down onto the lawn as the evening shadows lengthened. The damp turf brushed against her ankles, against her supersensitive skin, and she nearly cooed at the contact. The ballroom had been wickedly hot. Jade would have liked nothing more than to kick off her shoes, walk in the cool grass, and explore the night.

She'd always been something of a creature of the night. Her mother said it was in her blood, that surely there must have been a vampire or two in the New Orleans side of the family. That wouldn't surprise her. Jade had a passion for vampire novels. Not the gooshy ones with lots of blood and bodies, but the romance ones where the vampires actually had sex.

She wouldn't want to be a vampire if she couldn't have sex.

She laughed softly, knowing what her always-striving-to-be-proper mother would think of tonight's adventure, not to mention Jade's own thoughts. She'd be horrified. So it was a good thing she'd gone off on a cruise with her new husband, leaving Jade to take care of Aunt Lula Mae. And this Ryan Stoddard business.

Then she spied the perfect spot for tonight's interlude. "The fountain," she murmured, beelining toward the little corner area on the east side of the property.

It was shaded by willow, oak and magnolia trees, and curtained by loops of gray Spanish moss, which glistened with the same late-night moisture that clung to the grass. Once upon a time, it had probably been a place where ladies took tea in the afternoon and met their lovers late at night.

Unfortunately, though it did a good impersonation of one, the area was no longer a perfectly private and secluded haven. Back in the days of ladies and tea parties, there hadn't been those nice, powerful spotlights on the back corners of the house and on either side of the French doors. They were mostly pointed toward the statue of the general in the center of the lawn. But when the rear lights were turned on, the entire back yard was also well lit. Certainly anyone standing on the porch would have an excellent view of the antique fountain, complete with angels and seraphs, splashing an endless cycle of cool greenish water.

Not to mention anyone standing next to that fountain.

And the lights *would* be on. Right at midnight, when the entire party would come outside to raise a glass to the statue of the general. This grand reopening had been scheduled for his birthday, just so they could make the annual toast.

"Perfect," she murmured as she sat on a stone bench beside the fountain, waiting for Ryan Stoddard.

He'd think they were unseen. And they would be.

"Until the toast," she said with a grin.

"Toast?" a voice said.

Jade quickly schooled her features into a welcoming look, giving Ryan a smile. "What shall we toast to?"

He joined her on the bench, handing her a glass.

"To new acquaintances?"

"To Savannah?"

He thought it over, then lowered his voice suggestively. "How about to a glass of wine and a half an hour?"

She noted the wicked twinkle in his eye, reflected by the tiny lawn lights outlining the fountain and bench area. Not understanding his reference at first, she lifted the glass to her lips. Jade bit back a sigh of resignation and steeled herself against the bitter taste of beer. But what crossed her lips was a fine, heady, full-bodied red wine.

"Mmm." She closed her eyes and swallowed, appreciating the flavor and the warmth. Now she understood what he'd meant by his toast.

"I didn't take you for the beer-drinking type." He sipped his own, then added, "And I think we've officially known each other for more than a half hour now."

She thought about her comments earlier on the dance floor. A half hour and a glass of wine until she could determine if she was attracted to a man. It had taken less than that with *this* man. Not for the first time this evening, she wondered if she might be in over her head.

It didn't matter, even if she was. She owed it to her sister to see this through, no matter how personally uncomfortable it was becoming. And her attraction to her victim was making things *very* uncomfortable.

"You're very sure of yourself." She inhaled the aroma of the wine and sipped again.

"Just determined."

There was that confidence again. That certainty of her—of the situation, of his own charm—both intrigued her and angered her. Because the same charm had been used on a woman much less adept at handling it than Jade.

"I don't know that I needed the half hour," she said, her voice almost a purr as she hid her flash of anger.

"You want me for my wine, hmm?"

"It *is* good."

He nodded his agreement. "Found it in a tiny local grocery store. I figured they'd only carry six-packs and screw-top bottles."

"Savannah takes its food and wine almost as seriously as it takes its history."

Jade sipped again, daring only a small bit more as the stuff was heady. The warmth pervading her wasn't helping to remind her of her purpose. Nor was the hot summer evening, thick with the smells of moss, freshly-mown grass, and the sweet scent of magnolia from the profusion of trees in the yard.

Not to mention his cologne. Or maybe that was just the natural scent of his skin filling her head.

"Spicy," she murmured, taking a deep breath to appreciate all the scents.

"The wine?"

She rested her glass on the bench and looked at him through half-lowered lashes. "The air."

He gave her a quizzical look, then turned his head and closed his eyes. He remained silent for a moment or two, breathing deeply, then nodded. "You're right. Fragrant's not the right word. Spicy. It fits." Then he set his own glass on the ground, and turned slightly to face her. "Both the air…and *you.*"

"Me?" she asked with an air of feigned surprise that every Southern girl had learned by her fifth birthday. She didn't need to add the "li'l ole" part to the sentence. The meaning was clear enough.

"Yes, you. Spicy and dark and exotic." His voice was husky and thick, the low, masculine timbre echoing in her ears for a moment longer than it should have.

It wasn't the first time a man had called her exotic. Her thick brown hair, jet-black lashes and chocolate eyes had invited the description before. She'd inherited the looks from her great-great-grandmother, an acclaimed beauty and granddaughter of a slave. She'd been taken as a mistress by a Louisiana planter named Dupré at an Octoroon ball more than a century ago.

Exotic. Suited her bloodline. After all, she had descended from slaves and mistresses. Women who'd shaped their own destinies in spite of what the men in their lives had demanded.

But Jade had never liked the word exotic as much as she did when it came off this man's perfectly shaped lips.

Cool it. Those lips whispered promises that broke your sister's heart!

And, she reminded herself, they were the ones she needed to kiss. Soon. Very soon. Part of the plan, after all. But even as she moved her mouth to his, being the aggressor, she wondered if this was an entirely altruistic kiss.

When their lips met, she realized something.

No. It wasn't.

Then she couldn't think at all. She could only feel. The touch of their mouths—soft, dreamy. The teeny hitch in her throat as they drew a hair's width apart and shared a breath. Then intense pleasure as he moved forward again, capturing her lips and coaxing them apart with smooth, sweet caresses of his tongue.

She moaned, trying to remember what she was doing here. Trying to remember who she was and what she wanted, when all she could focus on was the new place they'd created with the meeting of their mouths.

"You're not what I expected, Jade," he whispered when they drew apart again.

She immediately stiffened and tried to regain her senses and put her thoughts in order—nearly impossible while still under the spell of his kiss.

Finally she managed to say, "Expected? What could you have expected after an evening's acquaintance?"

His eyes shifted slightly and he bent to retrieve his glass. "I meant, when I saw you inside, I'd expected a cool Southern beauty. Not an impulsive woman I'd be kissing in a private garden within a few hours."

She watched his face, gauging the truth of his words. Again, she couldn't help the tiny moment of wonder about just how easy this was. How quickly he'd fallen into her trap.

"You expected cool, and you got hot instead, is that it?" she asked, tilting her head back in pure provocation, inviting him to look at the line of her neck.

He responded. As if reading her mind, he lowered his mouth and pressed one hot, wet kiss to that hollow. His thick hair brushed her face and she couldn't resist raising her hands to tangle her fingers in it.

Then he moved up to kiss her again, his lips still tasting of the wine. The kiss was deeper, harder than before as they both acknowledged the buildup of passion between them.

And suddenly Jade began to wonder if she was really going to be able to go through with her plan after all. Because, somehow, letting this revenge-only seduction turn into a real one seemed altogether too appealing.

RYAN HADN'T KNOWN WHAT he'd find when he came outside into the garden. An armed woman demanding his money? A trickster telling him a sob story and begging him for a way out of some financial trouble?

Certainly not *this*. Certainly not a seductress. God help him, never a wanton, irresistible lover.

He'd fallen right into her web, been totally suckered

by the moonlight on her hair, the way the red wine drenched her lips, darkening them with a seductive moisture until he had to kiss them or go crazy.

She'd tasted amazing. Even better than she had inside, on the dance floor, because this time she'd initiated the kiss. She'd wanted it. Demanded it.

And he'd been more than happy to give it to her.

Now, however, he was finally regaining his senses. He needed to step back, to regroup. To remember who he was and why he was here before he did something stupid like have sex on a public lawn with the woman who'd robbed his helpless old grandmother.

That stiffened his spine. He pulled his mouth away, resisting the urge to inhale one more deep breath of that intoxicating scent she wore, and slid away on the bench. She pulled back, eyeing him through half-lowered lashes. The fullness of her lips nearly pulled him back into another kiss. Nearly.

He resisted the urge by reaching over and thrusting his fist into the cool water of the fountain. "Cool. Feels good on a night this hot. I didn't know what the term *sultry* meant until I came here to Georgia."

She quirked a brow. "We're talking about the weather now? Sultry as in hot and humid?"

Hot, yes. Sultry, yes. And he'd be willing to bet she was more than a little humid after the passionate kiss they'd just exchanged. His body had certainly reacted with sexual predictability, which made his pants uncomfortably tight across his lap.

"Yes, as in hot and humid *weather*."

Her bottom lip curled out in a tiny pout. "My, I think that's the first time I've ever been kissed by a man who then proceeded to talk about the weather." Her curved lips hinted at disappointment, but her eyes were sharp, studying him with wonder and a bit of disbelief.

He'd miscalculated. A woman with Jade's experience would be suspicious if he put up too much resistance, particularly when she had to have, um...*felt* how interested he was in her.

Trying to steel himself against reacting, he moved close again. The key was to win her trust until he could find out what she'd done with the painting. Hopefully without losing either his pants or his mind in the process.

"Sorry," he whispered, reaching over to run his fingertips over her jaw, then across her full, bottom lip. She quivered beneath his hand, and he felt an answering flush of heat.

"I wanted to make sure you weren't falling into something you didn't want. The moonlight, the wine..."

She stared at him intently, as if gauging the truth of his words. Then she slowly nodded. "Maybe you're right. We can talk about the weather for a little while. You should see how things will heat up next month. July's nothing compared to August."

Sounded like she expected him to be around a while. But he planned to be long gone as soon as he retrieved his family's property.

"How'd you know your way around back here?" he asked as he shifted to focus on the stone angels instead of the fantasy woman who'd just been in his arms.

She didn't reply for a moment, merely watching with a measured glance. It was as if she was testing his resolve, wondering if he was really pulling away, or merely building the tension through verbal small talk.

Neither. He was merely trying to hold on to his san-ity before he did something insane like haul up her dress to see whether she was wearing anything underneath.

From what he already knew about Jade Maguire, he suspected not.

Jade finally answered. "I'm pretty familiar with the city. Especially the historic buildings…like this one."

He knew a lot about her—her tour company—but wanted to see how much she'd reveal about herself. "You're a native?"

She nodded. "Born and raised. As were my parents, grandparents, great-grandparents and so on."

That surprised him. "You can really trace your genealogy back so far?"

She nodded. "Right back to the plantation."

The detective hadn't mentioned anything about that. "You're descended from some local plantation? From a long line of Southern belles?"

She laughed, but her laughter sounded more forced than amused. Shrugging, Jade rose from the bench, walked around toward the stone wall and leaned against it. She continued to sip her wine slowly. Then, seeming almost unaware she was doing so, she casually lifted one foot, slipping off one shoe, then the other. She arched a foot, stretching her leg, then her whole body, as sinuously as a cat. "Mmm, that feels wonderful."

Damn, even her feet were sexy. High-arched, delicate, with hot-pink-tinted nails. His mouth went dry as he pictured running his hands from those delicate ankles all the way up her legs. Up. Up. Under that black dress to find all her mysteries laid bare, waiting for him.

He closed his eyes as he drew in another deep breath

of hot night air. When he opened them, he found Jade watching him, a matching look of intensity on her face.

So, he wasn't the only one feeling it. This strange, instant attraction had affected them both.

If only he didn't have to hate her.

Trying to find something to distract himself with, he glanced at her wickedly high-heeled black shoes lying on the patio. He didn't understand how on earth women could contort their feet into such unnatural shapes. "Why do women wear the things if they're so painful? Do you really care what men think of your shoes?"

Shoes. A perfect topic of conversation for any woman. That heated look left her eyes as she gave him a pitying look. "No, of course we don't care what men think of our shoes. We care what *women* think of our shoes because we *all* love them."

She was right, though he still didn't get it. His own mother and sister felt the same way, as had every woman he'd ever dated. "All a man needs are two pairs of dress shoes, brown and black. Plus a casual brown pair for jeans, and some athletic shoes for sports."

Jade's shudder was almost comical. "You don't strike me as the type of man who has only four pairs of shoes in his closet."

"Ah, you can add," he said, not admitting she was right. "Most of the women I've met here tonight didn't look like they'd be able to."

This time, her surprised laughter sounded real, not forced. He found himself entranced by it, by the way her eyes lit up and crinkled a bit in the corners when she was really amused. She didn't look calculating now. Didn't look the seductress. Merely like an attractive, normal twenty-six-year-old. One who, under normal circumstances, he'd have been trying to get naked by now.

Naked. Bad thought. He swallowed hard, forcing it away.

"Oh, suh," she said, mimicking a thick accent, "I'm so awful lucky you don't have more shoes than I have little ole fingers," she retorted.

"Good thing," he said, getting up and moving to her side. He leaned his shoulder against the wall, turned sideways so he faced her. "Now tell me about your family's grand and glorious past on the plantation. Did your ancestors raise tobacco or cotton?"

"Cotton. And they *picked* it as much as raised it."

Good humor still kept her lips wide as he thought about her comment and finally understood it. "Really?"

She nodded. "We came from the wrong side of the Lancaster family tree. Via the mulatto mistress of the grand and valiant General Lester Lancaster, my great-great-great-great-grandfather." Then she added, "My great-great-great-great-grandmother, on the other hand, was a field hand who came to the attention of lecherous old Lester."

Descended of slaves. Fascinating. "I'm amazed you can track your family back so far."

"Many of the true locals can. That's why I know so much about the city—every bit of history, every piece of land." Her voice dropped, growing thick with intensity. This was a subject she truly cared about. "The architecture, the artifacts, the people, places and events. I've studied it all, read about it, been enthralled by it for as long as I can remember, examining it from both sides of my life to try to understand where I came from."

She seemed passionate about the subject. It sounded like he'd found the woman's real weakness. Beyond money, beyond sex or stealing, she was enthralled by the past. "Are you a historian?"

A mysterious smile widened her lips as she shook her head and returned to her seat, patting the bench until he sat down, too. Close to her. Very close. "Not exactly. But I do…dabble."

Dabble. He swallowed hard, wondering what other things the woman liked to *dabble* in. Naughty things?

"I like to explore things that interest me."

The way she said the word interest, combined with a slow lick of her lips and the way she watched him, sent his blood roaring through his veins.

He turned slightly so their faces were only a few inches apart. As were their bodies. "Things that interest you. You like to *study* them?"

She nodded, her gaze never straying from his face. "I like to study. And to touch." Her voice grew breathier. "To feel and to savor."

The heat was back, instant and unrelenting. He'd fought it valiantly for the half hour they'd been outside, but it surged back inside him. Every one of his senses was on alert, reacting to her nearness. Unbidden, his body moved closer. Closer. Close enough so they were sharing breaths and warmth and a physical desire that hung between them like a curtain.

"What about taste? Do you explore with your mouth?" He lifted his finger and brushed it across her full lower lip, tracing the soft skin in an intimate caress.

She licked at his skin, then bit the tip of his finger with her sharp white teeth. The contact was as exciting as it was unexpected. Jade was a little wild. He'd known that before they met. Now that wildness appeared to be driving her right back into his arms. And he didn't know if he'd be strong enough to step away this time.

"We done talking about the weather?" she asked, her whisper not taunting, not too assured, but full of a kind of hunger he hadn't heard in her voice before.

As if she, too, had recognized that, whatever had brought them both out here before, now there was nothing but pure, physical attraction.

He was as completely unable to resist it as any drowning man could resist grabbing on to a life ring. He needed her. To keep breathing. To keep surviving. To keep *living*.

So he took what she offered. He pulled her close, held her tight and lost himself in another deep kiss.

Whatever happened was going to happen, there was no escaping it anymore. Logic and tight control had evaporated under a mindless want and wild excitement he'd never experienced with anyone before.

He should be furious…with *himself*. But he had to acknowledge the truth. He planned to enjoy every blasted moment of it.

5

Now, Jade. Now.

It was time to act, to go ahead with her plan. If she didn't act now, she might lose all sense of purpose and forget that this wasn't a real seduction, a real interlude in a secret garden.

Besides, it was nearing midnight. Not pumpkin time. But toasting time. "Do you like to play sweet, wicked games, Ryan?" she asked when they drew apart for air.

He pressed his mouth to her neck, nibbling her pulse point. "Games? Fantasy games?"

She couldn't hold back a moan as his kiss grew hotter, deeper, and her mind filled with a dark fantasy of seductive vampires in shadowy Southern gardens.

"Yes," she finally replied, shifting on the bench so they were face-to-face. Her legs splayed, and the tight dress pushed higher up her thighs. She lifted them over his legs and slid closer, driving them both to the brink of pure sexual surrender.

"Wicked, naughty games. Fantasies. I've been having them ever since I saw you inside."

True. He just didn't have to know some of those fantasies included him being strung up by his private parts.

Speaking of private parts…his were definitely rising

to the occasion. She felt his heat, his thickness, against her leg, and nearly shuddered. Her revenge plan did not include actually getting to sample that impressive bulge of his in any way.

More's the pity.

"Tell me your fantasy, Jade. Are you a Southern belle stealing away to meet a forbidden lover?"

His whisper was husky, telling her he was just as affected by what was happening as she.

"Do you want me to be a dark stranger you stumble across in the dark? That isn't very far from the truth."

"No." *A vampire, a vampire*, she mentally answered, but she couldn't let the words escape her lips. Vampires weren't known to get naked in the moonlight.

"Tell me," he ordered. He lifted his mouth and brushed his lips against hers. She understood his tactic. He was taunting her, withholding more of those delightful kisses, nips and tastes until she admitted what she was thinking.

Good thing she'd thought this out in advance or she'd admit what she was really thinking—pulling her dress high enough to reveal her nakedness underneath, then unzipping his clothes and rubbing against all his hot skin until she came right on his lap. Then taking him for the ride of his life.

Not the plan, Jade. He's the one who's got to get caught and humiliated, not both of you.

Damn.

"You'll make my fantasy come true?"

He nodded, nipping at her lips, rubbing the tips of his fingers delicately along the neckline of her dress.

The contact electrified her and shot the tension up another notch. "I picture you naked in the moonlight."

"Not much of a fantasy," he replied as his fingers dipped lower, making incredible contact with her breast, but pulling away so quickly it nearly pained her instead of pleasuring her.

"There's more," she whispered, as they kissed again and again and she lowered her hand down his body.

She toyed with the buttons of his dress shirt, slipping them out, one by one. When she reached the waistband of his pants, she undid his belt and tugged the shirt free.

"Oh, God," he whispered as she ran her hand up his naked stomach and dug into those impossibly broad shoulders.

Focus. Focus, Jade, she told herself as he began to work the same magic. His hands were expert, smoothing here, pressing harder there, until he had her ready to go out of her mind with the need for a more intimate touch. He finally kissed her deeply again as he tugged the strap of her dress down and moved his hand to her breast.

She couldn't prevent a tiny cry from escaping her lips. "Oh, Ryan…"

He pulled away to look at her, then lowered his mouth to her breast. The touch of his fingers on her nipple had her writhing.

If this was going to happen, it had to happen immediately, or she was going to lose her resolve and have wild sex with a stranger in Mamie Brandywine's garden.

"Strip for me," she whispered.

He raised his head and looked at her, a half smile on his lips. "What?"

She looked at his body, not feigning a pure feminine appreciation for the long ridges of muscle and perfectly toned skin. "I want to watch you take off your clothes. I want you to reveal every inch of your body to me, with no touching. The anticipation is going to drive me out of my mind."

He began to laugh and tried to kiss her again. She put her hands over his lips. "I mean it, Ryan. I have this...this visual thing. I have extraordinary night vision and all my life I've been a creature of the night. I need to fill my eyes with you."

And she did. She longed to. Especially knowing that's all she could ever have.

"Because then when I fill my body with you," she continued, letting him hear her shaking arousal, "the pleasure will be so intense I don't know if I'll survive it."

He didn't respond for a moment. Then, without another word, he stood up and backed away from the bench. She wondered if she'd pushed too far, overplayed her hand.

When he dropped his white dress shirt off his shoulders, she knew she hadn't.

"Oh, my goodness," she whispered, not faking the response to seeing his thick arms, impossibly broad shoulders and hard, massive chest. "You hid so much beneath your suit."

He smiled. "You hide a lot behind your brown eyes."

"So we're even," she said on a breath, waiting for him to continue.

He reached for his waistband. But, heaven help her, Jade wasn't ready for that. She didn't know if she'd be able to withstand full-frontal without jumping on the man. Or at least tasting him a bit.

She shook her head, thrusting the sensual image from her mind, and pointed to his feet. His answering laugh said he knew what she wanted. "Anticipation, right?"

She nodded.

He took off his shoes and his socks, standing in bare feet and trousers just inches away, right in front of the gurgling fountain.

Reaching for his waist, he paused before unzipping. "Fair's fair, though. I don't think I got much of a glimpse of you."

She'd expected this. Giving him a mysterious smile, she reached for the other strap of her dress and pushed it down. Then, around her back, undoing the zipper just low enough to make the dress loosen across her breasts.

But before she let the black fabric drop away, she whispered, "I like to see, but I'm a little shy about being seen."

A snort of disbelief was his only answer.

"All right," she admitted. "Not shy...I like being mysterious." She showed him what she meant by drawing her red scarf around her shoulders and letting the two ends drape down her front. Then, and only then, did she allow the front of her dress to drop.

He watched, his expression hungry, as she moved the silky scarf across her taut nipples, almost cooing at the sensation.

"You're right," he whispered, wonder and surprise in his voice. "Anticipation is a wonderful thing."

She didn't know whether to be glad or disappointed that he hadn't insisted she remove the scarf. A big part of her—actually, two smaller, incredibly *sensitive* parts of her—were dying for his full attention. His eyes, his hands, his mouth. She wanted them all on her breasts.

Not in the plan.

"Now, Ryan?" she asked, not having to fake her sudden frenzy. She had to get this over with. It was nearly midnight. She could already see shadows of people moving into the solarium, where they'd gather to fill their champagne glasses for the toast.

He reached for his pants. Unzipped. Pushed them down. Jade watched through half-lowered lashes, not sure whether to be relieved or disappointed that he was wearing boxers underneath. Then it was time to move. She couldn't wait here, couldn't possibly watch him go one more step…couldn't get an eyeful of what she was leaving behind.

This was close enough.

She rose to her feet and approached him, still running the scarf across her nipples, keeping his attention firmly focused there.

"You done anticipating?" he asked.

"I have to touch you."

And she did. She stroked his shoulders, his stomach, all the while pushing him back, closer to the fountain. "Do you feel the spray against you?"

He nodded, leaning down to nip her neck, trying to nudge the scarf away from her breasts.

"It's so cool, isn't it?" she whispered. "Feels good against your hot skin."

Then she stopped speaking and simply let her body take over. She pressed against him, rubbing the silk between them with perfectly delicious friction. His groan told her how much he liked it.

It was so easy to rise on tiptoe, using a stone step below the fountain to bring her breasts closer to his mouth. She drew the scarf away slowly, inch by inch. Sliding it up over his head, she had it behind his back within a brief moment.

He didn't even notice. He was completely focused on her bared breasts. Focused on licking them, tasting them, drawing a nipple into his mouth with a suction so strong, so pleasurable it almost pained her.

"Just your mouth," she ordered when he tried to move his hands up to cup her.

He laughed against her chest, letting her capture his hands in her own, the scarf still sliding behind him.

Right around the back of one of the fountain cherubs. Through a loop over its wing. Then two quick twists around Ryan's hands and she was done.

"Jade?" He sounded only slightly alarmed.

"Don't you love this? Doesn't the silk feel amazing?" she replied, a little lost herself as he continued to lick her breasts.

Then she saw the lawn grow brighter, illuminated with the first of the floodlights, and knew it was time.

"Jade, I think someone's coming outside."

She didn't answer. She couldn't answer, she was suddenly so torn over what she was doing.

She wanted him, wanted him so badly. And what she was about to do would put him forever out of her reach.

Amazing sex with a fabulous stranger.

Or avenging her little sister.

As always in her life, family—loyalty to the other Dupré women—won out.

Without another word, she pulled away, bent down and yanked at his boxers. She had to pull them away from his body to get them over the massive erection, but Jade wasn't a strong enough woman to look. She kept her eyes firmly shut until the cotton hit the ground. Then she pulled up her dress.

And ran.

HE WAS GOING TO KILL her. Wrap his hands around her pretty pale throat and wring her conniving neck.

Ryan had never been so completely...*bested* by anyone.

Thankfully, her scheme to embarrass the hell out of him hadn't been a complete success. Yes, he'd been caught naked and alone, aroused, exposed and tied to a frigging statue.

But he hadn't been spotted by the entire crowd, as Jade had obviously hoped.

No, thankfully the only people who'd gotten the full view of him were Mamie Brandywine, owner of the inn, and Tally Jackson. The two women had stood framed in the doorway of the house, staring at him from across the yard. Their mouths had dropped.

So had their eyes. Down—straight down.

"Shit." The thought still made him cringe hours later in his bed.

Luckily, the two women had immediately backed into the house, telling the crowd some nonsense story about a sudden burst of rain falling on the lawn. So Ryan had had time to work free of the red scarf and pull on his clothes while cloaked in the shadows of the huge trees nearby.

Then he'd gone looking for Jade, slipping out of the garden through the back gate she'd used. But she'd disappeared like...a thief in the night.

Lying in his room late that night, he realized that, as furious as he was, he also had to hand it to her. She was good at what she did. Even if what she did was lie and cheat and steal and seduce.

Seduce. God in heaven, she really had. He'd gone down to that garden prepared to make her trust him, to reveal her secrets, so he could get some insight as to what she might have done with the painting.

Instead she'd kissed him. She'd invited him to touch

her. Her smell and the night air and the wind in the trees had successfully robbed him of all logic and made him give in to the most sensuous desire he'd ever felt. *Still* felt.

"Damn," he muttered in the darkness. He still wanted her, was rock hard again just thinking about how close they'd come.

"How close *you* came, moron. She was *a*cting the entire time."

But even as he whispered the words, he wondered if they were true. Jade might have set him up for a fall, then walked away—shoeless—laughing when he fell. But he'd guaran-damn-tee her legs had been wobbling a little bit during that walk.

He dangled one of her strappy, spike-heeled sandals—which he'd found on the patio where she'd left them—from the tip of his finger. "Cinderella you're not. And I'm sure as hell no Prince Charming."

She probably didn't realize he knew all about her— her full name, where she lived, how to find her, and how to get revenge. He didn't need a shoe to track down the girl who'd run away at midnight.

He'd give her her shoes back. No question about it. While he was at it, he'd force her to admit the truth. "She wanted me," he whispered aloud, certain he was right.

She had wanted more. She'd been just as lost as he had for a few minutes. Lost in that strange, powerful reaction they'd created in one another. If the light in the window hadn't come on...if there hadn't been a threat of exposure...if she'd been thinking only with the lower part of her body—as he had been—they might both have been caught in her spider web.

A knock sounded on his door, soft, tentative. "Now what?" he muttered.

"Mr. Stoddard? Would you like some company? Someone to talk things over with? May I come in for a little while?"

Good lord, his landlady. Ever since he'd returned to the house tonight, going in through a back kitchen door to avoid seeing anyone, she'd been tracking him. The look in her eyes when she'd seen him naked and hard was going to give him nightmares.

Good thing he'd locked the door. And put a chair under the knob, just in case the owner of the house decided to try testing her luck with a master key.

She knocked once or twice more. He remained silent, not wanting to have to change inns in the middle of the night.

Finally her footsteps moved away and he breathed a deep sigh of relief. He'd leave early tomorrow morning. No way was he going to stay here and risk getting attacked by an overly amorous old married lady who'd seen what he had to offer and wanted to take a closer look.

"I'll get you for this, Jade Maguire," he whispered softly so the inn owner wouldn't hear.

He'd come here to retrieve his grandmother's stolen property. That had been serious enough. Now things had gotten *really* personal. This battle had turned downright intimate.

Jade might have won the first skirmish. She might even have seen his…*weapon.*

But he had not yet begun to fight.

JADE NOTICED THE obnoxious tourist immediately upon meeting her tour group at the cemetery the following night. She couldn't stand the type. Loud, inconsiderate, not caring about the history of the area he was about to visit, but only wanting to act manly and disbelieving of the haunted stories he'd paid to hear.

She knew what he was thinking. His whole demeanor demanded, "Scare me or I'll want my money back." She'd met his kind before and, on every occasion, they'd nearly ruined an otherwise successful tour.

"I'm going to kill Freddy for this," she told Daisy, her employee, the guide who'd just completed the early evening ghost tour of Savannah.

"I think this is the fifth time he's called in sick this month," Daisy said, sounding disgusted. "You know I'd take it if I could."

Jade looked at her best worker and good friend. "I know you would. I'm sorry, I'm not blaming you. I know how you've been looking forward to your boyfriend coming home."

Jade didn't add the next words that crossed her mind—from jail. But Daisy probably knew she'd thought them.

The young girl was a doll. Supportive, hard-working. Much too good for the car-stealing jerk she loved.

So what if Daisy was a goth, transplanted from New Orleans, who was still into the Louisiana vampire culture? The black clothes, black spiked hair, black nails and black circles around her eyes worked well for the night tours. That's why Daisy had become the most popular guide Jade employed. Worth every penny it had taken Jade to lure her away from her second cousin, who ran a similar company down in New Orleans.

Freddy, on the other hand, wasn't worth the trouble it was going to take to fire him. She'd already started looking for someone else, not only because Freddy wasn't dependable. He also had a nasty habit of hitting on the unattached women in his tour groups.

"Are we going on this thing or what?" the loud man in the back asked.

Jade smothered a sigh. She'd known he'd be trouble when she saw his long shorts, coupled with shin-high white socks with the requisite red stripe around the elastic top. She hadn't even needed to see the brightly-flowered Hawaiian shirt, camera slung around his neck, big ugly glasses and ball cap to know he had "difficult" and "tasteless" written all over him.

"We'll be departing in a few minutes," Jade told the audience, implicitly telling the man to be patient.

The crowd was a big one tonight. Mostly college-age kids and young adults. The families typically came to the early tour, not this one, which wouldn't end until ten-thirty, at the Winter Garden inn.

Pushy tourists, however, seemed to show up at every single one. Lucky her.

"We gonna actually see any ghosts on this tour? Or just hear made-up stories about them?"

Jade shot the gum-chewing loudmouth a look that told him to shut up. He merely smirked, his long mustache covering his top lip so that he looked like a walrus.

"Don't give the city any more ghosts tonight," Daisy said, sounding amused. "We have enough murder victims for the tour. And I can't afford to be out of work because my boss is doing ten to twenty for justifiable homicide."

"Justifiable being the key," she replied, giving Daisy a wry look.

Daisy grinned, the happy look somewhat incongruous given her blood-red lips and paste-white skin, but the goodness shone through. Daisy was the first to admit she wasn't a vampire wannabe, merely a player.

She liked the look, but nothing else that went with it. That was one of the reasons she'd left New Orleans, which sometimes took its "playing" a little too seriously.

Jade was so glad she had. She valued Daisy's friendship, and squeezed her hand to let her know it. "If things don't go well tonight…"

"They will," Daisy said, not letting anything spoil her vision of her reunion with her ex-con boyfriend.

"I mean *if* they don't…then come by, okay? I'm sure I'll be up late."

Daisy smirked. "If I thought you'd be up late for the right reason—because you actually had a man in your bed, instead of a juicy book and a vibrator—I wouldn't come anywhere near your place."

Rolling her eyes, Jade didn't admit that Daisy's description was probably closer to the truth than anyone would realize. Except for the vibrator part. She wouldn't dare such a thing with Auntie Lula Mae staying with her. The old woman had ears like a hawk and would demand to know what the buzzing sound was. And once she'd seen the cute little toy—which Jade had bought off an Internet site when she'd hit fifteen months straight without sex—she'd probably want to know how to get one of her own.

Eeew.

But once Lula Mae returned home to Mama's house…well, Jade predicted her vibrating friend would get a good workout. She certainly could have used it after her incredible interlude with Ryan Stoddard the night before.

She still shook, remembering the intensity of feeling—of pleasure—they'd shared in the Medford garden. If the light hadn't come on, she might very well have been the one caught bare-ass naked by the fountain. Because she'd wanted nothing more at that moment other than him. Nothing. But. Him.

"Have fun," Daisy said as she walked off down the street.

Jade grimaced, waved goodbye, and led the group past the cemetery. She'd have to keep a smile on her face and ignore the troublemakers on the tour. As well as put any and all evil, distracting thoughts of sex out of her mind. This was her livelihood, after all.

There was one surefire way to make sure she kept a smile on her face. All she had to do was think about Ryan Stoddard, tied up, naked and discovered by fifty or so tuxedoed millionaires.

Naked. Humiliated. Embarrassed. Paid back. Unfulfilled.

Okay, that wasn't so satisfying, since they'd *both* been unfulfilled. Anyway, somehow, *naked* and *Ryan Stoddard* were three words she shouldn't have put in the same sentence.

God, he'd been glorious. Impossibly big and hard and toned and perfect. Covered with smooth skin that still made her fingers itch to touch, nearly twenty-four hours later.

Walking away had been about punishing him. But it had punished her as well. She'd never been as physically aroused by a man as she had in those moments before she'd remembered she was out for revenge. Not orgasms.

Though, those would have been pretty nice, too.

No, not from him. Vibrators were just as efficient, and they didn't go around seducing twenty-one-year-olds.

Or, if they did, at least they could be put back in a drawer.

"Next week. A woman can survive one week without a man or a vibrator," she told herself.

Though, to be honest, she found herself wishing Aunt Lula Mae were a little more hard of hearing, as were most people her age.

"Where's the ghosts?" she heard from a dozen people back.

Mr. Obnoxious.

Pasting a smile on her face, she thrust the incredible memory of Ryan Stoddard's body and face and hands and mouth out of her mind. He was out of her life. Probably out of Savannah after the embarrassment he'd suffered the night before. She'd never see him again, and he'd think twice about the women he went after.

All's well that ends well.

But that still didn't dispel the hint of emptiness inside her when she imagined what might have been.

6

SHE HADN'T RECOGNIZED him. She'd noticed him—oh, he'd made absolutely sure she'd notice him. If he'd tried to blend in and be unobtrusive, she'd probably have paid more attention. Deceptive people were sneaky and untrusting that way.

So Ryan had gone out of his way to be as obvious as possible.

If any of his buddies, clients or former girlfriends could see him now—dressed like one of those old farts who cruised the mall, looking for high school girls in tight shorts to drool over...

It was a perfect disguise.

Ryan had even begun to enjoy the tour once he'd let down his guard a bit. Jade stayed far away from him after his one attempt to move up front. He'd almost laughed when he'd sidled up behind her. He'd been right under her nose, hidden behind some saggy, hideously ugly clothes, a ball cap, thick eyeglasses complete with ugly black rims and a fake mustache.

She'd never even realized. She'd moved away, putting several people between them, and hadn't paid him a bit of attention since.

He had to hand it to her—she wasn't bad at her job. She had a natural theatrical flare, not surprising since she'd proven herself such a consummate actress last night.

But there was more than performance. She seemed passionate about her work. She answered questions about the history and architecture of the area without a moment's hesitation.

So she knew her stuff. Big deal. Any thief would have to have a good memory. The better to maneuver through dark houses. Or dark gardens.

"And here," she was saying somewhere ahead of him, "is the famous bar where an infamous pirate is rumored to demand his rum, even to this day."

A drink. That sounded good. If only to steel himself for what he was about to do to this woman very, very soon.

Last night she'd been the one who'd had the upper hand, and he'd ended up naked and restrained. Tonight, it was her turn.

By the end of the tour, when they reached the Winter Garden House, Ryan had made sure to be as much of a pest as he could. He was definitely the most noticeable one on the tour.

So she'd definitely notice when he disappeared.

He wondered why Jade included the house on the tour, considering it was owned by the wealthy side of her family. According to the tour, the place had been on that side of the family for decades. Did Jade come here night after night to look at what her side had been denied? Perhaps to see the kinds of things—paintings, jewelry, antiques—that she'd coveted but never had as a child?

Damn, he really needed to stop this psychoanalyzing stuff. It was stupid and he was no expert. He knew next to nothing about the woman, so why he'd started pegging her as a poor relation out to right the wrongs done to her ancestors, he had no idea.

Maybe because he didn't want her to be just an average, avaricious thief. Maybe because he wanted to *allow* himself to like her.

Or at least to get involved with her.

"Stupid, stupid," he muttered to himself as the tour finished up. Henry, Jade's uncle, had greeted them briefly, then disappeared somewhere inside the depths of the house. A uniformed waitress supplied everyone on the tour with a complimentary cognac or champagne as Jade wrapped up her story about the ghost who haunted the attic of the building.

Time to act. Now, while the guests tipped her, thanked her, and exited to the street. She was still in the parlor, and a cluster of people were moving through the foyer to the door.

He made his move. "I want to look at the upstairs rooms," he grumbled aloud, scratching his belly and being as disgusting as possible.

His words earned him a look of disdain from one of the women on the tour.

"Paid a lot of money, I should get to see upstairs!" He said the words loudly enough to be overheard, then sauntered away.

From behind him, he heard a buzz of conversation. Ryan merely strolled down the hall as if he owned the place. And up the stairs he went.

It would take about thirty seconds for one of the other customers to rat him out to Jade. Sixty more to usher everyone else out of the house. She'd be looking for him immediately thereafter.

Lucky for him this was a weeknight and the inn was relatively empty. Only two other upstairs rooms were occupied and both had their doors firmly shut. After darting into his own room, he turned on a light, sat in one of the antique frou-frou chairs…and waited.

"Sir. Sir, you can't be up here!"

A minute and a half. Damn, she was quick.

"Huh?" he asked, rising to his feet as Jade rushed into the room, her fists clenched, her face red.

"You cannot come upstairs to the private rooms. Mr. Porter allows us to visit the downstairs rooms only. You need to leave immediately."

Keeping his cap down in case the mustache and big, ugly glasses weren't a good enough disguise, he lifted his camera. Continuing to mimic the guy with the thick Bronx accent who'd done some repair work for him last month, he said, "I just wanted to get some pictures of this here old bed. People musta been sleepin' awful cozy in the old days." Then he cackled. "And I bet it squeaked when the getting got good."

She sighed heavily, looking disgusted. Ryan didn't know whether to be delighted with his own performance, or offended that she really thought he was some tasteless, tacky tourist.

"I must insist that you come with me right now."

She stepped closer. Closer. One step more. Until he *had* her.

Quick as he could, he moved behind her and shut the door. The old-fashioned lock worked—he'd tested it earlier. It was easy enough to twist the lock and drop the key into his pocket.

"What do you think you're doing?" Jade asked, looking more outraged than afraid.

He didn't answer. Instead he reached for the long strap of his camera and carefully lifted it over his head, not removing the cap.

"Unlock the door right now, or I'll call for help."

"Will you?" he asked, no longer trying to hide his real voice.

He reached for the top button of the hideous Hawaiian shirt and began to undo it. Jade's eyes widened as she began to realize the kind of trouble she could be in.

He was tempted to let her be afraid, but something inside him resisted. He wanted her afraid of *him*. Of his retribution. But not that some whacked out stranger was about to rape her.

"I know karate and I have a wicked herpes outbreak," she said, her voice thready. She curled her fingers into fists at her sides, obviously prepared to fight him in spite of her fear.

Ryan couldn't help laughing as he finally lifted the ball cap from his head and pulled the glasses from his face. "Well, then, I guess I should count myself lucky you stopped things where you did last night."

Then she got it. Her jaw dropped and she stepped back, wrapping her fingers in the velvety antique curtains behind her.

"Ryan…"

He peeled off the mustache, wincing a little as the spirit gum stuck to his lip. "Hello, Jade."

"How did you find me?" she asked, her voice breathy. She looked more nervous now than when she'd feared he was a rapist.

He didn't answer at first, merely letting the tension build as he unfastened another button. Then another. She never took her eyes off him and he'd swear her breathing picked up its pace as more and more of his body was revealed.

He'd been right—she hadn't faked her responses

last night. She'd wanted him. Badly. Which would definitely work to his advantage now.

"Did you really think you were going to be so hard to track down?" He could hear the tightly controlled anger in his own voice as the memory of what had happened between them last night returned full-force.

He'd been totally focused on what she'd done, leaving him there naked and humiliated. Now he was remembering more. How she'd felt in his arms. How her lips had tasted. The way her hands had touched him.

He didn't know whether to tear her clothes off and finish what they'd started or lock her in the closet for tormenting him.

"I, uh, figured you'd leave the city this morning. As soon as you were able."

He stepped closer. She stepped back. "You figured wrong. And by the way, your scheme didn't exactly work."

For the first time, she looked less nervous and more surprised. "It didn't?"

Shaking his head, he quirked a half smile, full of condescension, not amusement. "Your friend Tally spotted me. She made sure the guests didn't come out for their toast."

He didn't tell her about the amorous old innkeeper spying him, too. That would have given her too much satisfaction.

"So, all's well that ends well," she said with a nervous laugh, and he sensed the irony in her words. She tried to step around him. "Just a little joke and no harm done, right?"

He moved yet again, blocking her way with his body. After undoing the last button of the hideous shirt, he pushed it from his shoulders.

"Wh-what are you doing?" she asked. The lick of her lips and the shake in her voice indicated where her thoughts had gone.

To him. Undressing. In a bedroom. One night after they'd been so incredibly intimate in so many ways.

"Do you know how unpleasant it was to wear this disguise?" he asked. "I had to buy this shirt at a used clothing store."

The shirt dropped to the floor. Her eyes dropped to his chest, his stomach.

When he reached for the fastening of the ugly old-man shorts, her eyes dropped again. "You can't…"

"Can't what? Can't take off the ridiculous disguise I had to wear in order to get you alone again?"

Her stare never wavered as he unbuttoned the shorts, unzipped the zipper, and dropped them to the floor.

"Oh, my God," she whispered, reaching up to clutch her throat.

"Nothing you haven't seen before, is it, Jade? Though, you didn't stick around long enough to really see how you affected me last night."

She could see now, though. Her whole face was flushed, her lips parted and wet as she stared at him. All of him, including the erection he wasn't trying to hide.

He'd always assumed he was a normally built man. But the shocked hunger in her eyes told him he'd caught her off guard.

"No, you're right. I d-didn't see you that well," she stammered.

He kicked off the ugly shoes, then bent to peel off the socks. Then he rose, standing in front of her completely naked. Uncaring, not bothering even to pretend to be self-conscious.

She looked like she wanted to run. She looked like she wanted to jump on him. She looked like she needed someone to tell her what to do.

So he did.

"Take off your dress and get into the bed, Jade."

Noooo, no, this couldn't be happening. Not to her. Not here. Not with *him*.

But it was. She was so hungry, so full of want for this man that she couldn't think, couldn't move, couldn't breathe.

He'd just ordered her to strip and get into bed. Jade didn't take orders from anybody. And yet she wanted to do as he said more than she'd ever wanted anything.

She wanted *him*. All of him. His mouth, those incredibly thick arms. The flat washboard stomach, rippled with muscles, slimming down into a pair of lean male hips. And, oh mercy, *lower.* He was thick and hard and throbbing and he hadn't so much as touched her.

Lucky thing she hadn't looked carefully last night before she'd mustered up her last bit of willpower and escaped through the back gate. Because if she'd seen what she was giving up, she might never have left.

For one moment, a shot of gladness swept through her that no other woman at the party last night had seen him either—other than Tally, who was notoriously vain about her looks and hadn't been wearing her glasses. So she couldn't have gotten too good a look.

Why she felt territorial over this man—a man she'd sworn she hated—she had no idea. But she did. She *did*.

"You can't force me," she whispered, trying to come up with some resolve.

"You owe me."

"I owe you sex?"

He shook his head. "Sex isn't the right word."

"An apology? Okay, I'm sorry."

"That's not it, either, though I'm glad to hear you say it."

He obviously hadn't heard the sarcasm in her voice.

"Even though I know you don't mean it."

Maybe he had.

"I mean, you owe me a chance."

A chance for…revenge? To punish her? Hurt her in some diabolical way as she'd hurt him? "To do what?"

He lifted his hand to her face and ran his fingers across her lips. She couldn't resist nipping at them. The frustration inside her required the outlet. It was incredibly tense to stand here fully clothed, with a fully aroused, powerful, gorgeous naked man.

"I mean," he continued softly, "you owe me a chance to convince you to stay this time."

That rocked her right in her shoes. But before she could respond, he curled his hand around her head, wrapping his fingers in her hair. Not giving her time to refuse, he pulled her close, capturing her mouth in a kiss full of heat and anger, desire and lust. His tongue swept over hers as he nearly drank from her, consuming every bit of energy she might otherwise have used to protest.

When he finally pulled away, he looked down at her with wide eyes. His lips were parted, his breathing ragged. And between him, the hard, living proof of his hunger grew even harder. Stronger. Until she couldn't help but reach down and encircle him with her hand.

He groaned, low and long, as she caressed him, stroking his length with her fingers, giving out a helpless little whimper of her own at the feel of all that satin skin around that rock-hard heat.

"Give me a chance to make you *unable* to walk away this time," he whispered hoarsely.

Jade could no more resist than she could have said no to a chance for eternal happiness. There was no thinking. No logic. No revenge, remorse or family loyalty.

Nothing but overpowering *want*.

Stepping back, she reached around and unfastened her long black skirt. It fell to her feet and she kicked it aside. Ryan's eyes devoured her as hers had done with him. She hadn't gotten this far undressed last night.

"Ahh...I never got to find out what you were wearing under your dress," he murmured as he reached for her hip. He toyed with the elastic strap of her silky black thong, tugging it away from her skin and caressing her with his fingertips. "Was it something like this?"

She shook her head, reaching up to tug her tight tank top up and over her head. "Actually," she said as she threw it to the floor, "it was nothing like this. I mean *nothing*."

He smiled, catching her meaning. "Somehow I knew you were bold enough to come to that party without any underwear."

She smiled back. Then the lightness faded away and he simply stared at her clad in her black sandals, the panties and a matching lacy black bra that pushed her breasts up in pure invitation.

"You're beautiful," he said, wrapping his arms around her waist and pulling her close. He nuzzled her chest, running his tongue over the curves of her breast. When he slipped lower, to tease one achingly sensitive nipple, she shuddered. Her legs felt weak, unable to support her, and she leaned into him.

"To bed, Jade," he said, sweeping her up into his arms and carrying her across the room.

"Please tell me you didn't just steal this room," she whispered before she was completely lost to sensation.

He chuckled. "I'm registered. It's my room."

"Thank heaven."

Then she gave herself over to it, to the insane frenzy she'd felt for this man since the moment she'd laid eyes on him.

He slowly stripped off her sandals and her panties, stroking her long legs, running his hand teasingly across her curls until she shivered.

"Please…"

"Absolutely."

He reached for the front clasp of her bra and undid it with two fingers, watching as it popped open. A deep groan told her how much he liked what he saw.

"Lie back," he ordered, nudging her over on the bed as he knelt beside her. She did, raising her arms above her head and writhing on the sheets, loving the coolness of them against her skin.

"Tell me you wanted me last night," he murmured against her breast. "That whatever the hell made you do it, it was just as painful for you to walk away as it was for me to see you leave."

She couldn't lie. Not now, when he was touching her like this. Not when he was absolutely right. "I wanted you," she admitted, her voice breaking as he lavished attention on one sensitive nipple with his mouth, and the other with his fingertips. "So much I sat in my car and shook for ten minutes afterward."

"Yeah? Well I stood in my shower and jacked off for ten minutes afterward."

She groaned, inflamed by the hot, exciting words,

just as she was inflamed by the amazing things his hands and mouth were doing to her.

She closed her eyes, savoring it all. Every sensation built upon the last one. His touch, his smell, the way his lips felt…there, oh, yes, there on her neck…and on her jaw. The way his strong, rough hands slid up each arm as he covered her. The clasp of their fingers.

And then…

"What are you doing?" she said when she felt the first chill of cold metal against her wrist.

Before she had her answer, the second one was equally enclosed.

"Handcuffs?" she said, realizing he'd restrained her. He'd handcuffed her to the bed.

Under other circumstances, she might have enjoyed something so naughty. But this was their first time. And he hadn't asked. He'd simply gone ahead with something that was usually reserved for a bit later in a relationship. Like at least past the first date!

"I'm not comfortable with this, Ryan," she said, looking him in the eye to convey her seriousness.

He met her stare intently, then pressed one quick kiss against her lips. "I'm sorry, babe," he said. "You don't have a choice."

She only began to understand when he rose from the bed and reached for a pair of jeans draped on a nearby chair.

No, he couldn't be doing this. Couldn't possibly have done this to her all for…

"Paybacks are hell, Jade."

She heard the regretful tone in his voice but chose to ignore it, focusing only on her rising fury. "Unfasten me right now, you bastard."

He shook his head, calmly pulling on a black T-shirt.

He watched her strain and twist against the cuffs. If he'd smirked, if he'd looked triumphant, she probably would have found the adrenaline to rip the frigging headboard apart. But he continued to look sorry so she tried to calm down. "Okay. I probably deserved this. I did something pretty wicked to you last night."

Not that he hadn't deserved it, too.

"Someday you'll have to tell me why you did it."

Over her dead body. So he could go off and torment Jenny with the same kind of revenge? Not a chance.

God, the thought of him with her younger sister made her sick. She couldn't believe she'd forgotten, in these few intensely erotic minutes, that she couldn't have him. She hated the idea of him sharing anything this intimate with Jenny. Hated imagining Jenny seeing him, being touched by him.

But probably *not* being handcuffed by him.

"I…I thought you were too cocky," she said, scrambling for something that sounded reasonable. "I was trying to bring you down a peg. Teach you not to be so overconfident with women."

He leveled a stare on her, thankfully keeping his attention focused on her face and not on her naked body so completely at his mercy. "And I suppose you've never heard of just telling a guy no?"

Okay, lame story and he wasn't buying it. "Look, you're right, it was awful and I regret it." She wiggled the handcuffs. "Really, *really* regret it. So let's call it even. Okay?"

He sat in the chair, pulling on some shoes. "Sorry. Too late." Without another word, he stood and walked over to her pile of clothes. "Just in case you somehow manage to make like Houdini…" He picked them up—skirt, top, sandals, undies and all—and headed toward the door.

"Dammit, Ryan, get back here! You can't do this to me." She couldn't imagine anything worse than being left here, exposed, naked, vulnerable.

He looked over his shoulder. "I think you need a lesson. Be thankful I'm not leaving the door open so you can be spotted by anyone happening along."

Okay, *that* would be worse.

When he reached for the knob, her hope plummeted, and she tried one last desperate trick. "Ryan," she said, keeping her voice low and seductive, "look, you made your point, just like I did last night. Are we going to let these silly little games get in the way of what we could have together?"

That got him. He froze, hand on knob, and turned to look at her. She stretched sinuously, knowing gravity and a flat surface were helping her body look its absolute best.

He devoured her with his stare. Pure sexual hunger shone on his face and she had to twist a little on the bed as sensations she'd thought he'd killed with the snap of a handcuff returned full-force.

She didn't know what she'd do if he changed his mind. Brain him, or welcome him. Push him off her or dive on top of him herself.

In any case, she felt sure she had succeeded in changing his mind. Right up until the minute he opened the door.

That killed the moment. "You son of a bitch, I'll scream. If you do this, you'd better come back armed, because I'm going to kill you when you unlock me."

His laugh was wicked and made her even more furious. "You won't scream because I don't think you want your uncle Henry finding you like this."

He was right. The fiend.

"And you won't kill me, Jade." He walked the few steps back to the bed. Then he bent down, sliding his hand around her head and capturing her mouth in another of those incredible hot, wet kisses that fed her desire even as it fueled her anger.

When he lifted his mouth, she couldn't say a word, could only stare at him in disbelief.

"Once you're sufficiently paid back for last night," he said, "maybe then we can finish what we started."

While she still panted, reacting from their kiss, trying to decide whether she was bloody furious or aroused enough not to care, he bent down and retrieved something from the floor. "Here. I won't leave you without any of your belongings."

She held out hope that he'd at least give her a shirt or something to cover up. When he dropped her black, spike-heeled shoes—the ones she'd forgotten in the garden the night before—she could only groan. And try to kick him.

He easily evaded her foot. Then he got up, walked to the door and left the room. Leaving her, the always put-together Jade Maguire, naked and handcuffed to his bed.

7

A MONK WOULDN'T HAVE BEEN able to walk out of that bedroom without regretting it the minute he'd shut the door. And Ryan was no damned monk.

"She's gonna be furious," he whispered, leaning against the door, knowing he'd be facing an enraged woman when he returned to the inn. Even more enraged by his parting shot and final kiss. A woman with pride as great as hers would *never* let him take up where they'd left off. She'd be stewing over it, getting herself good and worked up and ready to rip him apart the minute he walked back in the room.

No second chance. No forgiveness. Certainly no body-rocking sex, which he needed right now like a starving man needed food.

But only with her. How could he deal with that? The only woman he wanted—the only woman he literally hungered for—was doomed to hate his guts forever and ever, amen.

Maybe it was just as well. He would need her hatred, her anger, to keep his defenses up. He'd come here to Savannah to expose her as a thief. To retrieve his family's property.

Not to become her lover. Not to worship every inch of her body, starting with her curved foot and those endlessly long soft legs. Not to kiss the hollow of her stomach or sample again the dusky sweet nipples he could still taste on his tongue. Not to find her secrets buried behind the curly patch between her legs.

Not to discover why he was affected by her as he'd never been affected by any other woman in his whole life.

"Moron," he called himself, thrusting away from the door to stalk down the stairs, trying to shake off his lust with every pounding step. He was going to lose it in his pants if he let his mind go down that road again. Once he got back from his mission, freed her and was alone again, he'd take care of himself. His hand would be a poor substitute for any part of the body he'd left lying on his bed. But it would have to do.

Almost not realizing he was doing it, he lifted Jade's shirt to his face and breathed in her sweet, flowery scent. How twisted was that? He was a total idiot. He'd let a con woman make him start fantasizing about the kind of sexual relationship he'd never known. And maybe about even more.

No way could he ever like, respect and enjoy the company of someone he couldn't trust an inch. Yet those were the feelings he had with Jade whenever he let down his guard, let himself forget why he'd sought her out in the first place. It was easy to forget. Especially when she was in his arms.

Or naked.

Balling her clothes in his fist, he reached into the pocket of her skirt and found what he'd hoped to—a small key ring. He knew her address. The P.I. had given him that. But the keys were a lucky break. Now he wouldn't have to actually break anything while he did his nighttime breaking and entering.

Fifteen minutes later, he was parked on a small,

quiet tree-lined street in an older part of town. Formerly townhouses for the wealthy, the buildings all around had been converted into apartments or condos. Jade's building wasn't exactly shabby, but it had the same worn, run-down feel of the rest of the street. Not for the first time, he wondered about her motives for stealing.

"Maybe she really just needed the money," he mused aloud.

Coming from a wealthy family, and having a good job, he'd never been put in the position of needing money. He liked to think he'd never resort to stealing, but until he was actually tested, he didn't know what he'd do if, say, a loved one needed food, medicine or shelter. It was something to consider, anyway.

He got out of his car, closing the door quietly behind him. As he slipped through the shadows of overgrown trees and bushes, he again noted the condition of the building. The lawn was wild and unkempt, a tangled profusion of vines climbing up one entire wall. Pretty, but dingy-looking at the same time.

He wondered again about her finances. How much money could a tour guide operator make? How much did her family rely on her? The mother was the talk of the town—the poor relation to the wealthy cousin living in the Winter Garden House.

He began to see the possibilities. Perhaps Jade had gone on this stealing spree to support her unusual family, from the man-hopping mother to the self-absorbed actress sister in New York to the old voodoo priestess aunt. It sounded like her mother liked to live the good life. With Jade's father's job as a bartender, perhaps that lifestyle had come at too high a cost.

Now, with Jade's mother having married some guy

and gone off on a cruise, maybe Jade wouldn't be on the hook for everyone else. Supporting herself on a tour guide's salary shouldn't be difficult. Maybe she could give up her other, illegal life.

Like she'd give it up for *him?* A near-stranger? A man who'd left her naked and helpless in a hotel room?

Fat friggin' chance.

Still, the thought that Jade had done what she'd done to help her family made it slightly less awful to imagine. Maybe even more forgivable. And for some crazy reason, he found himself *wanting* to forgive her.

Entering Jade's ground-floor home as quietly as... well, a burglar, he found himself in a dark living room. He paused, letting his eyes adjust to the low light, provided by a single lamp lit deeper inside the apartment.

The hint of light cast enough of a glimmer to let him get a quick layout of the room. Sofas and loveseats, one would think. But not for Jade. She had a few groupings of uncomfortable-looking chairs, but the center of the room was dominated by, of all things, a fountain.

He groaned. Ryan never wanted to look at another fountain again as long as he lived. But he couldn't help giving it a second glance. Talk about your unusual room décor. This one looked like it should have been outside, in a garden. Or, considering the crying angels, maybe even in a graveyard.

The woman had issues.

Moving further into the apartment, he again noticed that, though clean and colorful, Jade's home didn't offer much in the way of standard comforts. He didn't see a television. No stereo. In the kitchen, he found only the basics, devoid of any fancy appliances—no dishwasher at all.

"So where do you stash the good stuff, Jade?" he whispered.

He turned to leave the kitchen, determined to find out, and was shocked to see two white eyes staring back at him from about five feet above the floor.

He blinked. Looked again. They were still there.

"I'm not seeing this."

The eyes spoke. "Don' min' me, Mr. Tief. No silver, no jewels, but don' take my word. You go ahead an' look around."

Holy shit. He knew without a doubt who was speaking to him. Not a ghost. This was the voodoo witch. The one Tally had been talking about at the party. "It's not what you think..."

"How you know what I tink?" Her voice held a rhythmic cadence and her words rolled off her tongue, hinting of island secrets and mysteries.

"I'm not a thief."

Hearing a click, he was caught off guard when she turned on the overhead light. The sharp illumination hurt his darkness-accustomed eyes, and he had to close them.

He was nervous about reopening them, wondering what he'd see. If he had to be discovered, he'd almost prefer to be caught by a gun-toting redneck than a witch.

Finally he steeled himself for anything—including shrunken heads or chicken claws around her neck—and opened his eyes.

She grinned.

So did he. He couldn't help it. She looked very, *very* normal. "Hi."

"Hi, Mr. Tief."

Her polished brown skin was much darker than

Jade's. He wasn't surprised by her race, given what he knew about Jade's family. Her face was smooth and nearly unlined. But her hair was a wiry mix of black and gray, with gray appearing to be the winner. Her smile was accentuated by the whitest, largest teeth he'd ever seen. And she wore an old-lady housecoat that fell to just above a pair of very knobby brown knees. On her feet were bunny slippers.

Okay, no one with bunny slippers on her feet was going to chant a few words and cause all his hair to fall out or make his nuts stop doing their job.

"You find anyt'ing good?" she asked, as matter-of-factly as she'd ask an invited guest.

He shook his head. "You don't understand. I'm not a thief."

"You come here to take something from us?"

"Well…"

"Den you a tief. A good-looking one, though."

"So why haven't you called the police?"

She shrugged. "You not a dangerous man. I can tell as soon as you come in the front door."

She was right, though he felt mildly insulted that he didn't have even the tiniest bit of danger written anywhere on his aura.

"How you get in?"

"I used Jade's key," he admitted.

That didn't seem to phase her, either. She simply nodded. "Where is she?"

He hesitated. If he could get the old woman to help him somehow, maybe he could end this thing tonight. But it probably wouldn't be easy if she found out what he'd done.

She crossed her skinny arms over her old-lady chest and gave him a sideways smile. "What you do with

Jade? And don' lie." She wagged her eyebrows. "I'll know if you lie."

"She's handcuffed to my bed at the Winter Garden House," he found himself saying. Then he groaned, wondering how the hell he'd let those words spill out of his mouth. Maybe she *had* hexed him because he'd had no intention of telling the truth.

The old woman's eyes widened and she let out a bark of laughter that made her whole body shake. The white smile became even whiter. She clutched a chair, almost snorting with laughter, then clapped a hand to her mouth. "Oh, no," she lisped, "there go my good teefs."

He didn't know what she meant until she spat out a full set of dentures into her hand, giving him a wide, gummy grin. He began to laugh with her.

"Din' have time to glue 'dem in right when I hear you comin' in to steal from us." Before he protested, she held up a hand, smooth and work-worn, but still strong and capable. "Don' worry. I know now who you are. You flash de folks at de fancy party last night."

Oh, God, so much for his hope that Tally Jackson and Mamie Brandywine hadn't told their tale. "You heard about that, hmm?"

She shrugged, not explaining. "So you getting even?"

He shrugged. "Sort of."

The old woman casually retrieved a glass, filled it with water and dropped her teeth into it with a little plop. Then she put a pot of water on the stove, retrieved two mugs and a container of tea leaves. "We talk over a drink."

And somehow, though he'd come here to steal what had been stolen, he found himself sitting in a quiet kitchen, drinking a cup of delicious and strangely spiced tea, with Lula Mae Dupré, voodoo priestess of Savannah.

JADE FUMED, CURSED and muttered for the first ten minutes after Ryan had walked out of the room, leaving her helpless on the bed.

Helpless. What an unbelievably awful feeling. Jade hadn't felt helpless, ever. Her mother's romantic life had been a nonstop adventure, but otherwise Jade had been the product of a normal home. Her family—both close and extended—was a secure one. She'd always felt loved, both before and after Daddy's death, and had been raised to believe she could be anyone, achieve absolutely anything.

Except make handcuffs magically open.

"You sneaky S.O.B.," she whispered, finally allowing a bit of reluctant admiration for her adversary to enter her mind. He'd gotten her, but good.

After last night, he had to have figured she had it coming. *She* knew why she'd abandoned him in the garden at the Medford place—because of Jenny. But he didn't know. He must have figured her for some game-playing sexual psycho who got her kicks leading men on, building them up—way, way up, in his case, she recalled with a gulp—then letting them crash and burn.

His retribution was pretty fair, considering he'd at least shut the door to the room. Nobody would be seeing her here, unlike where she'd left him last night.

"That still doesn't mean I'm not going to kill him," she muttered through tight teeth.

But for now, she focused only on covering herself. Bad enough to have to face the man when he got back, knowing he'd won this round. She didn't want to have to do it while stark naked, laid bare for his perusal.

Or his *pursual*.

She couldn't handle that. Couldn't even think of him coming back into the room and doing what he'd threatened—counting the score even and trying to finish what they'd started.

She dreaded that. Not because he couldn't do it but, she was very much afraid, because he *could*.

The outraged sister in her insisted she could resist. The incredibly aroused woman who'd practically begged him to take her knew better.

It took a while, but eventually she was able to grasp the end of the folded-down sheet with her toes and drag it up her body. A contortionist she wasn't. But by lifting her legs all the way up in the air and toward her chest, she managed to drop the covering so it at least reached her midriff. All the wiggling, jiggling, cursing and bouncing wouldn't bring the blasted thing up over her breasts, however. So the man was going to get some peek-a-boo nipple action, but at least nothing farther south.

She'd just begun contemplating whether she should hit him before she got dressed, or after, when the door creaked open.

Jade held her breath, praying it was Ryan, even as she hated the idea of seeing him again.

"Still here, I see," he said as he came into the room.

She shot him a glare. "Like I was going to be able to go anywhere?"

He shrugged. "You're very resourceful."

"Resourceful wouldn't help me drag this eighteenth-century cherrywood bed over to the bathroom."

"You needed to go?"

She glared. "No, I hoped I might be able to find something in your shaving kit so I could unlock these things." Then she added, "And maybe a pair of scissors to attack you with."

He quirked a sideways grin, then began to look her over, head to foot. But he didn't get far, his gaze lingering somewhere below the throat. Her standing-at-attention nipples clued her in on where.

She swallowed a lump of rising awareness. "Unlock me."

"Are you going to attack me?"

"Not sexually," she snapped.

"Bummer," he said with a lift of his shoulders. "How about violently?"

"I'm debating."

"On?"

"On how loud it would be if I crack your head open with that lamp on the dressing table."

He glanced at it and tsked. "Porcelain. Pricey. And probably loud. Not to mention that these floors are wood. The thud would probably be heard all the way to your uncle Henry's room."

He was right. And somehow, drat the man, he was making her want to laugh with the matter-of-fact way he was trying to help her figure out how to attack him. Then again, since she was still handcuffed, he did hold a certain position of power.

"Please unlock me."

"I'm making sure you've calmed down," he replied, returning his gaze to her face and staring at her with a kind of quiet intensity he hadn't shown before.

Jade felt heat rise in her body, up her cheeks. The heat inside her was nothing compared to the expression on his face.

He wanted, all right. Still wanted.

"If you won't unlock me, you can certainly be decent enough to pull the sheet all the way up." Sakes alive, even to her own ears, her tone sounded more provocative than pleading.

"Can I?"

His voice was low, almost a purr, as he approached the bed. She couldn't read the look on his face. No smile, no twinkle in his green eyes to help her gauge his intentions.

Was he about to unlock her? Or strip naked and climb into bed beside her? And which was she really, deep in the innermost part of herself, hoping for?

He knelt on the bed, his knee close to her side, pulling the sheet tighter across her tummy and hips. Then he reached up, already holding a small silver key, and unlocked the cuffs.

She immediately pulled her hands free. Lowering her arms, she rubbed her wrists and shrugged her aching shoulders.

"Let me," he said.

"Hands off. Don't try your tricks on me again."

His expression said he was hurt. "I only wanted to ease the knots."

He reached his hands up again as Jade clutched the sheet to cover the front of her body. She had to tug it a little since he was still kneeling on the bed. He shifted, freeing the sheet and also sitting down beside her.

Then, only then, did Jade give a short nod. A shoulder rub was the least the man could do considering he'd caused the discomfort.

He began to stroke her upper arms, kneading, deep strokes that eased the tight muscles there. Then he moved higher, working on her shoulders, his hands moving over her with both strength and gentleness, as if he knew which she needed when. Jade couldn't help relaxing, dropping her head to the side. From behind her, she heard his breathing grow deeper, slower. More intimate.

Oh, so much more intimate.

She wanted that, so very much. But the thought of those hands, those strong, tender hands, having already touched her sister in the same way was just too much.

It wasn't so much about him *hurting* Jenny. It wasn't even about him locking her up naked and disappearing for an hour. Now this had become much more personal, with so much more at stake.

She simply didn't want to sleep with a man who'd been in bed with her sister. Period.

"I can't do this," she said, her voice shaking.

He didn't remove his hands, but they did pause on her shoulders, touching her with gentle possession but demanding nothing.

"I have to go."

He instantly removed his hands and slid off the bed to stand next to her. It took a moment before she could work up the nerve to turn her head and lift her eyes to meet his.

He looked serious. Intense. Maybe even a little sorrowful.

"I understand." He tossed a bag onto the foot of the bed. "Here are your clothes. Maybe…maybe once you can forget about my, uh, getting even tonight, we can meet again. Start over."

Start over. How lovely that sounded. She wished they could, considering he was the first man she'd ever known who'd both aroused her and completely matched her, wit for wit, in a hot, playful game of up the sexual ante. She had to admit it, if only in her mind, she'd liked their games. Ryan could be a very exciting playmate. In bed, and out of it.

If only she could pretend he was just an incredibly attractive man she'd recently met. That there was no baggage, no revenge schemes between them.

No Jenny.

She wanted to wail at the loss. She wanted this man more than she'd ever wanted anyone. In her life.

Sudden frustration rose and she clawed at her clothes, yanking her tank top on over her head, then tugging the sheet out from under it. Staying under the covers, she maneuvered her panties toward her feet and slid into them.

Clad in that much, at least, she felt a little more confident about her ability to face him. She stood up beside the bed. "It's impossible, Ryan."

"Nothing's impossible." His low, hypnotic voice almost made her believe it.

"I can never be with someone I don't trust and respect," she said. "Or someone who doesn't trust and respect me."

His brow shot up and his mouth dropped open. "Trust and respect?" he said, sounding completely offended. "This from the woman who tied me naked to a statue in a public place?"

"It wasn't public," she retorted.

"About as damn close as you can get."

"You said nobody saw you except Tally. And she wasn't wearing her glasses."

His face turned red and he leaned close. "Mamie Brandywine saw me as well. I had to stick like glue to other people leaving the inn this morning so she wouldn't corner me."

She snickered. Mamie's appetites were well known in Savannah. Half the town pitied her husband. The other half wondered what he wasn't doing to keep her satisfied at home.

Such ran the gossip mill.

She reached for her skirt, bunching it and stepping into the waist, still not trusting herself to look at him.

"Why, Jade? Why can't we even try to make something happen when we both know it's what we want?"

"Maybe we could," she replied without thinking about it, "if only you weren't such a womanizing reprobate."

He gave her a look of such shock and confusion that she almost felt sorry for him. The feeling quickly disappeared when he stepped closer, crowding her until the backs of her legs were against the bed. He'd stepped onto the bunched-up fabric of her skirt, so she was stuck there, with her feet inside it and the material puddled around them.

Grabbing her shoulders, he glared at her. "You've got a lot of nerve. I wasn't the one begging you to get naked in the moonlight. You wanna talk about people moving a little fast…"

She blinked. Was that a tiny bit of fear creeping up her spine? A bit of concern at the fury she heard in his voice and saw in his stiff form? Or maybe it was just excitement at seeing his raw masculine power unleashed.

Ryan had been in many moods since they'd met, but she'd never seen him truly angry. "Do you really want to compare notes on who was the aggressor here?" he asked, his voice shaking.

She jerked away from him, forgetting that her feet were tangled. There was only one way to go—down.

She wound up on her butt on the bed, eye level with his waist, and realized his anger hadn't done much to tamp down his arousal.

Wow. Not much at all.

She blinked her eyes and forced herself to look up toward his face. Sticking out her jaw, she hit him with the accusation she'd meant to keep to herself. "I'm not talking about *me*. I'm a grown woman. I know how to take care of myself around smooth-talkers like you."

He leaned over her, so close she could see the crisp black hairs in the open vee of his black cotton shirt. See the sheen of sweat on his skin and the bunching of his muscles. Slick. Bulging. Powerful. She gulped and tore her stare away.

Fisting his hands, Ryan bent close and put them on either side of her on the mattress, effectively trapping her. "You're not making any sense. You don't know a thing about me. Not about my past, who I've dated. Nothing."

"I know about Jenny," she snapped, trying to keep her wits about her when what she wanted to do was ask him if he knew there were tiny flecks of gold scattered across the green of his eyes. She regretted it as soon as the words left her mouth.

"Who?"

She tried to backpedal. "Never mind."

"No, I do mind. What aren't you telling me?"

"Look, it doesn't matter." Forcing a laugh, she tried to change the subject. "Why are we arguing anyway? It's not that big a deal never to see each other again. You can't want *me* too much if you had me naked and chained to a bed and still walked out the door."

This time, he was the one who barked a laugh. A disbelieving grunt of a laugh. "Not want you? Babe, a man would have to be gay, castrated at birth or had his nads blown off in an industrial accident not to have wanted you."

She sucked her lips into her mouth, both amused and a little mollified at the tormented tone in his voice. Okay, walking out hadn't been easy. That was a relief.

He straightened and crossed his arms, but remained threateningly close, as if silently ordering her to stay seated. "I did it to teach you a lesson about playing games with men you don't know."

"Yeah?" she said, scoffing at him with her tone. "Well, maybe I did that to you for the same reason."

He quirked a brow. "I don't play games with men."

"I sure hope not."

"So what makes you think I play games with women? Go back to what you were saying earlier— about Jenny."

She didn't want to, didn't mean to, didn't plan to. But somehow the words burst out of her anyway. "Jenny Maguire, from New York? She's my sister."

He continued to stare, then nodded slowly. "The waitress who wants to be an actress?"

He didn't even try to deny it, the dog. "Yeah. I guess she got some great acting lessons from you. How to act like you have a heart."

His jaw tightened and the amusement left his face. "Since I only met the girl twice in my life, I don't know what the hell you're talking about."

"Of course you know what I'm talk…" Then she paused as his words sunk in. "Twice?"

"Yeah, twice. Once in the diner where she worked. Once when we went out for lunch. Twice. End of story."

"Twice," she repeated dumbly, wondering what to believe, who to trust. "Jenny said she…she cared for you."

He ran a hand wearily through his hair, rumpling those dark waves into a sexy, bed-tousled disarray. "I don't know what she told you, Jade. But here's the truth. I met her at the diner when she waited on me. I invited her to lunch at one of those tourist traps where you sit in a stage-shaped booth. We ate. We talked. We had our picture taken. We left. I've never seen or spoken to her again."

"Why not?"

"Good grief, she's got to be all of what? Twenty? And I'm supposed to have developed some great passion for her? This is nuts!"

"So why'd you ask her to lunch in the first place?" she shot back.

For the first time, Ryan looked away. He thrust his hands into the pockets of his jeans. Through the worn blue fabric, she could see his fingers curl into fists. "It was a bad idea at a bad moment." He looked up at her through half-lowered lashes, his frown screaming his discomfort at the topic of conversation. "Haven't you ever had a bad idea?"

Oh, good heavens, yes. Like tracking down this guy. Getting involved with him. Getting him naked and tying him up to a little winged cherub statue. And getting herself naked and handcuffed to his bed...*without* him in it.

"I seem to have had nothing *but* bad ideas at bad moments since you and I met," she admitted.

They both fell silent for a long moment. Jade didn't look at him. She merely looked at her hands, trembling against her bare thighs. That slight trembling told her more about her emotional state than her own brain had been able to.

Jenny had lied. Or at least exaggerated. She didn't

seem to recognize the difference. Never had, probably never would.

Once again, the drama queen at the center of her own drama.

The next time she saw her spoiled sibling, Jade was going to have to make her work on that. Or else just slap her silly.

Ryan remained standing a few feet away, obviously as lost in thought as she. "So you thought I was involved with your sister," he finally said.

She corrected him. "I thought you *hurt* my sister. And I was out to, um…correct the injustice."

He merely shook his head. "I'd hate to see how you correct the injustice if someone actually harmed *you*."

She shrugged. "I wouldn't. I can take care of myself. At least usually." She glanced at the handcuffs.

He met her eye, understanding her meaning. Jade wasn't vengeful, not on her own behalf, anyway. But damned if anyone was going to hurt anyone she cared about.

"Point taken," he finally replied.

Then it was her turn to understand. "You thought I was some sick woman who liked picking up men and humiliating them for no reason, which is why you paid me back tonight. Here." She looked at the bed and softly added, "Like this."

"Yeah. We really made a mess of things, didn't we?" he asked.

"A major mess. I'd say this one would have to go in the record books for strange starts to relationships."

"Relationships?" His tone was hopeful. Or maybe Jade just read hope in his voice because she wanted it to be there.

Forgetting that her skirt was tangled around her

feet, she tried to stand up but immediately stumbled. It certainly wasn't by design that she landed right against his body, his warm, *welcoming* body.

His arms instantly reached to steady her, one hand landing below her waist, the other on her arm. Only a tiny scrap of elastic separated his hand from her bare hip and the skin there instantly felt hot and tender.

"What have we done?" he whispered, looking at her for answers she didn't have either.

"We certainly started out all wrong. But we started *something*," she said, not sure where the words had come from but knowing they were the right ones. And she knew, without a doubt, it was something she wanted to continue.

His thumb slid beneath the elastic, caressing her hipbone. The fingers of his other hand scraped delicately up her arm, to her shoulder, then to the nape of her neck.

"So where do we go from here?" He stepped even closer, his warm breath touching her hair as he continued to caress her gently with his fingertips.

"We could go the normal route. You ask me to dinner. I say yes and play hard to get when you walk me to the door."

He continued to delicately touch her neck, so lightly she wondered if she was feeling his fingertips or a bit of breeze stirred up by the lazily turning ceiling fan.

"Considering we've seen each other naked and touched each other as intimately as lovers, I'd say the normal route's a bit of a step backward," he murmured.

She already knew that and was glad he concurred. She hesitated for no longer than a heartbeat. Her voice wasn't the least bit uncertain when she replied. "Okay, then, now I guess we make love."

8

RYAN HAD PICTURED HAVING sex with Jade from the moment he'd first laid eyes on her. His desire for her, mixed with his anger at what she'd done, had filled his mind constantly. Nearly every waking thought had been full of hot sexual images where lust and hunger merged with anger and revenge until he couldn't think of anything else.

His nighttime mind hadn't been much different. Crazy, wicked dreams he hadn't experienced since he was a kid had left him trembling in his bed the previous night. And had left him wondering if he was really capable of doing the things to and with her that he'd dreamt of.

This, however, this moment which had finally arrived, was *nothing* like that. He didn't know who was more surprised—he or Jade—that the crazy anger and palpable heat had somehow evaporated, leaving in their place a kind of sweet, aching need that he'd never felt before.

Tonight was suddenly about nothing other than pure desire. He wasn't prompted by anger, but rather by a completely unexpected feeling of languorous want.

Even more amazing, he didn't hate himself for wanting her so much, knowing about her what he did. Instead, he gave himself over to it, glad he had the chance before she slipped out of his life—as quickly as she'd slipped into it. She was like a dark, sleek cat, one you spotted in the moonlight moving through the shadows until it disappeared out of sight. And then you wondered, long after it was gone, if you'd ever really seen it at all.

He didn't want her to disappear. To her real life, to her crazy family or her strange apartment or her life of crime.

He wanted her here. Now. In his arms. For at least one night.

"Ryan?" she whispered, sounding as confused as he felt. Amazingly, the mindless fury had evaporated, leaving them both wrapped in a kind of warm, sultry comfort that spoke of long slow loving on a hot summer night.

That's what he wanted. More than anything else. He wanted a sultry, slow, unhurried and completely sensual night of lovemaking with Jade Maguire—a woman he'd been prepared to hate. But one he'd come to understand much better in the twenty-four hours since they'd met. Particularly after his conversation with her unusual great-aunt, who hadn't helped him as far as the painting went, but *had* made him realize he didn't know the whole story.

She'd convinced him that he should give Jade a chance to prove him wrong about her. The old woman had encouraged him to get closer to Jade in order to understand the things she did, the choices she made. He had the feeling Lula Mae had meant *more* than understanding why Jade might have become a thief.

That issue remained for later. Not now.

"Jade," he whispered, drawing out her name on a

long, exhaled breath. "How can you make me so insane and yet so calmly certain all in a single night?"

Her eyes widened in surprise, then in understanding. So he felt it, too—something had changed for both of them.

Jade seemed to have dropped her guard, looking like the beautiful, charming young woman he'd glimpsed a few times since they'd met. The defenses were down, perhaps because she'd learned he hadn't hurt her sister.

He didn't question tomorrow, which would dawn with the same myriad of problems they'd had since the moment they'd met. But tonight wasn't about those things. It was just about *this*. This world the two of them had created, and which they now had to explore fully. This was the only thing he felt certain of.

A slow smile widened his lips as he reached one hand out to gently cup her waist. He didn't pull her toward him. He didn't drive her back onto the bed and let the subdued passion between them erupt into the final conflagration they'd both probably have predicted an hour ago. Instead he moved toward her mouth, her beautiful, perfect mouth, going slowly enough to give her the chance to turn away, if she wished to do so.

She didn't move, merely waited, anticipation gleaming in her eyes and a soft sigh the only sound as his lips brushed hers.

"Stay with me tonight," he whispered, gently licking at her lips until they parted for him. Then their tongues met in a slow, lazy exploration. The kiss told him, more than anything else, that she'd experienced a change in mood which matched his own.

"I'm not going anywhere," she confirmed, her voice husky but a little stunned.

He understood how she felt—suddenly unsure of

something that had seemed straightforward a few minutes ago. This hadn't happened to him before. His relationships usually started out frenzied and picked up steam. He'd never wanted to slow down and savor every step of a first exploration. Never. Not like this.

"I don't want you handcuffed to my bed," he whispered, moving to kiss the corner of her mouth, then the fine line of her jaw. Then he laughed lightly. "At least not *yet*."

She moaned and arched her head back, twining her fingers in his hair and caressing his earlobe. "What *do* you want?"

Easy one. "I want to touch every inch of you. Feel your skin and wonder again how it can be softer than any flower I've ever touched. And how you can smell more intoxicating."

She moaned, reaching up to slip her arms around his neck and tug him to her for another kiss. Ryan complied, sipping of her mouth, tasting the unique combination of sweet and spicy that so perfectly described the woman in his arms.

Their clothes came off slowly. He was sliding Jade's black tank up and over her shoulders almost before he realized he was doing it. They parted for a moment so he could pull it over her head. After tossing it to the floor, he moved in for another deep, wet kiss. He couldn't resist touching that supple skin, and he smoothed his palms up her sides until he could cup both of her breasts. She shivered a little, then pressed against him as he teased her dark, taut nipples with his fingertips.

"You're so beautiful," he whispered as he looked down at her, clad in nothing but her lacy black panties.

"You're not going to walk out on me this time?"

He shook his head, knowing he'd sooner put a gun to his head than walk out now, before finishing what they'd started the previous night in the garden. Hell, even *earlier*. This intensity had been building since their first look.

She seemed to believe him because she immediately reached for his shirt, tugging it free from his jeans. She pushed it up, her hands doing crazy, heavenly things to his chest and shoulders on the way.

"Wait," he said when she reached for his waistband. He had to feel her, skin to skin, first. So he drew her closer, groaning in pleasure when her nipples scraped his chest. She rubbed back and forth lightly, touching him with nothing but those two sensitive spots. Sucking in a slow breath between her teeth, she heightened the tension for both of them by teasing her own puckered skin with the hair of his chest.

Then she grasped his shoulders, her whole body shaking a little in reaction. The shaking, that hint of unsteadiness—as if she had no more power to resist what was happening between them than a flower could resist the sun—sent a surge of pure male satisfaction through him.

"Why do I feel like I've been building up to this all my life instead of just a few minutes?"

He shook his head and tsked. "We've been building up to this for more than twenty-four hours."

She shrugged, conceding his point, then reached for his waistband. She made short work of his jeans, unfastening them and pushing them off his hips. Ryan's breath caught in his throat when she tugged his briefs away, trailing her hand across the tip of his erection in a move too teasing to be accidental.

"I can't wait, and yet I don't even want to start because I don't want it to be over," she said, her voice choked with desire and a hint of desperate laughter.

"Ditto. So I should probably tell you," he said, "I haven't gone six times in one night in a long time." Then he gave her a sideways grin. "However, I have to admit, something's sparking inside me tonight. I'm feeling unstoppable." His own wolfish chuckle startled him. Wondering where this incredible surge of both sexual energy and sexual patience had come from, he added, "And *very* potent."

She laughed until their mouths met in another deep kiss full of shared breaths and tongue-tangling passion. Their kisses grew deeper and wetter. Then all clothes were gone, disappearing beneath frantic hands.

They gently fell onto the bed, still wrapped around one another, exchanging kiss after kiss. Each touch sucked Ryan deeper into a well of physical pleasure until he was sure he'd drown in it. Drown in her.

Unable to resist anymore, he slid his fingers into that hot, wet flesh between her legs, teasing those soft, pretty curls, feeling her shudder in response.

"So wet," he groaned as he played with her slick opening. He toyed with her, gauging her responses, filling her tight heat with one finger, then another, until she began to gasp and writhe. And finally he flicked at her pert little clit until her whole body shook and she began to beg in tiny whimpers and pleas.

"Ryan, do you have any protection?" she managed to bite out between gasps.

"Yeah," he said, needing every bit of control he had to pull away and reach toward the bedside table. "This wasn't planned, but I sure wasn't going to take any chances."

"Just in case?" she asked, amusement blending with the stark hunger in her eyes.

"Just in case."

Then he sheathed himself and slid into her warm, welcoming body. Jade rocked up to meet him, lifting her legs, taking him deeper.

He should have known she'd be as passionate in bed as she was about everything else. She wrapped her legs around his hips and her arms around his shoulders, already starting to gasp and breathe hard. He ground against her, seeing the unmistakable signs that she was, incredibly, already close to the edge.

"Oh, yes," she murmured, "I've been thinking about this since last night. Please…a little more…oooh."

Then she stretched, arched her back, and shook slightly. Ryan waited, watching, seeing the flush of color rise in her beautiful cheeks and her lips part as she sucked in shallow breaths. Her wildly tangled black hair provided exactly the contrast to his white sheets that he'd pictured when he'd first seen her. But having her here, in his arms, with their bodies together, exceeded anything he could have imagined.

She was tight and wet and hot and in the throes of pleasure. No way could he stop himself from moving.

Her eyes flew open. "Yes. Yes. You need to catch up."

He chuckled at her demanding tone and sunk into her again, deeper, until she gasped and twisted her hips to accommodate him. "I didn't mean to get ahead of you," she said between choppy breaths. "I'm not usually so, um…quick…."

"I don't feel left behind." He pulled out of her slowly, feeling the exquisite sensation not only in his groin but everywhere else in his body. "As long as you're not really *finished* when you reach that finish line, I don't consider this a race at all."

Smiling, she pulled his face down for another kiss. "I feel so sorry for men," she said, sounding anything but as she squeezed him deep inside her body, eliciting a guttural groan from his throat. "You only get to cross the finish line once."

He gave her an evil look. "We'll see about that." He felt completely up to the challenge of a long, erotic night.

She surprised him by suddenly pushing at his chest, rolling him over and climbing on top. He stared up at her, loving this sight most of all. Jade, her hair wild and loose around her face, her lips swollen from his kisses, looking down at him with pure feminine pleasure.

She rocked on him, taking and giving, and he rose up to meet her every downward stroke.

"This is good," she said hoarsely. She reached up to cup her own breasts. Ryan moaned at the sight, then tugged her close to capture one dark nipple between his lips. He sucked deeply, feeling her jerk against him in response.

He suckled harder as she set the pace she needed. When her breathing grew frantic, he held her hips, taking over from below while she came again in a blaze of glorious, satisfied cries. Then she collapsed on his chest, trying to regain her breath but still joined with him.

"You know, I believe this Southern air—or Southern *tea*," he said, remembering the brew Lula Mae gave him, "is doing me some good." He stroked her hair and her smooth back. "Because I think I'm going to have to watch you do that at least a half-dozen more times tonight."

"Deal," she whispered as she licked at his chest.

Rolling over, she dug her fingers into his hips, her whole body straining up toward him as he entered her again.

Nothing felt this good. Had *ever* felt this good.

"Maybe we'd better make that an even dozen," he said as he gave himself over to the pleasure they created once again.

And by the early predawn hours, he realized he hadn't missed by much.

JADE WOKE UP FIRST the next morning, unused to the long, hard body curled up against her back. When her cat, Jinx, curled up against her, he was usually right beside her face where, Aunt Lula Mae often said, he could steal her breath.

This definitely wasn't Jinx. No, this warmth wasn't soft in any way. It was all hard. Solid. Strong.

After a moment and a rapid blink of her eyes, she remembered where she was. And with whom.

It was true. She'd spent the night in Ryan Stoddard's bed, in a room at Uncle Henry's inn. All those lovely dreams of someone worshipping her, cherishing her, kissing every inch of her and making love to her until she couldn't remember her own name hadn't been dreams.

He'd made them real.

She closed her eyes, taking in a deep breath as she remembered their long, erotic night. She'd never experienced anything like it. She didn't imagine many women did.

"Perfect," she whispered, then she smiled.

Seeing the pinkish-gray light of a new morning sky slanting in through the center of the heavy drapes, she held out hope that she could get out of here without being seen. She didn't want to have to explain this. Not yet. Maybe because she didn't completely understand what had happened herself.

Carefully turning around until she was face to face with her sleeping lover, she studied him carefully. The long lashes resting on his cheeks. The tiny scar on the bridge of his nose. The shadow of morning stubble on his cheeks. His curved mouth, with those perfect lips slightly parted.

The sheet was tangled around his legs and she took the opportunity to look further. Her breaths grew deeper as she saw the visible proof of the strength she'd felt last night. The cut of muscles in his arm, the ripples in his chest—no wonder he'd carried her so effortlessly. She noted another small scar above one rib—she'd felt that during the night. Then lower. Oh, yes, she'd felt *that*, too.

She knew his body intimately, but she didn't really know the man. She wanted to, though. Desperately.

Jade had never in her life had a one-night stand. Something deep inside her rebelled against the idea that this might have been one. She wanted to laugh with him and talk with him in the moonlight again. Wanted to give him hell for the ridiculous costume he'd worn last night on the tour.

But to what end? He lived in another state. In another world, really. His life was as foreign to her as if he'd come from outer space. She should let him go. Kiss him goodbye. Be content with the few incredible memories they'd created. Geography said they had no future, even if her heart—along with other more *tender* body parts—was saying she should try to find out.

She still hadn't decided what to do when he opened

his eyes and smiled. That crooked smile made his eyes crinkle and spark with light, his lean face turn boyish and playful, and sucked the breath right out of her lungs.

How could she have thought she could just walk away?

"Morning," he growled.

"Good morning."

He pulled her close, draping an arm around her waist. "What are you thinking?"

She wasn't about to tell him the truth. "I was wondering what time it is."

"Too early. Go back to sleep." Then he lazily caressed her hip, teasing the upper curve of her bottom. "Better yet, let's stay awake."

She chuckled. "You're insatiable. I have to go to work."

"You're staying," he said, sounding supremely confident.

"No."

He leaned closer, kissed the tip of her nose and whispered, "Yes."

Her response was slightly weaker than before. "No."

When his hand moved up to cover her breast, tweaking her nipple into instant awareness, she gave a soft, helpless moan.

"Yes," he said again, dropping his mouth to her throat. "Yes." He nibbled his way lower. Then, *oh, God,* lower.

She groaned in anticipation, seeing his head between her legs, knowing the pleasure he wanted to give her. "Yes," he whispered once more before his tongue began to do incredibly wild and wicked things to her, making her gasp and whimper.

He toyed and nibbled and licked at her until she lost control and shook as hot waves of intense pleasure roared through her entire body.

Then once more he ordered her to give herself over to him, to let him have his way. "Yes."

She could no longer even try to resist. "Yes."

TWO HOURS LATER, however, she refused to allow him to coax her into staying. It was 8:00 a.m., and she could hear people moving around the house. She hoped she could escape while Uncle Henry visited with his guests during breakfast.

"When can I see you again?" Ryan asked as she emerged from the bathroom pulling her top on over her head.

He watched her from the bed, the sheet draped across his lap. Looking at him, she forgot to move for a second, with her head stuck out of her tank top and her arms tangled inside it. His thick arms, tousled hair and crooked smile had her wanting to crawl right back between the sheets and spend the day doing everything all over again.

Lord, she was becoming a sex maniac.

She finally remembered what the heck she'd been doing and pulled the top in place, then reached for her skirt.

"You, uh, want to see me again?" she asked, cursing the little squeak in her voice. Hopefully he hadn't heard it.

No such luck. He rose from the bed, striding toward her, his body lean and powerful. Her mouth went dry remembering the feel of him on top of her. Beneath her. Inside her. She closed her eyes, then opened them again.

"You're damn right I do," he said, taking her jaw in his hand. "I don't know what last night was about for you, but it was only a beginning for me."

A beginning. Of something that wasn't likely to have a happy ending. A wiser woman would have backed away, ended things now. Jade had always considered herself pretty smart. But as Aunt Lula Mae often said, particularly about Jade's mama, "Da heart don' always like to listen to what da head has to say."

"All right," she whispered.

His relieved smile was gratifying. "Spend the day with me."

"I just spent the night with you."

"So the rest will be easy."

She nibbled her lip. "I have to work."

"Aren't you the boss?"

She nodded. "But I have to do some things. Including going home and checking on Aunt Lula Mae." She looked down at her shirt and crumpled skirt. "Not to mention changing clothes."

"Then spend the afternoon with me."

"I can't."

He got out of the bed and approached her. Jade threw her hand up, palm out. "Don't try to persuade me."

He gave her an innocent, "who me?" look, and kept right on walking, until he was flush against her. Neck to knee. Breath to breath. "Meet me this afternoon."

"I ca…."

He kissed the end of the word right out of her mouth, taking her lips against his and licking his way inside so he could tease her tongue into saying yes.

"Say yes," he whispered when they drew apart.

"Do you always get your way?"

He nodded. "Always."

At least the man was honest. "All right. Just this afternoon. But no more playing hooky for me—I have a business to run."

He put two fingers straight up in the air and vowed, "Absolutely. Just today."

She didn't trust the humor in his eyes.

"And the next day."

"Ryan…"

"And the day after that."

She was laughing as she left the room. Laughing, and suspecting he might be right.

"SO, WHO'S THE GUY?"

Jade looked up from her desk the next morning, seeing Daisy framed in the doorway of her downtown office. Her all-black clothes and stark white makeup looked especially out of place on such a bright, beautiful summer day.

"I don't know what you mean," she replied, nibbling her lip at the lie.

Daisy smirked and entered the small, one-room office that Jade had rented last year when the record-keeping and phone calls had become too much to handle at home. She plopped down on the seat opposite the desk. "You are so full of it. I know you, Jade. This is the 'I-got-laid Jade' I'm seeing here."

Jade couldn't prevent a tiny smile. Daisy was so outrageous, but also a very intuitive friend. Jade had definitely gotten laid. Oh boy, oh boy, oh boy, had she!

"I think we're supposed to be talking about you and, uh, your formerly incarcerated friend," she replied, forcing her mind out of the bed she'd been sharing with Ryan for the past couple of nights.

Daisy shrugged. "I dunno. It's okay, except all he ever wants to talk about is how bad it was inside without a real fast-food burger for eighteen months. All we've done is hit every drive-thru in Savannah. Cripes, you'd think the key to getting some psycho to confess to anything is withholding his daily Whopper."

Jade met Daisy's eyes, they shared a salacious look, and both burst into laughter.

"Okay, so other than being sick of fast-food, what else is going on?"

Daisy shrugged. "He's changed. Or I've changed. Whatever. We just don't seem to have much in common anymore. He's even mentioned wanting to go back to Iowa and live off his folks on the farm. I'd rather have somebody stick flaming toothpicks up my nose than do that."

"Lovely," Jade murmured.

"I don't know if we'll make it. Seems kind of silly since I moved all the way up here to be close to the prison."

As much as she'd hate losing Daisy, Jade would much rather have the girl get the loser ex out of her life. "You don't want to go back to New Orleans, do you?"

Daisy crossed her arms across her chest, leaned back in her chair and lifted one boot-covered foot onto her other knee. "Nah. I've gotten used to it here in Savannah. Genteel freaky instead of raunchy freaky."

Jade nodded in rueful agreement. That kind of summed things up.

"So, tell me about your guy. Who put that look on your face?" Daisy asked, not distracted from her original question.

"What look?" The I-met-an-amazing-man-and-we've-spent-nearly-every-minute-together-for-the-last-two-days look?

She swallowed hard and lifted her water bottle to her lips, still trying to divert Daisy's attention. The water had been here all morning and was now somewhere between tepid and bathwater, but it was better than having to try to explain the crazy relationship she'd fallen into with a practical stranger.

An amazingly delicious relationship, but a crazy one nonetheless.

"Spill," said Daisy.

"It's not a big deal."

Daisy reached over and helped herself to a handful of peanut M&M's, which Jade kept in a dish on her desk. She picked out all the green ones, munched them, and dumped the others back in the bowl. "Puh-lease. You got some, I can see it all over you."

Jade quirked a brow and pointed to her loose yellow skirt and sleeveless top. "In case you haven't noticed, I'm not wearing a dress from the Gap."

Quick-witted Daisy immediately got Jade's Monica Lewinsky reference and snorted a laugh. "Is it anybody I know?"

Jade shook her head knowing she might as well come clean. Daisy was like a kid digging through a cereal box for a toy. Relentless, thorough, and not caring what spilled onto the floor. "He's someone I just met. And we're…"

"Having wild sex?"

"We're getting to know one another."

"In bed."

"And out," Jade shot back.

Daisy chortled. "Aha, so there was a bed in there somewhere!"

Oh, yes. A bed. A garden. The bathtub at the hotel Ryan had checked into yesterday afternoon—not wanting to stay at another cozy B&B where Jade was well-known.

She didn't mind people knowing she had sex—most people made a regular practice of it. She *did* mind people hearing anything, um, unusual from another room, in an old house with more old layers of paint than nails holding up the walls.

One thing was for sure—whether it was the Southern air or something else— Ryan was definitely the most potent man she'd ever known. His appetites perfectly matched hers.

They were both insatiable.

Ryan. Just thinking about him made her feel the most unusual feeling of elation. Jade had considered herself much too…well, *jaded* ever to turn into one of those giddy women who gauged their happiness by the barometer of their love life. Like her mother and her sister.

Her sister. That had been an interesting conversation. She'd called Jenny yesterday morning when she'd gone home for a change of clothes. Jenny had been rattling on about auditions and a big tipper at the restaurant. When Jade had asked about Ryan, her sister had responded with an unexpected, "Who?"

A few more words and Jenny had confirmed she'd blown a lunch date into gargantuan proportions.

Typical Jenny, their mother's daughter. A whirling bundle of energy who loved being at the center of attention and treated every aspect of her life as if she were the star performer and everyone else merely supporting players.

Jade was much more like her father. Danny Maguire had been a black-haired Irishman whose stoicism had hidden a deeply vulnerable emotional side. Not that he'd often let anyone see it. He'd been the stable element in their family. He'd put up with Mama's flamboyance and with two outrageously different daughters. He'd never protested the presence of a live-in great-aunt—a voodoo priestess who wasn't even technically a blood relation, since Lula Mae had been adopted by Jade's great-grandfather decades ago.

He'd done it all with quiet wisdom and a good-natured laugh. Right up until the end when he was dying of the kind of cancer that brought men to their knees, robbing them of life long before it actually killed them. Even now, more than twelve years later, she missed him every day. Tears rose in her eyes, as they always did when she thought about him.

Jade had been thinking about him a good deal over the past few days, and she didn't question why. It was because she'd finally begun to wonder if she was like her mother after all, able to experience love strong enough to last a lifetime. Hungry for love, wanting it desperately. Not because she'd *lost* it, as Patty Jean had, but because she'd never truly experienced it at all.

So far.

She couldn't imagine what Daddy would be thinking of her latest situation. Little Miss Common Sense, involved in a passionate affair with a man whose address she didn't even know. He'd be surprised, she was sure, because she'd been described from childhood as the calm, introspective, thoughtful one. The one who never let her emotions rule her head. Just like Daddy.

"You okay?" Daisy asked, interrupting Jade's long moments of silent thought. "The sex was so good that you're still crying over it a day later? Or was it that *bad?*"

Jade quickly wiped at the tears she hadn't realized

were there and was about to reply when she realized someone else had entered the office. Her nerve endings all perked up in reaction, so she knew before even looking who it was.

Ryan.

9

"SHE'S DEFINITELY NOT crying because it was bad," Ryan said with the kind of casual confidence some men never achieved in their entire lives. He strode into her office, filling up the small space with his mere presence.

Even Daisy did a double-take—and she was tough to impress.

"Well, hello," she said. "I think we were just talking about you. Brought out the emotional side of Jade."

Never one to allow anyone to be too sure of her, Jade merely shrugged. "I had something in my eye."

Ryan crossed the room in a few steps and looked down at Jade with visible concern. "You're sure? Is anything wrong?"

"Yeah," Daisy said, standing up and crossing her arms in front of her chest. "She's crying because she's finally realized all she missed out on by not having sex for a couple of years."

Oh, man. Jade was really going to kill her now. "Go away."

Ryan looked amused. "Years?"

"I'm gone." Daisy gave Ryan a thorough once-over, nodded and winked her approval, then sauntered toward the door.

Before she escaped, Jade came up with a decent

comeback. "You're one to talk considering where your boyfriend's been for the past year and a half!"

Daisy gave her a half smile and Jade realized that probably hadn't been the right retort. The young woman didn't seem the type to wait around for eighteen months for any man.

God, she felt old. Though only twenty-six to Daisy's nineteen, she'd played the mother to Jenny for so long that she didn't remember *ever* being as reckless as the younger women.

"Years?" Ryan asked again once Daisy was gone.

"She was exaggerating."

He waited.

"Greatly."

Still waited.

"Not *years,* plural."

Then he sat on the corner of her desk, looking completely at ease in his casual jeans and T-shirt as he waited for more details. He wasn't getting them. Instead, she went on the offensive. "Want to talk about *your* previous sex life?"

"Nope."

"Then don't ask about mine."

Boring as it's been.

He bent down and gave her a quick, possessive kiss on the lips. "Not talking about former sex lives. That's a sign of a relationship, isn't it?"

"There's that word again."

"Sex?"

"Relationship," she retorted. "That's not what we have."

He got off the desk and squatted next to her. Swiveling her around, he pulled the rolling chair closer until her knees touched his chest and his hands covered hers. "We don't have to put a name on it, Jade."

Good.

"But we both know we've fallen into something."

Fallen in. Naked, tied and handcuffed, but definitely fallen. "It's not like it can go anywhere," she said, determined not to get attached to this man and the things he made her feel.

"Why not?"

He looked really curious and a little confused, as if he hadn't noticed the minor problems of geography and their vastly different lifestyles. He was a responsible big-city architect who worked with millionaires on renovating their Fifth Avenue penthouses. She was a two-paychecks-away-from-broke tour guide operator who scared tourists for a living.

"We don't seem to have much common ground," she finally said, considering it the understatement of a lifetime.

His evil grin told her his mind had gone right into his pants.

"Other than that," she added, a laugh on her lips.

Oh, yeah, they had *that*. They had sexual compatibility coming out the yin-yang. But they didn't have anything else.

So they'd managed to fill a day or two and enjoy each other's company out of bed, as well. He liked her kind of music. She liked his kind of buildings. They both liked sushi and loathed catfish. They had fun window-shopping on River Street and liked people-watching in the Victorian District.

That didn't mean they were compatible, or anything. He was strictly northeastern white-bread conservative and she was Southern mixed-race bohemian.

"I can't believe I let you talk me into taking another afternoon off," she muttered as she led him outside and locked up the office.

"You're the perfect guide for these old plantation houses."

"And you're relentless about getting what you want. You must have driven your parents crazy, you spoiled brat."

He shrugged, unrepentant. "You like getting your own way, too. You're just a little more *genteel* about it."

True. She did like getting her own way. She'd had to. She'd been pretty much in charge of her little family since she was a teenager, and had become used to her mother following her advice. "Okay, so we're both used to being the boss. Both oldest kids—"

"And oldest grandkids," he added.

"Correct. We both like to be the one in the driver's seat."

He leaned close to her ear. "Right. And sometimes we both want to be on top. But I think we've managed to compromise and work things out there, don't you?"

Oh, lordy, she had set herself up for that one. She gulped, pushed a long strand of hair off her face and ordered herself not to blush. Not now, when other business owners she knew were walking by, nodding their hellos as she stood there, getting wet and aroused because of this man's wicked whisper.

"We have already established sexual compatibility," she conceded, keeping her voice low. "I'm talking about elsewhere. We don't have much else in common."

He rolled his eyes and made a sound of disgust. "We don't know that. Why do you think I've been insisting you spend your days with me? So we could get to know each other better. Like today, we'll be seeing headstones and houses full of dead people when what I want to do is go back into your office, lift you on top of your desk, flip up your little skirt and take you right there in front of Savannah and the world. Because maybe if I come inside you, again, you'll begin to believe there's something real happening between us."

She dropped her purse—literally dropped it out of her weak fingers—and stood there staring up at him, wide-eyed, on the sidewalk. Two women walked by, women she recognized. They giggled, then one of them picked up her handbag and put it in Jade's shaking fingers.

"Have a nice day, y'hear? 'Bye, honey," she said after giving Ryan a thorough head-to-toe examination. Then the women moved on.

Jade still couldn't say a word.

Finally, he tipped her gaping jaw closed with his index finger. "Do we go back in your office?" he asked, one brow quirked. "Or do we go visit those old museums you so love?"

Swallowing the first answer, the impulsive one from the deepest, most sensual part of her, she snapped, "Let's go."

WHILE DRIVING OUT OF Savannah for their day visiting historic houses of the South, Ryan and Jade maintained a comfortable silence. The hum of the engine droned beneath the hiss of the air conditioner, which tried to bring the stifling outside air to a breathable temperature. Her hand rested on the seat, his close to it, so that just their pinkies touched. That slight touch told him she'd forgiven him for the sexy taunt outside her office.

Hell, he was the one who'd lived to regret it. It'd

taken ten minutes of their drive for him to will his hard-on back down.

The tension was gone, though the awareness remained. There was more, though. If anyone had told him a few days ago that he could be falling for this woman, Ryan would have laughed in that person's face. But it was true. Somewhere between the sex and the anger, the schemes and the desire, they'd started to enjoy one another. To like one another. And, at least on his part, maybe more.

How twisted was that? He cared for a woman he believed was a thief. He was intrigued by her like he'd never been intrigued by anyone. He liked her intelligence and her caustic wit, her smile and her dark, mysterious eyes. Even the hint of vulnerability she'd hate to have anyone notice.

He'd noticed. He'd paid attention to the slight weariness in her shoulders after she'd worked out this weekend's tour schedule last night in his bed. The wistful tone in her voice when she spoke of missing her mother and sister told him more about her than any conversation about their families could have. The sadness when she spoke of the father she'd lost at such a young age broke his heart a little. The exasperated fondness when Lula Mae's name came up merely cemented what he'd figured the night he'd met the old woman.

Jade was the glue that held them all together. He knew that now, without ever having met most of her family. And he liked her even more for it.

None of it reconciled with a deceitful con woman who'd steal from the elderly. None. So he had decided to do exactly what Lula Mae had told him to—get closer to Jade. Much closer. And try to either win her trust, so she'd confide in him, or figure out all on his own how her mind worked.

"So why did you want to go on this field trip today, anyway? Aren't there enough old houses in the city for you to explore?" She shot him an amused look. "Or are you just trying to get away from Mamie Brandywine? She has to have tracked you down by now."

He grimaced. "She left a message for me at the hotel."

"She's relentless."

"She's a hundred and two."

"More like sixty."

"Who could tell?" he asked, wanting to change the subject to a much more pleasant one. "Besides, today gives me a chance to be alone with you, with no cell phone, no pager, no tourists recognizing you and asking questions about where to visit."

She reached to turn up the AC and a thick blast of cold air emerged from the vents. Jade leaned toward it, almost cooing her appreciation. She was such a creature of her senses, and watching the delight she took in so many things drove him crazy. She savored rich smells, decadent desserts, sultry whispers, or coolness against her overheated body.

His touch.

Ryan swallowed hard, knowing he had to get a grip before he drove off the road.

"We've been alone for the past two nights," she said, one brow lifted as she gave him a secretive smile.

So much for getting a grip. That comment put his brain right back into his lap. "I'm gonna get into a wreck if we start talking about the past two nights."

"They were fabulous."

Witch.

"It's a good thing it's not possible to overdose on orgasms, because I'd be a dead woman right now."

He growled and shifted again. "Shut. Up. Jade."

She giggled. "Just getting even for what you said back in front of my office. But I'll shut up now."

Unfortunately, it was too late. Her comments had his mind focused only on the hot, sensual encounters they'd shared. He could not get enough of her. No matter how many times he touched her, his hands felt empty when she wasn't in them.

He'd half wondered if her Aunt Lula Mae had slipped something into his tea that first night. But whatever the spell had been, it hadn't worn off, hadn't decreased in intensity at all. She was all he thought about while awake, all he dreamed about when asleep.

"Well," he said, trying to change the subject to a safer one, "the nights have been *private*. But yesterday was a little crowded."

"Crowded?"

He nodded. "Everyone knows you. Everywhere we went, people have been asking you questions, wanting your advice. I can barely exchange ten words with you before we're interrupted."

From vendors selling brightly-colored T-shirts to sweaty tourists, to artists peddling ten-dollar caricatures, she stopped to talk to them all. Old and young. Male and female. She had a ready smile, a word of support, an answer for every question.

"That happens in a place like this. You see the skyline and think we're a big city. But when you walk the old squares, you know it's still a very small town."

"Still seems strange to me," he said with a shrug.

"There's a whole history here," she said. "So many families have been here for a long time. We grew up together. Went to school together. Went to the same birthday parties and the same Southern colleges. Lifelong friends who grow up, marry and stay put so their children can be lifelong friends. That's Savannah."

So much for thinking Jade wasn't liked at the party the other night. Because she was obviously very well-liked among *her* people, as she called them—the modern, hard-working businesspeople of a thriving modern city. They didn't just like her. They admired her, looked up to her. Hell, they *loved* her.

How on earth she could be the thief he knew her to be, he had no idea. It didn't make sense. He'd thought it over a dozen different ways since their first night together, but no matter how he looked at it, the idea of Jade actually stealing from someone seemed impossible.

But his grandmother had told him she had. And the painting was missing.

The frustration of not knowing what to believe was driving him insane. He wanted to get the whole thing out in the open and done with. Whatever kind of trouble Jade was in—whatever would lead her to such a desperate choice—he wanted to know. To help her solve it, and to move on.

Until she trusted him enough to open up to him, however, he didn't think he'd be getting the answers he wanted. Not without giving her enough reason to disappear from his life for good. Like the fact that he'd been lying to her from the minute they'd met.

"How's your article coming?" she asked, giving him something else to think about.

The article. The one he was supposed to be writing about the architecture of old Georgia. The one he hadn't even started yet. "It's okay. Today should give me some new angles."

"Good. You'll love the Martinique place. The man who built it back in the mid-eighteen hundreds had every stone in the garden wall brought over from the ruins of an ancient castle in France."

"Probably because his wife asked him to, huh?"

She looked disgruntled. "Now how did you know that?"

"Isn't every romantic story about walls being moved or Taj Mahals being constructed somehow related to a man totally out of his mind over a woman?"

"Pessimist."

"Romantic," he shot back.

"I don't think anyone's ever called me that before. Pragmatist, yes. Romantic, no."

"Wicked," he offered.

"Without question."

He couldn't help twining his fingers in hers and bringing her hand to his mouth for a quick kiss. "I wouldn't change a thing."

Except maybe her side job as a thief.

"Have you studied any of the guidebooks to get a history of the area?" she asked.

He nodded, but didn't elaborate on what he already knew. He wanted to see Jade's world through her eyes. She was the ultimate tour guide—a woman who could trace her ancestry right back to the slave quarters *and* the mansion of a Southern plantation. Unbelievable.

"Is the place lecherous old great-great-grandpa Lester used to own still around?"

"Four greats," she corrected. Then she shook her head. "And no, it burnt to the ground. Sherman spared much of Savannah, but not a lot outside it." She wrapped her arms around herself. "I did visit the site once. Lots of ghosts there." She didn't sound like she was being fanciful, merely introspective.

"How were you able…"

"To track down the family tree?" she asked, as if reading his mind. "I didn't have to do anything. The members of my family all like to keep records. And to talk."

"Including Lula Mae?" he asked, not letting on that he'd actually met the woman. He wasn't ready to share that tidbit with Jade yet because it would invite a discussion about why he'd been at her place.

"She's not a blood relative," she explained. "My great-grandfather married Lula Mae's mother, a Jamaican immigrant, when my grandmother was a little girl. He adopted her. The two girls were raised like sisters, which scandalized the Old Guard. It got so bad they had to leave Savannah for several years." Her voice held a tinge of hurt for her elderly relative, for the pain she'd experienced decades ago.

"But she's here now."

"Home. With her family. We love her dearly. She's been like another grandmother to Jenny and me since we were little." Then she rolled her eyes. "That voodoo stuff is highly exaggerated, but she gets a kick out of the rumors."

Their conversation was interrupted when they arrived at their destination. Ryan turned the car off the main road, following Jade's directions and some small white signs. Martinique Plantation might be a popular tourist spot, but it was well hidden behind enormous groves of pecan trees, which lined the road leading to the parking lot.

"Beautiful," he said, whistling as he looked at the facade of the building.

"Wait 'til you see the inside."

And she was right. The inside of the place was perfectly decorated and furnished, every item either unique to the period or a fine replica. Ryan hadn't been too surprised when they'd been allowed to enter the museum without an escort. The woman at the entrance had called Jade by name, chatted about the summer heat and parties and hairdos, and ushered them in without asking for the usual donation.

Though he wouldn't have believed anything could capture his interest as much as the woman at his side, he found himself getting caught up in the ambiance. Little touches of elegance and pride of workmanship shone in the mellowed oak of the floor, polished to a high sheen. Some unusual angles used in the balustrade deserved closer attention, as did the wainscoting in the dining room. The magazine planned to send a photographer to some of the buildings he mentioned in the article. The grand staircase to this place might make a nice center spread.

Strangely, when they entered what had once been a grand drawing room, he began to feel a sense of familiarity. He cast his eyes around the room, focused on nothing, but taking it all in. A large room, tastefully furnished. Groupings of red velvet sofas and cherrywood tables stood at either end. A harpsichord sat next to a set of French doors leading out to the expansive veranda.

"Come look at this," Jade said, tugging at his arm. "Here's the bride of the man who built this house. She was a renowned beauty in her time. Maybe you'll understand a little more about his grand gesture."

Then he saw it—the familiar sight that his subconscious had recognized before his eyes had even been aware of. He gaped, his jaw falling open as he beheld the painting hanging over an enormous fireplace.

The one he'd last seen on a wall at his grandparents' house in upstate New York.

RYAN SOMEHOW MANAGED to keep himself from confronting Jade about the painting right there in the drawing room of the Martinique house. It wasn't easy. He'd stood there, slack-jawed, staring at the thing, knowing for sure it was the same painting he'd gazed at so many times in his grandmother's house. Mainly because the attractive woman in it was wearing a very low-cut gown. For a twelve-year-old boy, it had been about as close to titillation as he could get in an old-people house that didn't have so much as a *National Geographic* to ogle.

He hadn't known how to react—whether to confront Jade, accuse her, try to reason with her or take the painting off the wall and run like hell. Fortunately, Jade hadn't noticed his preoccupation with the portrait. She'd bought his story that he was deep in thought about the article, when in truth he was trying to figure out what was going on.

He was still a little shell-shocked a couple of hours later, sitting alone in his hotel room. He'd made an excuse—an important interview—and driven them back to the city right after they'd finished at the first house. Jade had seemed surprised, but she hadn't objected. Only when he'd dropped her off in front of her office had he noticed her look of confusion. It had probably been matched by his own, but there hadn't been anything he could do about it.

He had to think. To be alone. To have a drink from room service.

A double.

As he sipped his gin and tonic, he tried to piece it together. Jade had stolen the painting. The painting was now in a Southern plantation house on display for everyone to see, not hidden away. He knew there was a black market for stolen art, particularly anything by the Impressionists. But he'd never have thought a legitimate museum would be involved with a shady transaction. So it was likely they hadn't known the painting was stolen when they'd purchased it from Jade.

Seeing the glaring, full-color reminder of his purpose in being here, it was impossible *not* to let the reason for his trip here interrupt the happy, lust-filled daze he'd been living in. He'd come to Savannah to track down his grandmother's property, and to get vengeance on the woman who'd stolen it.

His lover.

"What a mess," he muttered as he sat on his hotel bed, sifting through notes, maps and brochures he'd been collecting for the article. Some of the brochures were for the local homes, including Martinique Plantation.

Even here he couldn't get away from the problem. Front and center on the Martinique brochure was a color picture of the LeBeuf painting. Below it, in fancy text, was an invitation to come see the painting that had long ago been lost.

The museum was touting its return to its rightful home because it had been…"Stolen during the Civil War?"

That widened his eyes and had him reaching for his drink again. He couldn't imagine what Grandmother would think about having stolen goods in her house.

Ryan continued to read. "The piece has recently been donated by a generous and anonymous benefactor, and is on display during regular operating hours."

Donated. On display.

"Dammit, Jade, what have you been doing?"

But he knew. He didn't even have to think about it. Jade was doing what she always did. Taking control. Righting a wrong. Getting justice, even if she had to go about it by stepping outside of the law.

She'd stolen the painting so she could return it to its original home.

Foolish. Risky. Daring. Honorable in a twisted sort of way. How like Jade.

He finally understood all the pieces that hadn't made sense—Jade's innate sense of justice, her love of history and tradition and culture. She was doing her part to set things right, in the only way she could.

The realization sent a feeling he couldn't quite define rushing through him. Relief? Gratitude?

Above all, happiness. Because while she *was* a thief, she wasn't necessarily an immoral person. She was living by her own code of right and wrong. Which was, really, all that could be expected of anyone when you came right down to it.

He'd expect nothing more from the woman he believed he was falling in love with. The one he knew he cared for more than he'd ever cared for anyone in his life.

The realization cleared things in his mind. He didn't have to feel guilty for caring for her. Jade was every bit the eccentric, dynamic, exotic, amazing woman he thought she was. And she stole stuff when she felt she had a good reason. Case closed.

So he now had only two problems to deal with. First, how to deal with his grandmother's painting.

And second, how to extricate Jade from her life of crime.

10

"I CAN'T BELIEVE YOU kidnapped me," Jade said.

Ryan ignored the disgruntled tone in Jade's voice as he drove toward Tybee Island the next afternoon. Because she wasn't disgruntled. She was just pretending to be. "When's the last time you took a vacation?"

She tapped her finger on her lips, thinking about it.

"I rest my case."

"This isn't exactly a typical vacation day. You practically carried me out of the office."

She was right, and he smiled at the memory.

Jade had at first refused to take more time off work, since she'd been out the previous day. But because one of her least reliable tour guides had come up with an excuse, she'd had to work the night tour again. She deserved the afternoon off, and he was making sure she got it. So he'd grabbed her around the waist and nearly dragged her to the door, with the aid and assistance of Daisy. After a quick trip to her house to pick up some essentials, they'd headed for Tybee Island.

"You do realize tourists are the only people crazy enough to go to the beach on a day like this."

"Why?"

She shot him a look and rolled her eyes. "It's blazing hot. Ever clued in to the whole *siesta* concept? Sleeping in the afternoon during the hottest part of the day?"

He immediately leapt on the opening. "Are you saying you want to go back to the hotel and go to bed for the afternoon?"

She chuckled. "No, you lusty man, I'm saying you're going to fry yourself like a pickle if you don't go heavy on the sunscreen."

The pickle comment probably would have elicited a reaction if he hadn't already seen the fried pickles on the menus of several local restaurants. "I already lotioned up. High SPF."

"My father used to say the same thing. And he'd fry as only an Irishman can under a Georgia summer sun." She was smiling, but he heard a wistful sound she couldn't quite hide. "I was thinking of him earlier," she added, "when you picked me up and I smelled the suntan lotion you'd put on."

"Why?"

"Coppertone. It has such a distinct smell. Makes my mind trip right back to my childhood and fills my head with warm and happy thoughts. One of those scent memory things, you know?"

He didn't follow. Obviously seeing his inquisitive look, she explained. "There are some smells that trigger memories, emotions. Haven't you ever experienced that?"

He couldn't say he had, but knew Jade was very serious about it. She appeared both lost in thought but very much aware of every word they spoke, every breath she took.

Reaching over, he dropped a hand on her leg. "No, I don't think I have."

She covered his hand with one of her own. "Have you ever lost someone, Ryan? Someone you *really* loved?"

Again he shook his head. "I've been lucky. Product of a normal childhood, all my grandparents still living, no tragedies in the Stoddard family tree."

"Ah." She nodded as if completely understanding, even though he still wasn't following her.

"Then you wouldn't get it." She reached into the back seat, retrieving a large beach bag, and pulled out a familiar brown bottle of suntan lotion. Flipping open the top with her thumb, she brought it to her nose and inhaled deeply.

He was shocked to see tears suddenly sparkling on her long lashes. She blinked rapidly. Then she held the bottle out so he could smell it.

"Smells like lotion to me."

"And to me it smells like my father." She reached up to touch the corners of her eyes and wiped away the moisture there. "You see, the innermost mind still mourns before the logical one has the chance to realize what we're grieving."

He suddenly understood and his heart broke a little for her. "I guess I do see," he admitted, lacing his fingers through hers. "Maybe that's why whenever I smell cinnamon I think of my grandmother's Christmas tree. She always hung spiced pine cones inside the branches and her whole house smelled of cinnamon every December. Someday that smell is going to give me flashes of sadness, isn't it?"

"Exactly," she said with a nod. "But happiness, too."

He pulled her fingertips to his lips and pressed a kiss to them. "I wish I'd met your dad."

She was quiet for a moment. "So do I. I think he's been on my mind so much because of you. Because of how much he would have liked you." Then she chuckled. "I've also been thinking how happy he'd be that there's apparently a little of my crazily romantic mother in me after all."

He wondered at her comment, but before he could ask about it, she continued. "By the way, for the rest of my life when I smell night-blooming jasmine with a hint of magnolia, I'll think of you. And the night we met."

So would he. He already wanted to drench himself in the scent and never let it go.

In the passenger seat, Jade stretched in the sunlight blazing through the sunroof, like a cat taking in the heat. Her whole body seemed to savor the warmth. So much for her grumbling.

"You're *glad* we're going to the beach. Admit it."

"Maybe," she said with a chuckle. "Why'd you want to do it, anyway?"

"Because I'm hot."

"That's bright," she said, a hint of dryness in her voice.

He took no offense. "At least this way I can get my whole body wet in the ocean, with very little on, instead of just getting my *clothes* wet because I'm dripping sweat in the heat and humidity."

He wasn't lying but it wasn't the only reason Ryan had suggested an afternoon at the beach. He also wanted to see the wind whip her long dark hair off her face. To watch her lick saltwater off her lips. To drown in need as he saw her hands on her skin, rubbing lotion onto her body with the unconsciously seductive movements that were second nature to her.

To talk to her, delve into her emotions and her past. Get to know her better by understanding just how deeply her feelings ran, how much sadness she'd had to deal with in her young life and what might drive her to do the things she did.

Lots of reasons.

"Pretty empty," he mumbled as he parked his rented car in a public lot near the dunes.

"Yes it is," she replied. "Like I said, only tourists come out on a day as hot as this. And usually just the British ones whose summers last two minutes."

When they got their stuff from the trunk of the car and walked down to the public beach, Ryan realized Jade was right. The place was nearly deserted. The long stretch of white sand meeting the frothy blue-green waves of the Atlantic was occupied by only a few groups of people, one with young children. It was a workday, but he'd expected at least a few more out-of-towners as crazy as himself.

"Hope they lotioned up," Jade murmured.

Choosing a spot a few yards from the water, Ryan put the cooler down and opened their two chairs while Jade spread out the rest of their gear. Kicking off his shoes, he prepared to revel in the rough sensation of sandy beach against his feet.

It felt more like burning charcoal. "Sonofa...."

"On the towel," she said quickly, pointing to a safe place to step.

"Okay, maybe this wasn't such a great idea. Should have gone closer to the water. Now we're stuck here, on Towel Island, unless we swim with our shoes on."

"It'll make running into the surf that much more exciting." She laughed softly, then pulled her sundress off, dropping it to the blanket she'd spread between their chairs.

When Ryan saw her in the hot pink bikini, he couldn't contain a soft wolf whistle. "Okay, maybe we'll stay awhile. If you run into the surf, I'll definitely withstand the burning coals and run after you."

"My hero." She lifted a pair of sunglasses to her face, staring out at the water as she slid them on. "It's beautiful."

He still hadn't taken his eyes off her. "Very."

The surf didn't pound, it merely washed up and back, and somehow it seemed Jade's body moved to its rhythm. She lowered herself to the chair, stretched out her legs, leaned back and watched the ocean. Every movement was graceful, in sync with some inner beat, as if part of her was, as always, in tune to her sultry surroundings.

She was loving it. Loving this.

"You complained, and warned me, but you like this intense heat, don't you?"

She nodded lazily. "I do like it hot."

Ditto.

"I love the sizzle on my skin," she added. "The brightness of the sky over the ocean."

Retrieving a bottle of water from the cooler, she flipped off the top and sipped it. The moisture brought a shine to her lips. Her pink tongue flicked out as she licked it away. Then she sipped again, moaned softly, and lowered the bottle.

Such a sensual woman. She nearly brought him to his knees.

He needed a cold drink. Pronto. Just watching Jade's mouth around the tip of a bottle had him thinking of all kinds of wicked things her mouth could do.

After peeling off his shirt, he dropped it on the ground, grateful for the sunscreen. The heat baked right in, bringing instant sweat which was cooled only by the light breeze blowing off the ocean.

"How do you do it?" she asked.

Looking at Jade, he found her staring up at him. Her

glasses were down on the tip of her nose and she watched his every move from above the rim.

He thought the sand was hot? Her eyes were on fire, roaming over his body as if she was seeing him bare-chested for the first time. Actually, considering their shadow-wrapped interludes of the past few nights, he supposed she was, at least in full light. "Do what?"

"How do you keep that body when you work behind a desk nine-to-five?"

He laughed softly, liking that appreciative look on her face. He understood. That pink bathing suit of hers had him thinking of nothing but getting her out of it. He'd love to take her by the hand and lead her into the water, neither of them wearing a thing. Unfortunately, with the pasty tourists a dozen yards away, he wasn't going to get his wish.

"I work out some."

"Some?"

He shrugged. "I run with my dog a few times a week."

She cocked a brow. "You have a dog?"

He nodded. "A drooling Lab I affectionately call Mutt."

"I have a cat."

"Mutt likes cats."

"For lunch?"

He shook his head and sat next to her. "He's a big goofy drooler who loves to play with anyone. People. Cats. The mouse that got into my kitchen last year."

She grinned. "Who's taking care of him?"

"He's staying with my grandparents."

He immediately stiffened as the image of his grandmother came to mind. What on earth would she think about him sitting here, engaged in casual conversation with the woman who'd stolen from her?

What *could* she think? He couldn't explain it to her, at least not until he figured out what to do about it. And he couldn't do that until he got Jade to open up to him.

He couldn't allow anything to upset this careful balance of friendship they had during the day while being passionate lovers at night.

"Can you hand me my bag?" she asked. "I need to put some lotion on before I fry."

"You must be kidding."

She tilted her head in confusion.

"This is straight date-at-the-beach stuff, Jade. You must know I'm not going to let you put on your own lotion. I'm going to insist you let me rub it on for you."

"I don't react well to orders," she murmured.

"How about to requests?" He leaned close to her chair, until their faces were a few inches apart, and they stared at one another through their dark sunglasses. "Will you *let* me put lotion on you?"

She nibbled her lip, then slowly nodded.

He gave her a kiss, licking the tiny bit of water still clinging to the corner of her mouth. Salty, sweet, hot. Jade.

Smiling in anticipation, Ryan retrieved the bottle she'd dropped beside her sundress. He poured a healthy amount of it into his hands, then knelt beside her chair.

He started at her throat. After dribbling some of the white liquid on that hollow, he gently smoothed his fingers against the skin he'd kissed so many times in the dark of night. Then he worked his way across her collarbones, using both hands until he could cup each slim shoulder. "Your skin is already so hot."

"So's the lotion," she replied.

She didn't seem to mind. In fact, her eyes were

closed, her head tipped back and her face turned toward the sun. She was savoring this. As was he.

He spread more lotion down her arms, gently turning them to protect the lighter, more vulnerable skin underneath. As he lifted one, he paused to press a hot kiss in the hollow of her elbow, then he draped her hand across his shoulder.

"Mmm," she said on a sigh.

He moved down her body. Silently counting the few adorable, tiny freckles on her chest, he licked at one, tasting the salty sheen of sweat on her body.

"That doesn't feel like lotion," she murmured.

"How about this?"

He kissed again, sucking her skin slightly, then rubbing his tongue over the spot.

"You're going to shock the British."

"They won't be the ones coming if I have my way."

She snorted a laugh at his reference to the "The British are coming." But she still didn't open her eyes.

"Get on with it, or I'm going to burn to a crisp and you won't be able to touch me without inflicting pain."

"I only want to inflict pleasure," he murmured, then returned to the task at hand.

He dispensed more lotion onto his hand, then rubbed it on her upper chest until it disappeared. He didn't trust himself to go near those perfect breasts of hers, merely sliding his hand over the curves and moving down to cup her midriff. He thoroughly coated her flat belly, and below it to the hem of her pink bikini.

"God, I have to touch you," he muttered. She didn't react, not even when he smoothed more lotion onto his fingertips then slid them below the elastic waistband of her swimsuit.

She moaned, low in her throat, not protesting as he dropped his fingers down, lower and lower.

When he reached the soft curls between her legs, her eyes flew open. "Ryan!"

"Shh," he whispered, turning slightly to shield her from view of the other people down the beach. No one was north of them. No one south would see anything except his back as he knelt beside her.

"What are you doing to me?" she asked.

"I'm giving you another scent memory. Coconut and citrus."

"Yes, you definitely are," she whispered. "I'll never be able to use this lotion again unless you're here to put it on me."

"I'm doing a good job, aren't I? Making sure you're well covered so you don't get a sunburn."

He pressed a lethargic kiss to her neck. Then he couldn't resist going further. Jade shivered when he moved his hand down, lower, seeking that hot, wet place where he so loved to lose himself.

She was drenched. Open, soft and moist against his fingers. This time he was the one to moan. "You're wet."

"You're evil," she choked out, staring straight up at the sky.

He knew why she wouldn't look at him. One look and they'd both be lost to where they were and who was nearby. She'd want his mouth, he'd need her tongue, and his hand wouldn't be contained for long by her swimsuit.

"Stop," she protested.

He chuckled. "That sounded convincing."

"Okay, don't stop." She punctuated the demand with a tilt of her hips, inviting his further exploration.

He gladly complied, sliding one finger deep into her wetness until she shuddered.

"Shh," he whispered, licking at her earlobe, rubbing his face against her silky hair. Then he kissed her, his tongue mimicking the movement of his finger, setting a quick, heady rhythm that he knew was driving her mad.

"Ryan, please," she whimpered.

He finally gave her what he knew she wanted and flicked his thumb onto that sensitive little nub of flesh that throbbed for attention.

"Yes!" Her cry wasn't too loud, but he still hoped the tourists were hard of hearing. Or that they thought seagulls' cries sounded like a woman having an orgasm.

Which, he realized when she shuddered, clenched her fists and arched her back, she was.

SOMEHOW, MAYBE BECAUSE of the heat of the sun, the sound of the surf, or the amazing afterglow of the things Ryan had made her feel with his incredible touch, Jade drifted off to sleep.

She dreamed. Short, choppy dreams full of laughter and heat, smiles and wet kisses. The warmth of someone's hand holding hers. Just that clasp of hands made her feel more happy than she'd ever felt before.

When she opened her eyes to the brilliant blue sky and a few puffy white clouds, she instinctively flexed her right hand and found it clasped with Ryan's.

He squeezed back. "I was about to wake you up to make sure you have enough sunscreen on."

She turned to face him, still slow and lethargic from her little nap, and smiled. "And if I don't, were you going to put more on for me?"

"I don't think I'm a strong enough man for that."

She took in a deep, comfortable breath, honey-sweet satisfaction oozing through her body. Letting her mind trip back to moments ago when all she could see was the sky, all she could hear was the churning of the waves and her own choppy breaths. All she could feel was *him.* "How long was I asleep?"

"Just a little while. Twenty minutes or so. But long enough that the beach traffic has thinned out a bit."

Glancing over his shoulder, she saw that the family with the young boy had gone. Nibbling her lip, she asked, "Do you think they left because of us?"

He shook his head. "I think it had something to do with the kid lying about putting on some sunscreen. His mother was screeching something about him being red as a lobster as she dragged him up the beach."

"Thank goodness," she replied with a chuckle. Then she rose from the chair and extended her hand. "Let's go for a swim."

"I thought you'd never ask."

They dropped their sunglasses onto their chairs then dashed, hand in hand, into the surf. The shock of cold water against her ankles made Jade moan in appreciation. Her whole body was sticky hot, and the cool waters of the Atlantic provided exactly the relief she needed.

They dove under the next wave, rising a few yards out beyond the break.

"Have I thanked you yet for suggesting this?" she asked as they treaded water.

"Not with words."

"Thanks," she replied. Then she gave him a saucy grin. "With words."

"Have I thanked you, yet, for tying me up naked to a statue in Mamie Brandywine's garden?"

She laughed aloud. "Not with words."

He swam closer, shaking water off his hair as he pulled her into his arms. "Thanks, Jade. I'm beginning to think this trip to Savannah might be one of the best things I ever did."

She studied his face, gauging his meaning. His voice had sounded husky, but also sincere. He stared back at her, as if not seeing the sopping hair and sun-reddened face. His expression said a lot about what he was thinking, what he was feeling.

The same things she was?

Whatever crazy feelings were swirling around here about this—this *thing* they'd fallen into—she wasn't the only one feeling them.

A wave washed over them, pushing them closer to shore until they could stand chest-deep in the water. Ryan slid his arms around her shoulders and pulled her close. "No children or harried moms to be shocked if we kiss."

She snorted a laugh. "I think we did a little more than kiss on the beach."

Instead of replying, he lowered his mouth to hers, sweeping his tongue along her lips. Salty. Minty. Delicious.

She kissed him back and tilted against him, sliding her wet body against his beneath the surface of the water.

He groaned against her lips. She knew why when she felt his instant reaction. "It's pretty deserted," she said. Her voice was low, wicked.

"You're so bad."

"Isn't that why you like me?"

He nodded. "One of many reasons."

One of many. That implied he liked her a lot, didn't

it? Darn good thing. Because she suspected she more than liked this man. Amazing, really. Someone she'd set out to destroy might turn out to be the man she'd been waiting for all her life.

"So what are you suggesting?" he asked, slipping his hands down to cup her waist, then her hips. Then lower, until he was playing with the waistband of her bottoms.

"What do you think I was suggesting?" She wrapped one leg around him, curving herself more intimately against him until he sucked in a harsh breath.

"I don't exactly have condoms in the pocket of my trunks."

"Shucks." She rubbed against him again, drawing out the torture for both of them.

"I'm not going to be able to walk out of the water for a good ten minutes now."

She glanced toward the beach. Now, with the full afternoon heat blazing down, more people had left to escape the sun. "Unless those two guys fishing down there have a pair of binoculars, they're not going to have any idea what we're doing under the waves."

"I like how you think."

"You're gonna like my next move even better," she promised. Without warning, she reached into the waistband of his trunks and captured his thick, throbbing erection in her hand.

"Oh, yeah," he managed to croak out between ragged breaths. "I definitely like that."

She liked it, too. Liked the solid, heavy weight of him in her palm. Liked how he moaned when she squeezed. Liked feeling so wicked and wanton and elemental with the roll of the waves and the far-off cry of seagulls in the background.

"If a wave comes and knocks us down, I'm gonna end up bare-ass naked on the beach with my trunks around my knees," he said, weakly trying to protest. She knew he didn't want her to stop. The way his head was thrown back and his lips parted told her he loved what she was doing. Each stroke brought another slight groan. Each roll of her thumb over the tip of his erection made him shake.

"Do you really care?" She rose on tiptoe to press a kiss against the base of his throat, the taste of salt water mixed with the salty essence of man completely intoxicating her.

He could only shake his head, then lower his mouth to hers to grab a deep, wet kiss even as he grabbed another deep breath. Without a single protest, he gave himself over to Jade as she took him to the same heights of pleasure where he'd so recently taken her.

By the time they came out of the water, he could only think that he was damned glad he'd used the waterproof sunscreen.

11

A FEW NIGHTS LATER, Ryan was ready to confront Jade about her secret life of crime and offer to help her work through it. Because he'd come to a few conclusions.

First, he couldn't keep up the deception. He hated lying, *hated* it. And lying to someone he cared about was proving too much to bear.

Second, until he figured out how to extract Jade from the sticky legal situation she'd gotten herself into, he wouldn't feel safe loving her.

Loving her. God, that sounded dramatic. He'd known the woman only slightly more than a week and he'd fallen in love with her.

Well, why not? He'd been engaged to a woman for a year and had never felt one moment of the pure joy he shared with Jade.

Besides, he'd simply followed in the footsteps of his family, hadn't he? His grandparents, parents and sister—they'd all met their one-and-only, their soul mate—and had never been willing to settle for anything else.

His grandmother had been warning him for years that he came from passionate stock. That when the right woman came along, he'd know, down to his bones, that she was the one person in the world he couldn't do without.

"What you t'inking, boy?"

Ryan looked up from the fabulous fried-chicken-and-okra dinner Aunt Lula Mae had made for them tonight and caught the old woman watching him with a knowing smile. Jade had invited him over to meet her much-loved relative. Neither Ryan nor Lula Mae had admitted that they'd already met. Lula Mae seemed to enjoy conspiracy—she'd given him several broad smiles and surreptitious winks throughout the evening.

"You know what I'm thinking about," he replied, knowing he was right. Whether she was truly into anything supernatural, the old woman had an uncanny ability to read people.

"You wonderin' how Jade gonna react when she fin' out you came here 'dat night. Because you don' trust her."

He glanced around the sparse dining room, furnished only with a small table and four chairs, to make sure Jade hadn't returned from her bedroom, where she'd gone to take a call during their dinner.

"*Didn't*," he clarified. "I understand her much better now."

Lula Mae nodded, setting the thick strand of beads around her neck clicking against her throat. No bunny slippers tonight. No chicken claws, either. She was dressed in a brightly-colored, loose dress with an island pattern. A red bandanna covered her spiky gray hair, and on her fingers she wore a number of large rings. She pointed one of those ringed fingers in his direction. "You see? You understan' the truth now?"

He nodded. "Jade doesn't think she's doing anything wrong."

Lula Mae nodded. "She never do anything she know is wrong."

"But she could get herself into trouble."

The woman cackled. "Didn't she already, when she hook up wid' you?"

Trouble? Maybe at first. But not now. Having spent nearly every hour in each other's company for the past several days, troublesome was not how he'd describe their relationship.

Exciting. Passionate. Playful. Sultry. Oh, yes, all those things. Things he'd almost forgotten he wanted and now knew he couldn't do without. Just like he couldn't do without her.

His grandmother, as it turned out, was right.

"I'm supposed to go back to New York tomorrow," he told Lula Mae, letting her hear his genuine anxiety.

He hated to make that trip for another reason as well. Because he'd have to go face Grandmother and tell her that if she wanted her stolen painting back, she was going to have to fight the Savannah Historical Society. Not to mention one more little tidbit—that if he had his way, she was going to be setting one more place at the table come Thanksgiving.

For Jade, the con woman his grandmother had sent him to find. The woman he planned to spend the rest of his rich, exciting, passionate life with.

How did I ever get by without her.

He didn't voice his question aloud, but Lula Mae seemed to know to answer, anyway. "Jade, she's like you. Not bein' true to herself, not lettin' anyone too close because she feel she got to protect all of us. Now, though, she doesn't have her mama and Jenny to play mama to. So time for her to have a life of her own."

With you.

This time, he was the one who heard the words the old woman didn't say.

"Well, it sounds like we met each other at exactly the perfect time in both our lives, doesn't it?"

He didn't even realize Jade had entered the room until she answered. "Absolutely."

She greeted him with the kind of open, genuine smile that made him shake under its power. Jade when sultry and wicked was deadly. Jade when happy and sunny was simply beyond resisting.

And he had no intention whatsoever of doing that.

"Lula Mae, if I could ever get my grandmother to visit Savannah, I want you to cook these greens for her."

The woman waved off his compliment with an airy hand.

"Speaking of which," he said, turning his attention to Jade, who'd settled back in her seat, "I have to go home tomorrow. Got to get back to work, pull an article out of my Jade-fried brain and meet my deadline."

"Wonderful," she replied, not looking at all dismayed by the prospect of him leaving.

Her response was deflating, to say the least. Then he saw the grin on her lips and knew she was toying with him.

"Because," she continued, "it just so happens that I need to make a trip up to New York, as well."

"Really?"

She nodded, then nibbled delicately at a piece of chicken. She remained silent, licking her lips and tasting the meat. She shot a look at Lula Mae. "You used something different in this."

The old woman merely smiled and shrugged before getting up to clear the table. "What fun is spice if you can't play with it?"

"She's always trying out different things," Jade said

once the older woman had left the room. "I'm some-times afraid to ask where she gets this stuff."

"As long as it doesn't come from midnight flowers blooming on a grave on a moonless night, I have to say I approve of her cooking."

"I think midnight flowers only bloom in graveyards when there's a full moon."

"The better for the werewolves?"

She tsked. "There's nothing as gauche as were-wolves in Savannah. Maybe vampires." She gave him a heated look, telling him where her thoughts had gone. "Have I ever told you about my vampire fan-tasies?"

He shook his head. "No, but I think I'd like to hear about them."

"I think you'd love to hear about them," she retorted with a definite lick of her lips.

He shifted in his seat, trying to remember that Lula Mae was in the next room. "I don't remember hearing you mention vampires on any of your tours."

She shrugged. "I don't. Only ghosts. Weren't you paying attention?"

He'd gone on three of Jade's tours now and learned as much as he wanted to about the ghosts who popu-lated the most haunted city in the U.S. "Yes, I was pay-ing attention. But today I kept getting distracted by the wiggle of the woman walking in front of me during the tour."

She shot him a glare. "That blonde had a lot of wig-gle in her walk."

"She had a lot of wiggle in a good stiff breeze," Ryan replied, sparing barely a thought for the bimbo who'd made a play for him today right in front of Jade.

Jade hadn't so much as batted an eyelash. But she'd

gotten her revenge, telling a particularly gruesome story about the murder of a blond tart who preyed on other women's men back in the twenties. Ryan hadn't known whether to feel sorry for the woman, who'd blanched red, or laugh his head off at Jade for being jealous.

Leaning across the cluttered table, he pressed a kiss on her shiny lips. "I was talking about my tour guide. The woman who's taught me quite a lot this past week."

"Like, not to go to the beach in the middle of a July afternoon unless you want to become as crispy as this chicken?"

He snorted. "Are you kidding? That was the best trip to the beach I ever had! I'll never want to go in the ocean again if you're not with me."

"I think you mean *come* in the ocean," she replied, completely deadpan.

He barked a laugh. "Oh, did I ever set myself up for that." He pulled Jade from her chair and onto his own lap. "You are so bad."

"And so are you," she replied, pressing a kiss against his lips before tucking her head against his neck. "Thank goodness."

He liked holding her. Liked feeling her in his lap, curled up in complete trust and comfort.

"Now, tell me why you're coming to New York. When we can leave. How long you can stay. And promise you'll wait outside my apartment door for ten minutes when we get there so I can change the sheets, hide my stash of porn, and make sure the toilet seat's down."

He should have known she wouldn't focus on the sheets.

"Porn?"

"I was a bachelor in my former life."

"A naughty one."

"Why do you think we go together so well?"

"Like Bonnie and Clyde."

Whoa, that comparison cut a little too close for comfort. But it was a perfect opening. "Jade—"

Lula Mae came back into the dining room before he could open up the conversation about Jade's secret life as a stolen-art avenger.

Hmm…sounded like the name of a dark super-heroine. He could totally get into seeing Jade in a skin-tight spandex catsuit. He closed his eyes to appreciate the mental flash.

"Aunt Lula Mae, do you think you'd mind going and staying with Tally for a couple of days?" Jade asked.

The woman pursed her lips. "She doesn't have HBO. I don' wanna miss any *Sex and the City* reruns."

"You've seen every episode. And Mama has the first season on tape anyway. We can pick them up from her place if you can't survive without them," Jade said with a roll of her eyes.

"You don' have to go out of state if you want to fool around with your man," Lula Mae said with a wag of her thin, gray eyebrows. "I got bad hearing."

"You hear like a guard dog," Jade retorted.

Lula Mae smirked.

"And I'm not going for that reason," Jade added as she rose from Ryan's lap to stand beside the table. "I just confirmed a meeting with someone who has something I've been looking for."

Ryan immediately went on alert. "What do you mean?"

Jade shrugged but didn't meet his eyes. "I've been investigating the disappearance of a famous pair of dueling flintlocks from the Harrison estate."

Oh, no. Dueling pistols. Sounded old, antique, Civil War–era.

"What does it have to do with you?" he asked, meeting Lula Mae's speculative stare over Jade's shoulder.

Jade busied herself by picking up the remaining dishes from the table. "It's a sideline. I like going on treasure hunts for the Historical Society. I'm going to visit the current owner, who happens to live up in New York. Seems like a whole regiment of New Yorkers spent some time in Savannah during the war."

Visit. Would she pose as a gun appraiser this time? A historian? A potential buyer? Or would she don all-black and creep into a strange house late at night to steal back what somebody stole more than a century ago? "Jade, you don't mean to—"

"Okay," Lula Mae interrupted. "I'll stay with Tally. And I bring Jinx, too."

Jade paused, dirty dishes in hand. "Tally hates cats. I can ask the neighbor to look in on him."

Lula Mae merely shrugged. "Jinx don't go, I don't go."

Jade groaned and glanced at Ryan. "She likes to scare Tally's housemaid. Voodoo priestess, black cat and all that stuff. She's as big an actress as Jenny." Then she sighed. "And Mama."

The old woman continued as if Jade hadn't spoken. "You go have fun on one of your treasure hunts." Turning to Ryan, she shook her finger at him. "And you make sure you stay close to keep my girl out of trouble."

"Trouble? Now why would I possibly get in any trouble?"

Ryan could think of a bunch of reasons—police, criminal charges and armed homeowners among them.

Lula Mae shot him another warning look. She seemed to be telling Ryan not to confront Jade about what she was doing. He wanted to, more than anything. He wanted to get things out in the open and do whatever he had to—including locking Jade in her room, if that's what it took—to get her to give up this crazy idea.

Again, though, when he opened his mouth, Lula Mae pointed an index finger at him and shook her head.

Maybe the old woman was right. Jade cared about him. He *knew* she did. He'd even go so far as to say he believed she was falling in love with him, as he was with her.

But she'd only known him a little over a week. She didn't entirely trust him yet, as evidenced by the way she was so evasive about her "treasure hunt." She'd already proven she was a woman who didn't like being told what to do. If he confronted her and demanded that she give up this crazy Robin Hood lifestyle of hers, she might become furious and have the opposite reaction.

She could run from him, from *them*, and get herself into even more trouble.

Which meant there was only one thing he could do. Stick to her like glue and save Jade from herself.

JADE LIKED NEW YORK. Even though her heart belonged in the South, she could appreciate the big thriving city that pulsed with life and excitement. What wasn't to love about a place that could turn its seediest areas into major tourist attractions? Savannah with its River

Walk. New Orleans with Bourbon Street. And New York City with Times Square.

They'd all adopted a take-charge attitude to overcome the past. They'd charged freely into the future, making a delight out of what had once been looked down upon. Kind of reminded her of some people she knew. Like herself.

Ryan was an incredibly attentive host. He rarely left her side the first two days, insisting he could do his work from home. He also wanted to accompany her wherever she went.

Funny, it was as if he was really afraid to leave her alone. She found herself touched by the protectiveness, since Jade had pretty much looked after herself from the time she was a kid. But she wasn't used to it, and finally told him one morning that she was going to meet her sister for breakfast, *alone*, whether he liked it or not.

"I don't like it," he grumbled as he leaned against his dresser, arms crossed in front of his chest.

She didn't look away from the mirror as she calmly continued to apply her makeup. "But—"

"But I know you have to leave and you're a big girl and you won't get lost and the Big Bad Wolf isn't going to gobble you up while you're walking down Fifth Avenue," he admitted.

"Correct," she replied after he rattled off the arguments she'd used with him moments before. "Now, I still haven't gotten a call back from Richard Brewer, the man I've been trying to see. I thought I'd have heard from him by now. Please take a message if he calls, okay?"

He merely shrugged, then got back to her day-trip. "You're just going for breakfast, right? You should take cabs there and right back so you don't get lost. This is a big city."

She slid some mascara over her lashes. "I've been in big cities before."

"You'll go straight to the restaurant and straight back?"

She closed the tube of mascara and rolled her eyes. "You bet." She finished up her lipstick, ran the brush through her hair one more time, then grabbed her purse. "Now, Mr. Overprotective, may I please go have breakfast with my sister?"

He lowered his eyes. "I'm being a caveman, huh?"

"Nah. Just a worrier."

He put his hands on her shoulders, holding her still so he could stare into her face. "I don't want anything happening to you. I don't want you to get into any trouble."

She quirked a brow. "Spoken like a man who stripped naked in a garden for a complete stranger just a couple of weeks ago."

"I think you hexed me," he replied. "Used some of Lula Mae's juju on me."

"You've been reading The Book again, haven't you?"

"Nope. Just wondering how on earth I left this apartment two weeks ago convinced I'd be a bachelor for a long, long time, and now I can't picture my world without you in it."

Jade froze, waiting for a funny remark, an offhand wink or something that would indicate Ryan was just playing around. He didn't laugh, didn't wink, didn't lighten the moment in any way. He merely stared at her with an intense, honest gaze that made his green eyes shine even brighter and made her heart thud in her chest.

Didn't most people think it took *time* to fall in love, time to decide when you'd found the person you wanted to spend your life with? Jade knew better. She was a Dupré, after all. The tendency to love fast and love hard was in her blood.

Fortunately, she was also a Maguire. Which meant she was like her father—emotional, deeply loyal, a believer in loving with her whole heart and holding back nothing. The kind of person who'd love only once. For a lifetime.

She also knew now that she was in love with Ryan Stoddard. She just hadn't been ready to admit it, nor did she think he was ready to hear it, much less that he was feeling the same way.

So his words came as something of a shock. "Ryan—"

"Come back soon, Jade," he said, pressing a kiss to her forehead, as if he recognized the door he'd opened with his words. "Promise."

Okay, he wasn't ready to talk. Neither was she, really. But just the things they'd hinted at had filled her mind with the most wonderful visions of a future for them, something she hadn't really dared think about before.

Giving him a soft kiss on the lips, she nodded. "I will."

Leaving his plush building, complete with uniformed doorman, Jade thought again about Ryan's background. They'd never talked about it, but there was no question the man had money. That could be an obstacle.

So could geography. Jade liked New York, but she didn't want to live here. She hated the thought of leaving Savannah.

"He's worth it," she whispered, drawing a stare from someone walking past her on the sidewalk.

The stranger, a young woman carrying a ton of shopping bags, paused, then gave her a broad, New York smile. "If he puts that look on your face, lady, he's definitely worth it!"

Good lord, even strangers were commenting on her love life. But she couldn't help smiling back.

When she reached the restaurant where Jenny worked, she sat in a booth and waited for her sister to show up. She didn't know why Jenny wanted to meet *here.* Jade would have figured she'd want to stay as far away as possible from her place of employment on her day off. But there was no second-guessing Jenny's motives about anything.

"You really are here!" her sister said when she arrived, bending down and giving Jade a kiss on the cheek. "I hadn't expected to see you for months. I'm so excited. But why aren't you staying with me? How long will you be in town?"

As usual, Jade found it hard to get a word in edgewise. When Jenny stopped for breath, Jade said, "Nice to see you, too. I'm here on business. I don't know how long I'll be around. And we have to talk."

Jenny's pretty face immediately pulled into the pretty pout that had always helped her get her way. "Am I in trouble?"

"That depends on your definition of trouble," Jade said dryly. "But you're certainly high on my shit-list right now."

Jenny's brows shot up. Jade had been mothering her sister for so long, she couldn't remember the last time they'd really argued. Jenny was probably also shocked that Jade had actually used a swear word—in public, no less. Jade had played the responsible one for so long, she'd seldom voiced her true feelings and emotions out loud.

Not until Ryan, anyway.

The last time she'd really erupted at her sister was probably when Jenny had decided to move to New York without a job or more than a hundred bucks. And Jade had informed her she was "out of her effing mind."

Jade had to hand it to her. Jenny wasn't starving. In fact, she looked just beautiful. Now, if only she'd grow up emotionally…

"Why are you mad at me?" Jenny asked, leaning close as if afraid to be overheard.

Jade quickly confronted her about the Ryan situation.

"I already told you on the phone I might have exaggerated."

"Might?"

Jenny rolled her eyes. "Okay, I did. Big deal. He was hot and I was ticked off that he never asked me out. Just that lunch, which was more like an interrogation anyway."

Confused, Jade said, "What do you mean?"

"I don't know. He just asked a lot of questions about where I was from and what I did for a living, when what I really wanted him to ask was how soon I could get naked with him."

"That's my prerogative," Jade said, her jaw tight.

Jenny didn't say anything for a minute. Then her mouth fell open. "Holy crap, is that why you're asking all these questions? Are *you* involved with him?"

All around them were chattering people ordering their omelets over the din of clanking dishes, and some guy was up on stage massacring a song from *Phantom of the Opera.* Jade still shot her sister a look that said "shut up" before replying. "I am. And I wanted to let you know it, face-to-face, just in case you have any left-over feelings or problems with it."

Jenny merely smiled. "No problem. He's too old for me anyway. And I'm infatuated with this new dancer at the studio. Man, if only he weren't gay."

"Oh, boy, that's a tough road to go down."

Jenny reached across the table and grabbed Jade's hand, squeezing it tightly. "I'm so happy for you. It's about time. If Ryan is what put this…this…glow around you, then I'll love him for always."

Jade quirked a brow.

"As a brother," Jenny said with a cheeky grin.

They clinked their coffee mugs together, then Jenny instantly hit Jade with a barrage of questions. Jade updated her on Lula Mae, and on their mother—whom they'd only heard from once since she'd left on her three-week honeymoon cruise in the Mediterranean. Fortunately, when Jenny zeroed in on Jade's relationship with Ryan, demanding details on how and where they'd met, Jade was literally saved by the bell—her phone.

"Sorry, I forgot to turn it off," she said, hating people who had loud cell phone conversations in public places. She planned to ignore it, at least until she saw the name of the person calling her. "Oh, no, do you mind? I've been trying to set up a meeting with this man. He e-mailed and said I could come one day this week, but I've never gotten a phone call confirming."

Jenny waved her off, probably completely oblivious to the rudeness Jade was trying so hard to avoid. Her little sister was completely occupied with picking the mushrooms out of her omelet. Same old Jenny— liked the flavor, not the texture, so she always ordered the things, then picked them out of whatever she was eating.

Jade had a quick conversation with Mr. Brewer, the man who now owned the famous Harrison dueling pistols. She'd been investigating the disappearance of the flintlocks for a long time, using her Internet resources to track them down. She'd expected it to be tough. Paintings were so much easier. But this particular set was so distinctive it had been mentioned in an old Savannah newspaper article as the finest pair of pistols in the state of Georgia. With the accompanying description, it hadn't been too tough to find Mr. Brewer through the gun collectors' circuit.

Jade had sent the gentleman a copy of the article, not to mention a lot of other background information, right down to the manufacturer of the pistols. So Brewer probably had a darn good idea why Jade wanted to see him.

Things would go one of two ways. Either he'd listen with interest, tell her it wasn't his problem that he had something that had been stolen a century and a half ago, and invite her out. There wasn't much the Historical Society could do in that case, and most people knew it.

Or, he could be like the nice old lady in upstate New York who'd returned the Impressionist painting just last month. He might immediately donate the stolen item, trying to right an injustice of the past.

She wondered which this Mr. Brewer would do. Thankfully, she wouldn't have to wonder for long. The man lived not too far from Ryan's place, and he was open to a visit that very morning.

Though she'd promised Ryan she'd only go out for breakfast, she had time for a quick detour. Besides, once she got this business taken care of, she'd feel much more comfortable settling in for a few days' *vacation*.

Then, if she had her way, they'd never leave Ryan's apartment—or his bedroom—during the little time they had left. And maybe they'd get around to finishing that conversation they'd started this morning.

12

Ryan didn't really start to worry until three hours after Jade's departure. Though he hadn't liked her going, he'd known she wanted to see her sister and hadn't been able to come up with a single good reason why she shouldn't.

He could have told her it was because he was afraid she'd make a side trip to steal, but didn't think she'd like that too much.

Until Jade confronted her sister over her lies about him, he certainly couldn't go with her. So he'd finally had to back down.

"They're just talking," he told himself. Given his firsthand knowledge of Jenny's gabbiness—which had driven him nuts from the moment they'd met—he'd expected Jade to be gone a while. But not *this* long.

Staring at the clock again, he smothered a groan. How could he focus on the article, which he was writing on the computer in his spare room? Or deal with the ton of e-mail, or check up on his day job? He couldn't keep his attention on *any* of it until he knew for sure Jade was okay—not in jail, or facing the end of an angry gun collector's pistol.

He shouldn't have let her leave. Lula Mae had warned him, plus his own instincts had been screaming at him. Not just to keep her in sight, but to confront her and get this business out in the open once and for all. But he'd hesitated, for what he now recognized were primarily selfish reasons.

Fact was, he didn't want to risk losing her. Didn't want to upset the tenuous balance of their new relationship. Didn't want her to walk out of here with a look of disgust on her face when she found out he was a liar.

Didn't want her to see a trace of dismay on his own face when she admitted she was a thief.

"Damn," he muttered, getting up again and prowling around his apartment.

It was while on the prowl that he thought to pick up the phone and call her on her cell. The double-fast dial tone told him he had a message.

Uh-oh.

Calling in to check the message, he cursed the twenty minutes he'd taken to grab a shower because during that time, two calls had come in. The first from Jade's potential victim, Mr. Brewer. He'd left a number, then said he would try to reach Jade on her cell phone.

"Oh, great."

The second call had come ten minutes later. From Jade.

"No, no, no," he muttered aloud as he listened to her soft voice with that underlying hint of Southern smoothness she hadn't completely eradicated. Brewer had tracked her down. She was going to see him.

After slamming down the phone, Ryan ran a frustrated hand through his hair. "She promised!"

In her message, she'd apologized for breaking that promise, tempting him by saying she wanted to get her business out of the way so she could devote every minute of the next few days to him. To *them.*

Unfortunately, there wouldn't be a next few days if she wound up in jail. Or hurt.

Thinking quickly, Ryan hurried into his office and pulled up a familiar Web site on his computer. Doing a reverse check on the phone number, he found the address for a Mr. Richard Brewer. Not believing his good luck, he realized the man lived only a short cab ride away.

Without giving it another thought, he left his apartment. Jade's days as a thief were over, starting now. Even if he had to steal the stupid guns back from her and return them to their owner, he was going to end this dangerous game she was playing.

Then he was going to see to it she was much too busy to play games with anybody but him.

MR. BREWER WAS A frail-looking old man, but he had a sharp-eyed stare that belied his slow movements. Jade sensed he'd been a business shark in his younger days. A widower, he lived in an apartment overlooking Central Park, so he'd likely been a *successful* shark. She figured he could afford to part with the flintlocks, at least financially.

When Jade had arrived, he'd played gracious host, serving her some iced tea before inviting her to join him in his beautifully decorated living room. He'd then spoken at length about his ancestor, an honored colonel in the Union army. His every word reinforced Jade's certainty that he did not even want to *consider* the idea that the flintlocks had been stolen.

But to Jade's surprise, he didn't seem perturbed at the idea of parting with them. He seemed more upset by the idea that his great-great-great-uncle might have looted them from a house in Savannah.

She had to tread very carefully.

"Well, of course, we have no way of knowing how

they came into the possession of Colonel Samuels, your ancestor. Perhaps he won them in a game of cards, or took them as payment from another Union officer who was responsible for the original theft."

That appeared to mollify him a bit.

"Perhaps. Do you have any children, Ms. Maguire?"

She shook her head. "No. I hope to, someday."

Then she thought of one more thing she and Ryan needed to discuss *someday*.

"My grandchildren come to visit all the time," he said as he freshened her tea. "My daughter hates guns, doesn't want her kids anywhere near them."

"Understandable," she said, bringing the glass to her lips. Horrid stuff, made with nasty-tasting powder. Then again, even freshly brewed tea tasted bad to Jade if it came from anywhere north of the Mason-Dixon line.

Mr. Brewer sat across from her, fixing his blue-eyed stare on her face. "I was thinking of *selling* the things. That's why I contacted an antique gun association to try to get more information on their worth."

Jade groaned inwardly. He'd been researching the value of the pistols. No way would she be able to offer him the kind of dollar figure they'd command at auction or private sale. Heck, she couldn't offer him *any* money at all.

The work she did on behalf of the Historical Society was on a donation or loan basis only. The society didn't have the money to purchase artifacts. Even if they could prove the items had once been stolen, the present-day descendents of the former owners usually couldn't afford the legal fees to pursue a lawsuit whose outcome was tenuous at best. If they could even be found.

Which was why Jade was so dedicated to what she did. She'd managed to talk a lot of people into donating a lot of items over the past few years. She could usually tell how things were going to progress as soon as she met the current owners, but this man had her stymied. She wasn't sure whether this was going to be a good day or a bad one.

"That is how I found you," Jade finally admitted. "Someone forwarded your posting from an antique gun Web site message board, and I began to do the research."

"Interesting line of work you're in, young lady," the old man said as he set his glass on a nearby coffee table.

"Not my line of work, exactly," she explained. "I'm a volunteer."

That seemed to surprise him. "You mean, you don't work for the Society?"

She shook her head and grinned. "I own a haunted sites tour company in Savannah. I just do this for fun."

He barked a laugh. "Some idea of fun."

The exchange seemed to have intrigued him, and he finally smiled. "All right, so tell me more about this Harrison estate. The family." Then he winked. "And the tax benefits of making such a valuable donation."

But before Jade could say another word, they were interrupted by a knock on the door to the apartment. Jade cursed the luck. She'd just about had Mr. Brewer in the right frame of mind to give away something he could sell for tens of thousands of dollars. Now, however, he was thoroughly distracted by the imperious knocking.

"One moment, young lady," the old man said as he rose from his seat. Using his cane, he carefully made his way to the entrance of the apartment. He peeked through the peephole, then opened the door only as far as the chain-lock would allow. "What do you want?"

"I'm sorry to bother you. I'm looking for someone. Miss Maguire."

That was Ryan's voice. Jade immediately rose to her feet, wondering what on earth he was doing here.

Mr. Brewer raised a curious brow, and Jade could only shrug in apology. Appearing satisfied, the old man unlocked the door and ushered Ryan inside. "Do I know you?"

Ryan strode toward the living room, answering over his shoulder. "No, sir, you don't. I'm sorry to intrude, but I have to take Miss Maguire out of here. Right now."

Her first thought was of bad news. An accident. "Something's wrong. Is it Jenny? Aunt Lula Mae?" she asked, her heart somewhere in the vicinity of her throat.

He sucked in a breath, instantly looking contrite. "No, darlin', nothing like that. But you, uh…you need to come with me. Right now." He lowered his voice and leaned closer. "Before this goes any further."

She whispered back. "Before what goes any further?"

"Yes, before what?" Mr. Brewer asked, banging his cane on the floor.

Ryan squared his shoulders. Even from a few feet away, Jade could see the pulse ticking in his jaw and the flush in his cheeks. No question something had happened. He looked more upset than he had since the night they'd met. "Sir, I'm sorry we've intruded on you. Miss Maguire and I are leaving now."

Jade's jaw fell open. From Mr. Overprotective to Mr. Freaking Neanderthal. She barely recognized this man as the flirtatious charmer she'd met at Mamie Brandywine's party.

She shook off his hand when he tried to take her arm. "Ryan, you're being ridiculous. I told you I had business to take care of."

"Not *this* kind of business," he bit out. Then he looked over his shoulder at Mr. Brewer. "Could you possibly give us a moment of privacy?"

The old man looked them both over, faint amusement evident on his face. He obviously thought they were having a lovers' quarrel.

He wasn't quite right. They were about to have a lovers' World War III if Ryan Stoddard didn't come up with a good explanation pretty darn quick.

As soon as Mr. Brewer had left them alone in the room, Jade threw Ryan's hand off her arm and put her fisted hands on her hips. "What do you think you're doing? I almost had him convinced to let me walk out of here with those flintlocks."

He took her by the upper arms and pulled her close. She felt the anger in his touch and saw the grimness of his tightly held lips. "I can't let you do it, Jade. I know you think you're doing something noble, but it's still wrong. I can't let you steal from that old man."

Steal. Steal? Had he just said *steal?*

This time her mouth didn't just open, she really thought for sure she'd heard the thud of her jaw hitting her own chest. "What are you talking about?" she managed to choke out.

"I know the truth," he said between clenched teeth. "I know you think you're being some kind of Robin Hood, stealing back stuff that was stolen and donating it to the Historical Society."

"I am *what*?"

He lowered his eyes, not meeting hers for a moment. Jade was still trying to take it all in.

Then he looked up, almost pleading with her. "You can't do it anymore. It's too dangerous and I won't let you risk it."

Wouldn't let her risk it…risk being a thief? That's what he thought she was doing here? A half-hysterical laugh, completely devoid of humor, escaped her lips. "This is crazy."

"Yeah, it is," he muttered, running a hand through his hair in frustration until it stuck up in all directions.

Her first impulse was to reach up and smooth it out. She squashed the urge. She'd be better off sticking her own fingers into a lit fire right at this moment. She suspected it might be less painful in the long run.

"I know you come from a crazy background," he added, "and that somehow you made it seem right in your mind. But you're playing a risky game, Jade, and your luck's not going to hold out. I can't stand by and watch you get caught."

"Caught," she murmured.

Heaven help her, she'd already been caught, hadn't she? Caught in a spell of love with a man who didn't know her at all. He'd nearly proclaimed his love for her a few hours ago. And now he was telling her he cared about her too much to let her get into trouble because of her *thieving.*

If he thought that…well, he didn't know her at all. She was a complete stranger to him. She had to be if he could think she was some kind of thief or con artist who'd steal from an old man because of some misplaced notions of Southern patriotism. Jade didn't know whether to laugh, cry or just pummel the distrusting louse.

The lousy man she loved.

"Wait a minute," she said, trying to put the pieces

together. "Is that why you went out with Jenny? She said you'd asked a bunch of questions." Then another thought struck. "Oh, God, that's why you came to Savannah, isn't it? You weren't there by chance—you were tracking me!"

It sounded ridiculous, but she knew by the look on his face that she'd scored a hit.

"I came after you to find something you took from someone I know," he explained tightly.

She shook her head, blinking rapidly to clear her eyes of gathering tears. "So it was all a lie. You pursued me on purpose, lying to me the whole time."

He fidgeted, then fired back. "You pursued me, too. I wasn't the one who tied you up naked to a statue in Mamie Brandywine's garden."

From the other room they heard a curious choking sound. Jade spared a second of concern for Mr. Brewer, but no more. She was too focused on what Ryan was admitting. "I already told you why I did that, because of Jenny. Which might have been the perfect time for you to admit the truth yourself."

He grabbed her hand. "I wish I had, Jade." He didn't elaborate. And frankly, she didn't really give a damn at this point.

"Tell me one thing," she finally said.

He waited.

She urged her voice to remain steady, not to crack as she voiced what might be the most important question she'd ever asked. "Tell me, knowing me as you do, do you really think I'm a thief?"

He met her stare and she silently pleaded with him to admit he was wrong. That there had been some colossal mistake, and he knew darn well she'd never be so dishonorable, so deceitful.

Instead, he just looked at her, his mouth opening, closing. But no words came out.

Without another word, she dropped his hand and walked out of the apartment.

"WELL, YOU CERTAINLY mucked that one up, didn't you, young man?"

Ryan had barely even remembered where he was—in a complete stranger's home—once Jade had stormed out. He'd been frozen, torn between what he knew to be true—based on his grandmother's words—and the look of absolute betrayal in Jade's eyes.

His head was spinning as he wondered what he'd just done.

"What did you say?" he finally asked the old man as he shook his head, trying to regain his equilibrium.

"Had the girl by the heart, and you chucked her away," Mr. Brewer said, shaking his head in disgust. "Youth is wasted on the stupid and insensitive."

He could only watch, slack-jawed, as the old gentleman sat down in a chair, pulling a wooden case onto his lap. He opened it, glanced at the items inside, then snapped it closed. "You'll take these with you and get them to her, won't you?"

Ryan stared, noting the emblem burned into the wood. "The pistols?"

"Of course the pistols," the man said with an irritated look. "Was about to give them to her when you busted in."

Ryan lowered himself into a chair opposite the old man. "Sir, you should know—"

"Should know what? That she was here on behalf of the Savannah Historical Society? That she asked me if I'd consider donating these flintlocks, which were stolen from a Southern plantation during the Civil War? That she knew they had no legal claim to them, but hoped I'd consider it as a good-faith gesture and an excellent tax write-off?"

Ryan sagged back into the chair, completely stunned. He could hardly take it in. Jade had come here in complete honesty? She'd asked the man to donate an antique, probably worth upward of fifty-thousand dollars, and he'd *agreed?*

Though, heaven knew, when Jade Maguire set her mind to have something, any man was hopeless to resist. Including this old guy.

"Do you mean to tell me she didn't come here saying she was some kind of buyer? Or gun expert? Or appraiser?" he asked, feeling two steps behind everyone else in the world.

"Course not," the old man snapped, rapping his cane on the wood floor. "Can't imagine why you'd think otherwise, but she contacted me weeks ago, telling me who she was and who she represented." Then he raised a sly brow. "But you didn't know that, did you? You thought she was here for some other reason altogether."

Yeah. To steal something that had once been stolen.

Ryan could only nod.

"And you've been lying to her all along about things? I heard that much." Then he cackled. "Naked and tied to a statue, eh? I'd like to know who this Mamie Brandywine is."

Ryan shuddered. "No, you wouldn't."

"That young lady, she got you good, didn't she?" He cackled again, then let out another sound, something like a harrumph. "But she didn't do it unscathed. Got herself hurt in the process."

Ryan, realizing all the implications of what the old man was saying, launched up out of the chair and began to stalk the room. "I can't understand this. She steals from my grandmother, but politely asks for something from you?"

He was speaking more to himself, so he wasn't quite prepared for Mr. Brewer to answer. "Your grandmother?"

Ryan nodded absently. "She called me for help, saying Jade had swindled her out of a painting."

"You a married man?"

The abrupt subject change didn't seem any more crazy than anything else that had happened in the past few minutes. Ryan shook his head. "No."

"In love with Miss Maguire?"

He merely nodded.

"Grandmother a matchmaking type?"

Then he froze and turned on his heel. Gape-jawed, he stared at the old man.

Mr. Brewer started to laugh. "Worried for a long time about my youngest boy getting hooked up with the wrong one. Tried everything to steer him toward a young woman who used to work for me, but he wouldn't have it." He nodded his head in obvious satisfaction. "'Til I locked 'em together in a storage closet at a Christmas party one year."

And suddenly, Ryan got it.

He closed his eyes, shaking his head, wondering when his brain had turned into a complete wasteland.

Suckered. He'd been completely suckered. Played like a kindergartner tricked into giving up his lunch money.

By his own grandmother.

13

JADE HAD STOPPED CRYING by the time she got home to her apartment in Savannah that night. She'd cried a lot while racing to the airport, not even caring about the things she'd left behind at Ryan's place. She'd tried to hide the tears behind dark glasses but probably hadn't fooled anyone on the flight home to Georgia.

And on the drive from the airport, she'd just given in and whined, right up until she'd entered her apartment.

"Damn him," she muttered late that night as she tore off her clothes and reached for a comfortable, familiar nightshirt in her top dresser drawer.

She couldn't believe how...how *raw* she felt, still, all these hours later. But those moments in Mr. Brewer's apartment—those few dangerous moments when she'd asked him to believe in her and he'd responded with silence—seemed like they were going to repeat in her brain for the rest of her life.

A thief, of all things.

She was used to the women in her family being called names. A witch, a terror, they'd called Lula Mae. A man-eater, her mother had been named. A tease, a bimbo they'd said about Jenny. As for her? Jade? The one who'd considered herself the reasonable, responsible, driven, hardworking one?

She'd heard seductress. She'd heard brazen. She'd even heard dangerous.

But, by God, she'd never heard thief. Not until the man she loved had called her that.

"Damn you, Ryan," she muttered as she curled up in her bed, hugging her pillow. She wished Jinx was around. He was a cat, therefore often aloof. He did, however, seem to know when Jade needed comfort. He gave her the sweetest kitty kisses when he knew she needed them the most. Right now, she wanted to cling to him like a drowning woman held a life preserver.

She couldn't pick up Jinx from Tally's, however, without picking up Lula Mae. Jade wasn't up to that. Commiserating with Lula Mae meant downing gallons of oddly spiced tea, hearing the old woman's riddles about love, and plotting payback.

"Maybe later."

For now she had to grieve, alone, over what she'd lost—something that she'd only this morning begun to believe she'd found. True love.

"Ha!" she snorted, thrusting the very idea of it away.

Sleep proving elusive, Jade lay in bed for a long time, still trying to put everything together. She knew the basics. Ryan had come to Savannah to seek her out, *after* he'd sought out her little sister up in New York.

He'd thought she'd stolen something and wanted… what? Recompense? Retribution? Revenge? All of the above?

She remembered that first night, all his intuitive questions, when she'd half-jokingly asked if he was a P.I. instead of an architect. If she hadn't just been in his home, seen the drawings and blueprints all over his home office, she'd suspect that he really was a private investigator. But she knew he wasn't.

No, he hadn't been hired to track her down. It had been entirely personal. She just couldn't understand why.

Finally, sheer exhaustion made her give in to a turbulent night's sleep full of disturbing dreams.

She still hadn't figured things out the next day. Ryan tried to call—she heard his voice on the answering machine, but she refused to pick up. His messages said he'd made a mistake, that he hadn't understood, had been misled. That he had to talk to her, to set things right.

But how could he set something like that right? How could they go back to the beginning and pretend he hadn't been lying to her and he hadn't believed her to be a completely different person than she was? How could she ever really believe he was honest when he said he needed her in his life, that he cared about her, when he obviously didn't know her at all?

Because she didn't want to see anyone and have to explain her tear-stained face, she didn't tell anyone she was back in town. Somehow, however, Daisy suspected. The young woman called late that afternoon, her voice sounding frenzied on Jade's answering machine. "Look, I know you're out of town, but if you pick up this message, please call me. Freddy called in sick, and we have this big private tour tonight, a special one leaving out of your uncle's place. And I have the regular group to take out. Help!"

Jade bit back a curse, vowing to fire Freddy first thing tomorrow even though the new people she'd hired weren't fully up to speed yet. Then she grabbed the phone. "I'm here, Daisy."

"Oh, thank you! I didn't know what to do."

"Freddy's now unemployed. I'm the camel and this is the last straw."

"About time," the young woman muttered.

"Now, what's this about a private tour?" They did private group tours on occasion, but Jade didn't remember scheduling any for this week. In fact, she'd felt comfortable going away for a few days precisely because she'd had the two new people, plus Daisy and Freddy, and no extra tours on the schedule.

"Sorry, it just came in. A group going out of the Winter Garden, because they're staying there or something. Tonight at nine. Freddy was supposed to take it, since I have the regular late-night tour. But he's a no-show. And those two new ones don't know the haunted stuff yet. They've just barely gotten the history for the day tours!"

Jade muttered a low curse, then sighed heavily. There was no escaping it. This was part of running her own business. "Don't worry about it, Daisy—I'll take the tour. Let the clients know I'll meet them in the parlor of the Winter Garden at nine sharp."

That's how Jade ended up knocking on the door to her Uncle Henry's place at 8:55 p.m. It was dark out, a steamy night full of the calls of cicadas and the scents of the South—wet earth, thick sweet perfumes of the night-blooming jasmine Henry grew around the place, and that spicy, late-night aroma of mystery that Savannah wore around itself like some women wore a heady perfume.

She hardly noticed as she pushed a pair of dark-tinted sunglasses over her puffy red eyes. Hopefully the tour group would think she was merely eccentric and mysterious. Not teary-eyed and heartbroken.

She only hoped she didn't break anything else by tripping over something in the dark.

"Right this way, Miss Maguire," Henry's maid said when she opened the door.

Mutely following the woman to the parlor, Jade stepped inside. Instead of coming in with her, the maid closed the door, leaving Jade alone. "Wait," she said, realizing no one else was in the room, "there's nobody…"

That's when she noticed the flowers. They were everywhere, filling antique vases and delicately cut crystal bowls. They rested on every surface in the room—each table, the mantelpiece, the baby grand piano.

Magnolias. Profusions of the giant flowers, white and moist as if they'd just been cut. And with them, great clumps of orange blossoms. The effect was intoxicating. A mix of sweet, heady perfume and citrus and…

"Coconut oil?"

She yanked her sunglasses off her face, scanning every corner of the room.

"Hello, Jade."

Ryan.

He rose from a chair in the corner, where he'd been sitting quietly since she'd entered.

She whirled around and reached for the doorknob. It wouldn't twist. "Uncle Henry," she said with a groan.

"I asked him to give us five minutes," Ryan said softly as he crossed the room. "Five minutes for me to try to convince you that even though I'm the biggest loser in the world, you should give me a second chance."

She clenched her jaw, then her fists, trying to gain control over her wildly swinging emotions. Jade wasn't ready to deal with this. Not now. Not here. Not while surrounded with these heady smells that reminded her of him. Of them.

The magnolias in the garden that very first wild

night. The citrus and coconut from their day at the beach. He'd had her heart clenching with the memories before her brain had the opportunity to force them away.

"You fight dirty," she whispered, still not turning around to face him.

He touched her shoulder, gently, not demanding, but silently pleading with her to look at him. When the tips of his fingers caressed the side of her neck, she let out a little moan, but remained frozen, staring at the dark wood paneling of the door.

"Let me talk to you, Jade."

"Go ahead," she said, fighting to remain stiff and unyielding. "Try to explain why I should believe a word a liar like you would say."

She could feel his entire body flinch—he was that close. But he didn't back off. "You're right. I'm a liar and an untrusting bastard. I came to Savannah to find you and get back a painting I thought you'd stolen from my grandmother."

She jerked her head to look at him over her shoulder. "What painting?"

He met her stare evenly. "The LeBeuf portrait hanging at the Martinique house."

The painting she'd acquired last month. The one she'd *legally* acquired last month.

"She told me you'd stolen it."

"Who?"

"The woman who gave it to you." He shook his head in disgust. "My grandmother."

That shocked her into finally turning around. But she stayed close to the door, backing against it to keep some physical distance between them. Thankfully Ryan didn't move forward or try to crowd her.

"Those nice people, the Graysons, are your grand-parents?"

He nodded.

"Why would she tell you the painting was stolen?"

"I'm not sure you'll believe this."

She crossed her arms. "Try me. I happen to be slightly more trusting than some people."

His eyes flared. She'd scored a hit. She wondered why that didn't give her even a moment of satisfaction.

"She wanted me to meet you."

Of all the things she'd expected to hear, that was no-where near the top five. Ryan's grandmother had re-ported her valuable painting stolen because she wanted her grandson to *meet* the woman who'd sup-posedly stolen it?

He must have seen her look of derision. "You don't understand my family. I come from a long line of pas-sionately romantic people."

Passionate. Oh, she could concede that. In spite of his cool, cultured, big-city facade, Ryan had exhibited depths of passion she'd never before seen in a man, as well as a daring spirit that had totally captivated her from that very first night. "Okay, I can believe that."

He looked relieved. "Unfortunately, I've never really accepted that about myself. My relationships have been okay. Nothing that knocked me off my feet. No one who ever inspired me to think I could fall madly in love, like my parents, grandparents and sister did. That happened to drive my rather controlling grandmother a little crazy."

She'd liked his grandmother quite a lot, but she could see the potential for controlling. The woman had asked Jade a ton of personal questions during their af-ternoon together. Including questions about Jade's love life. And marital status.

"I can't believe it," she whispered, bringing her hands to her lips as the truth dawned. "She was *match-making*?"

Ryan nodded, giving a helpless shrug. "She knew I'd never let her set me up. She's tried that too many times." He finally stepped closer, touching her arm—a featherlight touch that told her he was being honest but didn't intimidate. "She also knew you were perfect for me. That you were the soul mate I'd never really believed I had. That I'd fall madly in love with you and be unable to imagine my life without you in it."

Her heart thudded in her chest. Those green eyes of his, those beautiful eyes that darkened when Ryan was aroused, or sparkled when he was amused, shone clear and bright with the truth of his emotions.

"I love you, Jade. My grandmother's lie got me down here. But you…once I met you…I never wanted to leave." He raised his hand to cup her cheek, delicately stroking his fingertips over her cheekbone, wiping away a bit of moisture Jade hadn't even known had dripped out of her eye. "I'm sorry for what my family did to you. But I'm not sorry I came." His voice lowered, nearly shaking with intensity as he repeated, "I *love* you."

Her heart quivered again and her pulse sped up. Oh, she wanted to believe him. Wanted more than anything to believe him. His words were beautiful, his expression sincere, his touch divine. But it didn't erase everything that had happened.

"If you love me, how could you believe I'd…I'd be a thief?" Her voice broke a little, and she still kept her body stiff and straight, separated from his by mere inches as she demanded an answer to the most important question of all.

"I didn't, not really," he admitted.

"You did a good impersonation of it yesterday morning in Mr. Brewer's apartment."

He clarified. "I mean, at first, when my grandmother told me you'd stolen from her, I had no choice but to believe. As I got to know you, I realized I wasn't seeing the whole picture. Then when we visited the Martinique house, and I saw the painting, I began to understand."

She didn't quite follow, but she listened as Ryan continued, his fingers still gently caressing her face.

"I know you have a strong conscience, Jade. You have a strong sense of right and wrong, a strong loyalty to this place, its history and its culture. So it suddenly made sense to me, you see, that you'd want to return important artifacts to their rightful places. Like someone might want to return a statue from a looted tomb back to its pyramid in Egypt. You'd never steal for personal gain, only to right an old injustice."

She saw the honesty in his eyes, the tender smile he didn't try to hide.

"We were together both before and after we visited the Martinique house," she whispered, beginning to believe, to open up and take in the warmth radiating off the man.

He nodded. "Yes, we were. I was falling in love with you. Both before and after. But after, I began to understand you. To admire you for doing what you thought was right, even as I was terrified that you'd get hurt or get caught. I was determined to protect you."

The weight that she'd felt on her shoulders for the past thirty-six hours suddenly seemed to lift. Ryan might have thought she'd stolen something. His own grandmother, who he obviously loved, had flat-out *said* she had. But once he'd gotten to know her he'd never thought she was a common low *thief*. Even more, he hadn't judged her for it. Hadn't condemned her.

In fact, he'd loved her.

She took a deep breath, closing her eyes and trying to analyze her feelings. That breath filled her mind with the scents he'd surrounded her with. All the memories they'd created in the short weeks they'd known each other, the scent memories that would live inside her until the day she died. The ones that would remind her for the rest of her life that she loved this man, and *only* this man.

Her anger seeped away, replaced not only by understanding and forgiveness, but also heart-clenching love. She lifted a trembling hand and covered his hand on her face, then pulled it to her mouth to press a kiss on his palm.

"Oh, Jade," he whispered as he drew her close. "Can you forgive me?" He kissed her temple, rubbing his cheek against hers. "Can we call my doubt of you a mix of summer insanity and flower intoxication?"

She laughed softly.

"Not to mention," he added, "too much of your aunt Lula Mae's tea and a man who didn't believe in madness-inspiring love trying to find any reason to escape from his own destiny?"

Destiny. Sounded reasonable. Especially here in this rich, sultry place on this wicked, hot summer night.

"You're forgiven," she said, drawing his mouth close to hers for a long, lingering kiss. There was instant fire, as always, but also the slow, languorous, bone-melting emotion that had been present between them from the first night they'd made love—right in this very house.

"I think I can even forgive your grandmother," she added as they drew apart.

"I paid her back," Ryan said with a lift of his brow. "Right now she's so terrified her lies have cost me you forever that she hasn't even realized how successful her plan actually was."

Jade laughed softly, picturing the meddlesome woman in just such a state. "Let's not tell her for a while."

He joined her laughter. "You're a wicked woman."

"You wouldn't have me any other way."

"No, I wouldn't."

She curled her fingers into his hair to hold him close, meeting his stare so she could gift him with the same kind of declaration he'd given her. She'd never said the words to a man because she'd never felt them for anyone but Ryan.

The time had come. She was a Maguire. She loved hard. She'd love only once. She loved *him*.

"I love you, Ryan. I'll love you forever."

He showed her his pleasure by kissing her, tasting her, inhaling her as he held her tightly against his body as if he'd never let her go.

Maybe he wouldn't.

Which was just fine with Jade.

Epilogue

LYNNETTE GRAYSON SPOTTED the small jewelry box in her husband's shaving kit as they finished unpacking at the Winter Garden, where they were staying for Thanksgiving weekend. Edward was already anticipating Aunt Lula Mae's famous cornbread stuffing, so he wasn't paying attention as his wife began to dig through his things. "What's this?" she asked.

"That's nothing," he said with a harrumph as he tried to snatch the small velvet box from her hand.

She smiled, knowing at once what it meant. When she finally got him to open it and saw the lovely old wedding ring that her late mother-in-law had worn, she sighed in pleasure.

"Keep your nose out of it," Edward said, shaking his finger at her. "Let the boy propose in his own way. Ryan's just barely forgiven you for your shenanigans. And if you get yourself uninvited for Thanksgiving dinner tomorrow at Jade's mama's house, I'll…I'll go without you!"

He didn't mean it, of course. The sparkle in Edward's fine blue eyes told her he was just as happy as she that her scheme to bring Ryan together with the perfect woman had worked.

She wasn't one to brag…but she'd really *done* it.

She'd found the right woman for her boy. Ryan was madly in love with Jade Maguire, and she loved him right back. Anyone with eyes could see that.

The only problem was this whole moving to Savannah business. She hadn't anticipated that. Since when did the man move for the woman? Such things simply weren't done in her day.

But that's what had happened. Ryan had quit his job, packed his belongings, loaded that great slobbery dog of his in his car and driven south mere weeks after he'd first heard Jade Maguire's name. At least he'd found a job quickly, thanks to his work on the article about Savannah's architecture.

Ah, well, she supposed there were worse things than a grandson who lived several states away and served things like collard greens at Thanksgiving dinner.

Like a grandson who never found his soul mate, never fell madly in love, never truly glowed with happiness.

That would be worse. Much worse.

No worry of that anymore. Not for Ryan. Not for any member of her family. Which was exactly the way Lynnette Grayson planned to keep it.

"Are you ready?" her husband asked as he draped a wrap over her shoulders, giving her a slight squeeze that told her she was forgiven for being so meddlesome. How could he not forgive her, since she'd never known any other way to be?

"More than ready," she said, already bouncing on her toes with excitement about tonight's adventure.

Ghosts and murder. Vengeance and love affairs. Scandal and mystery. Yes, she was fully prepared to enjoy an evening with her future granddaughter-in-law, hearing Jade do what she did best—introduce Savannah. And make all who visited fall under her spell.

Just like Ryan had.

Sexy!

Three steamy, sultry reads to get the temperature rising this autumn

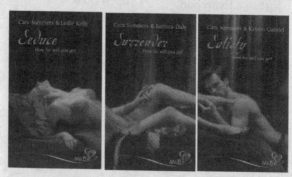

Seduce

The Proposition by Cara Summers &
Wickedly Hot by Leslie Kelly

Available 21st July 2006

Surrender

The Dare by Cara Summers &
Kiss & Run by Barbara Daly

Available 18th August 2006

Satisfy

The Favour by Cara Summers &
Good Night, Gracie by Kristin Gabriel

Available 15th September 2006

Escape to...

19th May 2006

16th June 2006

21st July 2006

18th August 2006

Available at WH Smith, Tesco, ASDA, Borders, Eason, Sainsbury's and all good paperback bookshops

www.millsandboon.co.uk

0806/14 V2

MILLS & BOON

Live the emotion

Blaze™

OPEN INVITATION? *by Karen Kendall*

The Man-Handlers, Bk 3

He's a little rough around the edges. In fact, Lilia London has
no idea how to polish Dan Granger. With only a few weeks
to work, she has no time to indulge the steamy attraction
between them. But he's so sexy when he's persistent…

TALKING ABOUT SEX…
by Vicki Lewis Thompson

Jess Harkins has always had a thing for Katie Peterson. He
could even have been her first lover…if he'd had the nerve to
take her up on her offer. Now Katie's an opinionated DJ and
Jess is determined to have her!

TEXAS FIRE *by Kimberly Raye*

Sociology professor Charlene Singer has always believed that
it's what's on the outside that counts. That's got her…nowhere.
So she's going to change her image and see if she gets any
luckier. Only she soon realises that she'll need more than luck
to handle Mason McGraw.

ABOUT LAST NIGHT… *by Samantha Hunter*

What really happened last night? Miranda Carter planned
to seduce best friend Colin Jacobs – till he got cold feet over
changing their relationship and left. Now he's got a puzzling
case of short-term amnesia. He *thinks* nothing happened, but
is that really the case?

On sale 1st September 2006

*Available at WHSmith, Tesco, ASDA, Borders, Eason,
Sainsbury's and most bookshops*

www.millsandboon.co.uk

0806/171 V2

MILLS & BOON®

Live the emotion

Modern

romance™
Extra

**Two longer and more passionate
stories every month**

WHITE-HOT! by *Trish Wylie*

When circumstance leaves Finn McNeill homeless,
her only option is the spare room of friend and
fire-fighter Shane Dwyer. Memories from Finn's
past refuse to let her act on her desire. And Shane
has promises to keep that mean Finn is forbidden to
him. But how long can they resist temptation? Is one
secret, white-hot night enough?

BEHIND THE SCENES by *Trish Jensen*

Gorgeous TV producer AJ Landry likes things done
his way – and he is used to getting what he wants! So
when sexy novice presenter Tanya Pierce arrives on
the set of a new make-over show with her own ideas,
the sparks begin to fly – in more ways than one…

On sale 1st September 2006

*Available at WHSmith, Tesco, ASDA, Borders, Eason,
Sainsbury's and most bookshops*

www.millsandboon.co.uk